A FOREIGN COUNTRY

Charles Cumming was born in Scotland in 1971. He has been described as 'the man who most successfully gets under the skin of Britain's intelligence agencies' (*The Times*). In the summer of 1995, he was approached for recruitment by the Secret Intelligence Service (MI6). A year later he moved to Montreal where he began working on a novel based on his experiences with MI6, and *A Spy By Nature* was published in the UK in 2001. *A Foreign Country* is his sixth novel.

In 2012, Charles won the CWA Ian Fleming Steel Dagger for Best Thriller and the Bloody Scotland Scottish Crime Book of the Year for *A Foreign Country*.

charlescumming.co.uk

twitter.com/CharlesCumming

facebook.com/AuthorCharlesCumming

CHARLES CUMMING

A Foreign Country

HARPER

Harper

An imprint of HarperCollins*Publishers*
77–85 Fulham Palace Road,
Hammersmith, London W6 8JB

www.harpercollins.co.uk

This paperback edition 2013

5

Copyright © Charles Cumming 2012

Charles Cumming asserts the moral right to be identified as the author of this work

A catalogue record for this book is available from the British Library

ISBN: 978 0 00 734643 1

Extract from *The Spirit Level* copyright © Seamus Heaney
Published in Great Britain by Faber and Faber 2001
reproduced by permission of Faber and Faber

Extract from *The Go-Between* by L.P. Hartley © 1953 Hamish Hamilton
reproduced by permission of Penguin Books Ltd

Extract from *Ashenden* by W. Somerset Maugham © 1928 William Heinemann
reproduced by kind permission of A P Watt on behalf of the Royal Literary Fund

Set in Meridien by Palimpsest Book Production Limited,
Falkirk, Stirlingshire

Printed and bound in Great Britain by Clays Ltd, St Ives plc

MIX
Paper from
responsible sources
FSC® C007454

FSC™ is a non-profit international organisation established to promote
the responsible management of the world's forests. Products carrying the
FSC label are independently certified to assure consumers that they come
from forests that are managed to meet the social, economic and
ecological needs of present and future generations,
and other controlled sources.

Find out more about HarperCollins and the environment at
www.harpercollins.co.uk/green

For Carolyn Hanbury

'There's just one thing I think you ought to know before you take on this job . . . If you do well you'll get no thanks and if you get into trouble you'll get no help. Does that suit you?'

'Perfectly.'

'Then I'll wish you good afternoon.'

W. Somerset Maugham, *Ashenden*

'The past is a foreign country: they do things differently there.'

L.P. Hartley, *The Go-Between*

Tunisia, 1978

1

Jean-Marc Daumal awoke to the din of the call to prayer and to the sound of his children weeping. It was just after seven o'clock on an airless Tunisian morning. For an instant, as he adjusted his eyes to the sunlight, Daumal was oblivious to the wretchedness of his situation; then the memory of it took him like a shortness of breath. He almost cried out in despair, staring up at the cracked, whitewashed ceiling, a married man of forty-one at the mercy of a broken heart.

Amelia Weldon had been gone for six days. Gone without warning, gone without reason, gone without leaving a note. One moment she had been caring for his children at the villa – preparing their supper, reading them a bedtime story – the next she had disappeared. At dawn on Saturday, Jean-Marc's wife, Celine, had found the au pair's bedroom stripped of its belongings, Amelia's suitcases taken from the cupboard, her photographs and posters removed from the walls. The family safe in the utility room was locked, but Amelia's passport, and a necklace that she had placed there for safekeeping, were both missing. There was no record at Port de la Goulette of a twenty-year-old British woman matching Amelia's description boarding a ferry for Europe, nor any airline out of Tunis with a passenger listing for 'Amelia Weldon'. No hotel or hostel in the city had a guest registered under her name and the few fresh-faced students and ex-pats with whom she had socialized in Tunis appeared to know nothing of her whereabouts. Presenting himself as a concerned employer, Jean-Marc had made enquiries at the British Embassy, telexed the agency in Paris that had arranged Amelia's employment and telephoned her brother in Oxford. Nobody, it seemed, could unravel the enigma of her disappearance. Jean-Marc's only solace lay in the fact that her body had not been discovered in some back alley of Tunis or Carthage; that she had not been admitted to hospital suffering from an illness, which might have taken her from him for ever. He was otherwise utterly bereft. The woman who had brought upon him the exquisite torture of infatuation had vanished as completely as an echo in the night.

The children's crying continued. Jean-Marc pulled back the single white sheet covering his body and sat up on the bed, massaging an ache in the small of his back. He heard Celine saying: 'I am telling you for the last time, Thibaud, you are *not* watching cartoons until you finish your breakfast' and it took all of his strength not to rise from the bed, to stride into the kitchen and, in his fury, to smack his son through the thin shorts of his Asterix pyjamas. Instead, Daumal drank from a half-empty glass of water on the bedside table, opened the curtains and stood on the first-floor balcony, gazing out over the rooftops of La Marsa. A tanker was moving west to east across the horizon, two days from Suez. Had Amelia left by private boat? Guttmann, he knew, kept a yacht out at Hammamet. The rich American Jew with his contacts and his privilege, the rumours of links to the MOSSAD. Daumal had seen how Guttmann had looked at Amelia; a man who had never wanted for anything in his life desired her as his prize. Had he taken her from him? There was no evidence to support his baseless jealousy, only the cuckold's fear of humiliation. Numb from lack of sleep, Daumal settled on a plastic chair on the balcony, a smell of baking bread rising up from a neighbouring garden. Two metres away, close to the window, he spotted a half-finished packet of Mars Légère and lit one with a steady hand, coughing on the first lungful of smoke.

Footsteps in the bedroom. The children had stopped crying. Celine appeared at the balcony door and said: 'You're awake,' in a tone of voice that managed to harden his heart against her still further. He knew that his wife blamed him for what had happened. But she did not know the truth. Had she guessed, she might even have comforted him; her own father, after all, had consorted with dozens of women during his married life. He wondered why Celine had not simply fired Amelia. That, at least, would have saved him from this season of pain. It was as though she wanted to torment him by keeping her in the house.

'I'm awake,' he replied, although Celine was long gone, locked in the bathroom under her ritual cold shower, scrubbing the child-altered body that was now repulsive to him. Jean-Marc stubbed out his cigarette, returned to the bedroom, found his dressing-gown discarded on the floor and walked downstairs to the kitchen.

Fatima, one of two maids assigned to the Daumal

residence as part of the ex-pat package offered by his employers in France, was putting on an apron. Jean-Marc ignored her and, finding a percolator of coffee on the stove, prepared himself a café au lait. Thibaud and Lola were giggling with one another in an adjoining room, but he did not wish to see them. Instead he sat in his office, the door closed, sipping from the bowl of coffee. Every room, every smell, every idiosyncrasy of the villa held for him a memory of Amelia. It was in this office that they had first kissed. It was at the base of those oleander trees at the rear of the property, visible now through the window, that they had first made love in the dead of night, while Celine slept obliviously indoors. Later, Jean-Marc would take appalling risks, slipping away from his bedroom at two or three o'clock in the morning to be with Amelia, to hold her, to swallow her, to touch and manipulate a body that was so intoxicating to him that he actually laughed at the memory of it. And then he heard himself entertaining such thoughts and knew that he was little more than a romantic, self-pitying fool. So many times he had been on the brink of confessing, of telling Celine every secret of the affair: the rooms that he and Amelia had taken in hotels in Tunis; the five April days that they had spent together in Sfax while his wife had been in Beaune with the children. Jean-Marc knew, as he had always known, that he enjoyed deceiving Celine; it was a form of revenge for all the stillness and *ennui* of their marriage. The lying kept him sane. Amelia had understood that. Perhaps that was what had bound them together – a shared aptitude for deceit. He had been astonished at her ability to finesse their indiscretions, to cover her tracks so that Celine had no suspicion of what was going on. There were the mischievous lies at breakfast

– 'Thank you, yes, I slept *very* well' – combined with a studied indifference towards Jean-Marc whenever the two lovers found themselves in Celine's company. It was Amelia who had suggested that he pay for their hotel rooms in cash, to avoid any dubious transactions appearing on Jean-Marc's bank statements. It was Amelia who had stopped wearing perfume, so that the scent of Hermès Calèche would not be carried back to the marital bed. There was no question in Jean-Marc's mind that she had derived a deep satisfaction from these clandestine games.

The telephone rang. It was rare for anybody to call the house before eight o'clock in the morning; Jean-Marc was certain that Amelia was trying to contact him. He picked up the receiver and said: '*Oui*?' in near-desperation.

A woman with an American accent replied: 'John Mark?'

It was Guttmann's wife. The WASP heiress, her father a senator, family money stinking all the way back to the *Mayflower*.

'Joan?'

'That's right. Have I called at a bad moment?'

He had no time to lament her blithe assumption that all conversations between them should be conducted in English. Neither Joan nor her husband had made any attempt to learn even rudimentary French, only Arabic.

'No, it is not a bad time. I was just on my way to work.' He assumed that Joan wanted to arrange to spend the day at the beach with his children. 'Do you want to speak to Celine?'

A pause. Some of the customary energy went out of Joan's voice and her mood became businesslike, even sombre.

'Actually, John Mark, I wanted to speak with you.'

5

'With *me*?'

'It's about Amelia.'

Joan knew. She had found out about the affair. Was she going to expose him?

'What about her?' His tone of voice had become hostile.

'She has asked me to convey a message to you.'

'You've *seen* her?'

It was like hearing that a relative, assumed dead, was alive and well. He was certain now that she would come back to him.

'I have seen her,' Joan replied. 'She's worried about you.'

Daumal would have fallen on this expression of devotion like a dog snatching at a bone, had it not been necessary to sustain the lie.

'Well, yes, Celine and the children have been very concerned. One moment Amelia was here with them, the next she was gone . . .'

'No. Not Celine. Not the children. She's worried about *you*.'

He felt the hope rushing out of him, a door slammed by a sudden wind.

'About *me*? I don't understand.'

Another careful pause. Joan and Amelia had always been close. As Guttmann had entrapped her in charm and money, Joan had played the caring older sister, a role model of elegance and sophistication to which Amelia might one day aspire.

'I think you do understand, John Mark.'

The game was up. The affair had been revealed. Everybody knew that Jean-Marc Daumal had fallen hopelessly and ridiculously in love with a twenty-year-old au pair. He would be a laughing stock in the expatriate community.

'I wanted to catch you before you went to work. I wanted to reassure you that nobody knows about this. I have not spoken to David, nor do I intend to say anything to Celine.'

'Thank you,' Jean-Marc replied quietly.

'Amelia has left Tunisia. Last night, as a matter of fact. She's going to go travelling for a while. She wanted me to tell you how sorry she is for the way things worked out. She never intended to hurt you or to abandon your family in the way that she did. She cares for you very deeply. It all just got too much for her, you know? Her heart was confused. Am I making sense, John Mark?'

'You are making sense.'

'So perhaps you might tell Celine that this was Amelia on the phone. Calling from the airport. Tell your children that she won't be coming back.'

'I will do that.'

'I think it's best, don't you? I think it's best if you forget all about her.'

The Present Day

2

Philippe and Jeannine Malot, of 79 Rue Pelleport, Paris, had been planning their dream holiday in Egypt for more than a year. Philippe, who had recently retired, had set aside a budget of three thousand euros and found an airline that was prepared to fly them to Cairo (albeit at six o'clock in the morning) for less than the price of a return taxi to Charles de Gaulle airport. They had researched the best hotels in Cairo and Luxor on the Internet and secured an over-60s discount at a luxury resort in Sharm-el-Sheikh, where they planned to relax for the final five days of their journey.

The Malots had arrived in Cairo on a humid summer afternoon, making love almost as soon as they had closed the door of their hotel room. Jeannine had then set about unpacking while Philippe remained in bed reading Naguib Mahfouz's *Akhénaton le Renégat*, a novel that he was not altogether enjoying. After a short walk around the local neighbourhood, they had eaten dinner in one of the hotel's three restaurants and fallen asleep before midnight to the muffled sounds of Cairene traffic.

Three enjoyable, if exhausting days, followed. Though she had developed a minor stomach complaint, Jeannine managed five hours of wide-eyed browsing in the Egyptian Museum, where she declared herself 'awestruck' by the treasures of Tutankhamun. On the second morning of their trip, the Malots had set off by taxi shortly after breakfast and were astonished – as all first-time visitors were – to find the Pyramids looming into view no more than a few hundred metres from a nondescript residential suburb at the edge of the city. Hounded by trinket-sellers and under-qualified guides, they had completed a full circuit of the area within two hours and asked a shaven-headed German tourist to take their photograph in front of the Sphinx. Jeannine was keen to enter the Pyramid at Cheops, but went alone, because Philippe suffered from a mild claustrophobia and had been warned by a colleague at work that the interior was both cramped and stiflingly hot. In a mood of jubilation at having finally witnessed a phenomenon that had enthralled her since childhood, Jeannine paid an Egyptian man the equivalent of fifteen euros for a brief ride on a camel. It had moaned throughout and smelled strongly of diesel. She had then accidentally deleted the picture of her husband astride the beast while attempting to organize the pictures on their digital camera at lunch the following day.

On the recommendation of an article in a French style magazine, they had travelled to Luxor by overnight train and booked a room at the Winter Palace, albeit in the Pavilion, a four-star annexed development added to the original colonial hotel. An enterprising tourism company offered donkey rides to the Valley of the Kings that left Luxor at five o'clock in the morning. The Malots had duly signed up, witnessing a dramatic sunrise over the Temple at Hatshepsut just after six a.m. They had then spent what they later agreed had been the best day of their holiday travelling out to the temples at Dendara and Abydos. On their final afternoon in Luxor, Philippe and Jeannine had taken a taxi to the Temple at Karnak and stayed until the evening to witness the famous Sound and Light show. Philippe had fallen asleep within ten minutes.

By Tuesday they were in Sharm-el-Sheikh, on the Sinai Peninsula. Their hotel boasted three swimming pools, a hairdressing salon, two cocktail bars, nine tennis courts and enough security to deter an army of Islamist fanatics. On that first evening, the Malots had decided to go for a short walk along the beach. Though their hotel was at full occupancy, no other tourists were visible in the moonlight as they made their way from the concrete walkway at the perimeter of the hotel down on to the still-warm sand.

It was afterwards estimated that they had been attacked by at least three men, each armed with knives and metal poles. Jeannine's necklace had been torn away, scattering pearls on to the sand, and her gold wedding ring removed from her finger. Philippe had had a noose placed around his neck and been jerked upright as a second assailant sliced through his throat and stabbed him repeatedly in the chest and legs. He had bled to death within a few minutes. A torn bed sheet that had been stuffed into her mouth had muffled Jeannine's screams. Her own throat was also slashed, her arms heavily bruised, her stomach and hips struck repeatedly by a metal pole.

A young Canadian couple, honeymooning at a neighbouring hotel, had noticed the commotion and heard Madame Malot's stifled cries, but could not see what was happening in the light of the waning moon. By the time they got there, the men who had attacked and murdered the elderly French couple had vanished into the night, leaving a scene of devastation that the Egyptian authorities quickly dismissed as a random act of violence, perpetrated by outsiders, which was 'highly unlikely ever to happen again'.

3

Taking someone in the street is as easy as lighting a cigarette, they had told him, and as Akim Errachidi waited in the van, he knew that he had the balls to pull it off.

It was a Monday night in late July. The target had been given a nickname – HOLST – and its movements monitored for fourteen days. Phone, email, bedroom, car: the team had everything covered. Akim had to hand it to the guys in charge – they were thorough and determined; they had thought through every detail. He was dealing with pros now and, yes, you really could tell the difference.

Beside him, in the driver's seat of the van, Slimane Nassah was tapping his fingers in time to some R&B on RFM and talking, in vivid detail, about what he wanted to do to Beyoncé Knowles.

'What an ass, man. Just give me five minutes with that sweet ass.' He made the shape of it with his hands, brought it down towards his circling groin. Akim laughed.

'Turn that shit off,' said the boss, crouched by the side

door and ready to spring. Slimane switched off the radio. 'HOLST in sight. Thirty seconds.'

It was just as they had said it would be. The dark street, a well-known short-cut, most of Paris in bed. Akim saw the target on the opposite side of the street, about to cross at the postbox.

'Ten seconds.' The boss at his very best. 'Remember, nobody is going to hurt anybody.'

The trick, Akim knew, was to move as quickly as possible, making the minimum amount of noise. In the movies, it was always the opposite way: the smash-and-grab of a screaming, adrenalized SWAT team crashing through walls, lobbing stun grenades, shouldering jet-black assault rifles. Not us, said the boss. We do it quiet and we do it slick. We open the door, we get behind HOLST, we make sure nobody sees.

'Five seconds.'

On the radio, Akim heard the woman saying 'Clear' which meant that there were no civilians within sighting distance of the van.

'OK. We go.'

There was a kind of choreographed beauty to it. As HOLST strolled past Akim's door, three things happened simultaneously: Slimane started the engine; Akim stepped out into the street; and the boss slid open the side panel of the van. If the target knew what was happening, there was no indication of it. Akim wrapped his left arm around HOLST's neck, smothered the gaping mouth with his hand and, with his right arm, lifted the body up into the van. The boss did the rest, grabbing at the legs and pulling them inside. Akim then came in behind them, sliding the door shut, just as he had rehearsed a dozen times. They pushed the prisoner to the floor. He heard the boss say: 'Go', as calm and controlled as a man buying a ticket for a train, and Slimane pulled the van out into the street.

The whole thing had taken less than twenty seconds.

4

Thomas Kell woke up in a strange bed, in a strange house, in a city with which he was all too familiar. It was eleven o'clock on an August morning in the eighth month of his enforced retirement from the Secret Intelligence Service. He was a forty-two-year-old man, estranged from his forty-three-year-old wife, with a hangover comparable in range and intensity to the reproduction Jackson Pollock hanging on the wall of his temporary bedroom.

Where the hell was he? Kell had unreliable memories of a fortieth birthday party in Kensington, of a crowded cab to a bar in Dean Street, of a nightclub in the wilds of Hackney – after that, everything was a blank.

He pulled back the duvet. He saw that he had fallen asleep in his clothes. Toys and magazines were piled up in one corner of the room. He climbed to his feet, searched in vain for a glass of water and opened the curtains. His mouth was dry, his head tight as a compress as he adjusted to the light.

It was a grey morning, shiftless and damp. He appeared to be on the first floor of a semi-detached house of indeterminate location in a quiet residential street. A small pink bicycle was secured in the drive by a loop of black cable, thick as a python. A hundred metres away, a learner driver with Jackie's School of Motoring had stalled midway through a three-point turn. Kell closed the curtains and listened for signs of life in the house. Slowly, like a half-remembered anecdote, fragments of the previous evening began to assemble in his mind. There had been trays of shots: absinthe and tequila. There had been dancing in a low-roofed basement. He had met a large group of Czech foreign students and talked at length about *Mad Men* and Don Draper. Kell was fairly sure that at a certain point he had shared a cab with an enormous man named Zoltan. Alcoholic blackouts had been a regular feature of his youth, but it had been many years since he had woken up with next to no recollection of a night's events; twenty years in the secret world had taught him the advantage of being the last man standing.

Kell was looking around for his trousers when his mobile phone began to ring. The number had been withheld.

'Tom?'

At first, through the fog of his hangover, Kell failed to recognize the voice. Then the familiar cadence came back to him.

'Jimmy? Christ.'

Jimmy Marquand was a former colleague of Kell's, now one of the high priests of SIS. His was the last hand Kell had shaken before taking his leave of Vauxhall Cross on a crisp December morning eight months earlier.

'We have a problem.'

'No small talk?' Kell said. 'Don't want to know how life is treating me in the private sector?'

'This is serious, Tom. I've walked half a mile to a phone box in Lambeth so the call won't be scooped. I need your help.'

'Personal or professional?' Kell located his trousers beneath a blanket on the back of a chair.

'We've lost the Chief.'

That stopped him. Kell reached out and put a hand against a wall in the bedroom. Suddenly he was as sober and clear-headed as a child.

'You've *what*?'

'Vanished. Five days ago. Nobody has any workable idea where the hell she's gone or what's happened to her.'

'*She*?' The anti-Rimington brigade within MI6 had long been allergic to the notion of a female Chief. It was almost beyond belief that the all-male inmates at Vauxhall Cross had finally allowed a woman to be appointed to the most prestigious position in British Intelligence. 'When did that happen?'

'There's a lot you don't know,' Marquand replied. 'A lot that's changed. I can't say any more if we're talking like this.'

Then why are we talking at all? Kell thought. Do they want me to come back after everything that happened? Have Kabul and Yassin just been brushed under the carpet? 'I'm not working for George Truscott,' he said, saving Marquand the effort of asking the question. 'I'm not coming back if Haynes still has his hands on the tiller.'

'Just for this,' Marquand replied.

'For nothing.'

It was almost the truth. Then Kell found himself saying: 'I'm beginning to enjoy having nothing to do,' which was an outright lie. There was a noise on the other end of the line that might have been the extinguishing of Marquand's hopes.

20

'Tom, it's important. We need a re-tread, somebody who knows the ropes. You're the only one we can trust.'

Who was 'we'? The high priests? The same men who had turfed him out over Kabul? The same men who would happily have sacrificed him to the public inquiry currently assembling its tanks on the SIS lawn?

'Trust?' he replied, putting on a shoe.

'Trust,' said Marquand. It almost sounded as though he meant it.

Kell went to the window and looked outside, at the pink bicycle, at Jackie's learner driver, moving through the gears. What did the rest of his day hold? Aspirin and daytime TV. Hair-of-the-dog bloody Marys at the Greyhound Inn. He had spent eight months twiddling his thumbs; that was the truth of his new life in the 'private sector'. Eight months watching black-and-white matinees on TCM and drinking his pay-off in the pub. Eight months struggling to salvage a marriage that would not be saved.

'There must be somebody else who can do it,' he said. He hoped that there was nobody else. He hoped that he was getting back in the game.

'The new Chief isn't just anybody,' Marquand replied. 'Amelia Levene made "C". She was due to take over in six weeks.' He had played his ace. Kell sat down on the bed, pitching slowly forwards. Throwing Amelia into the mix changed everything. 'That's why it has to be you, Tom. That's why we need you to find her. You were the only person at the Office who really knew what made her tick.' He sugared the pill, in case Kell was still wavering. 'It's what you've wanted, isn't it? A second chance? Get this done and the file on Yassin will be closed. That's coming from the highest levels. Find her and we can bring you in from the cold.'

21

5

Kell had returned to his bachelor's bedsit in a near-derelict
Fiat Punto driven by a moonlighting Sudanese cab driver who
kept a packet of Lockets and a well-thumbed copy of the
Koran on the dashboard. Pulling away from the house – which
had indeed belonged to a genial, gym-addicted Pole named
Zoltan with whom Kell had shared a drunken cab-ride from
Hackney – he had recognized the shabby streets of Finsbury
Park from a long-ago joint operation with MI5. He tried to
remember the exact details of the job: an Irish Republican; a
plot to blow up a department store; the convicted man later
released under the terms of the Good Friday Agreement.
Amelia Levene had been his boss at the time.

Her disappearance was unquestionably the gravest crisis
MI6 had faced since the fiasco of WMD. Officers didn't vanish,
simple as that. They didn't get kidnapped, they didn't get
murdered, they didn't defect. In particular, they didn't make
a point of going AWOL six weeks before they were due to
take over as Chief. If the news of Amelia's disappearance
leaked to the media – Christ, even if it leaked within the

walls of Vauxhall Cross – the blowback would be incendiary.

Kell had showered at home, eaten some leftover take-away Lebanese, levelled off his hangover with two codeine and a lukewarm half-litre of Coke. An hour later he was standing underneath a sycamore tree two hundred metres from the Serpentine Gallery, Jimmy Marquand striding towards him with a look on his face like his pension was on the line. He had come direct from Vauxhall Cross, wearing a suit and tie, but without the briefcase that usually accompanied him on official business. He was a slight man, a rangy weekend cyclist, tanned year-round and with a thick mop of lustrous hair that had earned him the nickname 'Melvyn' in the corridors of SIS. Kell had to remind himself that he had every right to refuse what Marquand was going to offer. But, of course, that was never going to happen. If Amelia was missing, he had to be the one to find her.

They exchanged a brief handshake and turned north-west in the direction of Kensington Palace.

'So how is life in the private sector?' Marquand asked. Humour didn't always come easily to him, particularly at times of stress. 'Keeping busy? Behaving?'

Kell wondered why he was making the effort. 'Something like that,' he said.

'Reading all those nineteenth-century novels you promised yourself?' Marquand sounded like a man speaking words that had been written for him. 'Tending your garden? Tapping out the memoirs?'

'The memoirs are finished,' Kell said. 'You come out of them very badly.'

'No more than I deserve.' Marquand appeared to run out of things to say. Kell knew that his apparent bonhomie

23

was a mask concealing a grave, institutional panic over Amelia's disappearance. He put him out of his misery.

'How the fuck did this happen, Jimmy?'

Marquand tried to circumvent the question.

'Word came through from Number 10 shortly after you left,' he said. 'They wanted an Arabist, they wanted a woman. She'd impressed the Prime Minister on the JIC. He finds out we've lost her, it's curtains.'

'That's not what I meant.'

'I know that's not what you meant.' Marquand's reply was terse and he looked away, as though ashamed that the crisis had happened on his watch. 'Two weeks ago she had a briefing with Haynes, the traditional one-on-one in which the baton gets passed from one Chief to the next. Secrets exchanged, tall tales told, all the things that you and me and the good people of Britain are not supposed to know.'

'Such as?'

'You tell me.'

'What, then? Who shot JR? A fifth plane on 9/11? Give me the facts, Jimmy. What did he tell her? Let's stop fucking around.'

'All right, all right.' Marquand swept back his hair. 'Sunday morning she announces that she has to go to Paris, for a funeral. Taking a couple of days off. Then, on Wednesday, we get another message. An email. She's strung out after the funeral and has decided to take some holiday. South of France. No warning, just using up the rest of her allowance before the top job sucks all of her time. A painting course in Nice, something that she'd "always wanted to crack".' Kell thought that he caught a vapour of alcohol on Marquand's breath. It could equally well have been his own. 'Told us that she'd be back in two weeks, reachable

24

on such-and-such a number at such-and-such a hotel in the event of any emergency.'

'Then what?'

Marquand was holding his hair in place against the buffeting London wind. He came to a halt. A blue plastic bag cartwheeled beside him across a patch of unmown grass, snagging in a nearby tree. He lowered his voice, as though ashamed by what he was about to say.

'George sent somebody after her. Off the books.'

'Now why would he do a thing like that?'

'He was suspicious that she'd arranged a holiday so soon after the download with Haynes. It seemed unusual.'

Kell knew that George Truscott, as Assistant to the Chief, had been the man lined up to succeed Simon Haynes as 'C'; as far as most observers were concerned, it was merely a question of the PM waving him through. Truscott would have had the suit made, the furniture fitted, the dye-stamped invitations waiting to go out in the post. But Amelia Levene had stolen his prize. A woman. A second-class citizen in the SIS firmament. His resentment towards her would have been toxic.

'What's unusual about taking a holiday at this time of year?'

Kell felt that he knew the answer to his own question. Amelia's story made no sense. It wasn't like her to attend a painting course; a woman like that didn't need a *hobby*. In all the years that he had known Amelia, she had used her holidays as opportunities for relaxation. Health spas, detox clinics, five-star lodges with salad bars and wall-to-wall masseurs. She had never spoken of a desire to paint. As Marquand contemplated his answer, Kell walked across the stretch of unmown ground, pulled the plastic bag clear of the tree and stuffed it into the back pocket of his jeans.

'You're a model citizen, Tom, a model citizen.' Marquand looked down at his shoes and gave a heavy sigh, as if he was tired of making excuses for the failings of other men. 'Of course there's nothing unusual about taking a holiday this time of year. But usually we have more warning. Usually it goes in the diary several months in advance. This looked like a sudden decision, a reaction to something that Haynes had told her.'

'What was Haynes's view on that?'

'He agreed with Truscott. So they asked some friends in Nice to keep an eye on her.'

Again, Kell kept his counsel. Towards the end of his career, he had himself become a victim of the paranoid, near-delusional manoeuvrings of George Truscott, yet he was still privately astonished that the two most senior figures in the Service had green-lit a surveillance operation against one of their own.

'Who are the friends in Nice? Liaison?'

'Christ, no. Avoid the Frog at all costs. Re-treads. Ours. Bill Knight and his wife, Barbara. Retired to Menton in '98. We got them to sign up for the painting course, they saw Amelia arrive on Wednesday afternoon, enjoyed a bit of a chat. Then Bill reported her missing when she failed to turn up three mornings in a row.'

'What's unusual about that?'

Marquand frowned. 'I'm not sure I follow you.'

'Well, couldn't Amelia have taken a couple of days off? Got sick?'

'That's just it. She didn't call it in. Barbara rang the hotel, there was no sign of her. We telephoned Amelia's husband –'

'– Giles,' said Kell.

'Giles, yes, but he hasn't heard from her since she left Wiltshire. Her mobile is switched off, she's not responding to emails, there's been no activity on her credit cards. It's a total blackout.'

'What about the police?'

Marquand bounced his caterpillar eyebrows and said: '*Bof*' in a cod French accent. 'They haven't scraped her off a motorway or found her body floating in the Med, if that's what you mean.' He saw Kell's reaction to this and felt compelled to apologize. 'Sorry, that was tasteless. I didn't mean to sound glib. This whole thing is a bloody mystery.'

Kell ran through a list of possible explanations, as arbitrary as they were inexhaustible: Russian or Iranian interference in some aspect of Amelia's personal affairs; a clandestine arrangement with the Yanks relating to Libya and the Arab Spring; a sudden crisis of faith engendered by something in the meeting with Haynes. In the run-up to Kell's demise at SIS, Amelia had been knee-deep in Francophone West Africa, which might have aroused interest from the French or Chinese. Islamist involvement was a permanent concern.

'What about known aliases?' He felt the dryness of his hangover again, the bluntness of three hours' sleep. 'Isn't it possible she's running an operation, one that Tweedledum and Tweedledee know nothing about?'

Marquand conceded the possibility of this, but wondered what was so secret that it would require Amelia Levene to disappear without at the very least enlisting the technical support of GCHQ.

'Look,' he said. 'The only people who know about this are Haynes, Truscott and the Knights. Paris Station is still in the dark and it needs to stay that way. This leaks out, the Service will be a laughing stock. God knows where it would end. She's due to meet the PM formally in two weeks' time. Obviously that meeting can't be cancelled without creating a gold-tinted Whitehall shitstorm. Washington finds out we've lost our most senior spy, they'll go ballistic. Haynes wants to find her within the next few days and pretend that none of this happened. She's due back Monday week.' Marquand looked quickly to his right, as though reacting to a sudden noise. 'Look, maybe she'll just show up. It'll probably be some smoothie from Paris, a Jean-Pierre or a Xavier with a big cock and a gîte in Aix-en-Provence. You know what Amelia's like with the boys. Madonna could take notes.'

Kell was surprised to hear Marquand talk of Amelia's reputation so candidly. Philandering, like alcohol, was almost an Office prerequisite, but it was a male sport, jocular and off the books. In all the years that Kell had known her, Amelia had had no more than three lovers, yet she was spoken of as though she had slept her way through seventy-five per cent of the Civil Service.

'Why Paris?'

Marquand looked up. 'She stopped there on the way down to Nice.'

'My question stands. Why Paris?'

'She went to the funeral on Tuesday.'

'Whose funeral?'

'I have absolutely no idea.' For a dyed-in-the-wool careerist, Marquand didn't seem unduly concerned about admitting to gaps in his knowledge. 'All this has happened very fast, Tom. We haven't been able to get a name. Giles thinks she went to a crematorium in the Fourteenth. Montparnasse. An old friend from student days.'

'He didn't go with her?'

'She told him he wasn't wanted.'

28

'And Giles does what Giles is told to do.' Kell knew all too well the mechanics of the Levene marriage; he had studied it closely, as a cautionary tale. Marquand looked as if he was about to laugh but thought better of it.

'Precisely. Dennis Thatcher syndrome. Husbands should be seen and not heard.'

'Sounds to me like you need to find out who the friend was.' Kell was stating the obvious, but Marquand appeared to have run out of road.

'Do I take that as an indication that you'll help?'

Kell looked up. The branches of the tree were obscuring a charcoal sky. It was going to rain. He thought of Afghanistan, of the book he was meant to be writing, of the vapid August nights stretching ahead of him at his bachelor's bedsit in Kensal Rise. He thought about his wife and he thought about Amelia. He was convinced that she was alive and convinced that Marquand was hiding something. How many other re-treads would be sent on her tail?

'How much is Her Majesty offering?'

'How much would you need?' It was somebody else's cash, so Jimmy Marquand could afford to splash it about. Kell didn't care about the money, not at all, but didn't want to appear sloppy by not asking. He plucked a figure out of the damp afternoon sky. 'A thousand a day. Plus expenses. I'll need a laptop, encrypted, ditto a mobile and the Stephen Uniacke alias. Decent car waiting for me at Nice airport. If it's a Peugeot with two doors and a tape deck, I'm coming home.'

'Sure.'

'And George Truscott pays my speeding fines. All of them.'

'Done.'

6

Kell caught a flight out of Heathrow at eight. As he was switching it to 'Flight Mode', a text message came through on his mobile phone:

> Don't forget appointment tomorrow. 2pm Finchley. Meet you at the Tube.

Finchley. The death throes of his marriage. An hour with a grim-faced guidance counsellor who offered up platitudes like biscuits on a plate. It occurred to Kell, clicking his seat belt on the aisle, that this was only the second time that he had left London in the eight months since his departure from SIS. In mid-March, Claire had suggested a 'romantic weekend' in Brighton – 'to see if we can be more than ships passing in the night' – but the hotel had played host to an all-night wedding party, they had slept for only three hours, and by Sunday were lost in a familiar blizzard of recrimination and argument.

A young mother was seated beside him on the plane, a

toddler strapped into the window seat. She had come prepared for the battle ahead, producing a bag stuffed with magazines and stickers, sugar-free biscuits and a bottle of water. Every now and again, when the boy fidgeted too much or screamed too loudly, his mother would offer up a knowing smile that was halfway to an apology. Kell tried to reassure her that he couldn't care less: it was only an hour and a half to Nice and he liked the company of children.

'Do you have kids of your own?' she said, the question that should never be asked.

'No,' Kell replied, picking up a green plastic figurine that had fallen on the floor. 'Sadly not.'

The mother was preoccupied throughout the flight and Kell was able to read the notes he had made from Amelia's classified file without being concerned about wandering eyes: the man in the seat across the aisle was engrossed in a spreadsheet; the woman behind him, over his left shoulder, asleep on an inflatable neck pillow. He knew most of Amelia's story already; they had swapped secrets during the strange intimacy of a fifteen-year friendship. Her journey into the secret world had begun at a young age. While working in Tunis as an au pair in the late 1970s Amelia had been talent-spotted by Joan Guttmann, a deep-cover officer with the Central Intelligence Agency. Guttmann had brought Amelia to the attention of SIS, which had kept an eye on her at Oxford, making an initial move to recruit soon after she had been awarded a starred First in French and Arabic in the summer of 1983. After a year at MECAS, the so-called 'School for Spies' in Lebanon, she had been posted to Egypt in '85 and to Iraq in '89. Returning to London in the spring of 1993, Amelia Weldon had met and quickly become engaged to Giles Levene, a fifty-two-year-old bond trader with thirty million in the bank and a personality described by one of Kell's former colleagues as 'aggressively soporific'. The file noted, with a passive anti-Semitism of the sort Kell believed had largely died out within SIS, that Levene was considered 'ambivalent' on Israel, but that his wife's 'attitudes in that area' should 'nevertheless be monitored for indications of bias'.

In such a context, Amelia's rise to power made for fascinating reading. There had been an astonishing amount of sexism directed towards her, particularly in the early phase of her career. In Egypt, for example, she had been over-looked for promotion on the grounds that she was unlikely to remain in the Service 'beyond child-bearing years'. The position had gone instead to a celebrated Cairo alcoholic with two marriages behind him and a record of producing CX reports lifted from the pages of *Al-Ahram*. Her fortunes began to shift in Iraq, where she worked under non-official cover as an analyst for a French conglomerate. An Irish passport had kept 'Ann Wilkes' in Baghdad for the duration of the first Gulf War, and her access to officials in the Ba'ath party, as well as to prominent figures in the Iraqi military structure, had been lauded both in London and in the United States. Since then, her career had gone from strength to strength: there were postings in Washington and to Kabul, where she had operational control of SIS operations throughout Afghanistan for more than two years following the toppling of the Taliban. In an indication of her ambitions for the Service, she had argued for a more robust British influence in Africa, a stance viewed as prescient by Downing Street in the wake of the Arab Spring, but one that had brought her into conflict with George Truscott, a corporatized bureaucrat with a Cold War mindset who was widely despised by the rank and file within SIS.

Kell closed the notebook. He looked at the child beside him, now sleeping in his mother's arms, and tried to relish some sense of being back in the game. Yet he felt nothing. For eight months he had been treading water, pretending to himself and to Claire that he had taken a principled stand against the double-think and mendacity of the secret state. It was nonsense, of course; they had turfed him out in disgrace. And when Marquand had come calling, the bagman for Truscott and Haynes, Kell had jumped back aboard like a child at a fairground, relishing the prospect of another ride. He realized that any determination he had felt to prove them wrong, to proclaim his innocence, even to create a new life for himself, had been built on sand. He had nothing but his past to live on, nothing but his skills as a spy.

Somewhere over the southern Alps the cabin lights dimmed like an eye test. The flight was on time. Kell looked out of the starboard window and searched for the glow of Nice. A stewardess strapped herself into a rear-facing seat, checked her face in a compact mirror and flashed him an air-conditioned smile. Kell nodded back, necked two aspirin and the remains of a bottle of water, then sat back as the plane banked over the Mediterranean. The landing earned the captain a round of applause from three drunken Yorkshiremen seated two rows behind him. Kell had no luggage in the hold and had cleared Immigration, on his own passport, by eleven fifteen.

The Knights were in Arrivals. Jimmy Marquand had told him to look out for 'a British couple in their mid-sixties', he 'a denizen of the tanning salon with a dyed moustache', she 'a tiny, rather sympathetic bird who's quick on her feet but permanently in her husband's shadow'.

The description was near-perfect. Emerging from the customs hall through a set of automatic doors, Kell was confronted by a languid Englishman with a deep suntan, wearing pressed chinos and a button-down cream shirt. A pistachio cashmere jumper was slung over his shoulders and knotted, in the Mediterranean style, across his chest. The moustache was no longer dyed but it looked as though Bill Knight had dedicated at least fifteen minutes of his evening to combing every strand of his thinning white hair. Here was a man who had never quite forgiven himself for growing old.

'Tom, I assume,' he said, the voice too loud, the handshake too firm, full lips rolling under his moustache as though life was a wine he was tasting. Kell toyed with the idea of saying: 'I'd prefer it if you referred to me at all times as Mr Kell,' but didn't have the energy to hurt his feelings.

'And you must be Barbara.' Behind Knight, lingering in what Claire called 'the Rain Man position', was a small lady with half-moon spectacles and a deteriorated posture. Her shy, sliding eye contact managed both to apologize for her husband's slightly ludicrous demeanour and to establish an immediate professional chemistry that Kell was glad of. Knight, he knew, would do most of the talking, but he would get the most productive information from his wife.

'We have your car waiting outside,' she said, as Knight offered to carry his bag. Kell waved away the offer and experienced the unsettling realization that his own mother, had she lived, would now be the same vintage as this diminutive lady with unkempt grey hair, creased clothes and soft, uncomplicated gestures.

'It's a luxury saloon,' said Knight, as if he disapproved of the expense. His voice had a smug, adenoidal quality that had already become irritating. 'I think you'll be quite satisfied.'

They walked towards the exit. Kell caught their reflection in a facing window and felt like a wayward son visiting his parents at a retirement complex on the Costa del Sol. It seemed astonishing to him that all that SIS had placed between the disappearance of Amelia Levene and a national scandal were a superannuated spook with a hangover and two borderline geriatric re-treads who hadn't been in the game since the fall of the Berlin Wall. Perhaps Marquand *intended* Kell to fail. Was that the plan? Or had the Knights come equipped with a hidden agenda, a plan to thwart Kell before he had even started?

'It's this way,' said Knight, as a young woman, under-nourished as a catwalk model, ran through the automatic doors and launched herself into the arms of a leathery lothario only a few years younger than Knight. Kell heard her say: '*Mon cherie!*' in a Russian accent and noted that she kept her eyes open when she kissed him.

They walked out into the humid French evening across a broad concrete apron that connected the terminal building to a three-storey car park a hundred metres to the east. The airport was gradually shutting down, buses nestled side by side beneath a blackened underpass, one of the drivers asleep at the wheel. A line of late arrivals were queuing for a connection to Monaco, all of them noticeably more chic and composed than the pint-swilling hordes Kell had witnessed at Heathrow airport. Knight paid for the car park, carefully folded the receipt into his wallet for expenses, and led him towards a black Citroën C6 on the upper level.

'The documents you requested arrived an hour ago and are in an envelope on the passenger seat,' he said. Kell assumed he was talking about the Uniacke legend, which Marquand had sent ahead by courier so that Kell would not have to carry a false passport through French customs. 'Be warned,' Knight continued, tapping his fingers on the back window, as though there was somebody hiding inside. 'It's a diesel. I can't tell you how many friends of ours come out here, rent a car from Hertz or Avis and then ruin their time in France by putting unleaded . . .'

Barbara put a stop to this.

'Bill, I'm quite sure Mr Kell is capable of filling up a car at a petrol station.' In the jaundiced light, it was difficult to see if her husband blushed. Kell remembered a line from Knight's file, which he had flicked through en route to the airport. 'Abhors a conversational vacuum. Tendency to talk when he might be wiser keeping his counsel.'

'That's OK,' Kell said. 'Easy mistake to make.'

The Knights' vehicle, parked alongside the C6, was a right-hand-drive Mercedes with twenty-year-old British plates and a dent on the front-right panel.

'An old and somewhat battered Merc,' Knight explained unnecessarily, as though he was used to the car attracting strange looks. 'But it does us very well. Once a year Barbara and I are obliged to drive back across the Channel to have an MOT and to update the insurance paperwork, but it's worth it . . .'

Kell had heard enough. He slung his bag in the back seat of the Citroën and got down to business.

'Let's talk about Amelia Levene,' he said. The car park

was deserted, the ambient noise of occasional planes and passing traffic smothering their conversation. Knight, who had been cut-off mid-sentence, looked suitably attentive. 'According to London, Mrs Levene went missing several days ago. Did you speak to her during the time she attended the painting course?'

'Absolutely,' said Knight, as if Kell was questioning their integrity. 'Of course.'

'What can you tell me about Amelia's mood, her behaviour?'

Barbara made to reply, but Knight interrupted her.

'Completely normal. Very friendly and enthusiastic. Introduced herself as a retired schoolteacher, widowed. Very little to report at all.'

Kell remembered another line from the Knight file: 'Not always prepared to go the extra mile. A feeling has developed among colleagues over the years that Bill Knight prefers the quiet life to getting his hands dirty.'

Barbara duly filled in the blanks.

'Well,' she said, sensing that Kell wasn't satisfied by her husband's answer, 'Bill and I have disagreed about this. I thought that she looked a little distracted. Didn't do an awful lot of painting, which seemed odd, given that she was there to learn. Also checked her phone rather a lot for text messages.' She glanced at Kell and produced a tiny, satisfied smile, like someone who has solved a taxing cross-word clue. 'That struck me as particularly strange. You see, people of her vintage aren't exactly glued to mobiles in the way that the younger generation are. Wouldn't you say, Mr Kell?'

'Call me Tom,' Kell said. 'What about friends, acquaint-ances? Did you see her with anybody? When London asked you to keep an eye on Mrs Levene, did you follow her into Nice? Did she go anywhere in the evenings?'

'That's an awful lot of questions all at once,' said Knight, looking pleased with himself.

'Answer them one at a time,' Kell said, and felt an operational adrenalin at last beginning to kick in. There was a sudden gust of wind and Knight did something compensatory with his hair.

'Well, Barbara and myself aren't aware that Mrs Levene went anywhere in particular. On Thursday evening, for example, she ate dinner alone at a restaurant on Rue Masséna. I followed her back to her hotel, sat in the Mercedes until midnight, but didn't see her leave.'

Kell met Knight's eye. 'You didn't think to take a room at the hotel?'

A pause, an awkward back-and-forth glance between husband and wife.

'What you have to understand, Tom, is that we haven't had a great deal of time to react to all this.' Knight, perhaps unconsciously, had taken a step backwards. 'London asked us simply to sign up for the course, to keep an eye on Mrs Levene, to report anything mysterious. That was all.'

Barbara took over the reins. She was plainly worried that they were giving Kell a poor impression of their abilities.

'It didn't sound as though London *expected* anything to happen,' she explained. 'It was almost pitched as though they were asking us to *look out* for her. And it's only been – what? – two or three days since we reported Mrs Levene missing.'

'And you're convinced that she's not in Nice, that she's not simply staying with a friend?'

'Oh, we're not convinced of *anything*,' Knight replied, which was the most convincing thing he had said since Kell had cleared customs. 'We did as we were told. Mrs Levene didn't show her face at the course, we rang it in. Mr Marquand must have smelled a rat and sent for reinforcements.'

Reinforcements. It occurred to Kell that exactly twenty-four hours earlier he was drinking in a crowded bar on Dean Street, singing 'Happy Birthday' to a forty-year-old university friend whom he hadn't seen for fifteen years.

'London are concerned that there's been no movement on Amelia's credit cards,' he said, 'no response from her mobile.'

'Do you think she's . . . *defected*?' Knight asked, and Kell suppressed a smile. Where to? Moscow? Beijing? Amelia would sooner live in Albania.

'Unlikely,' he said. 'Chiefs of the Service are too high profile. The political repercussions would be seismic. But never say never.'

'Never say never,' Barbara muttered.

'What about her room? Has anybody searched it?'

Knight looked at his shoes. Barbara adjusted her half-moon spectacles. Kell realized why they had never progressed beyond Ops Support in Nairobi.

'We weren't under instructions to conduct any kind of search,' Knight replied.

'And the people running the painting course? Have you talked to them?'

Knight shook his head, still staring at his shoes like a scolded schoolboy. Kell decided to put them out of their misery.

'OK, tell you what,' he said, 'how far is the Hotel Gillespie?'

Barbara looked worried. 'It's on Boulevard Dubouchage. About twenty minutes away.'

'I'm going to go. You've booked a room for me under "Stephen Uniacke", is that right?'

Knight perked up. 'That is correct. But wouldn't you like something to eat? Barbara and I thought that we could take you into Nice, to a little place we both enjoy near the port. It stays open well past . . .'

'Later,' Kell replied. There had been a Cajun wrap at Heathrow, a can of Coke to wash it down. That would see him through until morning. 'But I need you to do something for me.'

'Of course,' Barbara replied.

Kell could see how much she wanted to prolong her return to the spotlight and knew that she might still prove useful to him.

'Call the Gillespie. Tell them you've just landed and need a room. Go to the hotel, but wait outside and make sure you speak to me before you check in.'

Knight looked nonplussed.

'Is that OK?' Kell asked him pointedly. If Kell was being paid a thousand a day, chances were that the Knights were on at least half that. In final analysis, they were obliged to do whatever he told them. 'I'll need to gain access to the hotel's computer system. I want all the details from Amelia's room, arrival and departure times, Internet use and so on. In order to do that, I'll have to distract whoever works the night shift, get them away from the desk for five or ten minutes. You could be very useful in that context – ordering room service, complaining about a broken tap, pulling an emergency cord in the bathroom. Understood?'

'Understood,' Knight replied.

'Do you have a suitcase or something that will pass for an overnight bag?'

Barbara thought for a moment and said: 'I think so, yes.'

'Give me half an hour to check in and then make your way to the hotel.' He was aware of how quickly he was improvising ideas, old tricks coming back to him all the time; it was as though his brain had been sitting in aspic for eight months. 'It goes without saying that if you see me in the lobby, we don't know each other.'

Knight produced a blustery laugh. 'Of course, Tom.'

'And keep your phone on.' Kell climbed into the Citroën. 'Chances are I'll need to call you within the hour.'

7

The Citroën sat-nav knew how to negotiate the Nice one-way system and had led Kell to Boulevard Dubouchage within twenty minutes. The Hotel Gillespie was exactly the sort of place that Amelia favoured: modest in size but classy; comfortable but not ostentatious. George Truscott would have booked himself a suite at the Negresco and charged the lot to the British taxpayer.

There was an underground car park three blocks away. Kell looked for a secure place to stow his passport and the contents of his wallet and found a narrow wall cavity in a cracked breeze block about two metres above ground. Marquand had sent ahead full documentation for Stephen Uniacke, including credit cards, a passport, a driving licence, and the general paraphernalia of day-to-day life in England: supermarket loyalty cards; membership of Kew Gardens; breakdown cover for the RAC. There were even faded wallet photographs of Uniacke's phantom wife and phantom children. Kell discarded the envelope and took a lift up to street level. Uniacke – supposedly a marketing consultant with offices in Reading – had been one of three aliases that Kell had regularly employed during his twenty-two-year career in British Intelligence. Assuming the identity one more time felt as natural to him – indeed, in many ways, as comforting – as putting on an old coat.

The Gillespie was set back from the street by a short, semi-circular access road that allowed vehicles to pull up outside the entrance, depositing passengers and baggage. Kell walked through a pair of automatic doors and climbed a flight of steps into an intimate midnight lobby dotted with black-and-white photographs of Duke Ellington, Dizzy Gillespie and other musical legends of yesteryear. He had a deep and incurable aversion to jazz but a fondness for sober, low-lit lobbies with rugs on old wooden floors, decent oil paintings and residents' bars that tinkled with ice and conversation. A young man in a dark jacket with acne and cropped blond hair was organizing a large bowl of potpourri on the reception desk. The night porter. He greeted Kell with an effortful smile and Kell saw that he looked tired to the point of exhaustion.

'May I help you, sir?'

Kell put his bag on the ground and explained, in French, that he had reserved a room under the name 'Uniacke'. He was asked for his identification and a credit card, and obliged to fill in a brief registration form. There was a computer terminal at the desk on which the porter called up Uniacke's details. The keyboard was below the counter, out of sight, so that it was not possible for Kell to follow the keystrokes of any log-in password.

'I've stayed here before,' he said, scoping the small office at the back of the reception area where a second computer terminal was visible. There was a can of Coke adjacent to the screen and a large paperback book open on the desk. Kell had been looking for evidence of a CCTV system in the lobby but had not yet seen one. 'Do you have a record of that on your system?'

It was a prepared question to which he already knew the answer. Nevertheless, when the porter responded, he would have the opportunity to lean over the desk and to look directly at the reservation system in feigned astonishment.

'Let me have a look, sir,' the porter duly replied. A downy fur covered his pale, washed-out skin, a zit primed to burst on the chin. 'No, I don't think we have a record of that here . . .'

'You don't?' Kell ramped up his surprise and touched the side of the screen, tilting it towards him so that he could identify the booking software operated by the hotel. It was 'Opera', the most widely used reservations system in Europe and one with which Kell was reasonably familiar. Uniacke's details were laid out on a guest folio that itemized his impending expenses in a series of boxes marked 'Food', 'Accommodation', 'Drinks' and 'Telephone'. As long as the porter left himself logged in, accessing Amelia's information would be straightforward. Kell knew that she had been staying in Room 218 and that the tabs on Opera would take him to her personal details in two or three clicks of a mouse.

'Perhaps it's under my wife's name,' he said, moving his hand back behind the counter. A guest emerged from the bar, nodded at the porter and walked out of the lobby towards a bank of lifts. Kell took a few steps backwards, peered into the bar, and spotted a young couple drinking cognacs at a table in the far corner. A wide-hipped barmaid was picking peanuts off the carpet. The room was otherwise deserted. 'Never mind,' he said, turning back to the desk. 'Could I arrange a wake-up call for the morning? Seven o'clock?'

It was a small detail, but would give the porter the useful impression that Monsieur Uniacke intended to go to sleep as soon as he reached his room.

'Of course, sir.'

Kell was allocated a room on the third floor and walked up the stairs in order to familiarize himself with the layout of the hotel. On the first-floor landing he saw something that gave him an idea: a cupboard, the door ajar, in which a chambermaid had left a Hoover and various cleaning products. He continued along a short passage, entered his room using his card key, and immediately began to unpack. En route to Heathrow, Marquand had given him a laptop. Kell placed an encrypted 3G modem in a USB port and accessed the SIS server through three password-protected firewalls. There were two miniatures of Johnnie Walker in the mini-bar and he drank them, fifty-fifty with Evian, while he checked his email. Marquand had sent a message with an update on Amelia's disappearance:

Trust you have arrived safely. No sign of our friend. Peripherals still inactive.

'Peripherals' was a reference to Amelia's credit cards and mobile phone.

Funerals at crematoria in the Paris 14th on applicable days. Look for surnames: Chamson, Lilar, de Vilmorin, Tardieu, Radiguet, Malot, Bourget. Investigating further. Should have specifics within 24.

Crematoria. Trust Marquand to be fastidious with the Latin. Kell sprayed some aftershave under his shirt, switched the SIMs on his mobile so that he could check any private messages from London, and wolfed a tube of Pringles from the mini-bar. He then replaced the Uniacke SIM and dialled the Knights' number. Barbara picked up. It sounded as though her husband was doing the driving.

'Mr Kell?'

'Where are you, Barbara?'

'We're just parking around the corner from the hotel. We were a little delayed in traffic.'

'Did you get the room?'

'Yes. We rang from the airport.'

'Who made the call?'

'I did.'

'And did you say it was for two people?'

Barbara hesitated before replying, as though she suspected Kell was laying a trap for her. 'Not specifically, but I think he understood that I was with my husband.'

Kell took the risk. 'Change of plan,' he said. 'I want you to check in alone. I need you to leave Bill on the outside.'

'I see.' There was an awkward pause as Barbara absorbed the instruction.

'I'm going to create a diversion at two o'clock that will require the night porter to go upstairs and fetch a Hoover.'

The line cut out briefly and Barbara said: 'A *what*?'

'A Hoover. A vacuum cleaner. Listen carefully. What I'm going to tell you is important. The Hoover is in a cupboard on the first-floor landing. You'll be waiting there at two. When the porter comes up, tell him that you're lost and can't find your room. Get him to show you where it is. Don't let him come back to reception. If he insists on doing so, make a fuss. Feign illness, start crying, do whatever you have to do. When you get to the door of your room, ask him to come inside and explain how to work the television. Keep him busy, that's the main thing. I may need ten minutes if the log-in is down. Ask him questions. You're a lonely old lady with jet lag. Is that OK? Do you think you can manage that?'

'It sounds very straightforward,' Barbara replied, and Kell detected a note of terseness in her voice. He was aware that he was being brusque, and that to describe her as an 'old lady' was not, in retrospect, particularly constructive.

'When you check in, play up the eccentric side of your personality,' he continued, trying to restore some rapport. 'Get your papers in a muddle. Ask how to use the card key for your room. Flirt a little bit. The night porter is a young guy, probably speaks English. Try that first before you opt for French. OK?'

It sounded as though Barbara was writing things down. 'Of course, Tom.'

Kell explained that he would call back at 1.45 a.m. to confirm the plan. In the meantime, she was to check the hotel for any signs of a security guard, maid or member of the kitchen staff who might have remained on the premises. If she saw anybody, she was to alert him immediately.

'What room are you in?' Barbara asked him.

'Three two two. And tell Bill to keep his eye on the entrance. Anybody tries to come in from the street between one fifty-five and two-fifteen, he needs to stall them.'

'I'll do that.'

'Make sure he understands. The last thing I'll need when I'm sitting in the office is a guest walking through the lobby.'

8

'I simply don't understand it. I don't understand why he doesn't want me to be involved.'

Bill Knight was slumped over the wheel of the Mercedes, staring down at his beige patent leather shoes, shaking his head as he tried to fathom this latest, and probably final, SIS insult to his operational abilities. A passer-by, gazing through the window, might have assumed that he was weeping.

'Darling, he *does* want you to be involved. He just wants you to be on the outside. He needs you to keep an eye on the door.'

'At two o'clock in the morning? Who comes back to a hotel at *two o'clock* in the morning? He doesn't *trust* me. He doesn't think I'm up to it. He's been told that *you're* the star. It was ever thus.'

Barbara Knight had mopped and soothed her husband's fragile ego for almost forty years, through myriad professional humiliations, incessant financial crises, even his own hapless infidelities. She squeezed his clenched fingers as they gripped the handbrake and tried to resolve this latest crisis as best she could.

'Plenty of people come back to a hotel at two o'clock in the morning, Bill. You're just too old to remember.' That was a mistake, reminding him of his age. She tried a different approach. 'Kell needs to gain control of the reservations system. If somebody comes through the door and sees him behind the desk, they might smell a rat.'

'Oh *balls*,' said Knight. 'It isn't possible to get into any half-decent hotel in the world at that hour without first ringing a bell and having someone come down to let you in. Kell is fobbing me off. I'll be wasting my time out here.'

Right on cue, two guests appeared at the entrance to the Hotel Gillespie, rang the doorbell and waited as the night porter made his way to the bottom of the stairs. It was as though they had been provided by a mischievous god to illustrate Knight's point. The porter assessed their credentials and allowed them to pass into the lobby. Bill and Barbara Knight, parked fifty metres away, saw the whole thing through the windscreen of their superannuated Mercedes.

'See?' he said, with weary triumph.

Barbara was momentarily lost for words.

'Nevertheless,' she managed, 'it's best if they don't ring the bell. Why don't you buy yourself a packet of cigarettes and just loiter outside or something? You could still be very *useful*, darling.'

Knight felt that he was being hoodwinked. 'I don't smoke,' he said, and Barbara summoned the last of her strength in the face of his petulance.

'Look, it's perfectly clear that there's no role for you in the hotel. Kell wants me to play Miss Marple and make a nuisance of myself. If we go in as husband and wife, I'm automatically less vulnerable. Do you see?'

Knight ignored the question. Barbara finally lost her patience.

'Fine,' she said. 'Perhaps it would be better if you simply went home.'

'Went *home*?' Knight reared up from the wheel and Barbara saw that his eyes were stung with resentment; oddly, it was the same wretched expression that he wore after almost every conversation with their errant thirty-six-year-old son. 'I'm not going to leave you alone in a hotel with a man we don't know, working all hours of the night on some crackpot scheme to . . .'

'Darling, he's hardly someone we don't know . . .'

'I don't like the look of him. I don't like his manner.'

'Well, I'm sure the feeling is mutual.'

That was a second mistake. Knight inhaled violently through his nose and turned to stare out of the window. Moments later, he had switched on the engine and was beckoning Barbara to leave, purely by force of his body language.

'Don't be cross,' she said, one hand on the door, the other still on the handbrake. She was desperate to get into the hotel and to check into her room, to fulfil the task that had been given to her. Her husband's constant neediness was pointless and counter-productive. 'You know it isn't *personal*.' An overweight man wearing a tracksuit and bright white trainers walked past the Gillespie, turned left along Rue Alberti and disappeared. 'I'll be perfectly all right. I'll call you in less than an hour. Just wait in a café if you're worried. Tom will probably send me home in a couple of hours.'

'What *café*? I'm sixty-two years old, for goodness' sake. I can't go and sit in a *café*.' Knight continued to stare out of the window. He looked like a jilted lover. 'In any case, don't be so ridiculous. I can't abandon my post. He wants me watching the fucking entrance.'

It began to rain. Barbara shook her head and reached for the door. She didn't like to hear her husband swearing. On the back seat of the Mercedes was a sausage bag in which the Knights usually ferried bottles and cans to a recycling area in Menton. She had stuffed it with a scrunched-up copy of *Nice-Matin*, an old hat and a pair of Wellington boots. She picked it up. 'Just remember that we've had a lot of fun in the last few days,' she said. 'And that we're being very well paid.' Her words appeared to have no visible impact. 'I'll ring you as soon as I get to my room, Bill.' A gentle kiss on the cheek. 'Promise.'

9

Kell drained the last of the Johnnie Walker and picked up the landline on the bedside table. He dialled '0' for Reception. The night porter answered on the second ring.

'Oui, bonsoir, Monsieur Uniacke.'

It was now just a question of spinning the story. The wi-fi in his room wasn't connecting, Kell said. Could Reception check the system? The porter apologized for the inconvenience, dictated a new network key over the phone, and hoped that Monsieur Uniacke would have better luck second time around.

He didn't. Ten minutes later, Kell picked up the laptop and took a lift down to the ground floor. The lobby was deserted. The two guests who had been drinking cognacs in the bar had gone to bed, their table wiped clean. The lights had been dimmed and there was no sign of the barmaid.

Kell walked towards the reception desk. He had been standing there for several seconds before the night porter, lost in his textbook in the back office, looked up, jerked out of his seat and apologized for ignoring him.

'*Pas de problème,*' Kell replied. It was always advisable to speak to the French in their mother tongue; you earned their confidence and respect that much more quickly. He flipped open the laptop, pointed to the screen and explained that he was still having difficulty connecting. 'Is there anybody in the hotel who might be able to help?'

'I'm afraid not, sir. I'm here alone until five o'clock. But you may find that the signal is stronger in the lobby. I can suggest that you take a seat in the bar and try to connect from there.'

Kell looked across at the darkened lounge. The porter seemed to read his mind.

'It will be easy to turn up the lights. Perhaps you would also like to take something from the bar?'

'That would be very kind.'

Moments later, the porter had opened a low connecting door into the lobby and disappeared behind the bar. Kell picked up the laptop, quickly moved the bowl of potpourri on the counter six inches to the left, and followed him.

'What are you reading?' he called out, selecting a table with a partial view of the lobby. The porter was flicking a panel of lights beside a sign saying FIRE EXIT. Kell had still not been able to find any evidence of CCTV.

'It's for my college,' he replied, raising his voice to be heard. 'I'm taking a course in quantum theory.'

It was a subject about which Kell knew very little: a few half-remembered book reviews; the odd chat on *Start the Week*. Nevertheless, he was able to hold a brief conversation about black holes and Stephen Hawking while the porter fetched him a glass of mineral water. He introduced himself as 'Pierre'. Within a few minutes, the two men had developed that particular rapport which is characteristic of strangers who find themselves alone at night while the world around them sleeps. Kell could sense that Pierre perceived him as easygoing and without threat. It probably suited him to have a guest to talk to; it made the time pass more quickly.

'Looks like I've got a signal,' he announced.

Pierre, tucking in a loose section of shirt, smiled in relief. Kell navigated to a moribund SIS email account and began to read the messages. 'I'll be out of your way as soon as possible.'

'Take your time, Monsieur Uniacke, take your time. There's no hurry. If you need anything more, just let me know.'

Moments later, the bell rang at the entrance to the hotel. Pierre walked across the lobby, skipped down the stairs and briefly disappeared from view. Kell could hear a woman talking in flustered and apologetic English about the 'blasted weather' and how sorry she was for 'disturbing the hotel so late at night'.

Barbara.

'This way, madame.'

Pierre shouldered the sausage bag and led her up into the lobby with practised charm, passing behind the reception desk in order to process her details.

She checked in like a pro.

'Oh the flight was *terrible*. I'm not sure that the captain quite knew what he was doing. One moment we were in the air, the next he was bumping us down on the tarmac like a tractor. Do excuse me for not speaking French. I lived in the Loire as a young woman and used to be able to get by quite well, but at my age these things seem to disappear from one's brain, don't you find?'

'Is it just yourself staying with us, madame?'

'Just myself, yes. My husband, poor lamb, died three years ago.' Kell almost spat out his Badoit. 'Cancer got him in the end. You're so kind to have found me a room at such short notice. I am a nuisance, aren't I? There were several people at the airport with no idea at all where they were going to stay. I ought to have shared a taxi with them, but it was all so confusing. I must say this hotel seems *awfully* nice. My passport? Of course. And I suspect a credit card is required as well? They always are these days. So many PIN numbers. How is one supposed to *remember* them all?'

Kell grinned behind the laptop, screened from Barbara's gaze by a wall on which the management had hung a monochrome portrait of Nina Simone. Every now and again he would tap random letters on the keyboard to give an impression of honest endeavour. In due course, Pierre handed Barbara the card key for room 232, explained the timetable for breakfast and sent her on her way.

'Please push the button for the second floor, madame,' he said, as she walked towards the lifts. 'I wish you to pass a good night.'

Kell checked his watch. 1.35 a.m. He gave Barbara another ten minutes to settle in and to familiarize herself with the hotel, then sent a text message initiating the final part of their plan.

Time check 1.45. Lobby green. You?

Barbara responded immediately.

Yes. Will be in position from 2. Good luck.

Kell was putting the phone back in his pocket when Pierre emerged from reception and asked if Monsieur Uniacke needed anything further from the bar.

'Thank you, no,' Kell replied. 'I'm fine.'

'And how is the wi-fi? Still working to your satisfaction?'

'Completely.'

He waited until Pierre had returned to the office before texting Bill Knight.

Clear?

Nothing came back. Kell watched the clock on the laptop tick through to 1.57 and knew that Barbara would already be in position. He tried again.

Clear outside?

Still no reply. There was nothing for it but to proceed as planned and to hope that Knight had the situation under control. Kell disconnected the laptop from the socket in the wall, tucked it under his arm, took his now empty glass of mineral water to the reception desk and placed it on the right-hand side of the counter beside a plastic box filled with tourist brochures. Pierre was back in his chair in the office, drinking Coke, wallowing in astro-physics.

'Could I check something?' Kell asked him.

'Of course, sir.'

'What rate am I paying on my room? There's a confirmation email from my office that seems lower than I remember.'

Pierre frowned, approached the desk, logged into Opera and clicked into the Uniacke account. As he did so, Kell

56

lifted the laptop on to the counter and placed it approximately two inches from the bowl of potpourri.

'Let me see.' Pierre was muttering, squinting at the screen. 'We have you on . . .'

Kell put an elbow on to the laptop, let it slide along the counter, and sent the bowl of potpourri plummeting towards the floor.

'Fuck!' he exclaimed in English as it exploded in a cluster bomb of petals and glass. Pierre reared back from the counter with a matching '*Merde!*' of his own as Kell surveyed the delightful chaos of his creation.

'I am so, so sorry,' he said, first in English and then, repeating the apology, in French.

'It doesn't matter, sir, really it doesn't matter. These things happen. It can easily be cleaned up.'

Kell, bending to the floor in pursuit of the larger chunks of glass, searched for the French phrase for 'dustpan and brush', but found that he could only say: 'Do you have a vacuum cleaner?'

Pierre had now made his way out into the lobby and was standing over him, hands on hips, trying to calculate the best course of action.

'Yes, I think that's probably a good idea. We have a Hoover. I will clean everything up. Please do not worry, Monsieur Uniacke.'

'But you must let me help you.'

Pierre dropped to the floor beside him. To Kell's surprise, he even placed a consoling hand on his shoulder. 'No, no. Please, you are a guest. Relax. I will fetch something.'

'I think I saw one on the stairs on the way up to my room. Is that where you keep them? I can get it for you. Please, I'd like to help . . .'

It was the only risk in his strategy; that the night porter would be so concerned about the security of the front desk that he would accept a paying guest's offer of help. But Kell had read his personality correctly.

'No, no,' he said. 'I can fetch it. I know the cupboard. It's not far. If you wait here . . .'

The phone pulsed in Kell's pocket. He took it out as Pierre walked away. Knight had finally deigned to reply.

All clear out here Commander. Over and out.

'Prat,' Kell muttered, checked that Pierre had gone upstairs, and slipped behind the reception desk.

10

Barbara Knight had closed the door of her room, put the sausage bag on the floor outside the bathroom, poured a cognac from the mini-bar and telephoned her husband.

The conversation had gone better than she had expected. It transpired that Bill had begged a cigarette from a passer-by, found himself a seat at a bus stop thirty feet from the entrance to the hotel, and was busy killing time trying to remember the details of a love affair between the French Consul in Lagos and the daughter of an Angolan oil speculator which had been the talk of their three-year residency in Nigeria more than twenty years earlier.

'Didn't he eventually have a hand cut off or something?' Knight asked.

'Darling, I don't have time for this now.' Barbara closed the curtains and switched on one of the bedside lights. 'I think it was a finger. And I think it was an *accident*. Look, I'll have to call you later.'

She had then replied to a Kell text message – **Yes. Will be in position from 2. Good luck** – removed her blouse and skirt and, wearing only a pair of tights and a white Hotel Gillespie dressing-gown, walked out into the corridor. Less than a minute later, Barbara Knight was standing on a step halfway between the first- and second-floor landings, holding her shoes and listening out for the footsteps of the blond-haired porter with wretched acne who had only recently checked her in.

Pierre duly appeared at 2.04 a.m., jerking back in fright at the white apparition bearing down on him with a mop of wild hair, clutching a pair of shoes.

'Madame? Are you all right?'

'Oh, thank *goodness* you're here.' Barbara was shuddering in mock-frustration and had to remind herself not to over-cook the act. 'I'm afraid I'm rather lost. I was on my way downstairs to see you. I was trying to leave my shoes outside to be polished, you see, but I've only gone and locked myself out of my room . . .'

'Please, madame, do not worry, we can . . .'

She interrupted him.

'And now I can't remember for the life of me which floor I'm supposed to be on. I think you kindly put me in 232, but I can't seem to find . . .'

Pierre guided Madame Knight to a safe landing on the first floor. It was to the unanticipated advantage of the Secret Intelligence Service that the night porter's own grandmother was in the early stages of dementia. Recognizing a kindred spirit, he had put a kindly hand in the small of Barbara's back and informed her that he would be only too happy to escort Madame Knight to her room.

'Oh, you're so kind, such a nice young man,' said Barbara, brandishing a keycard from the pocket of her dressing-gown. 'I have the damned thing right here, you see? But of course *nowhere* does it tell you the number of one's wretched room.

Kell had worked quickly. The reservations software was open at a welcome page on the desktop; Pierre was still logged in. With the porter attending to Barbara's needs, he clicked 'Current' and was taken to a grid that gave him access to information on every guest in the hotel. The room numbers appeared in a vertical column on the left-hand side of the grid, the dates of occupancy on a horizontal line at the top of the screen. He found the matching dates for Amelia's stay, clicked on '218' and was taken to the details for her room.

It was a measure of Kell's self-confidence, as well as his conviction in Barbara's ability to detain Pierre, that he took the risk of printing out a three-page summary of Amelia's stay, including details of her room service orders, laundry bills and any phone calls she might have made from the landline in her room. He then returned to the welcome page, took the documents from a printer in the office, folded them into his back pocket and walked outside to the reception desk. There was a Magstripe Encoder beside the keyboard. Kell switched it on, followed the read-out to 'Check-In', typed in '218', set an expiration date of six days and pressed 'Create'. There was a small pile of white plastic cards to the right of the machine. He pushed one of them into the slot, listened as the information was written into the strip, then withdrew the card and placed it in the same pocket into which he had folded Amelia's bill.

By the time Pierre came back, more than five minutes later, Thomas Kell had removed almost all of the shards of glass that had fallen on to the floor in the lobby and was busy picking petals of potpourri out of the carpet.

'You should not have worried about this, Monsieur Uniacke.'

'I just wanted to help,' Kell told him. 'I'm so sorry. I feel terrible about what happened.'

11

The second-floor corridor was deserted. Kell walked towards Room 218 with only the hum of the hotel's air-conditioning for company. He was suddenly extraordinarily tired; the adrenalin of duping Pierre had dissipated from his body, leaving him with the remnants of a late night and a Hackney hangover.

He put the card key in the slot, watching as the light above the handle clicked to green, then passed into Amelia's room, closing the door quietly behind him. As he did so, he experienced a sudden flash image of her naked body sprawled across the bed, a nightmare of violence and blood, but it passed from his mind as no more than a brief and absurd hallucination.

The bed had been made, Amelia's clothes and personal effects tidied away by a chambermaid. The layout of the room was identical to his own: a television facing the bed, bolted to the wall above a writing desk; a sash window with a narrow balcony looking down on to Boulevard Dubouchage. Kell went into the bathroom and made a detailed assessment of its contents. No toothbrush or tooth-paste, but a plastic contact lens case and a bottle of ReNu cleaning fluid. No hairbrush, no glasses, no trace of Hermès Calèche, Amelia's preferred perfume. She had known that she was going somewhere specific and packed accordingly.

He looked in the wardrobe. There was a small metal safe on one of the shelves, the door closed. Ordinarily, an officer as experienced as Amelia Levene would never risk securing anything valuable behind a lock that could be opened by a concierge in under thirty seconds, but she would have gambled on zero threat from London. Kell pulled the safe away from the wall and turned it through one hundred and eighty degrees. There was a metal panel on the back with the make and serial number of the safe engraved beneath a film of dust. Kell wiped it clean and called Tech-Ops. He used the clearance code given to him by Marquand and requested a four-digit access pin for a Sentinel II safe, dictating the serial number to a sleepy technician somewhere in the bowels of Vauxhall Cross.

'SMS all right for response?' he was asked.

Kell said that would be fine.

Beneath the shelf was a large suitcase, but no sign of the leather carry-on bag that Amelia habitually took with her on most short-haul flights. A suit jacket and skirt were hanging in the next cupboard, but he knew of no woman who would travel to the south of France with fewer than three outfits; Amelia must have been wearing one of them and packed at least one other. He pulled the suitcase out on to the carpet and flipped it open. There were two crumpled shirts, some underwear and a pair of tights. She was using it as a temporary laundry bag. The lid of the case had a zip-up lining inside which Amelia had left a couple of paper-back books, a headset, an unopened packet of cigarettes and a copy of *Prospect* magazine. Kell felt around the edges of the case, probing for anything that might have been concealed in the lining, but there was nothing there. He put the suitcase back in the cupboard and sat down on the bed.

It was 2.47 a.m. Somewhere on the street outside a cat screeched. Kell thought of the Knights: Barbara in her room a few doors down the corridor; Bill on his way back to Menton. They had arranged to meet in Vieux Nice for lunch, an appointment Kell would almost certainly cancel. His work with them was done. He experienced an over-whelming desire to stretch out on the bed and to catch a few hours' sleep, but knew that such a thing was not yet possible. He checked the drawers on either side of the bed but found only an inevitable copy of the Gideon Bible and a couple of pillow chocolates, still in their silver wrappers. He checked under the bed for a laptop, a file, a mobile phone, lifting the mattress clear of the frame, but found only lint and dust. The drawers of the desk contained writing paper, as well as a guide to *Nice et Les Alpes-Maritimes* and some basic information about the hotel. Apart from the safe, Kell could think of nowhere else that Amelia might plausibly have hidden anything that would throw up a clue as to her whereabouts. His only other lead was the number of a French mobile phone listed on the printout from her room. He had called Marquand's contact at GCHQ for a trace on it five minutes after saying goodnight to Pierre in the lobby.

'It might take us a few hours,' a sprightly voice in Cheltenham had informed him. 'Gets busy this time of night with AF/PAK waking up.'

Kell wondered who would contact him first. Tech-Ops or GCHQ? It felt like a race to see who could be more indifferent to his circumstances. He returned to the bathroom and checked the toilet cistern as well as the pockets of two dressing-gowns hooked behind the door. On the basis that Amelia might have lifted them in order to conceal a passport or SIM card, he searched for loose tiles and areas of carpeting in both the bathroom and the bedroom. Nothing. He shook out the curtains, he tried to peer behind the television. Finally, he gave up.

Why the hell hadn't London called? Was it his clearance code? Tech-Ops might have rung it in, creating a dawn shitstorm for Marquand that would land both of them in trouble.

Kell was lying on Amelia's bed, planning to catch a few hours' rest, when the SMS finally came through. He climbed off the bed, punched the four-digit code into the safe and heard the satisfying grind of the lock pulling out, the door swinging open on a weighted hinge.

There was a single object inside the safe, positioned dead centre, the cat burglar's prize. A set of car keys. An Avis sticker on the plastic casing, two remote buttons to activate a central locking system, a metal key that swung out at the push of a button.

Kell locked the safe, put the keys in his pocket and left the room.

12

'You cannot sleep, Monsieur Uniacke?'

Kell was grateful for the ready-made lie. He braced his hands across the counter at reception, summoned a care-worn smile, and explained that insomnia had plagued him for years and that a brisk walk around the block usually cured it.

'Of course. Let me get the door for you.'

He noted the pristine carpet, cleansed of the remaining glass and potpourri, and again thanked Pierre for clearing it up as he followed him down the short flight of steps towards the entrance of the hotel. Five minutes later he was at the coded gate of his underground car park on Place Marshall, working on the assumption that Amelia would have left her vehicle at the same location.

He was wrong. Descending through four subterranean levels, along a yellow-lit corkscrew of silence and stale air, Kell searched in vain for the winking lights of Amelia's hire car, pressing repeatedly on the remote-control lock. In the basement of the car park he turned and walked back up to street level, following the same procedure, but again to no avail. A nightwatchman was snoozing in a hutch behind a parking barrier, his feet on the desk, arms folded across a copy of *Paris Match*. Kell tapped on the window and woke him up.

'*Excusez-moi?*'

No part of the nightwatchman's body moved save for his eyes, which flipped open like a child's doll.

'*Oui?*'

'I think I parked here this morning, but I can't find my vehicle. Is there another car park nearby?'

'*Etoile,*' the nightwatchman muttered, closing his eyes.

'I'm sorry?'

'*Nice Etoile. Rue Lamartine. Cinq minutes à pied.*'

The second underground car park was equidistant from the Hotel Gillespie, five minutes from Place Marshall. Kell walked there in the still of the night, a stranger on deserted French streets. He followed the same routine, going from floor to floor, pressing the infra-red key, looking for Amelia's car.

Finally he found it. She had parked on the second lower level. Kell was turning through three hundred and sixty degrees, eyes scanning every corner of the garage, when he saw a set of rear lights morsing in the distance. A dark blue Renault Clio squeezed in between a battered white van and a black Seat Altea with Marseilles plates. A film of dust on the windscreen. Kell went straight to the boot. There was an umbrella in the back and a pair of walking boots. He took them out, placed them on the ground, then lifted up the false floor in order to access the spare wheel. It was screwed in and secured by a plastic clip on a cable looped through the centre of the tyre.

Kell pulled the tyre free, let it spin and rock on to the ground, and immediately saw a cloth package concealed in the hollow. Wrapped in a pillow case from the Hotel Gillespie were Amelia Levene's passport, her driving licence, her credit cards and house keys. She had placed a SIM in a small protective cover, wrapped three hundred pounds sterling in an elastic band and put her BlackBerry, to which she was usually attached like a drip, inside a padded manila envelope.

Kell put the SIM and the BlackBerry in the pocket of his coat and searched the rest of the car. She had barely driven it. There was a nearly crisp sheet of paper, emblazoned with the Avis logo, still protecting the footwell on the driver's side. He could see mud on the surface, created by the soles of Amelia's shoes. Kell replaced the spare wheel, put the pillow case, the umbrella and the walking boots back in the boot, and locked the car. He returned to street level, walked three hundred metres east along Boulevard Dubouchage and rang the doorbell of the Gillespie.

'So, you feel ready to sleep now?' Pierre asked him, looking at his watch like a bad actor.

'Ready to sleep,' Kell replied, and thought about yawning for effect. 'Do me a favour, will you?'

'Of course, Monsieur Uniacke.'

'Cancel that alarm call. I'm going to need more than three hours' sleep.'

13

Yet sleep never came.

Thomas Kell took a shower, climbed into bed and tried to shut out the day's events, even as they replayed continuously in his mind. He had called Marquand for an update on the French mobile and requested tech support on the BlackBerry SIM. It was already past 4 a.m. He knew that Marquand would call back before seven and that Cheltenham would have a fix on the French mobile within a few hours. There hardly seemed any point even in closing his eyes.

The room then became strange to him, the quietness of it, the half-light. Kell felt his own solitude as intensely as he had known it at any stage since his departure from Vauxhall Cross. It occurred to him, as it often did in the depths of the night, that he knew only one way of being – a path that was separate to all others. Sometimes it felt as though his entire personality had grown out of a talent for the clandestine; he could not remember who he had been before the tap on the shoulder at twenty.

What had become of the life he had dreamed of, the life

he had promised himself on the other side of the river? Kell had told anyone prepared to listen that he was planning to write a book. He had convinced himself that he was going to study to become an architect. Both were notions that now seemed so absurd that he actually laughed against the silence of the room. He had tried, day after day in the grey winter months of a new year, to behave like an ordinary citizen, to become the sort of man who socialized and watched the football, who made small talk with strangers in pubs. He was determined to re-educate himself – to watch the films and the HBO box sets, to read the novels and the memoirs that had passed him by – but all he knew was the calling of the secret world. He had even believed, against all evidence, that he might finally become a father. But that particular dream was now as far away from him, as transient, as the whereabouts of Amelia Levene.

He thought then of George Truscott, the man who surely stood to gain the most from Amelia's continued absence. In the restlessness of his insomnia, Kell even wondered if Truscott himself had arranged for Amelia to disappear. Why else have her followed in Nice? Why else send Thomas Kell, of all people, to track her down? He opened his eyes to the blackened room and could make out only the faint yellow glow of a streetlamp in the window. He despised Truscott, not for his ambition, not for his cunning and trickery, but because he represented all that Kell loathed about the increasingly corporatized atmosphere within SIS; what mattered to Truscott was not the Service, not the defence of the realm, but his own personal advancement. With a lower IQ and a fractionally smaller ego, Truscott would likely have worked in some parallel career as a traffic warden or council inspector, dreaming at night of punching parking tickets and issuing directives against noise pollution. Kell would have laughed at the thought, but was too depressed by the prospect of Truscott ascending to 'C', bringing with him yet more apparatchiks, yet more corporate lawyers, while simultaneously sacrificing talented officers on the altar of his fastidiousness. Amelia Levene was almost certainly the last roadblock preventing SIS from turning into a branch of the Health and Safety Executive.

In the end, it was the hotel that rang. Pierre had forgotten to cancel the wake-up call. Kell's phone lurched him out of bed at exactly seven o'clock. He reckoned that he had been asleep for no more than half an hour. Ten minutes later, back in the shower, he heard the familiar ring of the mobile. His head swathed in shampoo, Kell swore under his breath, switched off the water and stepped out of the bath.

It was Marquand, sounding chipper.

'*Bonjour, Thomas. Comment allez-vous?*'

Rule One of SIS was never to moan, never to show weakness. So Kell mirrored Marquand's supercilious tone and said: '*Je suis très bien merci, monsieur,*' as though he was addressing a French teacher at a primary school.

'You found her BlackBerry?'

'In the boot of a hire car. It was parked a quarter of a mile from the hotel.'

'How did you get the keys?'

'She left them in the safe in her room.'

Marquand smelled a rat.

'Reason for that?' he asked.

'Search me. Maybe she didn't bank on George Truscott sending a team after her.' He let that one sink in and pictured Marquand nervously adjusting his hair. 'But she

72

had time to pack, she wasn't in a rush. There was no toothbrush in the bathroom, no perfume. Most of her clothes have gone AWOL as well. She's travelling on an alias, probably wearing her glasses and carrying a leather overnight bag. It's possible she left the key because she *wanted* me to find her, but that's a long shot. Her passport and credit cards were wrapped up with the BlackBerry, her house keys, SIM card, the lot. All in a hire car that she obviously wasn't worried might get nicked.'

Kell wanted to have both the BlackBerry and the SIM analysed by someone who could break their SIS encryptions. Marquand, despite the early hour, had already been in touch with a source in Genoa and explained that she would reach Nice at around midday.

'Elsa Cassani. Used to work for us in Rome. Freelance now. Worked out she can make a lot more money that way. Can do tech-ops, background checks, more contacts in more agencies than I care to think about. Feisty, smart, hyper-efficient. You'll like her. Comes highly recommended.'

'Tell her to call me when she gets into town.' Kell reckoned he could grab a few hours' sleep if Elsa left him undisturbed until twelve. 'What else have you got?'

'Cheltenham has been in touch. They've analysed the numbers you sent through. One of them was Amelia's house in Wiltshire. She rang it three times over the course of two days. Must have spoken to Giles on each occasion because he's been down there for the last week. As far as we know, he hadn't heard from her since she vanished. Each conversation lasted less than five minutes.' As an afterthought he added: 'Giles probably bored her into a persistent vegetative coma.' Kell was looping a DO NOT DISTURB sign on the handle of his room and was too strung out to acknowledge the joke. 'The French mobile isn't known to us. It's a new number, purchased in Paris four months ago. Registered to a François Malot. Amelia may have only left a message because the call lasted less than thirty seconds.'

Kell made the connection. 'Malot was one of the funerals in the Fourteenth.' He put the security chain on the door and remembered how Marquand had always been a beat behind the rest.

'Right, yes. Very good, Tom. I knew we'd hired the right man. I'll take a closer look. Watch this space.'

14

Elsa Cassani had the washed-out complexion of a young woman who had spent the bulk of her twenty-seven years sitting behind computer monitors in darkened rooms. A full-figured, lively Italian with stud ear-rings and a steady smile, she had called Kell's mobile shortly after twelve o'clock and arranged to pick up the SIM and BlackBerry from a café on the Rue de l'Hôtel des Postes.

The handover was straightforward. As instructed, Elsa had put on a hat, found herself a table and ordered a Campari and soda. ('Ah,' she had said, enjoying the trick. 'Because it's *red*.') Within a few minutes, Kell had strolled in, spotted the hat and the drink, handed over the hardware and told her that he needed the results 'by sunset'. He had then walked off in the general direction of the Mediterranean leaving Elsa alone at the table. Nobody had batted an eyelid. No need for the discipline of a formal brush contact. No need for Moscow Rules.

Kell had forgotten how much he disliked Nice. The city had none of the character that he associated with France:

it felt like a place with no history, a city that had never suffered. The too-clean streets, the incongruous palm trees, the poseurs on the boardwalks and the girls who weren't quite pretty: Nice was an antiseptic playground for rich foreigners who didn't have the imagination to spend their money properly. 'The place,' he muttered to himself, remembering the old joke, 'where suntans go to die.' Kell recalled his last visit to the city, an overnight stay in 1997, tracking a Real IRA commander who had struck up a friendship with an unsavoury Chechen money launderer with a villa in Villefranche. Kell had flown down on a soggy May morning to find a ghostly and sterile city, the cloistered cafés surrounding the old port deserted, the Café de Turin serving half a dozen oysters to half a dozen customers. It was different now, a tornado of summer tourists in the city, taking up every inch of sand on the beach, every changing room in the smart boutiques on Rues Paradis and Alphonse Karr. Kell began to wish that he had simply stayed in his hotel, lived off room service and watched pay-per-view movies and BBC World. Instead, he found a brasserie two blocks back from the Med, ordered inedible *steak frites* from a pretty Parisian waitress who smouldered for tips, and began to work his way through the copy of Seamus Heaney's *The Spirit Level* that he had packed at the last minute in London. Behind the bar, a fifty-something proprietor who appeared to have modelled his appearance on Johnny Hallyday was killing time on an iPhone, trying to catch his reflection in a nearby mirror. Kell had long ago concluded that all restaurants in the south of France were run by the same middle-aged proprietor on his thirty-fourth wife with the same paunch, the same tan and the same bombshell waitress whom he was inevitably trying to fuck. This one kept scratching an itch in the crack of his bum, like Rafael Nadal preparing to serve. When it was time to settle the bill, Kell decided to have some fun with him.

'The steak was tough,' he said in English.

'*Comment*?'

The proprietor was looking past his shoulder, as though it was beneath his dignity to make eye contact with a Brit. 'I said the steak was tough.' Kell gestured towards the kitchen. 'The food in this place is only marginally better than the stuff they served up in *Papillon*.'

'*Quoi*?'

'You think it's OK to charge tourists eighteen euros for medium-rare chewing gum?'

'*Il y a un problème, monsieur*?'

Kell turned around. 'Never mind,' he said. It had been enough to see Hallyday stirred from his complacency. The waitress appeared to have overheard their conversation and honoured Kell with a flirtatious smile. He left fifty euros of Truscott's money for her on the table and walked out into the afternoon sunshine.

A wise man once said that spying is waiting. Waiting for a joe. Waiting for a break. Kell killed time by wandering the streets of Vieux Nice and the Yves Klein galleries at the Museum of Modern and Contemporary Art. On a steel bench in the mezzanine he checked the messages on his London phone. Claire had left a series of increasingly irate texts from the waiting room of their marriage guidance counsellor. He had completely forgotten the appointment.

Thanks a lot. Total fucking waste of my fucking time.

He did not want to explain himself, to confess that Marquand had brought him in from the cold. Instead, texting quickly, he wrote:

Sorry. Totally forgot. Crazy 24 hrs. I am Nice.

It was only when she responded with a string of three bewildered question marks that he checked the outgoing message and saw his mistake. He called Claire to explain, but the line went direct to voicemail.

Sorry. I realize that I am not particularly nice. I meant to say that I am in Nice. As in France. Had to come here on business at the last minute. I completely forgot about the appointment. Will you apologize to . . .

But Kell could not remember the name of the marriage guidance counsellor; he could only picture her hair, a bob, her biscuits, the clock that ticked on the mantelpiece. He fudged it:

. . . the good doctor. Just say that I'm too busy. Call me back if you get the chance. I'm hanging around waiting for a meeting.

He knew that Claire would join the dots. She was too well versed in the euphemisms of the secret world not to read between the lines: 'last-minute business'; 'waiting for a meeting'; 'had to go to France'. Thomas Kell was a disgraced spook; he no longer had any business; he didn't *need* to go to any meetings. What possible reason would he have for flying to Nice at the last minute if not to run some errand for SIS? One of the features of his long career had been the necessity to lie to Claire about the nature of his work. Kell had enjoyed the brief respite from such fabrications, but was now back in the same cycle of concealment that he had spun for twenty years; back in the habit, so natural to him and so easily acquired, of keeping anybody who came close to him at arm's length. In this context, he wondered why Claire was keen on seeing a shrink. There was no 'structural flaw' in their marriage – a phrase the counsellor had used, time and again, with apparent relish. Neither was there any 'hard-wired animosity' between them. On the rare occasions that they met to discuss their future, Mr and Mrs Thomas Kell inevitably ended up in bed together, waking in the morning to wonder why on earth they were living apart. But the reason for that was clear. The reason for that was unequivocal. Without children, they were finished.

Elsa eventually rang at five and they arranged to meet outside the Negresco Hotel.

It was like meeting a different person. In the five hours that she had been analysing the hardware, Elsa appeared to have undergone a complete transformation. Her pale skin was suddenly ruddy with health, as though she had returned from a long walk along the beach, and her eyes, so lifeless in the café, sparkled in the dazzling summer light. Earlier, she had seemed nervous and closed-off; now she was animated and full of warmth. So easy was the rapport between them that Kell toyed with the idea that she had been ordered by Marquand to win his trust.

'How was your afternoon?' she asked as they walked in the direction of a dazzling sun.

'Great,' Kell lied, because he was glad of her company

79

after the long afternoon and did not want to appear negative by complaining. 'I had some lunch, went to a gallery, read a book . . .'

'I really do not like Nice at all,' Elsa declared, her English precise and musical.

'Me neither.' She looked across at him and smiled at the sudden fracturing in Kell's composure. 'It's inexplicable. I love everything about France. The great cities – Paris, Marseille – the food, the wine, the movies . . .'

'Blah blah blah . . .' said Elsa.

'. . . but Nice is like a theme park.'

'It has no soul,' she offered quickly.

Kell contemplated this and said: 'Precisely, yes. No soul.'

A long line of rush-hour traffic was held at a set of lights and they crossed the Promenade des Anglais, pushed together by two teenage boys running in the opposite direction. A hooker in stilettos and a black leather skirt was climbing out of a car on the nearside lane of the central reservation.

'There is nothing unusual on the SIM card,' Elsa said, picking her way through a flock of mopeds. 'I double-checked with Cheltenham.'

'And the BlackBerry?'

'It has been used to Skype.'

Of course. In the absence of a secure line, Skype was the spy's first port of call: near-impossible to bug, tricky to trace. A BlackBerry in this context was no different to an ordinary computer: all Amelia would have needed was a cheap plastic headset. She had probably borrowed one from reception.

'Do you know who she spoke to?'

'Yes. Always to the same account, always the same

number. Three different conversations. The Skype address is registered to a French email.'

'Is there a name associated with it?'

'It's to the same person. The name is François Malot.'

'Who *is* this guy?' Kell asked aloud, coming to a halt. He had assumed that the question was rhetorical, but Elsa had other ideas.

'I think I may have the answer,' she said, looking like a student who has solved a particularly knotty problem. She reached into her bag, rummaging around for the prize. 'You speak French, yes?' she asked, passing Kell a printout of a newspaper report.

'I speak French,' he replied.

They were leaning on a balustrade, looking out over the beach, rollerbladers grinding past in the heat. The story, from *Le Monde*, reproduced the grisly facts of an attack in Sharm-el-Sheikh. Middle-class couple. Dream holiday. Married for thirty-five years. Brutally assaulted with knives and metal bars on a beach in Sinai.

'Not such a nice way to die,' she said, with graphic understatement. She took out a cigarette and lit it with her back to the wind.

'Can I have one?' Kell asked. She touched his hand and caught his eye in the flame of the lighter. Theirs was the sudden intimacy of strangers who find themselves in the same city, on the same job, sharing the same secrets. Kell knew the signs. He had been there many times before.

'François Malot was their son,' she said. 'He lives in Paris. He has no brothers or sisters, no wife or girlfriend.'

'Cheltenham told you this?'

Elsa reacted haughtily. 'I do not need Cheltenham,' she

81

said, exhaling a blast of smoke. 'I can do this kind of research on my own.'

He was surprised by the sudden flash of petulance but understood that she was probably keen to impress him. A good report back to London was always useful to a stringer.

'So where did you get the information? Facebook? Myspace?'

Elsa turned and faced the beach. A man in a white shirt was making his way towards the sea, walking briskly in a straight line as though he intended to stop only when he reached Algeria. 'From sources in France. Myspace is not so popular any more,' she said, as if Kell was the last person in Europe not to know this. 'In France they use the Facebook or the Twitter. As far as I can see, François does not have a social networking account of any kind. Either he is too private or he is too . . .' She could not find the English word for 'cool' and used an Italian substitute: '*Figo*.'

An ambulance approached from the east, yellow lights strobing soundlessly through the fronds of the palm trees. Kell, since childhood, had felt an almost superstitious despair at the passing of an ambulance, and watched it accelerate out of sight with a feeling of dread in his gut.

'Is there anything else?' he asked. 'Anything unusual on the BlackBerry?'

'Of course.' Elsa's reply hinted at a bottomless reservoir of secret activity. 'The user accessed the websites of two airlines. Air France and Tunisair.'

Kell remembered Amelia's file, but could make no meaningful connection between her year as an au pair in Tunis and her sudden disappearance more than thirty years later. Was SIS secretly working on a leverage operation, possibly in conjunction with the Americans? Post-Ben Ali, Tunisia was ripe for picking. 'Did she buy a flight?'

'This is hard to say.' Elsa frowned and ground out the cigarette, as if Marlboro was to blame. 'It's not precise, but there was a credit-card transaction of some kind with Tunisair.'

'What was the name on the credit card?'

'I do not know. No amount in the transaction, either. When there is encryption by a bank, everything is much more difficult. But I have passed all of the details that I have found to my contacts and I am sure that they will be able to track the identity.'

Kell tried to fit together the remaining pieces of the puzzle. The fact that Amelia had left her hire car in Nice indicated that she had almost certainly flown overseas. It seemed logical, given the footprints on her BlackBerry, that she had gone to Tunisia. But why? And where to? Long ago, SIS had kept a small station in Monastir. Or was she in Tunis itself? Elsa provided him with the answer.

'There is one other thing that is vital,' she said.

'Yes?'

'The mobile telephone of François Malot. My contacts have tracked it. It would seem that he is no longer in Paris. It would seem that he is taking a holiday in Tunisia. The signal has been triangulated to Carthage.'

15

Kell took Amelia's BlackBerry and SIM back to the underground car park, replaced them in the boot of her hire car and returned to the Hotel Gillespie. He put the car keys back in the safe, ensured that the rest of the room remained as he had first found it, then booked a flight to Tunis on the Marquand laptop. By seven o'clock the following morning he was en route to Nice airport, dumping the Citroën at Hertz.

A French baggage handlers' strike was scheduled to begin at 11 a.m., but Kell's flight took off shortly after ten o'clock and he had landed in the white heat of Tunis-Carthage less than an hour later. GCHQ were certain that François Malot was staying in Gammarth, an upmarket seaside suburb popular with package tourists, financiers and diplomats looking to escape the bustle of downtown Tunis. The signal from Malot's mobile had been fixed to a short stretch of the Mediterranean coast in which two five-star hotels wrestled for space in an area adjacent to a nine-hole golf course. Malot could have been staying in either hotel. The first of them – the Valencia Carthage – had no record of a guest of that name in the register, but the second, the Ramada Plaza, which Kell called from a phone booth at Nice airport, was only too happy to connect him to Mr Malot's room. Kell got the number of the room – 1214 – but hung up before the call was put through. He then rang back three minutes later, spoke to a different receptionist, and attempted to book a room of his own.

There was just one problem. It was high summer and the Ramada was full. At Tunis airport, Kell tried again, calling from the tourism desk in Arrivals in the hope that there had been a cancellation while he was in the air. The receptionist was adamant; no rooms would be free for at least four days. Might she suggest trying the Valencia Carthage hotel, just along the beach? Kell thanked her for the tip-off, called the Valencia a second time, and booked six nights full board on a Uniacke credit card.

The Valencia should have been half an hour by car from the airport but Kell's taxi became congealed in thick traffic heading north-east towards the coast. Vehicles on the two-lane highway spilled out on to the hard shoulder, mounted the central reservation and even faced down oncoming traffic in an effort to escape the jams. *Africa*, Kell thought, and sat back to enjoy the show. His driver, an old man with a split windscreen and a taste for mid-period George Michael, weaved and shunted as best he could, views on either side of the cab of tilled fields bordered by the breeze-block shells of half-forgotten construction projects. Men, young and old, wandered at the sides of the road to no discernible purpose, the din of over-revved engines and horns, predictable and ceaseless.

Eventually they escaped the worst of the tailbacks and

arrived on the outskirts of La Marsa, Kell's taxi gliding along a coastal road dotted with diplomatic residences. Access to both the Ramada Plaza and Valencia Carthage was controlled by a roadblock at a roundabout on the highway. Three soldiers wearing khaki uniforms, each carrying an automatic weapon, had been ordered to check any vehicle approaching the complex of hotels and night-clubs that lined the beach; the last thing Tunisia needed in the wake of the Arab Spring was an Islamist fanatic setting off a suicide bomb in the car park of a seaside hotel. The youngest of the soldiers peered into the back seat and made studious eye contact with Kell. Kell nodded back, managed half a smile, and was duly waved on his way.

The Valencia was located on a forty-acre lot directly adjacent to the Ramada. Marquand had arranged for a Renault Megane to be left in the car park. Kell knew the colour and number plate and found it quickly, the keys nestled, as agreed with London, inside the exhaust pipe. A porter with closely cropped black hair, wearing dark trousers and a burgundy waistcoat, saw Kell coming towards the hotel and greeted him like a long-lost brother. Despite Kell's objections, his bag was placed on a trolley for the short journey up a ramp to the entrance of the hotel. Once inside, in the blessed relief of air conditioning, he tipped the porter, left the bag on the trolley and took a stroll around before checking in.

The lobby was vast: three storeys high and finished in custard yellow. To Kell's eyes it resembled a Mexican restaurant in a suburban shopping mall blown up to the size of an aircraft hangar. There were two dining areas on the ground floor, as well as a jazz-themed piano bar and a small, mocked-up Moorish café. Kell peered inside. A couple of baseball-capped tourists were drinking glasses of mint tea and smoking fruit tobacco from a shisha pipe, apparently under the illusion that they were experiencing the authentic Tunisian *souk*. Next door, Kell found a gift shop selling camels on key rings and overpriced bottles of suntan lotion. He bought a copy of the *Herald Tribune* then joined the queue checking in and out of the hotel. To the left of the reception desk, accessed through a second internal lobby, was a vast spa complex offering *hammams*, massage rooms and a saltwater plunge pool. More guests, most in white hotel dressing-gowns, were funnelling past. One of them had a bandage applied across her nose, as did a middle-aged Italian woman waiting in the check-in queue ahead of Kell. The bags beneath her eyes were black and bruised, as though she had been punched in a jealous rage. At the front desk, Kell asked what was going on.

'Why is everybody walking around with facial injuries?'

'Excuse me, sir?'

'The bandages,' he said, indicating his face. 'The guests with broken noses. It's like Jack Nicholson in *Chinatown*. What's the story?'

The receptionist, a young Tunisian woman wearing a blue headscarf, spoke good English and smiled as she replied:

'The hotel has a relationship with a plastic surgery clinic in Italy, Mr Uniacke. Their clients often come here in order to recuperate after an operation.'

Kell nodded, trying to remember the architecture of the Amelia Levene nose and concluding that it was beyond all possibility that the Chief-designate of the Secret Intelligence Service was hiding out in North Africa in the wake of a nose job.

His room was located towards the end of a three-hundred-metre-long corridor on the western flank of the hotel overlooking an outdoor swimming pool that boasted its own bar and restaurant and at least seventy sun loungers. Kell ordered a room service club sandwich and called Jimmy Marquand, updating him on the progress of the search. A database trawl at SIS had turned up just one photograph of François Malot, which Marquand sent as a JPEG to Kell's laptop and mobile.

'Good-looking bastard,' he said as he clicked on the attachment. The photograph showed Malot in a group of four other men, all wearing business suits; they were captioned as IT consultants. Malot was in his early thirties, with a full head of dark hair, parted to one side, five o'clock shadow on a strong jaw and the ghost of a self-satisfied smile playing at the edge of his mouth. *Just Amelia's type*, Kell thought and Marquand seemed to read his mind.

'You suspect an affair?'

'I don't know what I suspect.' Kell picked at a loose strand of fabric on the chair beside his desk. 'She may not even be here. Malot could be a wild-goose chase.'

'You don't think there's anything sinister in the murder of his parents, a connection of some kind?'

'Isn't that what I'm here to find out?'

The sandwich arrived and Kell rang off. Why was London so convinced that Amelia's disappearance had a sexual element? As far as Kell was aware, in her long career Amelia had been involved in serious relationships with only two men other than her husband: an American businessman, recently settled in Oregon, and a close friend of Kell's at SIS, Paul Wallinger, now Head of Station in Ankara. Yet that had been enough to earn her a reputation among the all-male inmates of the SIS asylum as a brazen seductress. Besides, how had she found time, on her schedule, to begin an affair with a Frenchman at least twenty years her junior?

There were other possibilities, of course: that Malot was a colleague in French Intelligence – either DGSE or DCRI – with whom she was running an operation. That would explain why there was so little information about Malot on the SIS database. But why comfort him in the aftermath of his parents' murder? There had to be some kind of emotional connection between them, something more than mere business.

His bags unpacked, his sandwich eaten, Kell decided to spend the late afternoon walking around the hotel, to familiarize himself with the layout, and to look for Malot at the Ramada Plaza. Wearing a sunhat bought from the gift shop, he took a path from the swimming pool down to the beach, where hotel staff were serving drinks to guests assembled on deckchairs and loungers set out in rows on the sand. Donkeys and emaciated camels were available for hire. A bikini-clad model with long black hair and bright red lipstick was having her photograph taken in the shallows; kite surfers were ripping past on broken waves in vain attempts to impress her. Kell took off his shoes and walked along the hot sand, a warm westerly wind against his back. Within two hundred metres he came across a similar scene, this time at the entrance to the Ramada: more guests sunbathing in dazed rows, staff preparing drinks and snacks in a wooden cabin erected on stilts, more donkeys, more camels, all of them touting for business. He thought of Philippe and Jeannine Malot, attacked on a stretch of beach similar to this one, murdered within a stone's throw of the sanctuary of a five-star hotel, beaten and robbed for a few pieces of silver.

The Ramada was visible from the beach as a white outcrop above a line of palm trees. Kell found himself on a narrow path bordered by dune grasses and clumps of bamboo. An elderly lady wearing a white headscarf, walking in the opposite direction, greeted him with a cheery 'Hello there' as if they were on Camber Sands. To his left, Kell could hear the slow, regularly interrupted thock of tennis being played badly, almost certainly by overheated geri- atrics. Eventually the path opened up at the edge of a crowded figure-of-eight swimming pool considerably larger than the one visible from his room at the Valencia. There were more plastic loungers and tables arranged around the perimeter, the great mass of the hotel surrounding it on three sides. As a man walking alone, neither dressed for the beach nor the pool, Kell was aware that he was conspic- uous, particularly in such an open environment. He stopped at a small hut at the side of the swimming area and took a seat at the counter. It was fiercely hot. An Italian-made coffee machine and some soft drink bottles were visible on a shelf at the back, ceramic ashtrays piled up beside a small sink. He scanned as many of the loungers as he could see, looking for Amelia, looking for a man resembling Malot. But it was almost impossible to pick out faces. At least half of the guests were tanning their backs or asleep on their sides; of the rest, many had heads obscured by novels or newspapers. Kell stood up and decided to keep moving, taking a side door into the main body of the hotel.

The lobby was an altogether more sober affair than the Valencia, akin to a business hotel in the centre of a large city. A couple in the reception area were arguing in Russian.

The woman, bottle blonde and upholstered in white leather, was far younger than her partner and wore the spoiled-milk look of a mistress growing tired of her role. The other clientele appeared to be mostly retired couples from the United Kingdom; five of them were perched on an L-shaped sofa in the centre of the lobby, surrounded by wheeled suitcases and plastic bags stuffed with booze and Tunisian bric-a-brac. Kell walked past them towards the automatic doors at the entrance of the hotel and found himself in a car park overlooking the southern façade of the Valencia Carthage. He walked towards the road dividing the two hotels, past a lone official in a whitewashed security booth operating a traffic barrier. Then he saw what he was looking for. Seven yellow taxis lined up in the street beyond him, waiting for guests to emerge from either hotel. Kell fell among the drivers, talking in French to the nearest of them about nothing more pressing than the length of time it would take to reach central Tunis by car.

'You are looking for a taxi, sir?'

The driver who had asked the question was in his late twenties and wore a Barcelona football shirt, a pair of white Adidas trainers and stonewashed jeans. Probably a veteran of the Jasmine Revolution, but certainly too young and excitable for the task Kell had in mind.

'Not right now. I'm just interested in how long it would take.'

His appearance had drawn the attention of an older man, bald and squat, wearing a collared shirt and pressed trousers. Kell nodded him over. Quick, intelligent eyes, a lazy smile and an ill-concealed pot belly attested to the sort of personality Kell was looking for. He needed somebody with experience of the world, somebody who wasn't going to go talking to his friends about all the money he was about to make.

'*Bonjour.*'

'*Bonjour,*' the man replied.

In the late afternoon sun, beneath the scarlet dazzle of a bougainvillea in full bloom, the three men had a brief conversation about tourist attractions in Tunis. In due course, the younger of the two drivers was distracted by a call on his mobile and Kell was left alone with the older man.

'You work these hotels on a regular basis?' he asked. They had switched to Arabic.

'Yes, sir.'

'What kind of hours?'

The driver shrugged, as though the concept of the nine-to-five was alien to him.

'Can you take me into La Marsa?'

It was a risk, of course, but Kell needed a driver on call, somebody who could keep tabs on Malot. Usually SIS would have provided a support agent, but with the Amelia operation off the books, Kell was obliged to improvise. It was just a question of whether or not this man could be trusted as a second pair of eyes. Kell climbed into the passenger seat of a well-maintained Peugeot 206 and instructed him to head towards the beach. He introduced himself as 'Stephen' and they shook hands over the gearstick.

'Sami.'

A mile from the hotel, beyond the security roadblock, Kell asked the driver to pull over. Sami kept the engine running for air conditioning and Kell turned square in his seat to face him.

'I want to offer you a business proposal.'

'OK.'

He liked this reaction: an easy nod, a half-glance at the meter.

'What are you doing for the next few days?'

'I work.'

'Would you like to work for me?'

'OK.'

Again, an easy nonchalance in the reply. Kell could hear a tractor running in the distance.

'I'm here on business. I'm going to need a driver on call at the hotel from first thing in the morning to late at night. Do you think you can manage that?'

Sami thought for a fraction of a second and said: 'OK.'

'I'll pay you five hundred dinars a day, first instalment up front.'

It was the equivalent of about two hundred pounds, a vast sum to a Tunisian who wouldn't expect to earn more than a thousand dinars per month. Kell handed over the money. Still Sami maintained his inscrutable cool.

'I'll pay you the other instalments at the end of every second day. I don't want you telling anybody about our arrangement and I may have to ask you to follow some people if they leave the hotel. Is that going to be a problem?'

'That will not be a problem.'

'Good. If I'm happy with your work, I'll pay you a bonus of a thousand dinars.'

'I understand.' Sami nodded gravely; he had absorbed the importance of keeping his mouth shut. The two men shook hands again and finally Sami managed a smile. There was a photograph on the dashboard of two young girls dressed in pink for a special occasion. Kell indicated them with his eyes.

'Yours?' he asked.

'My granddaughters,' Sami replied and it was as though mention of his bloodline sealed the bond between them. 'I have a son. In Marseille. In November I go to visit him.'

Kell took out his phone and scrolled through the photographs. He showed Sami the picture of Malot.

'This is the man I'm interested in. Do you recognize him?'

Sami had to put on a pair of reading glasses in order to bring the picture into focus. When he had done so, he shook his head.

'He's staying at the Ramada,' Kell explained. 'He may be with this woman. She's British, he is French.' He showed Sami the JPEG of Amelia. It was taken from a passport photograph and the quality of the image was not good. 'If either of them comes out of the hotel looking for a cab, try to get their business. If necessary, strike a deal with the other drivers so that you get to look after them. Let me know where they go and who you see them with. If you have to follow them, do so as discreetly as possible, but call me on this number before you leave. It may be that I can get downstairs in time and come with you or follow in a second vehicle.'

'You have a hire car?'

Kell shook his head. He didn't want to confuse him unnecessarily. 'I meant that I'll follow in another cab.'

They swapped numbers and Kell gave the Tunisian a basic timetable – seven until midnight. He then stepped out of the car, under the pummelling sun. He could see a path leading to the beach and decided to walk.

'You go back to the hotel,' he said. 'Get in the queue of taxis. If you see them, call me.'

94

'Fine,' Sami replied with a nonchalance that was by now characteristic. It was as though he was asked to undertake clandestine work of this kind all the time.

Half an hour later, Kell was back in his room. The remains of his club sandwich were still on the bedside table, shards of crisps mingled with lettuce and congealed mayonnaise. He opened the door, put the tray in the corridor, had a cold shower, then went outside on to his balcony.

The swimming pool at the Valencia was still busy. There were at least twenty people in the water, families with small children splashing and shouting in the shallows. Directly beneath Kell's window, a woman wearing a head-scarf and a long black dress was seated in a plastic chair reading a magazine. Kell looked at the guests on either side of her, the dying sun casting a shadow across the pool.

That was when he saw her.

Lying on her back on a lounger, wearing a one-piece bathing suit and a wide-brimmed hat. A beautiful woman in her early fifties reading a paperback, sipping from a cup of coffee.

Amelia Levene.

16

On a quiet Friday afternoon two weeks earlier, Amelia Levene had managed to slip away from Vauxhall Cross just after 5 p.m. and to wrestle through weekend traffic to her house in the Chalke Valley. She was all too aware, in the wake of her recent appointment as Chief of the Secret Intelligence Service, that this would probably be the last weekend that she would be able to enjoy in Wiltshire for many months; the responsibilities of her new position would soon require her to live in London on an almost permanent basis. That would mean making a home in Giles's house in Chelsea with roadworks for company and a protection officer on the door. Such was the price of success.

Amelia's house, which she had inherited from her late brother in the mid-1990s, was located along a narrow lane at the western edge of a small village about eight miles south-west of Salisbury. It was dark by the time she pulled up outside, leaving the key in the ignition so that she could hear the end of a piano sonata on Radio 3. Once it was finished, she turned off her mobile phone – there was no reception in the village – picked up her leather overnight bag from the passenger seat and locked the car.

Peace. In the darkness, Amelia stood at the gate of the house and listened to the sounds of the night. Lambs, newborn, were bleating in a field on the opposite side of the valley. She could hear the rushing of the stream that swelled in springtime, sometimes so deep that she had swum in it, borne along by the freezing current from field to field. She could see lights in the second of the three houses that shared this isolated corner of the village. The first, one hundred metres away, was owned by a twice-divorced literary agent who, like Amelia, shuttled between London and Wiltshire as often as she could. Occasionally, the two women would invite one another into their homes to share a glass of wine or whisky, though Amelia had remained discreet about her position, describing herself as little more than 'a civil servant'. The second house, hidden behind a steep hill, belonged to Charles and Susan Hamilton, an elderly couple whose family had been in the Valley for four generations. In the seventeen years that Amelia had lived in Chalke Bissett, she had exchanged no more than a few words with either of them.

It was cold to be standing outside after the warmth of the car and Amelia took the house keys from the pocket of her coat, switching off the burglar alarm once she had stepped inside. Her weekends usually adhered to a strict routine. She would switch on the Channel Four news, prepare herself a large gin and tonic with a slice of cucumber, find the ingredients to make a simple supper, then run a bath into which she poured oil from one of the three dozen bottles lining the shelves of her bathroom, all of them birthday and Christmas gifts from male colleagues at SIS who routinely gave books and booze to men and overpriced soap products to their female counterparts.

There was plenty of ice in the freezer, lemons in a bowl on the kitchen table. Amelia fixed the gin, sliced the cucumber and drank a silent toast in celebration of her husband's absence from the house: Giles would be in Scotland for the long weekend, earnestly researching a withered branch of his breathtakingly tedious family tree. Solitude was something almost unknown to her now and she tried to savour it as much as possible. London was a constant merry-go-round of meetings, lunches, cocktail parties, *connections*: at no point was Amelia alone for more than ten minutes at a time. For the most part she relished this lifestyle, her proximity to power, the buzz of influence, but there had been an increasingly bureaucratic dimension to her work in recent months that had frustrated her. She had stayed with SIS to *spy*, not to discuss budget cuts over canapés.

She lit a fire, went upstairs to run the bath and took a tub of homemade pesto from the freezer, setting it to defrost in the microwave. There was a pile of post beside the cooker and she flicked through it with one ear on the television news. Amid the bills and postcards were two copies of the Chalke Bissett magazine and three stiff-backed 'At Home' invitations to drinks parties in the county that she immediately co-opted as kindling for the fire. By eight o'clock, Amelia had changed into a dressing-gown, checked her emails, poured a second gin and tonic and found a packet of spaghetti in the larder.

That was when the telephone rang.

17

The envelope had borne a Parisian postmark and was addressed to *Mrs Joan Guttmann, c/o The Century Club, 7 West 43rd St, New York, New York*.

It had been forwarded by the club to Guttmann's apartment on the Upper West Side and brought up to the fourteenth floor by Vito, the doorman on whom Joan relied for everything from weather reports to grocery deliveries. The letter had been written in English.

> *Agence Père Blancs*
> *Rue la Quintinie, 147*
> *Paris 75015*
> *France*

Dear Mrs Guttmann
It is with the deepest regret that I must inform you of the deaths of Mr Philippe Malot and Mrs Jeannine Malot, who have passed away while on vacation in Egypt.

The next of kin has recently made contact with our agency, as a result of a clause inserted in the Last Will &

Testament of his late father. In accordance with the terms of our arrangement, the agency has therefore taken the decision to contact you.

Should you wish to take this matter further, I suggest that you either write to me at our Paris address or telephone me at a time convenient to you. Allow me to say that, according to the terms of French law, you are under no obligation to do so.

Yours, cordially
Pierre Barenton (Secretary)

Joan Guttmann had dialled the number.

18

The Stone Age answering machine picked up. Amelia heard her own voice, faded and scratched through repeated play-backs. The caller did not hang up, but remained on the line, and Amelia was startled to recognize the voice of Joan Guttmann, now surely in her early eighties, leaving a croaky smoker's message:

> *Amelia, honey. It's your old friend from New York. I have some news. You wanna give me a call sometime? I'd love to hear your voice.*

Her first thought was to pick up the receiver, but she knew that a call from Joan Guttmann meant Moscow Rules: no names on an open line; no talking about the past. That was why she hadn't identified herself. In case anybody was listening in. In case anybody ever found out about Tunis.

Amelia was out of her dressing-gown and into a pair of jeans and a sweater within two minutes. She grabbed a Barbour from the utility room, put on some Wellington boots, locked the house and went back to the car. She turned it around in the lane, drove into the village and parked a hundred metres from the pub on the Salisbury road. There was a telephone box on the corner, mercifully un-vandalized and still accepting coins. Amelia turned on her mobile and found Joan's number buried in the contacts. Then the long, drawn-out ring of an American telephone, the click of somebody picking up.

'Joan?'

The two women had not spoken for almost ten years. Their last encounter had been both brief and distressing: the funeral service of Joan's husband, David Guttmann, who had suffered a heart attack while working at his office in Manhattan. Amelia had made the journey across the Atlantic, expressed her condolences all too briefly at a service on Madison Avenue, then returned to the UK on a red-eye from Newark three hours later. Since then, there had been no contact between them, save for the occasional email or hastily scribbled Christmas card.

'Amelia, how are you? You're so clever to call back so soon.'

'It sounded important.'

It hadn't sounded important, of course. The message had been as deliberately mundane as any Amelia had ever heard. But 'news' from Joan Guttmann meant only one thing. Something had happened to François.

'It *is* important, honey, it really is. Are you OK to talk?'

'As long as you are.'

Joan cleared her throat, buying time. It was difficult to tell whether she was apprehensive about what she had to say, or merely searching for the right words. 'Did you happen to see the French newspapers at all this week?'

102

Amelia didn't know how best to answer. She kept abreast of events in France, but no particular developments had been flagged up in the previous few days. She began to respond but was interrupted.

'Something really quite terrible has happened. It's Philippe and Jeannine. They were on vacation in Egypt. They were mugged, attacked on a beach. They've been murdered.' Amelia leaned against the freezing glass of the phone booth, a hammer blow. 'The thing is, your boy has been in touch. He must have somehow traced me through the system at Père Blancs. I've had a contact at Langley look into it, run some background. He checks out. It's François. I guess he's reaching out or something. He's lost his parents and he's hurting. I couldn't keep it from you, honey. I'm so sorry. I really need to know what it is that you want me to do.'

19

Looking down from his balcony, Kell saw that Amelia Levene was not alone.

Ten feet in front of her, emerging from the Valencia hotel pool, came a fit-looking man in his early thirties wearing navy-blue shorts and a pair of yellow-tinted swimming goggles. He had a lean, exercised physique and moved through the shallows with a slow, self-conscious swagger, a man used to being stared at by women. He pulled the goggles down around his neck and Kell saw that his face precisely matched the image in the photograph of François Malot. The same firm jawline, the easy good looks, the lightly stubbled chin. Amelia, sensing him, looked up from her book and reached across to pull a towel from a neighbouring lounger. She then stood up and passed the towel to Malot, at arm's length, to prevent herself getting wet. Malot appeared to thank her and wiped his face clear of water. He dried his back and chest, wrapped the towel around his waist in the style of a sarong and sat on the edge of the lounger, looking in the direction of the pool.

Amelia appeared to be staring at him, as if trying to think of something to say, but then returned to her novel.

Kell went quickly into the room and retrieved his camera, firing off several shots with the telephoto lens tight on the scene. He had the opportunity to observe Amelia and Malot for some time and tried to reject the possibility that they were working together; surely Amelia would never allow her guard to drop to the extent of going swimming with a male colleague? Their body language was relaxed and familiar, but not overtly intimate: they did not project the heat of lovers. Amelia was attentive and oddly deferential towards him in a way that was unfamiliar to Kell, pouring Malot a glass of water from the bottle on the table, even offering him a cigarette as he walked to the edge of the water.

He began talking into a mobile phone. The dying light of the sun threw the musculature on Malot's back into sharp relief and he was smoking the cigarette with studied cool, head tilted to one side, lips set in an ironic smile. From time to time, he would allow the hand holding the cigarette to fall to one side and run his thumb across the dark hairs of his stomach, smoke drifting against the skin. Amelia, meanwhile, had come to the end of a chapter in her paperback. She closed the book and placed it on the low plastic table beside her, nestling it between the packet of cigarettes and the litre bottle of water. Kell caught the title in the telephoto lens: *Solar*, by Ian McEwan. She then signed the bill, pulled on a hotel dressing-gown, securing it with a cord around her waist. Kell found all of this compelling to watch; her beauty had long been a source of fascination to him. Amelia put on a pair of white hotel slippers and walked towards Malot, indicating that she was going to head indoors. The Frenchman broke off from his conversation, kissed her affectionately on the cheek and pressed his wristwatch, as if making an arrangement to meet for dinner. Amelia then turned and walked in the direction of the hotel, entering through a side door less than thirty metres from Kell's balcony. It was obvious that they were staying in separate hotels; another layer of obfuscation added by the veteran spy in order to cover her tracks. Less than a minute later, Malot strolled back to the lounger, brought his telephone conversation to an end, and stubbed out the cigarette in an ashtray. He removed the towel, allowed it to drop to the ground, and put on a pristine white T-shirt which he had produced from a bag. At one point, Kell thought that he caught Malot flirting with an attractive woman on the opposite side of the pool. The woman seemed to be smiling at him, but was then distracted by her young daughter and averted her gaze.

The Frenchman picked up the rest of his possessions. The bag, a book, a pair of sunglasses, the cigarettes and a bottle of suntan lotion. In the evening light he put on the sunglasses, like a matinee idol expecting to encounter a herd of paparazzi, and stepped into a pair of deck shoes. He then made his way towards the path that Kell had earlier taken to the beach.

Kell lowered the camera. He walked back into the room, threw the camera on to the bed, picked up his key and went outside into the corridor.

He was downstairs in fifteen seconds. Walking in the direction of the pool, he paused beside Amelia's lounger, leaned over – as if to stretch a muscle – and removed the bill from the low plastic table. He stood up, placed the piece of paper in the back pocket of his trousers and continued walking in the direction of the lobby.

20

The name at the top of the bill was A.M. Farrell. The room number was 1208.

Kell went back to his room and immediately called Marquand in London.

'I've found your missing girl.'

'Tom! I knew you would do it. What's the story?'

'She's staying at my hotel. The Valencia Carthage. Malot is across the road.'

'So they're shagging and staying apart so that nobody can trace them?'

Kell steered around the theory. He had learned to deal solely in facts. 'She's using a legend we haven't seen before. Farrell. Initials A.M. Can you run a credit-card check? Should be plenty of activity through Paris, Nice, Tunis.'

'Sure. Did you speak to her, Tom?'

'Now why would I want to do something like that?'

'Well, thank God she's all right.' There was a delay on the line, as though Marquand was trying to think of the appropriate thing to say. 'Fucking Frogs,' he offered eventually, 'always stealing our best women.' Truscott and Haynes would surely be told that Amelia was in Tunisia on little more than an extended dirty weekend. 'Can't Malot get his end away at home? Aren't there supposed to be thousands of beautiful girls in Paris?'

'You tell me,' Kell replied.

'What's the story?' Marquand asked. 'Is Malot married as well? We can't seem to find anything about him on the wires.'

'Hard to tell. I've only seen them from a distance, sunbathing by the pool . . .'

'Sunbathing by the pool!' Marquand sounded combustible with excitement. 'Imagine that.'

'He's what you might call a poser,' Kell said, trying to keep the conversation on an even keel. 'Wafts around the place like Montgomery Clift. Not exactly the grieving son.'

'Perhaps he's feeling cock of the walk about Amelia. What do they call the older woman nowadays? Cougars?'

Marquand had made himself laugh. It was the relief of a crisis averted.

'That's right, Jimmy,' Kell said. 'Cougars. Look, I have things I need to do. I'll take a closer look at Malot. There's always the possibility he's DGSE. Amelia might be running a joint op in Tunis.'

'And screwing a colleague on the side.'

Kell shook his head in disbelief. 'Have a drink, Jimmy,' he said. 'You deserve it.'

He hung up, put the phone back on the desk and retrieved his camera from the bed. Looping it over his shoulder, he went outside into the corridor. In the street between the two hotels he found Sami at the wheel of his cab, lazily turning the pages of a newspaper. He tapped on the window.

'Got something to show you.' Kell climbed into the passenger seat and handed Sami the camera, showing him how to click through the photographs of Amelia and Malot. A day's BO hummed around the cab. 'These are the people I'm interested in,' he said. 'The woman is staying at the Valencia. The man is a guest at the Ramada. Do you recognize them?'

Sami shook his head. Two other drivers, standing beneath the bougainvillea, were staring into the car with an almost insulted impatience, like girls at a party who have not been asked to dance.

'Maybe they'll go out for dinner tonight,' Kell said. 'They left the pool twenty minutes ago. If you see them, be sure to call me. If my phone doesn't answer, go through the hotel switchboard. I'm in room 1313. Follow them if they get into one of the other taxis. If you pick them up yourself, don't risk speaking to me in their presence. The woman speaks English, French and Arabic, all of them fluently. Send a text message with your destination.'

'Of course.'

Kell indicated the other drivers with his eyes. 'And if those two start asking questions about me, tell them I'm just a jealous husband.'

21

Joan Guttmann had given Amelia the telephone number of the adoption agency in Paris. Allowing for France being one hour ahead, Amelia had rung the agency at eight thirty on Saturday morning, only to discover that the office was closed for the weekend. A second number was given on the agency's website and Amelia had eventually spoken to a needlessly melodramatic woman who was 'fully aware' that Monsieur Malot's parents had been 'tragically and senselessly killed in Egypt' and had 'furthermore been apprized of the circumstances regarding Madame Weldon'. It was agreed that Amelia should not speak to François by telephone. Instead, she was advised to travel to France, to meet her son in Paris on Monday afternoon, and – at his discretion – perhaps to attend the private funeral service of Philippe and Jeannine Malot, which was scheduled for Tuesday morning in Montparnasse.

Amelia had taken twenty-four hours to carry out her own vetting on the Malots' murder and on François himself, with the assistance of an SIS asset in the DCRI, France's domestic intelligence service. When she was confident that he was their adopted child, she considered her strategy more fully. To bring her son into her life was to entertain the possibility that he could ruin her career, ushering in the reign of George Truscott. To travel to Paris with the purpose of consoling François was to risk any number of reactions: his anger, his contempt, his pity. She had no sense of her son's personality, only the plain fact that he had reached out to her in his hour of need. Yet such was her desire to help, and to encounter her lost child face-to-face, that Amelia quickly set aside all practical and professional considerations. She felt as though she had been given no choice; if her life was to have any meaning, any true and lasting happiness, she had to make her peace with the past.

Locking the Chalke Bissett house early on Sunday morning, she returned to London by car and went directly to Giles's house in Chelsea. The Farrell alias – a passport, assorted credit and SIM cards – was concealed in a small box behind a panel at the back of her husband's wardrobe. To access the panel, Amelia had to pull out more than a dozen plastic-wrapped shirts and dry-cleaned suits on hangers, piling them on the bed behind her. The cramped wardrobe had a throwback, post-war smell of mothballs and shoe polish. As well as golf clubs and hardback books, there were dozens of old newspapers stacked on the floor, hoarded by Giles as a means of keeping a permanent record of momentous events in his lifetime: the assassination of Yitzhak Rabin; the fall of the Berlin Wall; the Diana car crash; 9/11. The pages had yellowed and they crackled in Amelia's hands as she moved them. The box safely retrieved, she rang Santander, activating two of the bank accounts for use in Continental Europe, then charged up the battery on the Farrell mobile while packing a bag for France. Ringing Giles in Scotland, she told him that she was going to Paris 'on business'.

'How lovely for you,' he said, greeting the news with a characteristic wall of indifference. Amelia had the distinct impression that her husband was turning the pages of a historical document in some distant corner of Fife, busily filling in another branch of the family tree even as he spoke to her. 'Take care, won't you, darling? Perhaps we'll talk when you get back.'

She booked an evening ticket on the Eurostar and cancelled all of her appointments for Monday, Tuesday and Wednesday. Personal emails were sent out to senior colleagues explaining that she was required to attend the funeral of a close friend in Paris and would be returning to the Office on Thursday. Jimmy Marquand was the only top-tier officer to respond to these messages, expressing 'my condolences for the loss of your friend'.

Finally, at around three o'clock, Amelia walked up the King's Road to Peter Jones and bought two new outfits, one for the meeting with François, another for the funeral. Back at the flat, she packed them in a large suitcase, throwing in a couple of Ian McEwan paperbacks and a recent edition of *Prospect* magazine. She then walked outside and hailed a cab.

Sunday evening traffic, sparse under light rain. Within twenty minutes Amelia Levene was standing beneath the great vault of St Pancras station clutching a Business Premier ticket to Paris. The atmosphere in the station acted upon her like some romantic dream of the past: monochrome couples snatching final weekend kisses; liveried inspectors ushering passengers along the platform. Then a queue and the rigmarole of security, a female guard waving Amelia through on the assumption that she was just another chic bourgeois housewife shuttling between the two capitals. Amelia found her seat in the carriage, a forward-facing window at a table of four, and made a point of avoiding eye contact with any of her fellow passengers. The fewer people that noticed her, the better. She didn't want to be drawn into a conversation with a stranger. She wanted to be alone with her thoughts.

She had bought a copy of the *Sunday Times* at St Pancras and opened it up as the train pulled away from the platform. There was a story about alleged British Intelligence complicity in torture at the bottom of the front page and she immediately thought of Thomas Kell, but found that she could not concentrate on anything more than the opening paragraph. She knew the background to the case, knew that the story had been scheduled to appear, and would ordinarily have been interested to see how the facts had been reported. But it was as though François had switched off her professional antennae; none of it seemed to matter any more.

Amelia looked out of the window and might have been nineteen again, such was her sense of anticipation at the prospect of travelling to Paris. Over a period of more than thirty years, she had constructed a new personality around the wreckage of her teenage self. She caught her own reflection in the glass and wondered at the loss of Amelia Weldon. Did she even exist any more? The next twenty-four hours would provide some sort of answer. She was going on a journey into her future. She was going on a journey into her past.

22

Kell was shaving in his room when Sami called from the taxi rank.

'The Frenchman just came into your hotel. I asked him if he wanted a cab when he comes out. He said "yes".'

'That's great, Sami. Thank you. You're doing a terrific job.' The small compliments of agent-running were second nature to him. 'Keep in touch, OK? He's probably gone inside to collect Amelia. Let me know where they ask you to go.'

'Sure.'

The conversation had left a smear of shaving foam on the mobile phone. Kell wiped it clean and, with half a dozen sweeps of the razor, cleared his chin of stubble. He dried his face, sprayed aftershave on to his chest, and looked back at his own reflection in the mirror. A momentary reckoning before moving on. He found a clean shirt on a hanger, locked his passport in the safe and picked up the keycard for the Renault. As soon as Sami called to let him know that Amelia and Malot were on the road, he would follow in Marquand's car. If they were meeting third parties, Kell would need to get a look at their faces. That was basic operational behaviour, a tidying up of loose ends.

He sat on the bed and waited. His heart was thumping and Kell tried to remember when he had last felt such a rush of adrenalin. Not for months now. He took a beer from the fridge and popped the cap with his teeth, a party trick he performed, even in private. Claire always used to say: 'You'll lose your fucking molars.'

The text came through just after eight fifteen. Sami had written it in English.

Man and woman both. La Goulette.

Kell typed 'La Goulette' into a search engine on his phone and discovered that it was a coastal suburb between Gammarth and downtown Tunis with restaurants and bars that were popular in the evenings. Amelia and Malot were doubtless heading there for supper.

He grabbed the camera and walked quickly towards the entrance of the hotel. The same bellboy who had earlier accompanied Kell into the hotel was still on duty. This time there was no lobby smile, no courtesy; he clipped past bearing a tray of mint tea and biscuits. Kell, grateful for his own anonymity, went out into the sun-baked car park, unlocked the Renault from twenty metres, plugged the keycard into the ignition slot and threw the camera on to the seat beside him.

The car wouldn't start. He tried a second time, pushing his foot down on the clutch and again pressing the button marked 'Start'. Still no luck. For a moment he considered the possibility that he had been spotted by Amelia and that she had disabled the car, but the notion seemed too far-fetched for serious consideration. This was more likely an electrical failure. Kell tried a third time, removing the card, putting it back into the slot, pressing the clutch and again pushing 'Start'. Nothing.

'Why can't they just give you a fucking key?' he muttered, resolving to take a taxi to La Goulette.

There were no cabs on the rank. Worse still, eight pensioners were huddled beside the traffic barrier at the entrance to the Ramada, each of them seemingly impatient for a cab. Four guests from the Valencia were also lined up. One of them – a man of about Kell's age wearing chinos and a bright yellow Hawaiian shirt – began to walk towards the main intersection, in the hope of flagging down a taxi on the highway.

'Where are all the cabs?' Kell asked in French, rephrasing the question in English when he drew blank stares from the geriatrics.

'Something is happening in La Marsa tonight,' one of them replied. He was a genial, white-haired retiree with a walking stick and sweat patches under his arms. 'Some sort of festival.'

So Kell went back to the Renault. He tried the keycard one more time, to no effect. Finally, swearing at the wind-screen, he gave up on the possibility of making it to La Goulette. Sami could keep an eye on them. He had proved nerveless and efficient thus far; there was no reason to think that he would suddenly abandon the job, or confess to Amelia and Malot that he had been paid a small fortune to follow them. Besides, Malot's absence from the hotel had presented Kell with an opportunity.

He returned to his room and retrieved the copy of the

Herald Tribune. He then walked across the street to the lobby of the Ramada and installed himself on a sofa with clear sight of the reception desk. His plan was simple. He needed to be seen. He wanted the staff, albeit unconsciously, to think of him as a resident, perhaps a husband waiting for his wife to come downstairs for supper. To that end, Kell began to flick through the pages of the newspaper. He read an article about post-Mubarak Egypt, another on the forthcoming elections in France. Behind him, installed at a grand piano in the centre of the lobby, was an elderly British guest, pink as a balloon, playing Cole Porter tunes with the lifeless accuracy of a retired music teacher. She appeared to be a fixture in the hotel, attracting smiles from passing staff. Beside her, a letter on SAGA writing paper had been tacked to a notice board: 'Film Night. Monday. *Billy Elliot.*' Kell began to feel as though he had signed up for a week at Butlins. On the stroke of nine o'clock, a small crowd gathered around the piano and the pink lady was encouraged to embark on her pièce de résistance: a rendition of Rod Stewart's 'Sailing'. Kell decided to make his move. He tucked the newspaper under his arm, checked that the desk was clear of guests, and walked towards the receptionists.

There were two of them, a man and a woman. Working on a hunch that the woman looked more likely to cooperate, he stood in front of her and rolled his fingers on the desk.

'*Bonsoir.*' Eye contact, an easy smile. Kell spoke in French. 'I checked in this morning. Could you tell me what time the restaurant stops serving food?'

The receptionist could not have been more helpful. Drawing out a sheet of notepaper, she scribbled down an expansive summary of the hotel's mealtimes and amenities, suggesting that 'Sir' might like to take a drink at the bar before dinner, and hinting that breakfast was often extended into the morning beyond the official cut-off time. Kell was even given a map. He listened intently, expressed his gratitude, and returned to the sofa to read his newspaper for a further fifteen minutes.

At nine twenty, he enacted the second phase of his plan. Again, the strategy was simple: to give the impression that he was a guest in the hotel, returning momentarily to his room. He walked towards the bank of escalators on the north side of the lobby, waited until he was certain that he had been spotted by the receptionist, then made his way to the second-floor landing where he killed time by telephoning Sami.

As usual, the call was greeted not by a ringtone but by a cacophony of North African music. Sami's voice only became audible after several seconds of sustained wailing and screeching violins. It transpired that Amelia and Malot had arrived in La Goulette at half-past eight. Sami explained that they had gone for a drink at a bar on the beach and had asked him to wait until they had finished supper so that he could drive them back to the hotels.

'That's ideal,' Kell told him. 'Anybody else with them?'

'No, sir.'

'And are you OK? Have you had something to eat?'

'I am well, thank you.' Sami sounded guarded and tense, as though he was experiencing a sudden crisis of conscience. 'We had a long conversation while they were in the back of the car.'

'I'd like to hear about it.' Kell peered over the balcony and saw that the reception desk was clear. 'We can have a meeting in my room when you get back.' A teenage girl emerged from one of the lifts and looked at the ground as she passed him. 'Try to remember every detail of what they talk about on the way home. It could be important.'

'Of course, sir.'

Time to go. Kell took the lift to the ground floor, timed his approach to the receptionist, and produced a weary but apologetic smile.

'I have a problem,' he said.

'Yes, sir?'

'I can't find my room key. I rented a donkey on the beach this afternoon. I think it may have fallen out on to the sand. Would it be possible to have a replacement?'

'Of course, sir. What was the room, please?'

'Twelve fourteen.'

The receptionist keyed the number into the computer.

'And the name, sir?'

'Malot. François Malot.'

23

He was conceived as an act of love; to destroy him would be an act of hate.

Amelia remembered almost every word of the long-ago conversations with Joan, the to-and-fro of their arguments, her own steady conviction that she had no right to abort Jean-Marc's child without his knowledge. Joan had at first advised her to terminate the pregnancy, to fly back to London and to chalk up the experience to the cruelties of youth. Once Amelia had convinced her of her determination to give birth to the child, however, the American had proved a priceless ally and unshakeable friend. It was Joan who had installed Amelia in a one-bedroomed apartment just two blocks from the Guttmann residence, an arrangement so secret that only David, Joan's husband, had known anything about it. It was Joan who had put Amelia to work on American consular business so that she would have something with which to occupy herself in the seven months of the pregnancy. A few weeks after moving her into the apartment, the Guttmanns had taken Amelia to

Spain for a fortnight, treating her as the daughter they had never had, showing her the treasures of the Prado, the splendours of Cordoba, even a bullfight at Las Ventas, during which David had rested his hand gently on Amelia's stomach and said: 'You sure a lady in your condition ought to be *watching* this stuff?' And it had been Joan, once they were back in Tunis, who had first floated the notion of adoption through Père Blancs, an idea that Amelia had grasped at perhaps too readily, because she was so ambitious for herself at that age, so hungry for life, and terrified that a baby would rob her of all of the experiences and possibilities in her future.

Paris seemed to have been waiting for her. The humid summer streets were crowded with tourists, the pavement cafés alive with bustle and conversation. Sometimes, arriving in a new city, Amelia would feel an immediate and underlying sense of threat, as though she had been displaced into an alien environment, a home to bad luck. She was well aware that this was not much more than a hunch, a superstition, the sort of thing that her colleagues would laugh at if she had ever shared it with them. Yet a sixth sense – call it intuition – had been with her throughout her career, serving her, for the most part, very well. As an SIS officer working under diplomatic cover in Cairo, for example, or during her years in Baghdad, Amelia had reckoned that she needed fifty per cent more cunning and persistence than her male equivalents, simply to survive in such hostile environments. But France had always embraced her. In Paris she was always something close to her old self, the self before Tunis, the twenty-year-old Amelia Weldon with the world at her feet. As soon as they had taken François from her – it had been an immediate thing, she had never held or even seen her own child – the process of constructing a new and invulnerable personality had begun. Lovers were betrayed, colleagues discarded, friends forgotten or ignored. The double life of SIS had presented Amelia with what she looked back on as ideal laboratory conditions in which to re-make herself in the image of a woman who would never fail again.

Yet she was failing now. Failing to keep calm, failing to maintain whatever decorum she had brought with her across the Channel. She longed for the slow hours to quicken and to be in a room with her boy, just the two of them, and yet she dreaded what she might discover: a person unknown to her, a young man with whom she had nothing in common but their shared contempt for a mother who had abandoned him at birth.

There was a message waiting at her hotel, sent by the adoption agency and addressed to 'Madame Weldon'. The concierge had been reluctant to hand it over, because Amelia had booked her room under the name 'Levene', but when she explained that 'Weldon' was her maiden name, he relented. François had contacted the agency and requested that Amelia go to his apartment at four o'clock on Monday afternoon. He did not wish to speak to her by telephone beforehand, nor to communicate with her in any way prior to their first meeting. Without hesitation, Amelia rang the agency to confirm, because she was predisposed to cooperate with all of their instructions, yet she worried that the arrangement was a sign of François' anger. What if he told her, face-to-face, that she could never replace the mother who had been killed? What if he had lured her to Paris merely to wound her? All her life, Amelia had been blessed with an ability to assess people and to develop a quick and intuitive understanding of their circumstances. She could sense when she was being lied to; she knew when she was being manipulated. Some of this gift had been taught, as a necessary skill for a career in which human relationships were at the core of the work, but mostly it was a talent as innate as the ability to kick a ball or to capture the play of light on a canvas. Yet now, faced with what might become the most important relationship of her life, Amelia was almost helpless.

There was so much time to kill. The waiting was slower, the anticipation more sickening, than any intelligence operation she could recall. So many times in her career she had sat in hotel rooms, in safe houses, in offices that ticked like clocks, waiting for word from a joe. But this was quite different. There was no team, no chain of command, no tradecraft. She was just a private citizen, a tourist in Paris, one of ten thousand women with a secret. She had unpacked her suitcase and overnight bag within minutes of arriving, hanging the black suit from Peter Jones in a cupboard and putting the dress that she had picked out for the reunion on a chair in the corner of the room, so that she could look at it and try to decide if it was the correct choice for such an occasion. As if François would be concerned about her clothes! It was her face that he would want to see, her eyes into which he would pour his questions. For an hour Amelia tried to read one of the novels she had brought, to watch the news on CNN, but it was impossible to concentrate for more than a few minutes. Like a memory of her former self, she longed to speak to Joan again, to tell her what was about to happen, but could not trust the security of the line from the hotel. She thought

123

of Thomas Kell, of all people, her confidant in matters of marriage and children, the one colleague in whom she might have confided. But Kell was long gone, forced into disgrace and a stubborn retirement by the same men whom she had leapfrogged to 'C'. Would Tom even know about her triumph? She doubted it.

And then, finally, the meeting was upon her, the last hour before arriving at the flat passing as fleetingly as a face in the street. A vandal had scoured a deep scratch in the street door; a Chinese couple walking hand in hand smiled at Amelia as she walked into the lobby. Once inside, she felt as though she was going to be sick. It was as if the hole that had gaped inside her for three long decades was suddenly opening up. She had to steady herself against the door.

'Would a *man* behave like this?' she asked herself, a reliable maxim of her entire working career. But of course a man could never have known what it felt like to be in such a situation.

François lived on the third floor. Amelia ignored the lift and walked there, feeling as though she had never met any person in the course of her long life, had never climbed a flight of stairs, had never learned how to breathe. Reaching the landing, she felt that she was about to make a terrible mistake and would have turned and walked away if there had been any other choice.

She knocked on the door.

24

Kell knocked quietly on the door of 1214, heard nothing back, slipped the card key into the slot and stepped into François Malot's room.

A smell of shower gel and scorching sea air; a door had been left open on to a balcony overlooking the Mediterranean. Kell moved quickly in the heat, noting the open safe, the 35mm camera on a side table, a carton of Silver Lucky Strike, a gold cigarette lighter engraved with the initials 'P.M.', presumably for 'Philippe Malot'. Propped up on a table on the right-hand side of the double bed was a framed photograph of Malot's parents, smiling for the camera, not a care in the world.

A passport was lying on the bedspread. French, well worn, biometric. Kell opened it up. A nine-digit code was perforated into the bottom of each page; he scribbled the number down on a piece of paper and stuffed it into his back pocket. Kell then turned to the identity page which listed Malot's second name – Michel – his date of birth, the date of issue of the passport, his height, his eye colour and an address in Paris. On subsequent pages there were stamps for entry at JFK, Cape Town and Sharm-el-Sheikh, the last dated three weeks earlier. Kell photographed everything twice, checking that the flash had not reflected on the plastic seal. He then closed the passport and put it back on the bedspread.

Beside the framed photograph was a *roman policier* – a French translation of *Ratking* – as well as a wristwatch and a Moleskine diary. Kell photographed each page from January to the end of September, again checking the screen to ensure that the entries were legible. Though he knew that Malot was still miles away in La Goulette, this took time and his pulse was up. He wanted to move as quickly as possible. There was always the danger of a chambermaid stopping by to turn down the bed, even of a third-party guest with access to Malot's room.

Next he went to the bathroom. Shaving products, dental floss, toothpaste. Inside a washbag Kell found several loose strips of pills: aspirin; chlorpheniramine, which he knew to be an antihistamine often used as a sleeping aid; St John's Wort; a small bottle of Valium; insect repellent; a comb. No condoms.

Next he went through the pockets of Malot's jeans, careful not to disturb the layout of the room. In a black leather jacket he found loose change, a Paris metro *carnet* and a soft packet of Lucky Strike. It was an identical process to that which he had undertaken in Amelia's room, only now Kell felt a greater sense of the unknown, because he had no notion of Malot's character beyond his recent bereavement and the obvious vanity he had displayed beside the pool. Under the bed he discovered a Gideon Bible, open at a page in Deuteronomy, and a small box of matches. Underneath the copy of *Ratking* was an envelope in which Kell found a letter, dated 4 February 1999, written by Malot's father. Philippe's handwriting was an illegible scrawl, but Kell photographed both sides of it and replaced the letter carefully in the envelope.

When he was satisfied that he had thoroughly checked the contents of the room, Kell went outside into the corridor, discovered a side staircase leading to an exit adjacent to the swimming pool, and walked back to the Valencia Carthage via the beach. He found the number for Elsa Cassani and called her direct on the Marquand mobile.

To his surprise, Elsa was still in Nice, 'getting drunk and spending the money you gave me' at a bar in the old town. Kell could hear rock music thumping in the background and experienced an odd beat of jealousy for the men who were enjoying her company. He assumed that she was talking to him from one of the quiet cobbled streets south of Boulevard Jean Jaurès.

'I'm afraid you're going to have to stop getting drunk,' he told her. 'More work to do.'

'OK,' she replied. If she was disappointed by this, she did not betray it. 'What do you need me to do?'

'Got something to write with?'

He listened as she scrabbled around in her bag, found a pen and a piece of paper and announced that she had discovered 'a nice step to sit on and to take your dictation, Tom'. Kell began to flick through the images on his camera.

'I need enhanced traces on François Malot. Has to be off the books, through your famous contacts, not via Cheltenham.' It was an unusual request, but Kell wanted to avoid raising alarm bells with Marquand. 'You have ways of checking people in France, right?'

A knowing pause. 'Of course.'

'Good. I'm going to need full-spectrum background. Bank accounts, telephone records, tax payments, schooling and diplomas, medical history, whatever you can find.'

'Is that all?'

Kell wasn't sure if Elsa's question was evidence of sarcasm or over-confidence. He found one of the photographs of the passport and read out Malot's full name, his date of birth, his address in Paris. He took the piece of paper on which he had scrawled the passport number and checked that Elsa had taken it down correctly. 'He was in New York in January last year, Cape Town six months later, Sharm-el-Sheikh in July. I'm going to email you a series of photographs from his diary. I'll look at them, too, but you may find something useful there. Telephone numbers, email addresses, appointments . . .'

'Of course.'

'One other thing. It looks as though he's an I.T. consultant. Try to find out where he works. London had a JPEG of what looked like the Christmas party. I'll send that too.'

'When do you need all this by?' Elsa asked. It sounded as though she was making a concerted effort not to sound overwhelmed.

'As soon as possible,' Kell replied. 'You think you can pull it off?'

'This is why people hire me.'

25

The first thing that François reacted to was Amelia's beauty. He had not expected to find her so striking. Her remarkable appearance surprised him, because he had deliberately decided never to look at her photograph. Extraordinary dignity and strength of character in her face. She was elegantly dressed. The cut of her jacket brought out the fullness of her breasts and made her waist look slim and flat, as though she had never borne a child. He saw that she was wearing only basic make-up: a pale pink lipstick, light foundation, some definition around the eyes.

At first, because it was what he had decided on as the best course of action, he closed the door behind her and then reached out to shake her hand. Very quickly, however, he was drawing Amelia towards him into an embrace. She resisted this at first, and looked at him as though concerned that he might run off, like a frightened animal. He was touched by this. Her embrace, when it eventually came, was soft and hesitant, but as she reacted to the strength in his arms she squeezed much harder. She was not shaking, but he could sense that she was overwhelmed to be with him and he allowed her to rest her head briefly against his shoulder. François found that his own breathing was quick and lacked control, an irregularity that he put down to nerves.

'Do you mind if we talk in French?' he said, the line that he had practised and rehearsed many times.

'Of course not!' Amelia replied, and he heard the accuracy of her French, the flawless accent.

'It's just that I have never learned to speak English. I heard from the agency that you were fluent.'

'Well, that was flattering of them. I'm a little rusty.'

He had rehearsed the next part, too. My mother is British, and the British like to drink tea. Offer to make her a cup. It will break the ice and it will give me something to do in the first awkward minutes. To François' relief, Amelia accepted, and he led her through the small apartment to a kitchen that faced on to the street. He had already set out two cups and saucers and a bowl of brown sugar and could sense her watching him with forensic attention as he poured water into the kettle and retrieved a carton of milk from the fridge.

'Would you like a biscuit?'

'Thank you, no,' she replied, a lovely open smile. She was so impressive to look at; what his grandfather would have called 'sophistiquée'. He could see the euphoria in her eyes; she was trying hard to disguise it. He knew that she wanted to hold him again and to apologize for everything that she had done. Behind a British screen of nods and acknowledging smiles was a woman overwhelmed by the privilege of meeting him.

They spent the next four hours deep in conversation.

To his surprise, Amelia told him almost immediately that she worked for SIS.

'I can't bear the idea of any lies coming between us,' she explained. 'Obviously it's not something that I speak about very much.'

'Of course.' He was so surprised by her candour that he made a joke about it. 'I guess it's kind of cool to have a mother who's like Jason Bourne.'

She had laughed at this, but he realized that he had acknowledged her biological role as his mother before he had meant to. It was not a mistake, but it was not how he had wanted the afternoon to proceed. He suspected that the secret Amelia had shared with him had been intended, from her point of view, as a bond between them, something that even François' adopted parents had not known about her. And so it proved. Thereafter, he was surprised by how easy it was to talk to her. There were no awkward silences, no moments when he wished that she would leave so that he could be alone again in the apartment. They spoke about his career in I.T., they discussed the horror of the attacks in Egypt. Amelia appeared to be deeply sensitive to his loss, but she was not sentimental about it. He liked that. It showed that she had character.

In due course, he asked about Jean-Marc Daumal, but it transpired that Amelia knew very little about him. *The last time I saw him*, she said, *was the night that I left the house*. She confessed that in the face of near-constant temptation, particularly at the outset of her career, she had never run a trace on him, nor asked a colleague in Paris to peek into the French tax records.

'They would *do* that?' he asked.

'They would do that,' she told him.

Only once did he feel that she overstepped the mark, suggesting that their own reunion might be a precursor to François tracing his biological father, if indeed Jean-Marc was still alive.

'More than anything,' she said, 'I want you to feel that you have people in your life who care very deeply for you, despite what has happened.'

He had felt that this was crass and pushy, but disguised his reaction.

'Thank you,' he said. They had been standing, so he had allowed her to embrace him again. He could not place her perfume; he had a vague recollection that one of the girls in his high school class had worn it to a party at which they had kissed.

'I would very much like you to come to the funeral tomorrow,' he said.

'I would be honoured,' Amelia had replied.

Later, after she had gone, despite the remarkable success of their first meeting, François' overwhelming feeling had been one of exhaustion. This was only to be expected, he told himself. They were at the beginning of what he hoped would be a deep and rewarding relationship. In order to achieve that, he would be called upon to dig into reserves of strength and mental fortitude that were perhaps, at this stage, unknown even to him. It was part of the deal he had struck with himself. They were getting to know one another.

26

It was half-past eleven by the time Sami called again. Kell had eaten another club sandwich in his room and read a centimetre of Thomas Pakenham's *The Scramble for Africa*. There was that same cacophony of Arabic music on the line when he picked up, like a roomful of belly dancers having the time of their lives. Then Sami said:

'I have just let them out.' He still sounded tense, as though he had been confronted by the limits of his own decency. It was often the way with embryonic agents; the guilt and the adrenalin worked through them like poison and its antidote. 'François took her to the Valencia to make sure she was safely home. He said he was going to have a cognac in your hotel bar. Maybe I can meet you somewhere and tell you what happened between them. His mother, she is an interesting woman.'

Kell almost asked Sami to repeat what he had said, but the logic of it was suddenly as clear to him as the trajectory of a setting sun. Malot was Amelia's child, born to her in Tunis more than thirty years earlier. Was this *possible*? Kell

133

thought back to Amelia's file. The dates matched precisely. Malot had been born in 1979, only months after Amelia had finished working as an au pair in Tunis. How could he have missed the connection? Philippe and Jeannine must have adopted him at birth, with no trace of Amelia Weldon's name on the adoption papers or birth certificate. He marvelled at her ability to have kept the child a secret; SIS vetting was forensic, yet somehow François had slipped through the net. But who was the father? Somebody from the ex-pat community in Tunis? There had been no record in the pre-recruitment file of a boyfriend from that period of her life. Had Amelia been raped?

Kell looked up at the bare whitewashed walls of his room, down at the worn beige carpet, and rubbed his eyes. 'Come to my room,' he said quietly. 'We can talk here.'

He had not expected to feel resentment, but he was angry with Amelia because he felt that she had deceived him. Their shared childlessness, after all, had been the great private bond between them, a mutual absence that they had both quietly mourned. Yet all that time the master spy had concealed from him a simple tale of her youth. Then Kell began to feel enormous sorrow for his friend, because he could not imagine the agony of that separation, nine months of a body growing inside her body, the baby speaking to Amelia through her womb, then wrenched away to a life about which she would have known almost nothing. Kell wanted to knock on Amelia's door and to tell her that he was a friend to whom she could turn if ever she needed to speak about what had happened.

'You're going soft,' he muttered to himself, and stood up, as if he might regain a sense of professional decorum by doing so. He switched on the main overhead light in the room and poured himself the last of the glutinous red wine he had ordered from room service. Hannibal, the local poison. He retrieved his camera from the bed and began to click through the surveillance photos of the pool. In all, there were roughly fifty shots of Amelia and Malot. Looking at the images, Kell was sure that he could detect a family resemblance between the two and began to feel intrusive of Amelia's privacy. Their holiday in Tunis would be one of only a few occasions when they managed to spend time together. He had no right to be snooping on them. Throughout his long career, Kell's own privacy had been of the utmost importance to him; he knew that Amelia felt the same way about hers. As an intelligence officer, you had so little space in which to live a life free of scrutiny's gaze; moments of unguarded seclusion were sacred. Amelia's house in Wiltshire, for example, was a haven to which she would escape from the pressures of the secret world as often as she could. Kell had no comparable bolt-hole, and had instead shuttled between Claire and Vauxhall Cross until his personal and professional selves had seemed to bind together into a knot that would not be untied. On the one hand, a Service that had wanted his head on a plate for Afghanistan; on the other, a wife who would not release him from the cage of her resentment and frustration.

'To you,' Kell said aloud, raising the glass to Amelia. Then, more quietly: 'To being a mother.' And he drank.

27

There were only twelve mourners at the crematorium; a larger memorial service was planned for the autumn. François had insisted that Amelia sit beside him, with his mother's sister on her other side. Afterwards, at his uncle's apartment, François had introduced Amelia as 'an old friend of the family from England'. He had later apologized for this, saying that he did not yet 'possess the courage to tell everybody who you are'. Their decision to go to Tunis had been made that night. François explained that he was desperate to get out of Paris and Amelia could not bear the thought of leaving him so soon after they had met; when would there be another chance to be together? She had therefore contacted her assistant at Vauxhall Cross, announced that she needed time off in the wake of the funeral, and revealed that she would be in the South of France for a fortnight, using up the rest of her holiday allowance. As cover for the journey to Tunisia, she booked herself into a hotel in Nice, where she would be attending a painting course. There was a telephone call from Simon

Haynes, who understood that she 'probably deserved a break' and an irritable email from George Truscott pointing out the 'considerable inconvenience of abandoning the Office at twenty-four hours notice'. Otherwise her absence seemed to generate little in the way of comment.

By Friday, Amelia Levene was in Gammarth, living under the Farrell alias and staying in a package hotel located across the road from a Ramada, where François was installed for a probably needless second layer of secrecy. François himself had not questioned this strategy nor objected to the subterfuge; if anything, he seemed to relish the sense of intrigue and even joked that it might be 'hereditary'.

For Amelia to return to Tunisia after more than thirty years was, at first, melancholy and unsettling, but as the days went by and they visited many of her old haunts, the journey became emotionally satisfying in ways that she had not anticipated. On the surface, little had changed: she remembered the whistle of darting swifts in the evening sky, the fierce dry heat and the constant chatter of men. She recalled the garden at La Marsa, long nights in the arms of her lover, so contemptuous of Jean-Marc's wife and children, so cruel in her desire to possess him. She took François to Le Golfe, a restaurant that his father had never dared risk for fear that they would be spotted by one of his colleagues or friends. It was in Tunisia, before the pregnancy, that Amelia had begun to study Arabic, wandering the streets of the Medina on the way to class wearing a headscarf and skirt, gawping Tunisian boys clicking their tongues as she passed. She had been convinced, as all self-possessed young people are at such an age, that Amelia Weldon was different to all the other students and backpackers passing through Tunis, Mummy's boys travelling on Daddy's bank account. Now, more than three decades later, she felt a great nostalgia for that time, not least because she had long since ceased to be one of the most captivating girls in the city. In the second decade of the twenty-first century Amelia Levene was just another middle-aged tourist from England, a target for stallholders selling carpets and counterfeit polo shirts. It was as though the same men she had seen in 1978 were drinking the same cup of tea at the same café; identical women scrubbing identical vegetables lurked in the same alleys and tiled doorways of the Medina. The wedding baskets, pink and cream, the piles of tea and spice, they still lay unsold in the market. Nothing had changed. Yet of course it had. The young women now wore make-up and Dolce & Gabbana jeans. There were mobile phones attached to the ears of their boyfriends, and posters of Chelsea footballers on the walls of the cafés. The children that had run amok in the dust and the diesel of 1978 were now the adults who drove Amelia's taxi to the Boudu museum, or popped François' napkin as he sat for lunch at Dar el-Jeld.

'I was happy here,' she told him in an unguarded and sentimental moment, regretting it instantly, because how could she have been happy when she was about to give up her son? 'Before what happened,' she added, stumbling on the phrase in French. 'I loved the freedom of my life. I loved the sense of being away from England.'

'And yet now you work for England,' François replied.

'What a way to put it,' she said, raising a glass to toast him and staring into the refraction of the crystal. 'Yes, I suppose I do.'

28

A knock at the door, a soft tap-tap from the corridor. Kell slipped the security chain and invited Sami to come inside. A strange midnight encounter between men. Kell opened the door of the balcony to allow fresh evening air to blow into the room. There was a bottle of Macallan on the floor beside his bed, imported duty free via Nice, and he poured three fingers into two glasses from the bathroom. As he did so, Kell made a point of apologizing for the 'atmosphere of secrecy', a phrase that he had difficulty translating into Arabic.

'Not a problem,' Sami replied. 'I understand.'

A long evening at the wheel of the cab had left the Tunisian looking hunched and slightly immobile, but as he shuffled across the room, compacting himself on to a low-sprung sofa, Kell saw that his eyes were glinting with excitement.

'So they had a nice time?' he began, an ambiguous question that would allow Sami to fill in the blanks.

'Yes. An incredible story.' Sami was leaning forward in

his chair, bald and squat and full of news. 'You know about them?'

'Tell me,' Kell said. 'I've forgotten a lot of the details.'

And so it began. Thirty years before, 'Amy' – that was the name Amelia was going by – had been working in Tunis when she had fallen pregnant outside of marriage. Because she was still a teenager, and the daughter of strict Catholic parents, it had been decided that she should give up her baby for adoption. That baby was François, who was subsequently taken to France and raised in Paris by Philippe and Jeannine Malot. Tragically, his adoptive parents had been murdered only weeks earlier during a holiday in Egypt. It was only while reading his father's Will that François had been made aware, for the first time, of the circumstances of his birth. Without hesitation, he had contacted the agency in Tunis that had arranged his adoption.

Kell listened with less astonishment than might ordinarily have been the case; he had suspected as much. The story, after all, made sense in all the right places. The sole surprise was that Amelia had only met her son for the first time in recent days. For some reason, Kell had assumed that the relationship between them had been growing for several years. Why had he made such a baseless assumption?

'Who told you all this?' he asked. 'How did it come out?'

'François. I asked him what they were doing in Tunisia, so soon after the revolution, he tells me the whole story.'

'Amy didn't say anything? She left it to him?'

Kell wanted to know why Amelia was allowing François to be so indiscreet; perhaps her guard was down and she had seen no reason to distrust Sami.

140

The driver nodded. 'The lady, she is much quieter. He does most of the talking.'

'But she seemed happy? They were content together.'

'Oh yes,' Sami replied. He had seen off the three fingers of whisky and proffered his glass for more. 'So, can I ask you a personal question?'

Kell picked up the bottle from the carpet and obliged him. 'Sure.'

'Why did you want me to follow them around?'

Sami was a straightforward man, palpably kind and biddable, with a strain of romanticism in his nature that had evidently responded to the pathos of François' story.

'Someone is paying me,' Kell replied. In the next room, a man began to cough. He tried to move off the subject. 'You must be tired.'

Sami shrugged. In operations of yesteryear, even with Elsa in Nice, Kell had often tried to imagine the private circumstances of his contacts. It was one of the diversions of the trade, a way of passing time during the long periods of waiting. Elsa, he presumed, was into rock music and would take grateful, long-haired men with abundant tattoos to bed. But what about Sami? Who was he? An observant Muslim? Most probably not, judging by his thirst for whisky. A sports fan? A lover of women and food? Certainly his girth and bonhomie, the speed with which he had sunk his drink, spoke of a man with large appetites.

Kell returned to the conversation.

'Did François say why they were staying in separate hotels?'

'Yes.' The reply was quick and almost startled, as though Sami suspected Kell of intuiting something from his private thoughts. 'The Ramada was full, so she took a room here.'

He nodded in the general direction of the lobby. 'She leaves tomorrow. I'm taking her to the airport.'

'And they told you all this in the course of one cab journey?'

Was Amelia playing him? Did she know that Kell was in Tunis and had recruited Sami?

'Two,' he replied, making a stubby Churchillian 'V' with his fingers. 'People always tell me things. I like to ask questions. Tourists come to Tunisia, they tell you their secrets because they think they are never going to see you again.'

Kell's smile disguised his private doubt. 'And so now you're taking Amy to the airport?'

Sami suddenly looked embarrassed, as if he had spoken out of turn.

'Is that OK, Stephen?'

'Of course. It's fine.' He waved Sami's concerns away and thought about Marquand. What was he going to tell London in the morning? How was he going to finesse Amelia's secret? 'Just be careful not to slip up about our arrangement. We've never met, OK? You've never seen or talked to me. I've never given you money. The people who are paying my bills would be very angry if Amy found out that I was following her.'

'Of course.' Sami put his empty glass on a table beside the sofa and looked offended at being castigated for a sin he had yet to commit. 'Perhaps it's time I went home and got some sleep.'

'Perhaps.'

Moments later, Kell was ushering the Tunisian to the door, telling him to relax until it was time to take Amy to the airport. He watched as he shuffled down the corridor, wondering what he would say to François if they bumped into one another in the lobby, wondering if it would even matter if they did. The mystery, after all, had been solved. Kell's work was done.

He switched off the overhead light and lay on the bed, listening to the rasping coughs of his neighbour, to the fragmentary and indecipherable conversation of a man and a woman talking beneath his window. It was almost one o'clock in the morning. Unable to relax, he put on a jacket and walked down to the lobby, half-imagining that he would encounter Amelia in the bar. But, save for a young man at reception, the hotel was deserted and the bar already closed. On a whim, Kell went outside to the taxi rank. A driver asked if he wanted to be taken to La Marsa and Kell, surprising himself, agreed, because he needed to be away from the hotel, away from the claustrophobia of conceal-ment and strategy. Besides, it was time to celebrate. His driver, who did not utter a word during the ten-minute journey along the coast, dropped him at Plaza Corniche, a fashionable bar in the centre of La Marsa where the waiters dressed like pilots on a layover and caramel-tanned Italians made eyes at gangs of beautiful Tunisian girls. Kell had forgotten how much he disliked going out alone: he was too old for nightclubs, too wired to go to bed. Half an hour later, having drunk a single bottle of imported German beer, he went back outside to find his taxi driver waiting for him on the opposite corner of the street. As they were pulling away from the kerb, Sami called his mobile. The music, the belly dancers. Then:

'Mr Stephen?'

'Sami?' Kell looked at his watch. 'What's up?'

'I am sorry to ring so late. It's just that I forgot to tell you something important.'

'Go on.'

'Tomorrow. The ship. François is booked on the ferry from La Goulette. He is leaving, travelling overnight to Marseille.'

29

There was only one passenger ferry scheduled to leave for Marseille the following day. Kell went back to the Valencia, reserved an interior cabin via the SNCM website, cancelled his return flight to Nice and grabbed a few hours' sleep before ordering breakfast to his room. Sami called at eight to say that he was en route to the Ramada to pick up both Amelia and François.

'They want me to take Mrs Farrell to the airport. Then I drop François at the ferry terminal. They are close to each other.'

Kell assumed he was talking about the proximity of the airport to La Goulette, rather than offering an opinion on the status of Amelia's relationship with her son. He didn't trust Sami's sense of humour sufficiently to make a joke about it.

'Any idea why François isn't flying as well?'

'He said he likes to go by sea when he has a choice. Amy is going to Nice.'

Back to her painting course, Kell thought, and wondered

if the Knights were still dutifully attending classes, day after day, in the vain hope of catching sight of their mark. Chances were she would clear out her room at the Gillespie and be back in London by Sunday night.

'Call me when you've dropped François at the terminal,' he said. 'I'll leave your final payment in an envelope at reception. Fifteen hundred dinars. Is that OK?'

'This is very generous, Stephen.'

'Don't mention it.'

The port was a thousand concrete acres of cranes and trucks, seagulls twisting in the wind, ramps on to ferries banked with cars. Kell took a cab to the SNCM terminal and queued on an elevated walkway in the full glare of the sun behind a shuffling family of Tunisians who looked to have made their way in from the desert. A stooped old man cast Kell a slow, disdainful look before ordering a young boy – perhaps his great-grandson – to fasten a blue plastic bag stuffed with clothes and shoes that was threatening to slip free of its mooring on a rattling metal trolley. The old man's hands were long and dark, thick-boned through decades of manual labour. Kell wondered at the family's circumstances; were they emigrating to France? It looked as though their every possession was packed into three veteran suitcases and crammed into the soft cardboard boxes that drooped on the metal trolley like stomachs.

The queue moved quickly. Before long Kell found himself in an indoor waiting area, a high-ceilinged cube bordered on three sides by ticket desks, souvenir kiosks and a café selling pizza and pancakes. He collected his ticket from an SNCM official of Sami's vintage who looked as smart and urbane as any London spymaster. His was the sort of job

Kell had always dreaded: the confinement in one room; the day-after-day repetition of mundane tasks. He bought himself a coffee and sat at a window table overlooking the harbour, everything strangely damp to the touch, as if the morning sea had swept through the hall on a sudden, cleansing tide.

After five minutes, through the crowds of foot passengers gathered in the hall, he saw François standing at the security check fifty metres away. He was showing his ticket to a guard. Headphones were looped around his neck and he was holding a little leather clutch bag of the sort favoured by fashionable southern European men. Passport control indicated the expensive pair of designer sunglasses concealing François' eyes and Kell saw him pull them up over his head with what looked like an almost haughty disdain; perhaps a week spent in the company of the Chief-designate of the Secret Intelligence Service had fortified him in the presence of low-level power. He then turned left, out of sight, and Kell finished his coffee with no sense of rush or panic. He had twenty-two hours on the ship ahead of him: that was plenty of time to make the acquaintance of Monsieur François Malot.

The ferry was identical to many Kell had taken as a child across the English Channel on family holidays to the Normandy coast; a roll-on, roll-off passenger ship with stacked decks, open walkways on the port and starboard sides, a sun deck beneath the funnel. He located his cabin in the bowels of the ship, a tiny room squeezed among a hundred others along identical, criss-cross corridors in which he quickly lost any sense of direction. He could hear the voice of his father – 'No bloody cat small enough to swing' – as he pulled the bed down from the wall of his cabin, immediately reducing the available floor space by fifty per cent. He slid his luggage underneath. There was a small moulded shelf next to the pillow, beneath a scratched mirror; to the right of the door, a bathroom only fractionally larger than a telephone box. Kell sat on the bed, put the half-finished bottle of duty-free Macallan on the shelf, removed the memory card from the camera and headed back upstairs to look around.

No sign of François. He went from deck to deck, from salon to salon, mapping out the territory. Two veiled women were already camped out in a reception lobby on Level 6; they had laid out sponge mats and were fast asleep on the floor. A door connected the lobby to a seating area where roughly fifty North Africans had secured rows of leather armchairs in a sunlit lounge. It was lunchtime and they were eating picnics of boiled eggs, lettuce and bread. One man was slicing a tomato with a penknife and spreading a baguette with what appeared to be homemade harissa paste. The eggs were peeled white and Kell watched as he swept the broken shells carefully into a small plastic tub on the floor. He felt a pang of hunger and went looking for something to eat. Two floors up there was a restaurant, closed, and he was told by a genial French waiter that food would be served once the ship had left dock. So Kell went out on to the port deck, braced his hands on a chipped-paint railing, and watched as the last of the cars made their way into the stern of the ferry. It was a brilliant summer day, sun-glinting and clean, the salt light blinding to the eyes. Kell breathed the air deeply to clear what felt like days of indoor living. Beside him, an Algerian man with a moustache was taking photographs of the port; another was waving at a small family group clustered in a car park. He looked close to tears.

30

The years, as they say, had been kind to Jean-Marc Daumal. From Tunis, in the first months of the new decade, he had been posted to Buenos Aires, where he had enjoyed a front-row seat at the Argentine invasion of the Falkland Islands and embarked on a suitably tempestuous affair with one of the girls from the secretarial pool at his office in Avenida San Juan. In due course, his infatuation with Amelia Weldon had been, if not forgotten, then replaced by something closer to resentment and shame. It irked Daumal that a young woman should have exercised such a hold over his emotions; had he met her at a particularly vulnerable moment in his life? None of the other women with whom Daumal had become involved in the remaining twenty years of his working career had meant much more to him than brief, diversionary pleasures.

Daumal had finally solved the enigma of Amelia's disappearance some sixteen years after leaving Tunisia. At a wedding reception for a wealthy client in Atlanta, Georgia, who should Jean-Marc espy across the snow-white marquee but Joan and David Guttmann, the WASP and the Jew who had sheltered his lover on the night of her flight from La Marsa. In those first gruelling days in 1978, Jean-Marc had quickly abandoned his theory that Guttmann had stolen Amelia from under his nose, for the simple reason that he had been in Israel for six weeks either side of her disappearance. In fact, everything had later been clarified by Joan. At a lunch three days after Amelia had gone missing, she had vouchsafed to Celine that one of the English boys with whom Amelia had been spending time in the city had made her pregnant. According to Joan, she had taken the very difficult decision to fly home and to have an abortion. She hoped that the entire matter would now be forgotten and that the Daumals would find some way of forgiving their au pair for her rash and morally contemptible behaviour.

Jean-Marc had known, of course, that the baby was his, and in spite of his overwhelming feelings of love for Amelia, could not suppress a parallel sensation of intense relief that she had decided to abort the pregnancy. An illegitimate child would have steered Celine to the divorce courts, no question; the scandal would have ruined his chances of promotion to the Argentine office and had a deleterious long-term effect on the personal development of Thibaud and Lola. No, upon reflection, he was glad that Amelia had shown such maturity and good sense.

But there was a final twist. On that radiant summer afternoon in Atlanta, David Guttmann had had too much to drink. Forgetting the carefully assembled lies of 1978, he had assumed that Jean-Marc knew all about the long months that Amelia had spent in Tunis at an apartment near their house, as the baby grew inside her. Trying to disguise his astonished reaction, Jean-Marc had come to realize that Amelia had not aborted their child but instead given birth to a son. It was only when Guttmann had drunkenly registered the extent of his mistake that he grabbed a lie out of the clear Georgia air and tried to backtrack on what he had said.

'The great tragedy, of course, is that the baby passed away a few weeks later.'

'Is that true?'

'Sure. It was just a heart-rending thing. Some kind of blood poisoning. We never really got to the bottom of it. Joan will remember, but probably best not to bring it up tonight, huh? Far as I recall, the hospital wasn't as clean as it should have been. Some problem with septicaemia.'

By 1996, Jean-Marc Daumal was living back in Paris and flew home determined to find out what had become of his child. He found no trace of Amelia Weldon in the United Kingdom, despite employing the services of a private detective in Mayfair, at eye-watering expense. His various enquiries with adoption agencies in Tunisia drew a series of similar blanks. It was only a decade later, long since retired and living at the family home in Burgundy, that Daumal finally discovered what had become of Amelia. Daumal's son, Thibaud, now a journalist in Paris, had brought home one of his girlfriends, who happened to work in the Ministry of the Interior. Keen to impress the man whom she hoped might one day become her father-in-law, the girlfriend, whose name was Marion, had agreed to find out what she could about Mademoiselle Amelia Weldon. Her subsequent enquiries into a known officer of the British Secret Intelligence Service had attracted the attention of France's overseas intelligence service, which had promptly interviewed Marion in order to discover the reason behind her enquiry. She, in turn, had pointed the DGSE in the direction of Jean-Marc Daumal, who agreed to have lunch in Beaune with an officer identifying himself as 'Benedict Voltaire'.

'Tell me, Monsieur,' Benedict had asked, as their waiter snapped open a couple of menus at the outset of what was to become a memorable meal. 'What do you remember of your time in Tunis? Is there anything at all, for example, that you can tell us about a woman named Amelia Weldon?'

31

Spying is waiting.

Kell went back to his cabin, retrieved *The Scramble for Africa*, got lost in the switchback corridors on the sleeping level, eventually found his way to the restaurant and ate a decent lunch. The ferry, now pulling out into the open sea, appeared to be only half-full; no queue had formed outside the restaurant and there were enough spare tables to accommodate the mostly French passengers who had materialized en masse from the lower decks after parking their cars. There were no Africans in sight; the food was French, the prices in euros and the clientele exclusively white. Kell waited for François to make an appearance, lingering over his book and coffee, but by two thirty he had still not shown and Kell gave up, on the assumption that the Frenchman must have eaten in the self-service canteen. He paid his bill and walked upstairs, passing through the canteen as the low, whitewashed houses of Carthage narrowed to a chalk strip on the horizon. The entire area was deserted save for a young British couple on a damage-limitation exercise with two screaming toddlers and a new-born baby. The mother was spooning puréed food into the baby's mouth, the toddlers bombing the linoleum with plastic toys. A section of the floor was soaked with seawater. All of them looked exhausted.

Eventually, like stumbling on the right street without the aid of a map, Kell found François standing at the stern railings on the sun deck, gazing down at the churning wake of the sea, the distant Tunisian coast now obscured by a vapour of mist. Beside him was a taller man, bearded and dressed in jeans, wearing a button-down blue shirt. The man, who had lustrous black hair, almost certainly dyed, looked about fifty-five and was smoking a filterless cigarette, which he eventually flicked out over the stern; the wind failed to catch it and it dropped on to a lower deck. The conversation between them seemed relaxed and matter-of-fact, yet something in their physical proximity spoke of an established familiarity. Perhaps they had been talking for some time; perhaps they had met before. Kell positioned himself a few metres along the railing, caught the man's name – Luc – and heard a snatch of dialogue about 'hotels in Marseille'. But any hopes he had of overhearing more of the conversation were snuffed out by the low, perpetual roar of the ship's funnel.

He lit a cigarette of his own. He always carried a packet in environments that might require him to make contact with an agent or member of the public. A lighter could trigger a conversation; a cigarette was something to occupy nervous hands. Kell turned and looked at the plastic chairs on the deck, at the scattering of passengers taking siestas under the unrelenting Mediterranean sun. They were held in the suspended animation of travel, the no-man's-land of waiting to cross from one place to another. Nothing to do but read and sleep and eat. The wind was buffeting Kell's face and cracking a French flag at the stern of the ship. Still the two men kept talking, their voices low, their conversation a rumble of French unpunctuated by laughter. Eventually Kell took a flight of sea-greased steps to a lower deck and waited directly beneath them, hoping that the breeze might push more of their words towards him. But it was no good: the roar of the engine muffled every sound. At a loose end, he powered up his London phone, only to watch the last bar of reception flicker and vanish as the ship moved steadily north.

He did not see the bearded Luc again until dinner. François' companion was eating alone at a corner table not four feet from where Kell was seated. He had his back to the room and was hunched over a lengthy document that he read, with great concentration, between mouthfuls of rice and chicken chasseur. Kell had a glorious sunset and a copy of *Time* magazine for company and was beginning to wonder why he had bothered following François back to Marseille. Better, surely, to have tailed Amelia to Nice, to liaise with the Knights, send a full report to London and then invoice Truscott for his trouble.

He was mid-pudding when Luc stood up and walked towards a salad bar close to the entrance of the restaurant. He appeared to scan the selection: cucumbers in yoghurt; piles of shredded carrot; drained, tinned sweetcorn. As Luc was helping himself to a triangle of processed cheese, François walked into the restaurant, directly in his line of sight. Kell saw the two men make eye contact, plainly aware of the other's presence, but there was no further acknowledgment between them. Luc looked down at his plate; François immediately switched his gaze to a waiter, who led him to a table on the starboard side of the restaurant. Kell wondered what he had just seen. Were they ignoring one another? Was it a case of avoiding a fellow passenger for fear that they would be obliged to sit together. Or was there more to it?

François sat down. He flapped a napkin into his lap and picked up the menu. He was seated directly opposite Kell but paid no attention to him, nor to any of the other diners in the restaurant. The light of the sunset was pouring through the windows and coating the walls of the salon in a deep orange glow. It was curious to watch him in his solitude. Much of François' swagger and arrogance had diminished; he was somehow less striking, less self-confident than the man he had photographed at the hotel. Perhaps grief was upon him; Kell knew all too well how the loss of a parent could snatch at you for months, sometimes years afterwards. His own mother had died from breast cancer in the second year of his career at SIS, a loss with which he felt he had only recently come to terms. François had no book for company, no newspaper, and seemed content simply to eat his food, to sip his wine, and to allow his thoughts and gaze to wander. Once, sensing that Kell was staring at him, he caught his eye and nodded, in a way that reminded Kell so completely of Amelia that he was almost tempted to rise from his chair, to introduce himself as an old friend of the family and to share memories of his mother's life and career. Luc, meanwhile, had finished his meal and was gesturing impatiently at a waiter for the bill. Kell did the same, put the food and wine on a Uniacke debit card, and followed Luc out of the restaurant.

It was not easy to track him. One switchback, one curious turn of the head, and Luc would have seen him all too easily. The stairs were short and narrow, the corridors of the ship all but empty. Kell tried to maintain his distance, but had to be close enough to spot a sudden turn or a move to a lower deck. In due course it became apparent that Luc was heading for the sleeping cabins, descending four floors to the deck immediately below Kell's room. He was soon into the criss-cross corridors, all sense of direction lost. Halfway along one of the narrow, yellow-lit passages, Luc came to a halt outside his room. At a distance of perhaps fifty metres, Kell observed him punching a four-digit pin into the lock. The Frenchman went inside, securing a DO NOT DISTURB sign on the outer handle, then closed the door. Kell waited several seconds, walked past the cabin and made a note of the room number: 4571. He then went back to his own room and read again a Heaney poem that he had enjoyed in Tunis, in order to give François time to finish dinner. The name of the poem was 'Postscript', and on the inside back page of *The Spirit Level* Kell scribbled down a phrase – *the earthed lightning of a flock of swans* – that struck him as particularly beautiful. He left the book open on the bed, face down, then headed upstairs with no larger ambition than to sit among the passengers in the entertainment lounge, hoping that François would stop by for a drink. If he did so, he would make conversation; if he did not, he would try to speak to him in the morning, perhaps on deck as the ship closed in on Marseille. There was no future in tracking François from the restaurant, in trying to break the code to his room. All that he needed was the chance to talk to him and to make an assessment of his character. He wondered if Amelia had told him about her work for SIS. Though it was beyond the remit of the task Marquand had set, Kell wanted to be sure that François wasn't going to blow her cover, either by talking to random strangers on ships, or when he reached mainland France. If he was satisfied that her son was capable of keeping a secret, he would leave both of them in peace.

32

François Malot finished his dinner, paid the bill in cash and made his way to the entertainment lounge on the upper level of the ship. He wanted to meet a woman and yet he did not want to meet a woman. It was a strange split in his mood, a confusion of desires. He felt a need to be outside himself, to engage with a stranger, yet he did not want to become involved in the tiring and complicated rituals of seduction. In any event, what were the chances of meeting a girl on a ship like this? A ferry halfway across the Mediterranean was not the same as a nightclub in Paris or Reims. He would be better off waiting until Marseille and buying a girl, if he could get away with it. He couldn't have risked a prostitute in Tunisia, not with the laws as strict as they were, but a couple of times at the Ramada he had been so starved of sexual contact that he had booked himself in for a massage in the therapy centre, just to feel a woman's hands on his skin. It wasn't the same when Amelia did it, rubbing suntan lotion on to his back beside the pool. That wasn't what François had wanted. That sort of behaviour confused him.

He had been seated at the bar in the lounge for about ten minutes when he became aware of a man standing beside him, trying to attract the attention of the barmaid. François recognized him as the passenger he had seen in the restaurant reading a copy of *Time* magazine. They had nodded at one another and François had felt his gaze once or twice as he ate his pasta. He assumed, by the man's pale complexion and slightly unkempt appearance, that he was British. The collars of his shirt had lost their stiffness, he was sporting at least a day of stubble and his shoes were brown and scuffed. Before he knew it, he had caught the man's eye again and they were making conversation.

'Impossible to get a drink round here.'

François shrugged. Though he understood English, he was in no mood to stagger through a stilted conversation with a stranger. Besides, he loathed the British assumption that all foreigners could be spoken to in English. The stranger seemed to detect his reluctance and said: '*Vous êtes français?*'

'*Oui,*' François replied. '*Vous le parlez?*'

It transpired that the man's name was Stephen Uniacke and that he spoke excellent French. At first, François was slightly worried that he might be gay, but early in the conversation Stephen vouchsafed that he was 'happily married' and was making his way back from Tunisia after spending a week at a hotel in Hammamet.

'How did you find it down there?'

'Package tourism distilled to its essence,' Stephen replied. 'Kids on inflatable sausage rides, fish-and-chip shops, sunburned Anglo-Saxons everywhere you look. I might as well have stayed in Reading.'

The barmaid eventually came over. François had reached

the bottom of a gin and tonic. He wasn't surprised when Stephen offered to buy him another one and felt that he could not refuse.

'Thank you. That's very kind.'

'My pleasure. Are you travelling on your own?'

Perhaps he *was* gay. Perhaps Stephen Uniacke took holidays in Hammamet because he liked picking up boys on the beach.

'I am,' François replied, wondering whether he would be obliged to tell Amelia's story all over again. He was bored even of thinking about it.

'And you live in Marseille?'

'Paris.'

The deliberate brevity of his answer seemed to convince the Englishman that he should change the subject. He had settled at a stool alongside and now cast his eyes around the room, perhaps while thinking of something to say.

'This place looks like it was decorated by Grace Jones with a hangover.'

It was a very good description, very apt. François laughed and looked across the lounge. A man of about fifty was squeezed into a disc jockey booth with a pair of headphones clamped to his scalp. He was trying to entice a group of over-excited Marseillaise housewives on to the dance floor, but so far only a young boy of about ten seemed interested. One of the housewives had looked at François once or twice, but she was fat and lower class and he had paid her no attention. The lighting design was retro-purple, a disco ball spinning blurred stars around the lounge. The DJ started playing 'Let Me Entertain You' and Stephen mock-coughed into his drink.

'Oh Christ.'

'What is it?'

'On behalf of my countrymen, can I just apologize for Robbie Williams?'

François laughed again. It felt good to be engaged in a normal conversation with somebody who was bright and funny. Amelia was all those things, but their time together had been different, more like a series of interviews or business meetings in which they were working one another out. One evening in Tunis, when Amelia had gone to bed, François had felt like going out and had taken a taxi to a club in La Marsa. But the local nightlife had not been to his satisfaction. He had sat alone at the edge of a dance floor watching Tunis's smug, idle young rich trying to seduce Muslim girls who would surely never sleep with them. Sex in Islam was the ultimate sin for a woman before marriage. The boys wore big watches and preened their hair with vats of gel. One of the girls, wearing too much eyeliner, had flirted with François, and he had thought about approaching her for a dance. But you never knew who might be watching; he never knew what he could or could not risk. The Tunisian men all looked slightly overweight and sported sinister moustaches. One of them might have been her boyfriend or brother. He had felt sorry for the girl and wondered what would become of her.

'How did you find the food in Tunisia?' Stephen was asking.

He could tell that the Englishman was struggling for conversation, but this was a subject about which François was enthused. He replied that he had enjoyed an evening with his mother at an open-air fish restaurant in La Goulette, but that they had both been disappointed by the couscous at an undeservedly famous Tunisian restaurant in Sidi Bou-Said.

'I had a disastrous time with the food,' Stephen revealed. 'Ordered *"merguez"* in one place thinking it was fish, but ended up with a sausage. Tried to play it safe the next night by ordering *"tajine"*, but that turned out to be some kind of omelette. Hadn't been within a thousand miles of Morocco. You said your mother lives in Tunis?'

Now François was trapped. He would have to say something about Amelia or it would seem rude.

'It's a long story.'

Stephen looked at his drink, looked at the disco ball, looked at François. 'I've got all night.'

So he told him. The whole thing. The murder in Egypt. Trying to contact Amelia through the adoption agency. Their reunion in Paris. Then he described the week they had spent together in Gammarth. It was like telling a favourite anecdote; he embellished certain elements, skipped over the parts that no longer interested him, tried to depict Amelia in the best possible light. Stephen, as François had anticipated, was by turns appalled at the tragedy in Sharm-el-Sheikh and delighted that mother and son had been brought together so quickly in its aftermath. Yet François soon began to tire of his sympathy and questions. By eleven o'clock he had reached the bottom of a third drink, the one he had been obliged to buy for Stephen in return, and wanted desperately to be free of him so that he could return to his cabin. It was just a question of finding a way to escape. Thankfully, a woman on the opposite side of the bar had been staring at them for some time. At first, François could not tell with whom she was flirting. She was an attractive, if severe woman in her late thirties; he had seen her on the ship in the afternoon, reading a newspaper in the lobby. Usually, he would have assumed that any available woman on board would have preferred his company to that of the Englishman, yet increasingly she seemed to be directing her attention towards Stephen.

'Looks like someone likes you,' he said, flicking his eyes in her direction.

'Who?' It appeared that Stephen had not even noticed the woman.

'Across the bar. The lady with the dyed blonde hair. You want me to invite her over?'

Stephen looked across, startled. François noted a flush of embarrassment in his cheeks as he caught her eye. She looked away.

'I think she'll almost certainly be more interested in *you*,' Stephen replied.

It was a flattering observation but it was also the opportunity François had been waiting for. His glass was empty. There was a long day ahead. He had every excuse to leave.

'No,' he said, rising from his stool. 'I will leave you to her.' He shook the Englishman's hand. 'It was interesting to meet you. I enjoyed our conversation very much. Perhaps we will see one another again in the morning.'

'I hope so,' Stephen replied, and with that the two men parted.

33

It had been a long time since any woman had given Thomas Kell the eye and he was suspicious immediately. Why now? Why on the boat? With Malot out of the picture, the woman went full throttle with her disco seduction: a comely smile, an eyelash enticement, even a smothered, schoolgirl laugh when the middle-aged disc jockey in his sparkly booth started playing 'Billie Jean' at top volume. The approach was so gauche that Kell began to think she could only be a run-of-the-mill civilian: surely no intelligence officer – state-sponsored or private sector – would ever make such an obvious and direct approach?

As soon as François had left she was coming over, slipping off her stool, walking around the bar. Kell looked away in the direction of the portside windows, but there was soon a slice of dyed blonde hair in his peripheral vision, then the bottom of a skirt, a slash of thigh. She was standing beside him. Late thirties, slim, no wedding ring. Their eyes met and she produced a knowing smile.

'You don't remember me, do you?'

He didn't. The accent was scrambled, originally French, but with long periods of exposure to North America. He had no idea where or when they might have met. Did she know him as 'Thomas Kell', or as another man, one of the myriad pseudonyms he had adopted down the years? Was he a spy to this woman, or a consultant? Was he a lawyer or a civil engineer? Had he met her when he was 'attached to the Ministry of Defence' in London or was she a student from his long-ago days at Exeter University? He could not remember anything about her, and was usually expert at such things. Perhaps she was connected to him via Claire: Kell had always had a blind spot for his wife's colleagues, her cousins, her friends.

'I'm afraid I don't . . .'

'It's Madeleine. You remember? DC?'

Kell tried to keep his composure as his memory ran a showreel of highlights from numerous visits to the American capital: interminable meetings at the Pentagon; a rainy afternoon at the Lincoln Memorial; guided tours of the National Museum of American History; the firing range at Langley, where an over-excited training officer on the Farm had tried to instigate a shooting competition between SIS and the CIA. At no point could Kell recall a slim, bottle-blonde French woman with a scrambled accent playing any part in these proceedings.

'DC?' he repeated, buying time.

Had he met her at a dinner, in a bar, in a nightclub? Kell knew the names and faces of the eleven women he had been to bed with in the course of his life and this lady wasn't one of them.

'It's Michael, isn't it?' she said.

He knew then that she had made a mistake. He had

never used the legend 'Michael'. Stephen, yes. Tim, Patrick, Paul. Never Michael.

'I think you may have confused me with somebody else,' he said. 'I'm Stephen. Stephen Uniacke. From England. Good to meet you.' Kell extended a friendly hand, because he did not want to embarrass her. It was perfectly plausible that she had invented an entire phantom story simply to break the ice.

'How strange,' she replied. 'Are you sure?' Her neck flushed red and the thump of 'Rolling in the Deep', the energy in the bar, seemed to isolate her. 'I was certain it was you. I'm so sorry . . .'

She began to back away, heading towards her seat, as though she had asked a boy to dance and he had refused her. The barmaid seemed to be enjoying the atmosphere of embarrassment and was staring at the woman, probably storing up an anecdote for the later amusement of the crew. Kell was aware that any number of possibilities was still in play: 'Madeleine' could be part of a surveillance team watching François. If French Intelligence had found out about Malot's relationship with Amelia, they would almost certainly have sent people to track him. Kell's lengthy conversation with François at the bar would have been noted. Madeleine, on post in the entertainment lounge, would have known that she had a responsibility to find out more about him. Hence her ridiculous story about Washington: she had not had the time, nor perhaps the expertise, to think up a better cover.

'Please, let me buy you a drink,' he said, because it was now important for him to ascertain precisely who she was. He could not remember seeing Madeleine at either of the hotels in Tunisia, but that was of little consequence. Even a half-decent DGSE team would have remained under the radar.

'I don't want to bother you,' she said, with an expression of neediness on her face that precisely contradicted that statement. 'Are you sure?'

The barmaid was pretending to arrange glasses but was self-evidently still listening in. Kell was curt with her, ordering two red wines and hoping that they would be left in peace. He offered Madeleine the same stool that Malot had only recently vacated. If she was a spy, he could expect several things. Forensic initial questioning about his legend. *Who are you, Stephen? And what do you do for a living?* Then, perhaps, a period of small talk in which Kell would be able to relax and encouraged to drink more alcohol. Then further exchanges that would subtly test the integrity of his cover. For example: if he told Madeleine that Stephen Uniacke was a marketing consultant, he might expect later questions about the details of his job. If he mentioned Reading as his place of residence, an experienced spy would almost certainly say that she had visited the city and perhaps ask questions about local landmarks. If Kell hesitated on any answer, or was ignorant on a point of detail, it would untangle his legend.

Of course, this worked both ways. Kell had been presented with a similar opportunity to make an assessment of Madeleine. *What did you do in Tunis? Why are you coming back on the ferry?* If the alcohol on her breath was anything to go by, she might prove easy to break down. It was just a matter of asking the right questions.

And so it began. The game. The dance. Yet for the best part of forty-five minutes Madeleine Brive exposed Stephen

Uniacke only to the full glare of her blatant sexual desire. She was divorced. She had been on a 'boring' holiday in La Marsa with an 'alcoholic' friend whose husband had left her for a younger woman. She part-owned a clothing store in Tours that sold designer labels to rich Loire Valley housewives and was worried that her fourteen-year-old son was already smoking 'a lot of fucking cannabis'. Kell was struck by the extent to which she seemed almost entirely interested in her own personality and circumstances, rather than in asking questions of her own. He gave Madeleine ample opportunity to probe Stephen Uniacke for details about his profession, his marital status, his home, but she did not seize any of them. Instead, as a second glass of wine slipped down, quickly becoming a third, the clock drifted past midnight and she made it clear that she wanted to go to bed with him, even to the point of touching his knee, in the manner of a guest on a talk show trying to ingratiate herself with the host.

'I have a cabin,' she said, a little hiccupy giggle accompanying the pass. 'It's very *big*.'

'Me too,' Kell replied, trying to kill the offer at source. 'Mine is very small.'

It was a depressing, even emasculating feeling, but he had no desire to sleep with this woman, to thrash in the night on a bed only fractionally larger than a yoga mat. *No cat small enough to swing.* Madeleine Brive was beautiful, and lonely, and her perfume was the memory of other women. When she smiled at him, Kell felt the rush of her flattery, the relief of being taken for a normal man in normal circumstances engaged in the age-old cut-and-thrust of sex and desire. But his heart wasn't in it. His heart was still attached to Claire. He was a still-married man on a boat in the middle of the sea with a responsibility to honour his estranged wife.

'Look,' he said. 'I haven't been sleeping lately. Will you forgive me if I slip away?' It was an embarrassing excuse, but perhaps not out of character for Uniacke. 'It was so interesting to meet you. Maybe we could have lunch in Marseille?'

To his surprise, Madeleine appeared almost relieved.

'I would love that. I love Marseille. Will you be staying a night there?'

'I haven't decided.' This, at least, was the truth.

So they swapped numbers – on a napkin and pen proffered by the frowning barmaid – and made tentative plans to meet for breakfast in the canteen. Madeleine knew the finest restaurant in Marseille for *bouillabaisse* and promised to take him there.

She left the disco before he did. The barmaid watched her leave and glowered at Kell, as if she had seen it all before. *You think nobody knows what's going on? She's given you the number of her cabin. You'll head down there in five minutes when she's had time to get into her negligée.* Kell flicked her a look and she went back to arranging her glasses.

Five minutes later he was in the bowels of the ship, close to the spacious cabin of the tempting Madeleine Brive, but standing at the door of his own room, tapping in his four-digit code.

An unsettling feeling was upon him, as though he had been tricked or humiliated. Something was not right. Kell cast his mind back to what he had seen at dinner, to the strange encounter between Luc and Malot. Why had the two men ignored one another when François had walked into the restaurant? Because they did not want to eat

170

together – or because they did not want to be seen in one another's company? François himself had turned out to be an unusually remote and delicate man, sensitive and vain, yet possessed of a quick intelligence and an underlying melancholy that Kell put down to grief. Had he been approached by Luc that afternoon? Was that what Kell had seen – an offer of recruitment from the DGSE? Six figures to tell us everything you know about Amelia Levene? Stranger things had happened. Of course, it was probable that there was zero threat on the ship. Most likely Madeleine was exactly who she said she was: the owner of a clothes shop in Tours looking for a quick fuck on the high seas. And Luc? Who was to say that he and François had not simply shared a run-of-the-mill conversation on the sun deck and then gone their separate ways? Yet as Kell opened the door of his cabin, something felt out of place, something as yet unknown to him. Something was wrong, yet he could not identify precisely what it was.

He went into the tiny bathroom, ducking his head through the door. He brushed his teeth, he took off his shirt. He then retrieved the camera from his suitcase, took out the memory card from his pocket and replaced it in its slot. He picked up the bottle of Macallan and poured himself a tooth mug of whisky to ease him into sleep.

The Spirit Level was still open on the bed, face down, stretching the spine. Kell picked it up, planning to read 'Postscript' again in order to erase his questions, to change his mood and to shut out the operation for a few well-earned hours.

The earthed lightning of a flock of swans.

The book was on the wrong page. 'Postscript' was the final poem in the collection, but he was looking at 'At the Wellhead', four pages earlier. Somebody had picked up the book and put it back without due care. Somebody had been through the contents of his room.

34

If Kell was in any doubt that Madeleine Brive had been intent only on distracting Stephen Uniacke while a third party searched his room, it was dispelled by what happened next. As soon as he lifted the lid on the Marquand laptop, he saw that the encryption page installed by SIS had booted up: the small blue box in the centre of the screen was awaiting his sequence of passwords. A chambermaid, a cleaner, would not have done such a thing. Whoever had been into his room had attempted to boot the computer, only to encounter the password protection. Unable to shut it down, they had closed the lid and put the laptop back on the floor.

Kell lay on the narrow bed and considered his options. Was Uniacke blown? Not necessarily. If a DGSE team had control of the ship, they would know the names and cabin numbers of every passenger on board, including 'Stephen Uniacke'. Madeleine would have been instructed to distract him with her little dance of the honeytrap so that one of her colleagues – Luc, perhaps – could go through his belongings. Accessing Kell's cabin would have been as easy as breaking a pane of glass: a quick bribe of the concierge; a computer attack on the SNCM reservations system – either would have yielded the pin. And what would Luc have discovered? At worst, a camera with no memory card and a laptop with password protection. Hardly the stuff of conspiracy theories. The rest of his belongings were as mundane as they were blameless: clothes; toiletries; books.

Kell was suddenly aware – too late, perhaps – of a threat from visual surveillance. A basic, low-light camera might have been fitted in his cabin. He was still lying on the narrow bed, arms propped behind his head, and tried quickly to recall how he had behaved since entering the room. He had been into the bathroom and brushed his teeth. He had poured himself a whisky, opened and then closed the laptop. He had looked – too long and too hard, perhaps – at the book of poems. How would his behaviour have seemed to Luc, watching on a blurred surveillance screen in Cabin 4571? Suspicious? Kell doubted it. Any agitation he might have shown could more plausibly have been interpreted as regret for not following Madeleine to her cabin. Nevertheless, he set about going to bed, knowing, of course, that if there was a camera concealed in a light fitting, or hidden behind the mirror, that he could not go looking for it. Instead, he must behave naturally. Rising from the bed, as though he had been briefly distracted by an unsettling thought, Kell keyed the ten-digit password into the laptop and typed a random sequence of letters into the computer for several minutes, to give the appearance of writing up a report or filling in the pages of a journal. Next, he turned to *The Spirit Level*, studying a couple of poems intently, as though his earlier behaviour had been some indication of scholarly angst. He then stripped to his underpants, took a T-shirt from his suitcase, and climbed into bed.

It was a relief to turn out the light and to lie in the darkness unseen, a taste of whisky and toothpaste in his mouth. Kell's beating heart kept time to the thrumming of the engine and he felt enclosed by the womb of the ship. As soon as the ferry came within signal range of the European coast, Kell knew that he would be obliged to call London with an update. He had three options. He could tell Jimmy Marquand that Amelia Levene, the Chief-designate of the Secret Intelligence Service, had an illegitimate son. This was the truth of the situation and would fulfil Kell's formal obligation to SIS. He could also reveal his suspicion that French Intelligence had discovered Malot's identity, followed him to Tunisia and perhaps even attempted to recruit him en route to Marseille. Of course, these revelations would be catastrophic for Amelia and lead to her immediate dismissal from the Service. As a consequence, the revival of his own career would be stillborn; with Truscott in charge, Kell would remain *persona non grata*.

There was a second option. Kell could tell Marquand that François Malot was a fraud, that he was masquerading as Amelia's son and had returned to France by ship in the company of at least two French Intelligence officers. But was there any evidence for this? Kell had spent an hour talking to Malot in the bar and at no point felt that he was speaking to an impostor. Amelia's son bore a striking physical resemblance to his mother and his legend was watertight: a thorough search of his hotel room in Gammarth had failed to turn up anything suspicious. The purpose of the DGSE mounting such an operation – so fraught with risk, so difficult to carry off – was also not clear, but neither was it beyond the realms of possibility. Furthermore, the implications it entailed – that Malot's adoptive parents had been murdered and their funeral faked – were too wretched to consider. For this reason, Kell set them to the back of his mind and concluded that he had no proof of such a conspiracy.

He settled, with no great fanfare or embattled conscience, on a third course of action. Let London continue to think that Amelia Levene is having an affair. Let Truscott and Haynes assume that she merely slipped her moorings for a few days in order to enjoy a dirty weekend with a French lothario in Gammarth. It was what they wanted to believe, after all; it was what they *deserved* to believe. To lie to Marquand in this way was not something Kell would have considered twelve months earlier, but his loyalty to the newly minted high priests of SIS was close to non-existent. 'If I had to choose between betraying my country and betraying my friend,' he thought, remembering the words of E.M. Forster, 'I hope I should have the guts to betray my country.'

For the first time in his life, that notion made sense to him.

35

The safe house was located on the summit of a hill overlooking the southern expanse of the Ariège, about three
kilometres east of the village of Salles-sur-l'Hers in
Languedoc-Roussillon. It was approached from the south
by a single-track road leading off the D625. The track passed
the house in a tight loop and turned sharply downhill past
a ruined windmill before rejoining the main road to
Castelnaudary about two kilometres to the south-east.

There were usually only two guards at the house: Akim
and Slimane. That was more than enough to keep an eye on
HOLST. Each man had his own bedroom on the first floor
with a shelf of pirated DVDs and a laptop computer. In the
downstairs living room there was a large television equipped
with a Nintendo Wii, and the two men spent as many as four
or five hours every day playing rounds of golf in St Andrews,
games of tennis at Roland Garros or fighting al-Qaeda insur-
gents in the backstreets and caves of a cartoon Afghanistan.
They were forbidden to bring women to the house and lived
off a steady diet of roast chicken, couscous and frozen pizzas.

HOLST himself was locked in a small room between the entrance hall and a large ground-floor bedroom at the southern end of the house. There were two doors leading into his makeshift cell. The main door, linked to the entrance hall, was secured by a padlock. The second, which connected the cell to the bedroom at the back, was held in place by two metal bars mounted on hooks. The boss had built a sight-glass into both doors to monitor HOLST's movements and behaviour day and night. HOLST received three meals per day and was allowed to exercise for twenty minutes every afternoon on a small patch of grass behind the house. The exercise area was bordered on three sides by a twelve-foot hedge so that HOLST could not be seen by passers-by. He had never refused food and made no complaint about the conditions in which he was kept. If he needed to go to the bathroom, there was a bucket in his cell which Akim and Slimane emptied at meal times. From time to time, Slimane would grow bored and agitated and do things that Akim didn't think he should do. On one occasion, for example, Slimane took his knife and put a gag in HOLST's mouth, then heated the blade on the gas stove and got a kick out of watching HOLST wince and moan as he drew circles round his eyes. They never hurt him, though. They never touched a hair on his head. The worst thing, maybe, was when Slimane got drunk and told HOLST about a girl he had raped. That was a really bad story and Akim had gone in and got him to cool down. But generally Akim believed that the prisoner was being treated with dignity and respect.

After a week, on the instructions of the boss, HOLST had been allowed a television and some DVDs in his room, which he watched for up to sixteen hours every day. As a further gesture of goodwill, and against all protocol, Akim had let HOLST sit with him in the living room one evening – albeit while handcuffed to a chair – to watch a football match between Marseille and a team from England. He had given him a beer and explained that it would not be long before he was allowed to go back to Paris.

Akim's only moment of real concern arose in the middle of the second week when a neighbour happened to pass by the house and enquire if the owners would be returning in the autumn. The sight of a shaven-headed *Arabe* in the rural Languedoc had evidently surprised the man, who had quite literally taken a step backwards when Akim had opened the door. Only a few metres away, Slimane had stuffed a dish-cloth into HOLST's mouth and was leaning a gun into his groin to prevent him from shouting for help. Akim had said that the owner was a friend from Paris who would be arriving within the next few days. Thankfully, the boss himself did indeed turn up the following afternoon and any concerned neighbours with binoculars trained on the house would have been gladdened by the sight of a bearded white man mowing the grass in his shorts and later diving into the outdoor pool.

On a clear day, it was possible to see the distant foothills of the Pyrenees across the flat expanse of the Ariège, but on the morning of Akim's weekly trip to Castelnaudary, a storm had blown in from the Basque country and drenched the property in an inch of warm summer rain. Akim went first to the hypermarket at Villefranche-de-Lauragais to buy basic provisions, as well as Bandol rosé for Valerie and a bottle of Ricard for the boss. In a pharmacy in Castelnaudary, he fetched the asthma medication for HOLST and bought himself some deodorant and aspirin, both of which were running low in the house. Slimane had put in a request for several pornographic magazines, which Akim purchased in a *tabac* from an elderly woman who did nothing to disguise the fact that she considered the presence of an *Arabe* in her shop an affront to the dignity of the Republic.

'Scum,' she muttered under her breath as Akim left the shop and it was all that he could do to control his rage and to keep on walking. The last thing the boss wanted was any trouble.

He returned to the house to find HOLST watching *Diva* on DVD. Slimane was sitting in the kitchen smoking a cigarette in the company of two men whom Akim had never seen before.

'Boss wants us for a job,' he said. 'These guys are going to watch our friend.'

The two men, both white and in their early twenties, introduced themselves as 'Jacques' and 'Patric', names that Akim took for pseudonyms. Slimane had his laptop open on the kitchen table and swivelled it round so that Akim could see what he was looking at. There was a blurred surveillance photograph on the screen, taken in what looked like a disco or late-night bar.

'They're worried about some guy on the ferry,' he said. 'Luc's girl wants us to follow him. Get your stuff. We're going to Marseille.'

36

Kell was woken at seven o'clock by the sound of children running in the corridor outside his cabin. He had a shower in the tiny bathroom, packed his suitcase and took the camera up on deck. It was a grey morning, the French coast not yet visible through banks of cloud, but when he switched on the London mobile he discovered that he could get a signal. Kell immediately rang Marquand at home and found him awake and good-humoured, eating a bowl of cereal in the kitchen.

'Bran Flakes, Tom. Fibre,' he said. 'Have to look after myself. I'm not getting any younger.'

'No, you're not,' Kell replied, and told him what needed to be done.

'There might be some calls to Uniacke's office in Reading. The consultancy firm. Possible that his finances might be checked as well. Can you make sure everything is kosher, bank balances, tax returns, that there's somebody who knows the drill? Uniacke stayed in a hotel in Hammamet, so that will need to flash up, also ATM withdrawals and restaurant receipts. Can you fix it?'

Marquand was putting the details into a computer. Kell could hear the soft taps as his fingers hit the keyboard.

'Who the hell's doing the checking? Amelia?'

Kell was ready with the lie. 'Nothing to do with her. Different situation altogether. I spotted an old contact in Tunis. Decided to follow him to Marseille. I'm on the overnight ferry.'

'You're *what*? What does this have to do with our agreement?'

'Everything and nothing.' A sleepy-eyed African emerged from the interior of the ship, clearing her head in the brisk wind. 'It's a long story. Came at me out of thin air. I'll brief you when I get back. Just make sure the Uniacke backstops are in place. If somebody rings the Reading office and asks to speak to Stephen, I'm on holiday until Friday.'

Marquand repeated the word 'Friday' and then withdrew any suggestion of financial or technical support. 'Look, if you've abandoned Amelia to her fate, Tom, the Office isn't going to pay you by the hour to pursue an entirely new operation. They pushed you out, remember? To all intents and purposes, you were *fired*, for Christ's sake.'

'Who said anything about abandoning Amelia?' Kell was looking out at the eternal greys of the sliding sea, water fizzing against the sides of the ship. How typical of Marquand to think only of the money, to cover his back. A bureaucrat through and through. 'She kissed François goodbye at the airport yesterday morning. Squeezed his bum and bought a bottle of Hermès Calèche to cheer herself up. Should be back in Nice by now. Have the Knights do a drive-by of the Gillespie.' There was a grumble on the line, which Kell took as a sign that Marquand was backing down. 'I don't need paying,' he added. 'My work is done.

If something comes of this, maybe you can throw me a bone later on.'

'Who are you following, Tom?'

'Not until I get home,' Kell replied. 'Like I said. Just an old contact.' And he hung up.

Four hours later, no sign of Madeleine at breakfast, no glimpse of Luc or Malot, Kell was standing with his camera on the sun deck beneath the unceasing roar of the ship's funnel, the ferry pulling towards Marseille. The southern coast of France was now lit by crisp midday sunlight, boats easing east and west below the squat cream cliffs of the Calanques. Kell had deleted the pictures of Malot's room at the Ramada as well as the surveillance photographs of Amelia lying beside the pool. He now replaced them with a sequence of shots appropriate to the interests and sensibility of a lone, middle-aged marketing consultant on a roll-on, roll-off ferry: pictures of orange lifeboats; studies of laundry bags piled high behind paint-chipped portholes; weathered coils of rope.

Once the ship had docked in Marseille he queued with the other foot passengers, perhaps forty of them crowded into a narrow, increasingly stuffy stairwell leading down to the car decks. There was a long delay as the ship was cleared; only when every vehicle had funnelled out on to the mainland were the foot passengers permitted to leave. Kell fell in behind an Irish couple arguing vociferously about being late for a flight to Dublin. They shuffled en masse down a carpeted corridor towards a prefabricated building at the southern edge of the dock, where customs officials were inspecting random bags on formica tables. If the DGSE remained suspicious of him, Kell knew that he would now most probably be stopped and his luggage searched. That was page one of the operational handbook. He was confident that they would find nothing to link him to Malot. The photos were gone and he had destroyed the Uniacke receipts from the Valencia Carthage. As long as Marquand had generated a paper trail for Uniacke in Hammamet, he would be fine.

In the event, Kell was allowed to pass through the customs area without incident and found himself in a slow-moving queue for Immigration. There were no split channels for EU citizens and several of the foot passengers ahead of him were carrying Tunisian and Algerian passports. Kell, aware that Luc or Madeleine could be watching from behind a screen of one-way glass at the side of the Immigration area, was surprised by the extent of his own anxiety. To occupy himself, and to convey an impression of calm, he read a couple of pages of *The Scramble for Africa*, then checked the messages on his London phone.

Claire had called. A voicemail had been left in the early hours of the English morning. Kell could hear, by the rushed and surly tone of her voice, that she had been drinking. Her anger at his failure to appear in Finchley had now crystallized into a typical rant.

Tom, it's me. Look, I don't see why we're bothering any more. Do you? I think what we really need is to face this thing and to make a formal move towards divorce. It's obviously what you want . . .

There was a brief pause in the message, then silence. Kell pressed '9' to save what he had heard, then moved to a second message. It was Claire again, picking up where she had left off.

184

For some reason we were cut off. What I was trying to say, what I was about to say, is that it's what I want. A clean break, Tom.

She had probably been into her second bottle of red, a couple of gins, too, if history was anything to go by. There was another pause in the message, a gathering of thoughts. Kell knew what was coming. Claire had a standard game plan whenever she sensed that her husband was drawing away from her.

Look, Richard has invited me to go to California. He has a series of meetings in Napa and San Francisco and it only seems fair to tell you that I've booked my flight and intend to go. Or rather, Richard has booked my flight. He's paid for the ticket. I'll probably be gone by the time you get back, wherever you are, whatever's going on. It's your business, so . . .

Another cut-off. There was no further message. Kell, winded by shock and jealousy, put the phone in his back pocket as he was ushered forward by a moustachioed passport inspector with blond highlights in his hair. A quick glance at the passport and Stephen Uniacke was waved through. A consultant. A married father of two. Not a soon-to-be-divorced husband with a wife jetting off to California in the arms of another man. Not a childless spy on the trail of a friend's secret son. Not Thomas Kell.

He was soon outside, into the heat and thrash of Marseille. At the perimeter of a congested traffic area – a temporary roundabout taking vehicles in and out of the docks – Kell looked around, knowing that invisible eyes, in cars, in windows, would be watching Stephen Uniacke. 'There is no such thing as paranoia,' an SIS elder had once told him, many years earlier, 'there are only facts.' It had sounded like a clever thing to say, but in practice it was meaningless. In counter-surveillance, there were no facts; there was only experience and intuition. Kell merely had to put himself in the shoes of the DGSE to know that they would tail him for his first few hours in Marseille. If his cabin had merited a break-in, his movements on the mainland would be more than worthy of attention.

Marseille. He took in the high blue sky, the distant cathedral of Notre-Dame de la Garde, the blaze of sunlight on slate and terracotta roofs. Then, directly in his line of sight as he lowered his gaze, François Malot. The Frenchman was standing with insouciant cool on the far side of the roundabout, climbing into a taxi driven by a man in his fifties who was almost certainly of West African origin. A seagull swooped low over the roof as Malot ducked into the back seat. Kell had a clear sight of the number plate and committed it to memory. There was a phone number on the side of the taxi and he tapped it into his mobile, just as a vacant cab swung into view. He raised his free hand to hail it, but two elderly foot passengers stepped in front of him and attempted simultaneously to flag it down.

'My cab,' he shouted out, in French, and to his surprise they turned and conceded the point. The vehicle was a Renault Espace, more than large enough to accommodate three passengers, and Kell offered to share the ride. It was a decision taken solely for the benefit of the DGSE; he wanted Uniacke to look like a nice, considerate *rosbif* heading into town, not a suspicious British spy with instructions to follow François Malot wherever he went.

The couple turned out to be Americans – Harry and Penny Curtis – both retired former air traffic control officers out of St Louis who had glimpsed the chaos in the skies and vowed never again to travel anywhere by aeroplane.

'We spent a coupla weeks down in Tunisia, came back over with SNCM,' said the husband, who had the quick eyes and broad, fattened build of a former soldier. 'Visited the *Star Wars* locations, checked out the Roman ruins. You staying a while in Marseille, Steve?'

Kell concocted a story for the benefit of the driver, who might later be questioned by the DGSE. He had long since lost sight of Malot's vehicle.

'I think I'm going to stay in town for a night. Need to find a hotel. I met someone on the boat who promised to show me around and take me for *bouillabaisse*. I don't have to be home for a couple of days, so I'm hoping we'll spend some time together.'

'Sounds good,' said Harry. 'You mean some kind of a lady friend?'

'I mean a lady friend,' Kell replied, and flourished a knowing smile.

He was thinking, of course, of Madeleine, whose napkin-scrawled number was still nestled at the bottom of his suitcase. With Malot evaporated into the Marseille traffic, she was now his best lead. He wondered if she would call. If Madeleine hadn't made contact by the evening, he would try the number on the napkin. Most probably there would be no answer, in which case he would head out to the airport and try to run Malot to ground in Paris.

'We got a train leaving Marseille at five,' said Harry, scratching what looked like an infected mosquito bite on his forearm. 'TGV up to Gare Lyon.'

'Lee-on,' said Penny, because her husband had rhymed 'Lyon' with 'lion'. Kell smiled and she returned his grin with a wink. 'Then a whole week in Paris, can you believe it? The Louvre. Musée d'Orsay. All those shops . . .'

'. . . all that food,' Harry added, and Kell had a sudden, sentimental desire to join them on the five o'clock, to hear their stories of St Louis, to share in their joy at being in Paris.

'I hope you both have a wonderful time,' he said.

37

It did not take long for Amelia Levene to clean up the loose ends of her truncated visit to France. There was a chambermaid at the Hotel Gillespie who had agreed, for the sum of two thousand euros, to say nothing about Madame Levene's prolonged absence from her room. Amelia had paid her half in advance on the morning of her flight to Tunis and now settled the debt as she packed her belongings, the chambermaid having made a special visit to her place of work in mid-afternoon from her home in the suburbs of Nice.

Next, Amelia put a call through to the Austrian divorcee who had organized the painting classes. Brigitta Wettig accepted Amelia's effusive apologies for abandoning the course after less than two days, but assumed that she had been 'sick or something' and seemed concerned only that Mrs Levene would now demand a refund.

'Of course not, Brigitta. And one day I hope to be able to return. You really do have the most wonderful set-up here.'

Three hours after landing in Nice, Amelia was on her

way back to the airport, having retrieved her personal effects from the boot of the hire car in Rue Lamartine. By eight o'clock she was in London, en route by cab to Giles's house in Chelsea. They had arranged to eat supper together. Amelia had told her husband that she had something 'important' that she wished to discuss with him.

They picked a favourite Thai restaurant at the western end of King's Road. Giles ordered a green curry, Amelia a chicken and basil stir-fry. It was late on a Saturday evening and there were perhaps a dozen other customers in the restaurant, none within earshot and most on the point of asking for the bill.

'So you had something you wanted to say,' Giles began, hoping to get the more awkward part of the evening out of the way so that he could enjoy his curry in relative peace. Whenever Amelia called a summit meeting of this kind, it was usually to confess that she had 'slipped up again' with Paul Wallinger, her long-term lover. Giles was long past caring and, frankly, would have preferred not to know. It irritated him that his wife always chose one of their favourite restaurants in which to vouchsafe her indiscretions, thereby preventing him from giving expression to his rage with a full-scale row.

'I'm afraid I haven't been entirely honest with you about something in my childhood.'

That was a new line. Usually it was: 'I'm afraid I've behaved rather unkindly,' or: 'I'm afraid you're not going to be pleased.' This time, however, Amelia had opted for the enigma of her past.

'Your childhood?'

She dabbed her face with a napkin, swallowed a prawn cracker.

190

'Not my childhood, exactly. My teenage years. My early twenties.'

'You mean Oxford?'

'I mean Tunisia.'

And so it came out. The story of her affair with Jean-Marc Daumal; the birth of their child; the boy's adoption by Philippe and Jeannine Malot. Giles's curry arrived but he found that he could not eat it, so great was his sense of shock and near-revulsion. The first ten years of his marriage to Amelia had been a prolonged nightmare of fertility tests, of third trimester miscarriages, of interviews with adoption agencies which had offered the shattering verdict that Giles and Amelia Levene, despite their impeccable professional and personal credentials, were considered too old to take on the responsibility of caring for a young child. And now here was Amelia calmly informing him that, at the age of twenty, she had given birth to a healthy baby who had surfaced in Paris more than thirty years later to steal her heart and to draw her away from him still further. Giles wanted, for the first time in his life, physically to assault a woman, to send the whole edifice of their sham and sexless marriage crashing to the ground.

But Giles Levene was not the demonstrative type. He lacked physical courage and he hated making a scene. If he had been a more self-analytical man, he might have acknowledged that he had married Amelia because she was emotionally stronger than he was, intellectually at least his equal, and his social passport to the high tables that would otherwise have been denied him. Taking a sip of his white wine and a first mouthful of curry, he found himself saying: 'I'm glad you've told me this' and thought how much his

191

own conciliating voice sounded like his father's. 'How long have you known?'

'About a month,' Amelia replied, and took his hand across the tablecloth. 'As you can imagine, I don't know how I'm going to work things out with the Office.'

This astonished him. 'They don't *know*?'

Amelia chose her words carefully, as though picking out the chillies in a stir-fry. 'I decided never to tell them. I didn't want it on my record. I thought it would affect any chances I had of making a success of my career.'

Giles nodded. 'Obviously nothing turned up during the vetting process.'

'Obviously.' Amelia felt the need to expand. 'The adoption was arranged through a Catholic organization in Tunis. They had links back to France, but my name was never recorded in the paperwork.'

'Then how did François find you?'

More out of habit than calculation, Amelia decided to protect Joan Guttmann's identity.

'Through a friend in Tunis who helped me during that period.'

Giles leaped to a conclusion. 'The boy's father? This Jean-Marc?'

Amelia shook her head. 'No. I haven't seen him for years. In fact, I'm not sure he even knows that François exists.'

As the meal progressed, Giles's temper subsided and Amelia told him of her plans eventually to bring her son to London. They had talked about it at the hotel in Tunisia. With his parents murdered, François felt that he no longer had much of a life in Paris and would welcome a change of scene.

'What about his friends?' Giles asked. 'Is there a wife, a girlfriend? A job?'

Amelia paused as she recollected all that François had told her.

'He's never had a serious relationship. You might call him a bit of a loner. A rather melancholy soul, if I'm honest. Prone to the odd mood swing. Not unlike his father, in fact.'

Giles wasn't interested in pursuing this line of enquiry and asked how Amelia was going to clear things with SIS.

'I think the best thing is to present him as a *fait accompli*. It's hardly a sackable offence to have given birth to a child.'

Giles saw how proud she was to have uttered these words and felt the revulsion again, the returning sense of his own miserable isolation.

'I see. But they'll want to know that he's the real thing.'

It was the closest he could come to wounding her. Amelia reacted as though he had spat in her food.

'What does that mean?'

'Well, surely they'll want to vet him? You're about to become the Chief of the Secret Intelligence Service, Amelia. They can't have a cuckoo in the nest.'

She pushed her plate away from her, a sound of crockery meeting glass.

'He's *mine*,' she said, hissing the words as her napkin hit the table. 'They can test him all they fucking want.'

38

The cab driver dropped Kell at a three-star hotel en route to the Gare Saint-Charles. He bid the Americans goodbye, handed a twenty-euro note to Harry, waved away Penny's objections that he was paying 'way too much', then stood on the pavement with his bags while taking a non-existent call on his mobile. Turning to face the oncoming traffic, Kell looked carefully for vehicles pulling over, of possible watchers on foot or bike, for furtive movements of any kind, all the time reciting some favourite lines from Yeats into the receiver to give the impression of an ongoing conversation. When he was satisfied that there was no apparent threat, he walked into the hotel, booked himself a bed for the night, rode the lift to the third floor and unpacked his bags in a room that smelled of detergent and stale cigarettes.

Claire's message still scratched at him like the bite on Harry's arm, a calculated insult to his pride, to his fidelity. Richard Quinn, the hedge fund bachelor with two ex-wives and three sons at St Paul's, was the primary weapon in Claire's extra-marital armoury, a background threat to whom she would turn whenever Kell looked like leaving her on a permanent basis. Richard knew of Kell's background in MI6 and plainly viewed it as an affront to his ego, as though Her Majesty had made a grave error of judgement in failing to recruit him into the Secret Service some thirty years earlier. Now fifty-five and rich beyond imagination, he regularly tried to lure the newly single Claire to five-star hotels in Provence and Bordeaux, whenever his so-called 'professional interest in wine' took him overseas. In an unguarded moment, returning from one such trip to Alsace, Claire had begged Kell for forgiveness and confessed that she found Quinn 'boring'.

'Then why the hell do you fuck him?' Kell had shouted, to which his estranged wife, so shattered by unhappiness, had replied: 'Because he is there for me. Because he has a *family*.' Kell could summon no adequate response. The logic of her grievances was so chopped, her despair so wretched and apparently incurable, that he had simply run out of ways to console her. Quinn could no more give her a child than any of the other men she had turned to in her desperate promiscuity; the infertility was hers, not his. Kell loved her more deeply than perhaps he had ever said, but had reached the conclusion that their only viable future lay apart. The thought of such a failure, the thought of divorcing Claire, was enervating.

His mobile was ringing. Only a handful of people had the number.

'Stephen?'

The accent was unmistakable.

'Madeleine. How nice to hear your voice.'

'Of course!' It sounded as though she was calling from a residential street. Kell heard the wasp buzz of a passing moped, the larger echo of the city. 'So you would like to meet for dinner, as we talked about? Are you free? I can take you to have *la bouillabaisse*.'

'Sounds great. I'd love to. I've just checked into a hotel . . .'

'. . . Oh, which one? Where are you?'

Kell told her, because he had no choice in the matter. Luc and his pals would now have a fix on his position and would surely lose no opportunity in taking another crack at Kell's laptop. Though he was certain that the computer could not incriminate him, he would have to carry it with him and remove anything sensitive from his room whenever he left the building.

'I've got no idea what street it's on,' he said. 'A cab dropped me at the edge of the Arab quarter, about half a mile from the station . . .'

'Never mind,' Madeleine interrupted. 'I can find it. I will come to pick you up at seven o'clock and we can walk to Chez Michel. It's on the other side of the port. Not far.'

'Seven o'clock,' Kell confirmed.

That gave him five hours. After eating lunch in a café two blocks from the hotel, Kell returned to his room and used the telephone beside his bed to ring the backstop number for Uniacke's family, a line that existed solely as an answering service for the benefit of snooping spooks. Kell heard the pre-recorded voice of a female colleague at SIS masquerading as Uniacke's wife.

Hello. You've reached Stephen and Caroline Uniacke. We're not at home at the moment, but if you'd like to leave a message for us, or for Bella and Dan, please speak after the beep.

Kell did what he had to do.

Hi, sweetheart, it's me. Are you there? Pick up if you are. [An appropriate pause] OK. I just got off the boat and wanted to see how you are. I'm going to stay in Marseille tonight, then perhaps stop off in Paris on the way home. There's a client I want to see, but he doesn't know whether he's going to be in town. I might get a flight back to London tomorrow and be home for supper or I might be in Paris for a couple of days. Anyway, I'll let you know. Beautiful weather here, going for bouilla-baisse tonight. Call my mobile if you get the chance or try the hotel. Cheaper that way. It's the Montand. I'm in room 316.

He left the number of the hotel, blew a kiss to his phantom wife, told her that he loved her and that he missed 'Bella and Dan', then hung up and changed into a fresh shirt.

Five minutes later, carrying his laptop and mobile phones in a shoulder bag, Kell was en route to La Cité Radieuse, a Marseille landmark for architecture buffs, and the perfect place for the auto-didact in him to kill a couple of hours before meeting Madeleine at seven. The twenty-something cab driver he flagged down on Rue de la Republique was new in town and had never heard of Le Corbusier, so Kell put him in the picture.

'Every tower block in the world, every thirty-storey high-rise built to house the urban working class in the last sixty years, looks like it does because of the Cité Radieuse.'

'It's true?' The driver was looking at Kell in his rear-view mirror, eyes narrowed against the sun. It was hard to tell if he was interested or just being polite.

'It's true. From Sheffield to Sao Paulo, if you grew up on the tenth floor of a concrete housing scheme, Le Corbusier put you there.'

'I grew up outside Lyon,' said the driver. 'My father owns a shop,' which was where the more enlightened section of their conversation ended. Thereafter he was intent only on talking about football, pointing out the Stade Velodrome on Boulevard Michelet, home to Olympique de Marseille, and complaining that Karim Benzema, once the darling of Lyon's supporters, had 'whored himself to Real Madrid'. Moments later the driver had dropped Kell at the entrance to the Cité Radieuse.

'This is it?' he said, peering up at the building with evident suspicion. 'Looks like every other fucking tower in Marseille.'

'Exactly,' Kell replied. Two hundred metres back along the road, two men on mopeds had pulled over on Boulevard Michelet. Kell was certain that he had seen one of the drivers, wearing a blue crash helmet, tailing the cab on Place Castellane. The two mopeds disappeared out of sight down a side street and Kell paid the driver.

'Good to talk to you,' he said.

The Cité Radieuse was situated in a small, poorly maintained municipal garden, set back from Boulevard Michelet behind a screen of trees. Kell found the entrance and was soon in the third-floor restaurant eating a sandwich and drinking a cup of coffee. This section of the building operated both as an upmarket boutique hotel and as an area in which visitors to the complex could look at examples of Le Corbusier's work. The rest of Cité Radieuse was still a fully functioning apartment building, complete with a rooftop kindergarten and a row of shops. Kell, breaking a minor law of trespass, took an interior staircase to one of the upper storeys so that he could snoop around without feeling like a tourist.

This was a mistake. Emerging into a long, black-red corridor, dark as a throat, he found himself entirely alone, with little sound except the occasional murmur of a television or radio in one of the apartments. Halfway down the corridor, which was blocked off at the far end, Kell heard a noise behind him and turned to see two young Arab men in tracksuits moving towards him. He thought immediately of the moped drivers. One of them, brandishing a metal pole said, in English: 'Hello, mister, can we help you?' but Kell was under no illusion that they were residents. La Cité Radieuse was too affluent for a couple of migrant kids in tracksuits to be renting an apartment.

'I don't think so,' he said, replying in French but already setting his shoulder bag on the ground so that he could move and react more freely. 'I'm just looking around. Big fan of Corbusier.'

'What have you got with you?' said the older of the two men, nodding at Kell's bag. Kell saw the glint of a knife in his left hand, the blade briefly catching the dull yellow glow of a light in the doorway of an apartment.

'Why?' he replied. 'What's on your mind?'

Nothing more was said. They came for him. Kell picked up the bag and threw it very quickly across the floor, hard enough that the man with the knife was briefly knocked off balance. Rather than turn to retaliate, however, the man moved several paces back down the corridor and picked up the bag, leaving his friend to fight alone. The second Arab was older, but shorter and more agile than the first. Kell felt the numb slowness of his middle-aged bones as he wheeled to confront him. There was noise now, Kell shouting loudly in French to alert the residents, projecting strength, watching the metal bar and looking constantly for the flash of a second blade. He was effectively trapped at the end of the corridor, with nowhere to turn, no space in which to run. In front of him, about ten metres down the corridor, silhouetted by a distant whitewashed wall reflecting outdoor light, the younger man shouted out: 'OK, I've got it,' just as his accomplice moved in to strike. Rather than use it as a weapon, he hurled the bar, but Kell had time to duck as it whistled past him, clanging into a door at the back of the corridor. The Arab came at him now, throwing a punch that Kell took in the ribs. He was able to catch his attacker in his momentum, to grab at him. They were thrown to the ground and Kell, drawing on some vague and distant memory of a Fort Monckton fight class, pressed a finger into the man's left eye and drove it deep into the socket.

'Let's go!' his accomplice shouted. Kell saw the younger man at the edge of his vision, as he drove his hand up into his attacker's throat, pushing his neck backwards. At the same time, a knee thumped into his groin, slowly and almost without force, but pain was soon shunting into Kell's gut and spine so that he groaned and swore, again trying to gain a hold on the Arab's neck. His assailant somehow freed himself, days-old sweat like a taste in Kell's mouth, and launched a kick directly into his face. Kell brought his arms up around his head, trying to get to his feet, but the younger man had joined them and was standing above him, swearing triumphantly in high-pitched Marseille Arabic and landing heavy kicks repeatedly into Kell's arms and legs. He was terrified that he would now use the knife.

Just then, a commotion behind them, a door opening in the black-red corridor. There was a voice in the dark.

'What the fuck is going on?' a woman shouted in French and the two assailants ran, scooping up the shoulder bag and taking it with them, trainers squeaking on the linoleum. Kell swore after them, defeated and lying on the ground. They had the laptop, the camera, the Marquand mobile, the Uniacke passport. They had everything.

The woman came towards him.

'Jesus,' she said. 'Are you all right?'

39

There were police, there were paramedics, there were a great many concerned neighbours from all corners of La Cité Radieuse. There was also, of course, the shame of being mugged, that particular sense of humiliation which comes in the aftermath of a thorough defeat. But mostly Kell felt the dread of bureaucracy, of form-filling, of enforced visits to local hospitals, of the pity and fuss of strangers. He was obliged to see a doctor, who issued a Certificat Medicale which confirmed that Kell had suffered no serious physical damage save for a severe bruise on his left bicep and another on his left thigh, both already the colour of aubergines. His right kneecap had swollen slightly and he had a cut above the eye that did not require stitching. Both Claude, the French paramedic who examined him at the scene, and Laurent, the lugubrious police officer who had only that morning arrested '*trois putains de beurs*', recommended that Kell stay overnight and submit to a full medical examination in hospital. You could be in shock, said Claude. You ought to have a blood test, said Laurent. There was no way of knowing if Monsieur Uniacke had sustained internal injuries.

Kell, who had spent exactly one day in bed with illness since the age of fifteen, had always been a firm believer in listening to his own body, rather than to the risk-averse counselling of jaded public servants. On this occasion, his body told him what he wanted to hear: that he would be a little stiff in the morning, a little older, and that the injury to his knee would cause him to limp for several days. Otherwise the fight had damaged no more than his pride. It had also placed Thomas Kell in the awkward position of having to give a sworn Procés-Verbal to the Marseille police in the name of Stephen Uniacke. This was contrary to the spy's DNA, to every impulse he possessed to keep a low profile when conducting an operation overseas. Yet if the DGSE was going to send two Arab thugs to beat him up, Kell figured he didn't have much of a choice.

It took less than five minutes in Laurent's spruce Citroën Xsara to reach police headquarters half a mile away, thanks to the traffic-parting wail of a siren. The building was a sandstone, three-storey Hausmann throwback in an otherwise hyper-modern Marseille suburb with a predictable mix of late-afternoon clientele idling in the lobby: jumpy pickpockets; protesting drug dealers; breathalysed post-lunch businessmen; pensioners with a grudge. Kell was fast-tracked into an office on the second floor and interviewed formally by Laurent and his partner, Alain, a thirty-something hard man with salt-and-pepper stubble and a gleaming firearm, which he touched from time to time, like someone stroking a cat. Kell was asked for a full inventory of his shoulder bag and listed the contents as best he could, well aware that Jimmy Marquand and the beancounters at SIS would require a copy of the official police statement in order to reclaim the laptop and camera on insurance; such was the box-ticking small-mindedness that had overtaken the Service in recent years. After thirty minutes he was taken into a second room and shown a series of mug shots of local North African hoodlums, none of whom matched the descriptions of the two men who had assaulted him. It was already seven o'clock by the time Laurent was satisfied that he had covered every detail of the attack, asking Kell to sign the official 'Plainte Contre X' and apologizing, much to Alain's evident distaste, that 'as a British tourist' he had fallen prey to 'an immigrant crime'. Kell, who was in no doubt that his two assailants had stolen his laptop and phones to order, thanked both policemen for their 'patience and professionalism', and asked to be driven back to his hotel as soon as possible so that he could rest before travelling to Paris in the morning.

Laurent was on the point of agreeing when the telephone rang. He picked it up and said: 'Yes?' then embarked on what Kell assumed was an internal call. *'Oui, oui,'* the policeman muttered slowly, before a half-smile broke out on his face. Laurent nodded his head and made happy eye contact with Kell. Something had happened.

'It appears that your bag has been found, Monsieur Uniacke,' he said, hanging up the phone. 'It was dropped outside La Cité Radieuse and picked up by a member of the public. One of my fellow officers is bringing it to you now.'

Three minutes later there was a knock at the door and a third police officer walked into the room. He was wearing regulation black boots and a crisp, navy-blue uniform. Like Alain, he carried a firearm on his belt, but looked in every way a more imposing figure, thickset and pitiless. The beard had gone, taking as much as ten years off his face, but Kell recognized the man instantly.

It was Luc.

40

That Luc had bothered to shave off his beard told Kell everything he needed to know. Malot's companion from the boat intended to interview him while impersonating a police officer and did not want to run the small risk that Kell would recognize him. He said: '*Bonjour*' in an upbeat fashion, passed the shoulder bag to Laurent, and introduced himself as 'Benedict Voltaire', a pseudonym as preposterous as any Kell had ever encountered.

'So what happened here please?' he asked in English, settling into a chair that Alain had vacated, as though making way for a visiting dignitary. Kell noted the extra stripe on Luc's shoulder, outranking his two putative colleagues. He was either a senior police official or, more likely, a French Intelligence officer who had persuaded Laurent and Alain to let him masquerade as a cop.

'Monsieur Uniacke is a British national. He was visiting La Cité Radieuse when he was attacked by two Arab youths. They took his bag, but it looks like he got lucky.'

'It does look like that, yes,' Luc replied, this time in

French. He had the cracked, gravelly voice of a heavy smoker and was studying Kell's face intently, as though delaying the inevitable moment when he would expose him as a liar. Laurent had unzipped the bag.

'Would you like to check that nothing is missing?'

He passed the bag across the desk and Kell quickly began to remove the contents and to place them, one by one, amid the paperwork and mugs in front of him. The laptop was the first item to emerge, not damaged in any way. Next came the camera, then the Marquand mobile, which was still switched on. He placed it beside his London phone on the table. *The Scramble for Africa* was at the bottom of the bag, wedged in next to a tourist map of Marseille. Finally, from a zip-up interior pocket, he retrieved the Uniacke wallet.

'Two cell phones?' said Luc, a rising note of suspicion in his voice. Kell knew that he was in a scrap potentially far more dangerous than his earlier fight in the corridor. The SIM would have been checked and traced and he prayed that Marquand had erased Uniacke's trail through Nice. It was only by sheer luck that Kell's London phone had not been stolen; had Luc been given access to that, it would have been game over.

'That's right,' he said, picking up the Marquand phone and inspecting it. 'I have one for work, one for personal stuff.'

There was an unread text message on the screen and he opened it. It was from Marquand himself:

You were right. Everyone safely back in town. See you next week.

'Personal stuff,' Luc repeated, in English, as though Kell had employed a euphemism. The smell of a recently extinguished cigarette was on his breath.

'This is fantastic,' Kell said, trying to ignore Luc's cynicism by channelling the innocent relief and enthusiasm of Stephen Uniacke. 'Everything seems to be here. My laptop, my camera . . .' He checked the wallet next, flicking through the books of stamps, the membership of Kew, the various Uniacke credit and debit cards. Inevitably, more than four hundred euros had been removed. 'Fuck, they took all my fucking money,' he said. 'Excuse my language.'

Laurent smiled. 'No problem.' He looked quickly at Luc, as though tacitly asking permission to speak. 'You have insurance, yes?'

'Of course.'

'How much is missing?' Luc asked. 'How much did they take?'

'I think about four hundred euros. I took five hundred out of an ATM this morning but spent some . . .'

'Put a thousand on the form,' Luc said grandly, nodding towards Laurent. It was a smart, if obvious psychological move.

'I'm not sure I approve of that,' Kell replied, but the smile on his face belied any ethical reservations he might have possessed. He turned the smile into a grateful nod of the head, saying: 'Thank you' to Luc with as much sincerity as he could muster. To bolster his image as a family man, he then laid out the frayed photographs of 'Bella' and 'Dan', his phantom son and phantom daughter, and said: 'These are the most valuable things in my wallet. I'm just glad I didn't lose those.'

'Of course,' Laurent replied quickly, with what sounded

like genuine sincerity, and even Luc seemed moved by Kell's devotion to his family.

'What about the computer?' he asked. 'Is it damaged in any way?'

This was the most vulnerable moment in the interview, the point at which the DGSE could easily catch him out. They had stolen Kell's bag in order to examine the laptop. He was convinced of that. He was also convinced that they would not have returned the computer to him unless they had failed to crack the encryption. Even had they done so, it was unlikely that French tech-ops would have found anything incriminating. In the hotel, Kell had run an SIS-installed software programme that erased the user's digital footprints, replacing them with a series of benign cookies and URLs; the DGSE would have found only the emails and search engine history of Stephen Uniacke, marketing consultant and family man, reader of the *Daily Mail* and occasional gambler with Paddy Power. The Uniacke legend was so watertight it even had an account with Amazon.

'Is it working?' Luc asked, rising to his feet after Kell had flipped the lid and powered it up. It was obvious that he was coming round the desk in order to watch Kell typing in the password. Kell had no choice but to do so without complaint, tapping in the ten-digit code right under Luc's direct and unembarrassed gaze.

'Why do you have a password, if I may ask?'

'I work as a consultant,' Kell replied, again channelling his alter-ego's guileless integrity. 'We have a lot of high-net-worth clients who wouldn't want information about their businesses falling into the wrong hands.' He remembered the moments he had spent staring at the laptop screen in his cabin, under the possible surveillance of a DGSE camera, and found a way of explaining it: 'Trouble is, I always forget the code because it's so bloody long.'

'Of course,' said Luc, who hadn't moved an inch.

'Is there something you wanted to see?' Kell asked, looking back over his shoulder with what he hoped was the mild suggestion that Benedict Voltaire of the Marseille constabulary was beginning to encroach on his privacy. 'Everything seems to be working fine.'

This was enough to deter him. Reaching up to stroke the beard that was no longer there, Luc walked towards a double-glazed window at the southern end of the room and looked out over the back of the building. He tapped a couple of fingers on the glass and Kell wondered how he would make his next move. Surely the DGSE was now convinced of his innocence? Surely he had nothing to link him to Amelia or Malot?

'What were you doing in Marseille, Mr Uniacke?'

Kell's instinct was to insist that he had already answered such questions many times since the attack, but it was vital not to rise to Luc's provocations.

'I was in Tunisia on holiday. I came over on the ferry last night.'

Luc turned to face him. 'And was there anybody on the ferry who may have antagonized you? Who may have had a reason to follow you in Marseille and to attack you?'

It was not the line of enquiry that Kell had expected. Where was Luc going with this?

'I don't think so. I talked to a couple of people in the bar, to some others in the queue while we were waiting to disembark. Otherwise, nobody. I was mainly reading in my cabin.'

'No arguments? No problems on the boat?'

Kell shook his head. 'None.' It was almost too easy. 'No arguments,' he said, a sudden wince of pain in his knee.

In a room nearby, a man suddenly raised his voice in violent anger, as though enraged by a wild injustice. The building then became quiet again.

'You said to my colleague that you are on your way to Paris?'

This was a slip. Kell had told Laurent of his plan to leave Marseille before Luc had arrived. Clearly he had been eavesdropping on the formal police interview.

'Yes. I have a client in Paris who may be in town over the next few days. I was going to go up there to meet him. If he doesn't show up, I'll probably just go home.'

'To Reading?'

'To Reading via London, yes.'

Kell was suddenly tired of the second-rate interrogation, of Luc's supercilious machismo. It was obvious that they had nothing on him. He longed to be free of the now-stifling room, of a long afternoon of violence and bureaucracy. He wanted to find Malot.

'So I wish you good luck, Mr Uniacke,' Luc said, apparently arriving at the same conclusion. 'I am sorry for the trouble we have put you through. Truly.' There was a strange moment here, a look of intense hidden meaning directed towards him that Kell could not untangle. 'My colleague, Laurent, will take you back to your hotel. Thank you for your time. I do trust you will enjoy the rest of your visit to France.'

41

At Kell's request, Laurent dropped him at the corner of Rue Breteuil and Quai des Belges so that he could walk back to his hotel past the old port. He was already over an hour late for Madeleine Brive and wanted to cancel their plan for dinner, using the excuse that he had been robbed and beaten up. There was no advantage to be gained from meeting her: the DGSE held all the cards and she would simply oblige him to spend several more hours masquerading as Stephen Uniacke.

As it transpired, Madeleine was not answering her phone and Kell left a long message apologizing for cancelling the dinner and explaining what had happened at La Cité Radieuse. He hoped that they might have a chance to meet again one day and wished Madeleine a safe journey home to Tours.

The port at night was crowded with drifting couples, tourists in their best shirts, children tossing coins at the feet of weary buskers. The market stalls selling fish from ice-strewn tables at the eastern end of the marina had long since been packed away and the ferries had brought back the last of their passengers from sightseeing trips to the Calanques and Chateau d'If. At a *tabac* on the Quai des Belges, Kell bought a télécarte and went in search of a public phone. The first two were vandalized beyond repair, but at the north end of Rue Thubaneau he found a functioning France Telecom booth in a quiet side street opposite a shuttered pharmacy. He closed the door, set his bag on the ground and dialled the number for the taxi company Malot had used at the ferry terminal.

A woman answered, fifth ring, and Thomas Kell weaved his tall tale.

'Hello, yes. I hope that you can help me.' As a schoolboy, Kell had been told by a teacher that his spoken French sounded like a British Spitfire pilot who had crash-landed in Normandy. For the purposes of the conversation he tried to recreate a similar effect. 'I was in Marseille last week and rented one of your taxis outside Chez Michel at about half-past eleven on a Friday night. It was a white Mercedes. The driver was West African, an incredibly nice man . . .'

'Maybe Arnaud, maybe Bobo, maybe Daniel . . .'

'Yes, maybe. Do you know who I'm talking about? He was around fifty or fifty-five . . .'

'Arnaud, then . . .'

'Yes, that's right.'

'What about him?'

'Well, I'm British . . .'

'I can tell this . . .'

'And I work for Médecins sans Frontières. Arnaud gave me his card because I promised to get in touch with regard to some friends he was very concerned about in the Ivory Coast.'

'Oh, OK . . .'

That did the trick; the merest suggestion of possible human rights abuses had transformed the receptionist's previously indifferent attitude.

'It's just that I've lost the card and have no way of contacting him. Would you be able to ask him to ring me here in London or, if that's going to be too expensive, do you have a number or an email where I could reach him in Marseille?'

As a ruse, it wasn't watertight, but Kell possessed enough of an understanding of the French character to know that they would not refuse such a request purely on the basis of protecting Arnaud's privacy. At worst, the receptionist would ask for Kell's number and promise that Arnaud would call him back; at best, she would put them directly in touch.

'He's not working tonight,' she said, which gave him hope that a number might be forthcoming.

'That's fine,' Kell replied. 'I can always call him on Monday when I'm back at my desk. I have all the files on the computer in my office . . .'

'Hold on please.'

The line suddenly switched to an old Moby track; it wasn't clear whether the receptionist was taking another call or had gone in search of Arnaud's number. Within thirty seconds, however, she was back, saying: 'OK, do you have a pen?'

'I do.' Kell allowed himself a quiet smile of satisfaction. 'Thank you so much for going to all this trouble. I really think Arnaud will be pleased.'

Arnaud was in what sounded like a crowded restaurant or café and wasn't much interested in taking a call from a complete stranger at nine thirty on a Sunday night.

'Who?' he said for the third time when Kell told him that he was a British journalist looking for information about one of Arnaud's passengers, and willing to pay five hundred euros simply for the opportunity to sit down over a beer and talk.

'What, now? Tonight?'

'Tonight, yes. It's urgent.'

'This is not possible, my friend. Tonight I relax. Maybe you should too.'

A resident had emerged from one of the apartment buildings adjacent to the phone box. He turned the throttle on a motorbike and Kell had to shout above the noise of the revving engine.

'I'll come to you,' he said. 'Just tell me where you are, I'll meet you near your home. It won't take more than ten minutes.'

A contemplative silence ensued, which Kell eventually ventured to break by saying: 'Hello? Are you still there?'

'I'm still here.' Arnaud was enjoying all the attention.

'A thousand,' Kell said, running out of Marquand's money.

That did the trick. There was enough of a pause, then. 'Which passenger do you want to know about?'

'Not on an open line,' Kell replied. 'I'll tell you when I see you.'

A forty-five euro, forty-minute cab ride later, Kell was deep in the Quartier Nord, miles from the yachts and the Audis and the tennis court villas of the Corniche, in a thankless landscape of breeze-block towers and litter-strewn streets; everything that Le Corbusier, in the zeal of his idealism, had failed to imagine.

Arnaud was drinking pastis at a café in the basement of a slate-grey tower block patrolled by bored, undernourished youths wearing tracksuits and state-of-the-art trainers. One of the windows of the café had a pane of shattered glass; the other was obscured by a metal shutter daubed in graffiti: MARSEILLE. CAPITALE DE LA CULTURE ou DU BETON. Kell told his driver to wait on the street and ran a gauntlet of clicks and stares, entering the café in the expectation of total silence, of doors swishing behind him like a western saloon. Instead, he was greeted by the exclusively African clientele with half-interested nods of welcome. Perhaps Kell's pronounced limp and the cut above his eye leant him the air of a man who had endured more than his fair share of misfortune.

'Over here,' said Arnaud, seated at the bar beneath a collage of photographs of Marseille footballers, past and present. On a facing wall were pictures of Lilian Thuram, Patrick Vieira and Zinedine Zidane, clutching the 1998 World Cup; next to this, a framed cartoon of Nicolas Sarkozy in exaggeratedly stacked heels, his eyes scratched out by a knife, a biro-drawn phallus swelling from his trousers. Arnaud stood up. He was a tall, well-built man, at least seventeen stone. Wordlessly, he ushered Kell to a formica table at the back of the café. The table was positioned beneath a television that had been bolted to the wall. They shook hands over an ashtray swollen with gum and cigarettes and sat on opposite chairs. Arnaud's palm was dry and soft, his face entirely without kindness but not lacking a certain nobility. With his dark, indifferent eyes, he looked for all the world like an exiled despot of the Amin school. It made sense. Arnaud was probably losing face by talking to Kell but had calculated that a thousand euros for a ten-minute conversation was a price well worth paying.

'So you are journalist?'

'That's right.'

Arnaud didn't ask what paper. They were speaking in French, his accent as difficult to unpick as any Kell could remember. 'And you want to know about someone?'

Kell nodded. Somebody had switched on the television and his reply was partly smothered by the commentary on a game of basketball. Perhaps Arnaud had ordered this so that they might speak in confidence; perhaps it was the manager's way of expressing his disapproval.

'This morning, at the ferry terminal, you picked up a man in his early thirties off the boat from Tunis.'

Arnaud nodded, though it wasn't clear whether or not he remembered. He was wearing a button-down denim shirt and removed a packet of full-strength Winston from the breast pocket.

'Smoke?'

'Sure,' said Kell, and took one.

There was a pause while Arnaud lit their cigarettes – his own first. Then he leaned forward.

'You feeling nervous in this place? You look nervous.'

'Do I?' Kell knew that he didn't and that Arnaud was trying to wind him up. 'Funny. I was just reflecting on what a civilized place this is.'

'Huh?'

Kell looked back at the bar. There was a half-eaten plate of spaghetti on the next-door table, two old men playing backgammon by the door. 'You can get an espresso. You can smoke. The food smells good.' He made a point of looking directly into Arnaud's eyes, so that he wouldn't have to waste time playing any more of his games. 'I'm used to places where you can't drink alcohol, where they don't allow women to sit with men. I'm used to roadside bombs and snipers lining the white man up for breakfast. I get nervous in places like Baghdad, Arnaud. I get nervous in Kabul. Do you follow?'

The despot shifted in his chair, the plastic squeaking.

'I remember this guy.' It took Kell a moment to realize that the driver was talking about Malot.

'I thought you might. Can you tell me where you drove him?'

Arnaud blew a cloud of smoke past Kell's ear. 'That's it? That's all you want to know?'

'That's all I want to know.'

He frowned, the tops of his soft black cheeks tightening under the eyes. A mixed-race boy, not much older than fifteen or sixteen, came to the table and asked Kell if he wanted a drink.

'Nothing for me.'

'Have something,' said Arnaud.

Kell took a drag on the cigarette. 'A beer.'

'*Un bière*, Pep,' said Arnaud, as though Kell's order needed translating. He scratched at something on the side of his neck. 'It was a long journey, expensive.'

'How long?'

'Only got back about two hours ago. We went to Castelnaudary.'

'Castelnaudary? That's near Toulouse, right?'

'Look it up.'

Kell blew the smoke back. 'Or you could just tell me.'

'Pay me the money.'

He took an envelope containing the cash from his jeans and passed it across the table.

'So. For a thousand euros, Arnaud. Where's Castelnaudary?'

The cab driver smiled, enjoying the game. 'West of here. Maybe three hours on the autoroute. Past Carcassone.'

'Cassoulet country,' Kell replied, thinking of the Languedoc-Roussillon but not expecting much in the way of a reaction. 'Did you drop him in town? Do you remember the address?'

'There was no address.' Arnaud put the envelope in the hip pocket of his chinos and it was as if the weight of the money, the reality of it, jolted him into a greater cooperation. 'It was strange, in fact. He wanted me to leave him on the outskirts of a village ten kilometres to the south. In a lay-by, in the middle of the countryside. He said that somebody was coming to collect him.'

Kell asked the obvious question. 'Why didn't you just take him to where he needed to go?'

'He said that he didn't have an address. I didn't want to argue, I didn't really care. I had a long drive back to Marseille. I wanted to come home and see my daughter.'

Kell thought about enquiring after Arnaud's family, to soften him up a bit, but it didn't feel like a strategy worth pursuing. 'And what about the rest of the journey? Did you talk on the way? Did he have anything to say to you?'

The African smiled, more broadly now, and Kell saw that his gums were yellowed with age and decay. 'No, man.' He shook his head. 'This guy doesn't talk. He doesn't even look. Mostly he sleeps or stares out of the window. Typical racist. Typical French.'

'You think he was *racist*?'

Arnaud ignored the question and asked one of his own. 'So who is he? Why is a British newspaper interested in him? Did he steal something? He fuck Princess Kate or something?'

Arnaud laughed heartily at his own joke. Kell wasn't much of a royalist but refrained from joining in.

'He's just somebody we're interested in. If I had a map, could you show me exactly where you left him?'

Arnaud nodded. Kell waited for him to make a move. They sat in silence until it became clear that Arnaud was holding out for something.

'Do you *have* a map?' Kell asked.

Arnaud folded his arms.

'Why would I have one in here?' he asked, looking down at the floor. The crust of an old sandwich was hardening beneath a torn leather stool. Kell could not get a signal on his iPhone and had no choice but to stand up and leave the café, again running the gauntlet of track-suited youths and unleashed dogs outside. He found his waiting cab and tapped on the window, waking the driver from a brief sleep. The window came down and Kell asked if he could borrow a road map of France. This simple request was met with almost complete contempt, because it required the driver to step out of the vehicle, to open the boot of his Mercedes and to retrieve the map from the boot.

'Maybe you should keep it in the car,' Kell told him, and returned to his table in the café. Arnaud took the map, flicked to the index, found Castelnaudary and pointed to the approximate area where he had left François Malot.

'Here,' he said, a dry, nail-chewed finger momentarily obscuring the precise location. Kell took the map and wrote down the name of the village: Salles-sur-l'Hers.

'And it was a lay-by? In the middle of the countryside?'

Arnaud nodded.

'Anything distinctive about the area that you can remember? Was there a church nearby? A playground?'

Arnaud shook his head, as though he was becoming bored of the conversation. 'No. Just some trees, fields. Fucking countryside, you know?' He said the word 'countryside' as if it were also a term of abuse. 'When I turned around to go home, I remember I went past some recycling bins after maybe one minute, two, so that's how far I dropped him from Salles-sur-l'Hers.'

'Thank you,' Kell replied. He passed the number of the Marquand mobile across the table. 'If you think of anything else . . .'

'I'll call you.' Arnaud slid the number into the same shirt pocket in which he kept his cigarettes. The tone of his reply suggested that this would be the last time that Thomas Kell ever saw or heard from him. 'What happened to your eye? The passenger did this to you?'

'One of his friends,' Kell replied, rising from the table. His beer had arrived while he was fetching the map. He left a two-euro coin on the table though he hadn't touched it. 'Thanks for agreeing to meet me.'

'No problem.' Arnaud did not bother standing up. He shook Kell's hand and with the other, patted the wad of money in his pocket. 'I should say thank you to your British newspaper.' Another yellow-gummed smile. 'Very generous. Very nice present.'

42

Back at the hotel, there was a voice message on Kell's telephone from a petulant-sounding Madeleine Brive. She was sorry to hear about the attack at Cité Radieuse, but seemingly more upset that Stephen Uniacke had not possessed the good grace to call her earlier in the afternoon to warn her that their dinner at Chez Michel would not now be going ahead. As a consequence, she had wasted her one and only night in Marseille.

'Charming,' Kell said to the room as he hung up. He wondered if Luc was still listening.

He slept well, as deeply as at any point in the operation, and ate a decent breakfast in the hotel restaurant before checking out and finding an Internet café within a stone's throw of the Gare Saint-Charles. His laptop was now effectively useless; Luc's DGSE comrades would almost certainly have fitted it with a tracking device or key logger software. Kell saw that Elsa Cassani had sent a document by email, which he assumed – correctly – was the vetting file on Malot. A message accompanying the document said: 'Call me if you have any questions x' and Kell printed it out with the assistance of a hyper-efficient Goth with a piercing in his tongue.

There was a branch of McDonald's at the station. Kell bought a cup of radioactively hot coffee, found a vacant table, and worked his way through Elsa's findings.

She had done well, tracing Malot's secondary school, the college in Toulon where he had studied Information Technology, the name of the gym in Paris of which he was a member. The photograph of Malot sent by Marquand showed two of his colleagues from a software firm in Brest that had been bought out and absorbed by a larger corporation in Paris, at the headquarters of which Malot now worked. Elsa had traced two bank accounts, as well as tax records going back seven years; there were, in her opinion, 'no anomalies' in Malot's financial affairs. He paid his bills on time, had been renting his apartment in the 7th for just over a year, and drove a second-hand Renault Megane that had been purchased in Brittany. As far as friends or girl-friends were concerned, enquiries at his office and gym-nasium suggested that François Malot was something of a loner, a private man who kept himself to himself. Elsa had even telephoned Malot's boss, who informed her that 'poor François' was on an extended leave of absence following a family tragedy. As far as she could tell, Malot had no presence on social networks and his emails were regularly downloaded to a host computer that Elsa had not been able to hack. Without the assistance of Cheltenham, it had not been possible to listen to his mobile telephone calls but she had managed to intercept one potentially interesting email exchange between Malot and an individual registered with Wanadoo as 'Christophe Delestre' whom she suspected was a friend or relative. Elsa had attached the correspondence to the file.

Kell placed the rest of the documents in his shoulder bag, drained his cup of coffee and sent Elsa a text.

This is all first class. Thank you.

In different circumstances, he might have added one of her kisses – 'x' – at the end of the message, but he was the boss, and therefore obliged to keep a certain professional distance. He then proceeded to read the Delestre emails. They were in French and dated five days earlier, which placed Malot at the Ramada towards the tail-end of his holiday with Amelia.

From: dugarrylemec@wanadoo.fr
To: fmalot54@hotmail.fr
When are you coming back to Paris? We miss you.
Kitty wants a kiss from her godfather.
Christophe

From: fmalot54@hotmail.fr
To: dugarrylemec@wanadoo.fr
Enjoying Tunis. Coming back at the weekend but a lot of stuff to think about. Have taken sabbatical from work – they've been great about everything. Might come home to Paris next week, might go on the road for a while. Not sure. But give Kitty a kiss from her Godfather Frankie.
P.S. Hope you guys are starting to put things together again after the fire. Promise to get you those books to replace the ones you lost.

Kell put the email printout with the rest of the documents in his shoulder bag. He found a public toilet in the underground level of Gare Saint-Charles, went into a cubicle, tore up the entire file and flushed it in small pieces down the toilet. He went back upstairs, bought himself a ticket with a Uniacke credit card, and caught the ten o'clock TGV to Paris.

It was time to have a little chat with Christophe.

43

Four hours later, Kell was sitting alone at a table in Brasserie Lipp staring at a photograph of Christophe Delestre that he had culled from the pages of Facebook. In the photograph, Delestre was wearing an outsize pair of black sunglasses, cargo shorts and a burgundy T-shirt. He looked to be in his early to mid thirties, had a neatly trimmed moustache and goatee beard, with gel giving spiked life to thinning hair. The privacy settings on the account had been tight and it was the only picture of Delestre that Kell could find. On the basis that Facebook users generally gave a great deal of thought and attention to their profile picture, Kell assumed that Delestre wanted to convey an image of easygoing cool and bonhomie; he was laughing in the shot and holding a roll-up cigarette in his right hand. Nobody else was visible in the frame.

Lipp was an old-school Parisian brasserie on Boulevard Saint-Germain that had been a favourite of Claire's when she had lived in Paris for a year as a student. She had taken Kell there twice during their marriage and they had sat side by side, at the same window table, watching the *haute bourgeoisie* of Paris in full flow. Little had changed. The waiters in black tie, wearing white aprons and careful smiles, prepared plates of steak tartare at a serving station just a pace from the entrance. The manager, immaculately turned out in a silk shirt and single-breasted suit, reserved his customary *froideur* for first-time visitors to the restaurant and an unctuous Gallic charm for more regular customers. Two tables from Kell, an elderly widow, decked out in fourteen kilos of art deco jewellery, was picking her way through a salade Niçoise, her shoulders covered by a black shawl. From time to time, the tablecloth would part to reveal a loyal Scottish terrier curled at her feet; a dog, Kell reckoned, more cherished and pampered than the late husband had ever been. Further along the same wall, beneath framed caricatures of Jacques Cousteau and Catherine Deneuve, three middle-aged women in Chanel suits were deep in conspiratorial conversation. They were too far away to be overheard, but Kell could imagine Claire, still clinging to a stereotype of the privileged French, announcing that they 'probably have nothing better to talk about than sex and power'. He loved this place because it was the very soul of old world Paris and yet today he almost hated it, because he could only think of his estranged wife on her plane to California, sipping the same French wines and eating the same French food in a first-class seat paid for by Richard Quinn. At the Gare de Lyon, Kell had left a message on Claire's voicemail asking her to reconsider her trip to America. She had rung back to say that she was already en route to Heathrow. There had been a note of weary triumph in her voice and Kell, gripped by jealousy, had almost dialled Elsa's number in Italy and invited her

227

to Paris, just to be in the company of a young woman who might soften the blow of his humiliation. Instead, he had taken a cab to Lipp, ordered himself a bottle of Nuits-St-Georges Premier Cru and buried himself in strategies for Christophe Delestre.

An hour later, the bottle finished, Kell paid his bill, crossed the street for an espresso at Café Flore, then took the metro to Pereire in the 17th arrondissement, where he knew a small, discreet hotel on Rue Verniquet. There was a double room available and he booked it under the Uniacke alias, his seventh bed in as many days. The tiny room was on the second floor and had bright orange walls, a reproduction Miró hanging beside the bathroom door and a window looking out over a small courtyard. Beginning to feel the sluggishness of a lunchtime bottle of wine, Kell did not bother to unpack, but instead went out into the late-afternoon sunshine and walked east towards Montmartre. He carried his camera with him and took a series of photographs in the blinding summer light – of café life, of wrought-iron street lamps, of fresh fruits and vegetables displayed in the windows of grocery shops – using the camera as a means of turning in the street and photographing the pedestrians and vehicles around him. Though he was sure that the DGSE, post-Marseille, had lost interest in Stephen Uniacke, a camera was a useful deterrent against mobile surveillance; later he could check faces and number plates to ascertain if certain vehicles or members of the public appeared in more than one location.

By six, he was on Rue Lamarck, a main Montmartre thoroughfare in the foothills of the Basilique du Sacré-Coeur. According to Elsa's file, Delestre lived in a ground-floor apartment on the corner of Rue Darwin and Rue des

Saules. Kell began to descend a steep flight of stone steps leading to the junction of the two streets. He paused halfway down, looking back up towards Lamarck, and fired off a sequence of photographs in the manner of an amateur photographer trying his best to capture the idiosyncratic charm of Paris. He then turned and aimed the camera at the lines of cars stretching ahead of him on both sides of Rue des Saules. Using the telephoto lens, he looked for evidence of a surveillance team. All of the vehicles appeared to be empty; as Kell suspected, no agency would have the manpower to watch each and every one of Malot's relatives and friends. At the bottom of the steps, now only a few metres from Delestre's front door, Kell looked up at the facing apartments on Rue Darwin and judged that it would be impossible to spot a stakeout position; he would just have to trust to the odds and take his chances. He circled the block, walking down Rue des Saules and back up Darwin from the western side. It was a busy neighbourhood, old ladies coming home from the shops, children returning from school in the company of their parents. Kell approached Delestre's door in the hope that Christophe would now be home from work.

He heard the baby before he saw it, through an open window on the ground floor. In a small, dimly lit sitting room an attractive, dark-haired woman, perhaps of Spanish or Italian descent, was bouncing the baby up and down in her arms in an effort to stop it from crying.

'Madame Delestre?' Kell asked.

'*Oui?*'

'Is your husband at home?'

The woman glanced quickly to her right, then back at the stranger on the street. Christophe Delestre was in the room with her. He stood up and came to the window, standing in front of his wife and child in what may have been an unconscious instinct to protect them.

'Can I help you?'

'It's about François Malot,' Kell replied. He was speaking in French and extended a hand through the window. 'It's about the fire. I wondered if I could come inside?'

44

Facebook was misleading. Christophe Delestre had shaved off his moustache and goatee beard, put on a couple of stone in weight and was no longer wearing an outsized pair of black sunglasses. His brown eyes were large and candid, his puffy face bruised by a succession of sleepless nights. He was dressed in pale linen trousers, tennis shoes and a blue, button-down cotton shirt. Kell was ushered into the sitting room and invited to sit on a sofa covered by a moth-eaten blanket. Christophe closed the window on to the street and formally introduced his wife, who squinted at Kell as he shook her hand, holding the baby more tightly, as though she did not entirely trust this stranger in her home.

'Is it about the insurance?' she asked. Her name was Maria and she spoke French with a Spanish accent.

'It's not,' he replied, and nodded affectionately at the child to put Maria more at ease.

'You said your name was Tom? You are English?' Perhaps to alleviate the tedium of permanent childcare, Christophe had been all too willing to allow Kell into his home. His manner was now more reserved. 'How do you know about the fire?'

'I'm going to be frank,' Kell told them, and noticed that the child had stopped crying. Kitty. Malot's god-daughter. 'I work for MI6. Do you know what that is?'

There was a stunned pause as the Delestres looked at one another. Officers did not often choose to break cover, but in certain circumstances, and within certain psychological parameters, name-dropping MI6 was like flashing a badge at a crime scene.

It was Maria who spoke first. 'You are a spy?'

'I am an officer with the British Secret Intelligence Service. Yes. To all intents and purposes, I am a spy.'

'And what do you want with us?' Christophe looked frightened, as though Kell was now a direct threat to his wife and daughter.

'You have nothing to worry about. I just need to ask you some questions about François Malot.'

'What about him?' Maria's answer was quick, accessing some basic Latin impulse to disdain authority. 'Who has sent you here? What do you want?'

The small sitting room had become stuffy and Kitty began to moan. Perhaps she had sensed the gathering atmosphere of distrust, the hostility in her mother's usually gentle and consoling voice. 'I apologize for visiting your home without an appointment. It was important that the French authorities did not know that I was coming here today.'

Christophe elected to move his daughter next door, taking the baby from Maria's arms and walking through a kitchen area into what Kell assumed was a nursery or bedroom. Maria continued to stare at him, dark eyes cold with suspicion.

'Can you please tell me your name again,' she said. 'I wish to write it down.' Kell obliged her, spelling out K-E-L-L with slow precision. When Christophe came back into the room he seemed surprised to find his wife stooped over a table, scribbling.

'I'm not feeling comfortable about this,' he said, as though he had been coached by a third party and injected with greater self-confidence. 'You say that you are with MI6, this seems a lie. What do you want? I think it was a mistake for me to allow you to come here.'

'I mean you no harm,' Kell replied, the quality of his French momentarily deserting him. The nuance he had tried to build into his response was lost and Maria found her voice.

'I think you should leave us,' she said. 'We don't want to have anything to do with you . . .'

'No,' added Christophe, buoyed by his wife's courage. 'I think it was a mistake. Please, if you want to interview us, you must go through the police . . .'

'Sit down.' Kell's lingering, ceaseless irritation with Claire, allied to a general impatience with the Delestres, had caused him to lose his temper. He felt it flare inside him, the sudden snap of goodwill, and thought of Yassin naked in the chair in Kabul, his eyes wet with fear. The young French couple reacted to the sudden intensity in Kell's voice as though he had drawn a gun. Christophe stepped sideways and dropped into an armchair. Maria took longer, but was eventually persuaded by Kell's fixed stare to settle at the table.

'What do you want?' she said.

'Why are you so defensive? Is there something I should know?' Christophe began to reply, but Kell interrupted him. 'It's strange that you have no interest in François' whereabouts. Can you explain that? I was under the impression that he was your closest friend.'

Christophe looked dazed, like a commuter woken from a nap on a train. His tired, indoor face was motionless as he tried to unpick the meaning of what Kell had told him.

'I know where François is,' he replied, finding a certain courage. His right hand gripped the arm of his chair, knuckles white. A film of sweat had gathered around his widow's peak.

'Then where is he?'

'Why should we tell you?' Maria flashed a look of dismay at her husband, who shook his head, as though to warn her against further resistance. 'You say that you are a spy, but you could be working for the journalist who called us after the murder. We have already told him, repeatedly. We do not want to talk about what happened.'

Kell stood up, moving towards her. 'Why would a journalist pretend to be a spy? Why would anybody do anything that stupid?' The question became rhetorical, because the Delestres found no answer. 'Let me get something straight. There's a possibility that François is in a lot of trouble. I need to know if he's been in touch with you. I need to see your correspondence.'

Maria produced a contemptuous snort. Kell could not help but admire her guts. 'This is our private email!' she said. 'Why should we show you this? You have no right to . . .'

Kell stopped her mid-sentence. 'Is Kitty asleep?' he asked, moving towards the nursery as though he intended to take the child. It took only a fraction of a second for Maria to realize what Kell had said.

'How do you know my daughter's name?'

He turned towards Christophe, who looked to be weighing up the good sense of throwing a punch. 'What about the books François promised you in his email from Tunis? Did they ever show up? Did "Uncle Frankie" come through for his god-daughter?'

Delestre tried to stand but Kell went a pace towards him and said: 'Stay where you are.' He was back with Yassin again, the power of containment, the greed for revenge and information, and had to check himself from going too far. 'I don't want this conversation to become difficult, for either of us. What I'm trying to tell you is that I can get access to anything I want. I need your cooperation so that I don't have to go to the trouble of breaking the law. I would rather not spend days listening to your private phone calls. I would rather not tell MI6 Station in Paris to follow you around town, to hack into your computers, to watch your friends. But I will do that if I have to, because what I need to know is worth breaking the law for. Do you understand?' Christophe looked confused, like a child being bullied. 'I am trying to pay you the compliment of being honest. There is a hard way to do what I have to do and there is an easy way that leaves you free and unmolested.'

'Tell us the easy way,' Maria replied quietly, and it was as though her own private capitulation marked an end to the Delestres' resistance.

'I need to see a photograph of François,' Kell replied. 'Do you have one?'

He suspected that he already knew the answer to his own question, and so it proved. Christophe, adjusting his position in the armchair, shook his head and said: 'We lost everything in the fire. All the albums, all the photographs. There are no pictures of François.'

'Of course.' Kell went towards the window and glanced up Rue Darwin. A smell of diesel came in from the street. 'What about online?' he asked. 'What about Twitter or Facebook? Anything on there I could look at?'

Maria tilted her head to one side and stared at Kell in puzzlement, as though he had stumbled on a coincidence.

'Christophe cannot access his Facebook,' she said, a note of surprise in her voice. 'It hasn't been working for a month.'

'I've contacted them,' Christophe added. They were both looking at Kell as if they blamed him for this. 'I've tried to change my password. One time I managed to get in but all my Facebook friends had vanished, all my photographs, all of my biographical information.'

'Just wiped out?'

'Just wiped out. The same with emails, Dropbox, Flickr. Everything to do with my Internet since the fire has been no good. It's all gone. I just have this one account that I can use, my regular email to talk to friends. Everything else, no.'

Outside on the street, a motorbike sped past the window, braked at the corner, then burned off down Rue des Saules.

'Any idea why?' Again, Kell felt that he already knew the answer to his own question: a DGSE computer attack on the Delestre residence, wiping out all evidence of their association with François Malot. The fire was probably the icing on the cake; perhaps it had even been intended to kill them.

'We have no idea,' Maria replied, and asked permission to go into the bedroom to check on Kitty. Kell made a gesture of goodwill, his arms spread apart, his hands upturned, as if to say: *Of course you can. It's your house. You can do what you want.* She returned moments later carrying something behind her back. Kell thought for a split second that it was a knife, until she brought her hand forward and he saw that she was holding a bottle of baby milk.

'Tell me about the fire,' he said. 'Were you at home?'

They had been. Their top-floor flat four blocks away in Montmartre had gone up in smoke at two o'clock in the morning. An electrical fault, according to the landlord. They had been lucky to escape alive. If the fire brigade had not come as quickly as they did, Maria explained, Kitty would almost certainly have suffocated.

'And you don't know anybody else who might have a photograph of François? An uncle? An aunt? An ex-girlfriend?'

Christophe shook his head. 'François is a loner,' he said.

'He does not have any friends,' Maria added, as though she had long been suspicious of this. 'No girls, either. Why do you keep asking about photographs? What's going on?'

By now, she had sat on the arm of her husband's chair, her hand in his. Kell opened the window and sat in the chair that Maria had earlier occupied. The light outside had faded and there were children playing in the street.

'When did you last hear from him? You said that you'd received a number of emails.'

'It sounds as though you've already read them.' Christophe's quick response lacked malice. It was as if the fresh air blowing in from the street had cleared the last of the ill-feeling between them.

Kell nodded. 'MI6 intercepted an email that François

sent to your 'dugarrylemec' address three days ago. His situation is a concern to us. The email was sent from Tunis. That's how I know about Kitty, about Uncle Frankie, about the books. What else has he told you?'

The question appeared to unlock something within Christophe, who frowned as though poring over a puzzle.

'He has told me a lot of things,' he said, his soft eyes almost sorrowful in their confusion. 'I have to be honest with you. Some of it worries me. Some of what he has written does not make very much sense.'

45

It all poured out, and was later produced as a transcript thanks to a DGSE analyst who, five days later, conducted his weekly check on the microphones at the Delestres' apartment and came across evidence of the conversation with Thomas Kell.

The take quality was considered extremely high.

CHRISTOPHE DELESTRE (CD): He has told me a lot of things. I have to be honest with you. Some of it worries me. Some of what he has written does not make very much sense.

THOMAS KELL (TK): Tell me more.

CD: I know Frankie very well, OK? It isn't like him just to disappear and make a new life, even with everything that's happened to him.

TK: How do you mean, 'make a new life'?

MARIA DELESTRE (MD): In the other emails

he's talked about leaving Paris for good, how upset he is about what happened in Egypt, saying that he doesn't know when he'll be coming home . . .

CD: The thing is, Frankie was never that close to his mother and father. He was adopted, did you know that?

TK: I knew that.

CD: But now it's like he can't get out of bed in the morning. He won't talk to me, he won't go to work . . .

TK: What do you mean he won't talk to you?

CD: I can't get him on the phone . . .

MD: [Unclear]

TK: He doesn't answer the phone?

CD: No. He won't respond to my messages. We used to talk all the time, I'm like his brother. Now everything is SMS . . .

TK: Text messages.

CD: Exactly, which was never his style. He [expletive] hates SMS. But now I get maybe three or four every day.

TK: May I see them?

Pause. Sound of movement.

MD: [Unclear]

CD: Here. You can just click through them.

MD: It's difficult for you to know, but they aren't like him at all. What do they say? 'Starting new life'? 'Sick of France'? 'Too many memories in Paris'? All [expletive]. Frankie is not sentimental like this. It's as if he's joined a cult or something, some kind of therapy that's telling him to say these things, breaking him away from his old friends.

TK: Grief can do strange things to people.

CD: But [Traffic noise. Unclear.]

TK: [Traffic noise continuing. Unclear.] How did he behave at the funeral?

MD: It was like you would expect. Just awful. He was very brave but very upset, you know? We all were. It was Père-Lachaise, very formal, only close friends and family invited.

TK: Père-Lachaise?

CD: Yes. It's a cemetery about half an hour—

TK: I know what it is.

CD: [Unclear]

TK: Which arrondissement is that?

MD: What?

CD: Père-Lachaise? The twentieth, I think.

TK: Not the fourteenth?

CD: What?

TK: You're certain that the funeral was in the twentieth arrondissement? Not in Montparnasse?

CD [and MD partial]: Yes.

TK: Can you tell me the date?

CD: For sure. It was a Friday. The twenty-first or twenty-second, I think.

46

That two funerals had been arranged for Philippe and Jeannine Malot confirmed to Kell that Amelia had been the victim of an elaborate DGSE sting. The emails Christophe had received from François ('Frankie is not sentimental like this. It's as if he's joined a cult or something') had almost certainly been written by an impostor. Kell checked out of his hotel and prepared to return to London, where he would confront Amelia with the wretched truth of what had been done to her.

In the early years of his career, coming home had always given Kell a buzz. He might have been returning from a meeting in Vienna or Bonn, or from a longer operation overseas, but always there was the same slightly elevated sense of his own importance as he touched down on British soil. Passing through Heathrow or Gatwick, he would feel like a superior being among a rabble of lesser mortals, gliding invisibly through passport control on Her Majesty's secret service. Such arrogance, such hubris, had long since ceased to form a part of Kell's make-up. He no longer felt anointed or conferred with particular status; he was conscious only of being *different* to all the rest. Towards the end of his time with SIS, he had envied the uncomplicated lives of the men and women of his own generation with whom he came into contact. What would it be like, he wondered, a life without lies, an existence free of the double-think and second-guess that was a permanent feature of his clandestine trade? Kell had been recruited for his charm and cunning; he knew that. He had risen to the heights as a direct consequence of his imagination and flair for deceit. But the ceaseless demands of the work – the need to stay one step ahead of the competition – not to mention the increasingly burdensome bureaucratic dimension of spying in the post-9/11 environment, were exhausting. Sometimes Kell wondered if what had happened to him in Kabul had been a blessing. The scandal had forced him out just at the point at which he was getting ready to jump. In this sense, a forty-two-year-old spy was no different to a forty-two-year-old chef or accountant. Men reached a certain point in their lives and felt the need for change, to make their mark on the landscape, to bank some serious money before it was all too late. So the chef bought himself a restaurant; the banker started his own hedge fund. And the spy? The drop-out rate from SIS after forty-five was as alarming as it was unstoppable. The cream of the crop, like Amelia, stayed on, in the hope of making 'C'; the rest grew observably tired of the game and diverted their energies to the private sector, finding lucrative jobs in finance and oil, or opening up their contacts books to the grateful directors of boutique corporate espionage outfits which attended, at colossal expense, to the whims and schemes of oligarchs and plutocrats the world over.

Yet, while queuing for the Paddington Express at Heathrow, Kell was visited by a thought that had been troubling him throughout his journey across Tunisia and France: *I was wasting my time before this.* Thoughts of writing a book, thoughts of starting his own business. Why had he tried to deceive himself? He could no more function in the world beyond SIS than he could imagine becoming a father. He was like one of the grey, institutionalized men who had taught French or mathematics at his school, teachers who were still plying their trade in exactly the same fashion at exactly the same place more than twenty-five years later. There was no escape.

He had spoken to Amelia from a France Telecom booth in the Gare du Nord, using the télécarte purchased in Marseille.

'Tom! How lovely to hear from you.'

She had been in her office at Vauxhall Cross. He tried to keep the conversation brief, because you never knew who was listening in.

'I need to see you,' he told her. 'Are you free tonight?'

'Tonight? It's a bit late notice.' It felt like making a date with a girl who had six better offers. 'Giles has tickets for the National.'

'Can he go alone?'

Amelia had detected Kell's anxiety, something more than a bullish desire to get his own way.

'Why, what's happened? Is it Claire? Is everything all right?'

Kell had looked out at the bustle and thrust of the Gare du Nord and allowed himself a momentary pause for reflection. No, nothing was all right with Claire. She's putting me through the ringer. She's drinking Pinot Noir with Dick the Wonder Schlong in Napa. He would gladly have talked to Amelia about his marriage for hours on end.

'Nothing to do with Claire,' he said. 'Everything is as it was on that front. This is work stuff. Professional.'

Amelia misunderstood. 'Tom, I can't talk about Yassin until I take over next month. Then we can sit down and we work out how to clear your—'

'This is not about Yassin. I'm not worried about Kabul.' He realized that he had not formally congratulated her on becoming Chief. He would do it later, if and when the opportunity arose. 'It's about you. We need to meet and we need to do it tonight.'

'Fine.' Her voice was suddenly slightly hostile. Amelia Levene, in common with most driven and successful people of Kell's acquaintance, didn't like being pushed around. 'Where do you suggest?'

Kell would have liked to meet outdoors, but it had begun to rain. He needed a place where they could talk at length without risk of being overheard. Amelia's house and his own bachelor bedsit were out of the question, because any number of interested parties could have wired them for sight and sound. They might have gone to one of the private members clubs in Pall Mall to which he had access, if such places opened their doors to women. They could even have taken a room at a London hotel, if Kell had not been worried that Amelia would misread his intentions. In the end, she suggested an office in Bayswater to which SIS kept a set of keys.

'It's just behind the Whiteleys shopping centre,' she said. 'We use it from time to time. Nobody in the building after six o'clock except the odd cleaner. Will that do?'

'That will do.'

She arrived on foot and on time, wearing her habitual Office uniform: a skirt with matching jacket, a cream blouse, black shoes and a simple gold necklace. Kell had come straight from Paddington and was standing outside the building on Redan Place, his suitcase and shoulder bag set down on the steps behind him.

'Going somewhere?' Amelia asked, kissing him on both cheeks.

'Just got back,' he said.

47

The office was on the fourth floor. An alarm triggered as Amelia stepped inside; she knew the passcode and tapped it in. Kell followed her as she flicked a bank of lights, strobing rows of computers on desks in an open-plan office that stretched back to what looked like a kitchen. There were magazines and brochures on the desks, headsets and mugs of half-finished tea and coffee. Along the right-hand wall, rows of dresses wrapped in plastic were jammed on hangers like outfits in the backstage chaos of a fashion show.

'What is this place?' Kell asked.

'Mail-order catalogue.' Amelia walked to the far end of the room and immediately settled into a low red sofa near the kitchen. Kell closed the door behind him, put his bags on the ground and followed her.

'So,' she said, as he peered into the kitchen. 'What happened to your face?'

'Got into a fight. Mugged.'

'Christ. Where?'

'Marseille.'

Amelia tripped on the coincidence, a split-second reaction fleeting across her face like scudding clouds. She disguised her concern by saying simply: 'Poor you' and then waited for Kell to elaborate. There was nowhere for him to sit, nowhere to make himself comfortable. He paced back and forth, wondering how to begin. Amelia always had this effect on him; he felt jumpy and somehow incomplete in her presence, a generation younger.

'There isn't anything straightforward about what I'm going to tell you,' he said.

'There never is.'

'Please.' Kell found that he was anxious enough to ask Amelia not to interrupt. 'I'm just going to tell you what I know. The facts.'

'About the mugging?'

He shook his head. She had kicked off her shoes and was stretching the fabric of her tights with painted toes. He found himself staring at them.

'When you have had time to absorb everything, I hope you'll come to understand that I am on your side, that I am doing this to protect you.'

'Oh for God's sake, Tom, spit it out.'

He looked at her and remembered how happy she had seemed at the pool, so attentive towards François, so relaxed and unguarded. He wished he wasn't about to take it all away.

'Your trip to France raised some alarm bells.'

'I'm sorry?'

'Please.' Kell lifted a hand to indicate that he would explain everything, but in his own time. 'Simon and George got nervous. They couldn't work out why you had taken off at such short notice. So they had you watched in Nice.'

'How do you know this?'

He marvelled at the nonchalance of the question, as though Amelia was merely enquiring after a point of detail. In all probability she was already several stages ahead of him, seeing the problem in seven dimensions, anticipating everything that Kell was about to say and calculating its implications.

'Because when you disappeared, Jimmy Marquand hired me to come and look for you.'

Kell watched Amelia's face. 'I see.'

'Look.' He had sat at the edge of a large table, but stood again now and paced towards the sofa. 'Long story short, I got the keys to your hire car from the safe in your room at the Gillespie . . .'

'Jesus.' That caught her out. Amelia stared at the floor. Kell found himself saying: 'I'm sorry' and felt a fool for doing so.

'I got hold of your BlackBerry, traced some calls . . .'

'. . . and followed me to Tunis. Yes, I understand.' There was now a degree of hostility in her voice.

'The man you were with in Tunis,' he said, not wishing to prolong Amelia's suffering, 'he is not who you think he is.'

She looked up. It was as though he had stepped on her soul. 'And who do I think he is, Tom?'

'He is not your son.'

Four years earlier, Kell had sat with Amelia Levene in a control room in Helmand province when news came in that two SIS officers and five of their American colleagues had been killed by a suicide bomber in Najaf. One man in the room, still a senior figure in SIS, had broken down in tears. Kell himself had accompanied his opposite number in the CIA outside and comforted her for fifteen minutes in a passageway that buzzed with oblivious Marines. Only Amelia had remained unaffected. This was the price of war, she would later explain. Almost alone among her colleagues, she had been full-square behind the invasion of Iraq and incensed by the *bien-pensant* Left, on both sides of the Atlantic, who had seemed happy to leave Iraq in the hands of a genocidal maniac. Amelia was a realist. She didn't live in a black-and-white world of simple rights and obvious wrongs. She knew that bad things happened to good people and that all you could do was stick to your principles.

So it did not surprise Kell when she looked at him with an almost stubborn indifference and said: 'Is that so?'

He knew how she worked. She would do anything to maintain her dignity in front of him.

'I tracked down his closest friend in Paris,' Kell said. 'A man named Christophe Delestre. There were two funerals. Philippe and Jeannine Malot were cremated on July twenty-second at Père-Lachaise. That service has now been wiped from the public record, almost certainly by elements in the DGSE. You attended a similarly intimate funeral on July twenty-sixth at a crematorium in the Fourteenth. Is that correct?'

Amelia nodded.

'Did this man make the eulogy?'

He passed a photograph of Delestre to Amelia, taken on his mobile phone in Montmartre. She looked at the screen.

'This is Delestre?'

'Yes.'

'I've never seen him before. There was no eulogy. Just a Bible reading, some . . .' Her voice trailed off as she realized what had happened. 'The funeral was a set-up.'

Kell nodded. He did not like to see Amelia suffering, but had no choice but to press on. 'At the end of my meeting with Delestre and his wife, I showed them a photograph of François lying beside the pool at the Valencia Carthage. They didn't recognize him. He said the two men were similar in build, in colouring, but that was all. He had never seen this man before in his life.'

Amelia stood up from the sofa, like a physical rejection of what Kell was telling her. She went into the kitchen and poured herself some water. She came back holding two plastic cups, one of which she handed to Kell. It did not seem as though she was ready to speak, so Kell assembled the final points of his theory and put them as delicately as he could.

'It seems likely that Paris found out about your son at some point in the last few years, arranged for Philippe and Jeannine to be murdered, then put you alongside an agent whom you assumed, because you had no reason to doubt him, was François.'

Amelia took a sip of the water. There was an obvious question and it was as though she could not bear to ask it.

'What about François?' she said. 'What about my son?'

Kell wanted to come forward and to hold her. All through their long association he had been careful never to allow his affection for Amelia to cloud their professional relationship. He needed all of that discipline now. 'Nobody knows what's happened to him. Delestre has received emails and text messages which indicate that François may still be alive. There's a strong chance that he's being held captive by the DGSE, possibly at a safe house in the Languedoc . . .'

Suddenly, from the opposite end of the office, came the

ping of a lift and the distant sound of doors sliding open. Kell looked up as a middle-aged South American man emerged on to the landing, trailing a vacuum cleaner. Walking towards him across the open-plan office, Kell saw that the man had a set of keys in his hand and was preparing to unlock the door.

'What do you want?' he shouted.

'It's just the cleaner,' Amelia muttered.

Through the glass, the man lazily waved a hand and indicated that he would return when the office was empty. Kell walked back to the sofa.

'Held captive?' Amelia asked. Kell could see how hard she was working to mask her despair.

'It makes the most sense,' he replied, but found that he could not elaborate. His mind was momentarily blank. He had no clue as to François' whereabouts, save for the fact that the man impersonating him had been dropped off by a Marseille cab driver near a village south of Castelnaudary. Amelia pulled on her shoes, covering her painted toes.

'It's certainly an interesting theory,' she said. Kell still did not know what to say or do. Bending forward, Amelia flicked a speck of dust from her tights. 'But it rather begs a question, don't you think?'

'Several,' Kell replied, and wondered if she was preparing to leave.

'Such as *why*?'

'Why you?' he said. 'Or why kidnap François?'

Amelia produced a look of quick contempt. 'No, not that.' Kell felt momentarily insulted. 'I mean, why stage such an operation? Why murder two innocent civilians? God knows the *Service Action* has carried out quiet assassinations on foreign soil, but what did Philippe and Jeannine ever do to anyone? Why would the DGSE take another risk on the scale of *Rainbow Warrior*? To *humiliate* me?'

'You ever hear of a DGSE officer using the legend Benedict Voltaire?' Kell asked.

Amelia shook her head.

'Tall, mid-fifties, smokes filterless cigarettes. A lot of them. Sarcastic, a bit macho.'

'You could be describing every middle-aged Frenchman I've ever met.'

Kell was too tense to laugh. 'Dyed black hair,' he said. 'His real name may be Luc.'

Amelia flinched. '*Luc*?'

Kell moved a step towards her. 'You think you might know him?'

But Amelia seemed to back away from the coincidence, suspicious of any probable link. 'Must be a hundred Lucs in the Service. In the run-up to Iraq, I became entangled with a man who roughly fits that description, but we shouldn't jump to conclusions.'

'Entangled how?' Kell couldn't tell whether she was implying a romantic or professional relationship. Amelia quickly provided an answer.

'You remember in '02 and '03, the Office ran a fairly aggressive attack on the French team at the UN after Chirac turned his back on Blair and Bush.' Kell had suspected that such an operation had been put in place, but its secrecy had prevented it from ever being confirmed in his hearing. 'At the same time, I recruited a source at the Élysée Palace.'

'You personally?'

'Me personally. Known to us as DENEUVE.'

Kell was impressed, but not surprised. It was the sort of coup with which Amelia Levene had made her name.

'And Luc found out about it? That's the nature of the entanglement?'

Amelia stood up and began to walk towards the southern wall of the office, like a customer in a shop testing a new pair of shoes. Several seconds passed before she answered Kell's question.

'There was always a suspicion that DENEUVE was unreliable, but we were up against it in terms of time and needed whatever information we could get from Chirac's people. When the invasion began, the relationship with DENEUVE quickly came to an end. We noticed that, within a few weeks, she had lost her job. If Luc is Luc Javeau, he was the DGSE officer in Paris tasked with covering up the DENEUVE leak. We think she named me as her SIS case officer in order to save her skin. Javeau actually called me up in person and warned me off any further French targets.'

'That must have been an interesting conversation.'

'Let's just say that it didn't end well. I denied all knowledge, of course, but as far as Javeau was concerned, it was now "open season" on London.'

Kell moved closer towards her, shutting down the space. 'So you think there may be a possibility of payback in all this?'

Amelia was too smart, and too experienced, to pin the Malot operation on mere vengeance, without a greater burden of proof.

'What else have you got?' she asked.

'Africa,' Kell suggested.

'*Africa*?'

It was a thesis that Kell had been turning over in his mind since Paris. 'Arab Spring. The French know that Amelia Levene has prioritized greater British involvement in the region. They know that you have the ear of the PM. Either they were seeking to blackmail you, to get you to ease off Libya and Egypt, or they were simply going to expose you when François was subjected to vetting. Paris sees the Maghreb as their patch. They've already lost significant control of Francophone West Africa to the Chinese. The last thing they want is a new Chief of the SIS trying to roll back that influence still further.'

Amelia looked across the office at a shuttered window on the Queensway side. 'So they get rid of me, George Truscott takes over, and the Moscow Men go back to a pre-9/11 mindset?'

'Precisely.' Kell was warming to his theme. 'No movement on Libya, Egypt, Algeria when it falls. No meaningful strategy for China or India. Two officers and a dog in Brazil. Just keep kissing Washington's arse and preserve the Cold War status quo. It's no coincidence that the operation began as soon as you were appointed Chief. The DGSE may have known about François for years but only chose to act now. That tells us something. It tells us that they knew François' existence, if taken advantage of effectively, had the potential to compromise you. Expose him and it could end your career.'

'My career is already over, Tom.'

It was an uncharacteristically defeatist line.

'Not necessarily.' One of the strip-lights above Kell's head began to flicker. He reached up and twisted the tube until it cut out. 'Nobody knows about this. Nobody but me.'

Amelia looked at him sharply. 'You haven't told Marquand?'

'He thinks you were in Tunis on a dirty weekend. He thinks you and François are fucking. They *all* do. Just another one of Amelia's extra-marital affairs.'

Amelia winced and Kell saw that he had gone too far. Male hypocrisy writ large. Amelia took a sip of water, forgiving him with a glance, and Kell moved the subject on.

'We have options,' he said, because it had occurred to him, not for the first time, that he was saving her career as well as salvaging his own.

Amelia met his gaze. 'Enlighten me.'

Kell arranged his pieces on the board. 'We go after the DGSE,' he said. 'We go after the man who is masquerading as Malot. Let's call him what he is: CUCKOO. A cuckoo in the nest.' Kell drained his cup of water and set it on the table. 'You invite him to stay with you in Chalke Bissett this weekend, a little mother-and-son bonding time. We get a team together, we soak his phones, his laptop, we find out who's behind the operation. He eventually leads us to where they're holding your son.'

'You truly believe that François is still alive?' she asked.

'Of course. Think about it. They've known all along that they have an insurance plan. Even in the worst-case scenario, even if the operation gets blown, they still have François in captivity. Why would they kill someone who is so valuable to them?'

48

He was not afraid of dying, but he was afraid of Slimane Nassah.

He could stand the waiting, he could stand the loss of his privacy, but François feared Slimane because he was the only one among them who was completely unpredictable.

The tone had been set almost immediately, as soon as they had driven him down from Paris. Luc and Valerie keeping their distance, never looking him in the eye; Akim playing good cop with his soft, innocent eyes – and Slimane taking every opportunity that came his way to crawl under François' skin, to probe for weaknesses, to taunt him with threats and insults. It was worst when the house was deserted. On only the third day, Akim had gone for provisions, Luc and Valerie for a walk in the garden. Slimane had come into the cell, closed the door, indicated to François not to make a sound – then grabbed at his nose, blocking the air so that he was forced to open his mouth to breathe. Next thing François knew there was some kind of cloth or handkerchief stuffed into his mouth, a taste of petrol on his tongue; he thought that Slimane was going to light it and burn his face away. Then he had bound his hands and feet and François had started to struggle. He'd stood up off the bed and shuffled around the cell, falling over on the cold ground. Slimane had opened the door of the cell, walked outside and come back with a knife, the blade heated on the gas stove in the kitchen. He was smiling as he picked François up and sat him upright on the bed. Then he had drawn circles around his eyes with the black steel, the heat on the tip of the blade opening up a cut above François' left eye so that tears slipped down past his cheek and Slimane began to laugh, taunting him for crying 'like a woman'. A few moments later, the gag had been removed from his mouth, his hands and legs untied, and Slimane had gone next door, securing the bolt and putting some Arabic rap on the iPod in the sitting room, a smell of marijuana drifting into the cell.

François had always thought of himself as a brave person, difficult to unsettle, self-sufficient. At fourteen, his parents had told him that he had been adopted, that he was the son of an English mother who had not been able to care for him. So François had grown up with the idea that he was somehow uncherished and temporary; no matter how much Philippe and Jeannine adored him – and they had been wonderful parents – they could never have loved him in the same way as his natural mother. This had bred in François a certain stubbornness allied to a profound distrust of people. Terrified of being hurt and abandoned, he had always kept his friends and colleagues – with only one or two exceptions – emotionally at arm's length. He was an honest man, and liked for this by those who knew him, and, for the most part, his choice of a solitary life had suited him well. François had made sure to move around, from job to job and from place to place, so that he was not obliged to put roots down, nor to forge links with people for any length of time. What he hated most in his captivity was that Slimane understood a lot of this almost instinctively. François came to dread not the loneliness or the fear of his imprisonment, but the knowledge that Slimane could, at any moment, humiliate him for the accident of his birth.

'Think about it,' he had whispered to him one night through the door of the cell. 'Your own mother hated you so much that she was prepared to give you up, to abandon you. You ever think about that, about how ugly you must have been? A real cunt to do that to her son, too, don't you reckon?' It was perhaps three or four o'clock in the morning, the house asleep, not even the click of the cicadas outside to break the silence. François, lying on the bed, had wrapped the pillow around his ears but could still hear every word of what Slimane was saying. 'I've seen a picture of your mother,' he whispered. 'Good-looking woman. I'd like to fuck her. Akim wants to fuck her too. Maybe we'll both do it after we kill you. What do you think? You like that idea? We'll both fuck her in the ass for what she did to you when you were just a little kid.'

That was perhaps the worst night, the one that François always remembered. But Slimane's constant taunts were debilitating to his spirit. Whenever he brought food, for example, whenever he emptied the bucket, whenever he thought Akim was getting too close or too friendly to 'the little boy', Slimane would make a remark, put the gun in François' groin, come up behind him and rip at the hairs on the nape of his neck or slap him hard around the head. François wondered if a braver man would have fought back or tried harder to escape. It made sense to try to run. If they had killed Philippe and Jeannine, they were surely going to kill him.

Often, at night, when he was on shift, Slimane would wake François as a kind of sleep deprivation for kicks, a way of passing the time through the boredom of a night-watch. So François would sleep during the days, resting on his bed listening to the frogs and birds in the garden, dreaming of Paris, of his parents brought back to life and protecting him from what had happened. Then, in time, he began to dream of his real mother, of Amelia Levene, but had no picture of her in his mind's eye, nor of the man who was his father. Did he look like either of them? Perhaps François was now too old for any family resemblance to have lasted. He had never wanted to find them, not since Philippe and Jeannine had given him the news of his adoption, but towards the third week of his captivity François began to pray that he would be rescued by them, that his real parents would somehow pay the ransom and return him to his life in Paris. At times, François would sob like a child for the mother he had never seen, for the father he had never known, but not so that his captors would hear him or see his face, never so that Slimane could enjoy the pleasure of his distress. François at least kept that dignity. But everything was complicated by Vincent. Everything was made worse by the knowledge that another man had replaced him, stolen his life, and was already making a relationship with Amelia.

'Vincent's living in your house,' Slimane told him, day after day, night after night. 'He's wearing your clothes, he's fucking your girls. He even went on holiday with your mother. Did you know that? Luc says she *loves* him, they can't get enough of each other. He's going to go and live with her in England. How do you feel about that, François? Amelia's got the son she always wanted. So why would she ever think about cashing him in for a dumb prick like you?'

49

Amelia rang the man who was no longer her son, the man who had so humiliated her, less than an hour after meeting Kell in Queensway. She had made the call from the kitchen of the open-plan office using her private mobile. Kell, standing a few feet away, watched her intently, amazed by Amelia's ability to continue with the masquerade of maternal affection.

'François? It's Amelia. I've missed you, darling. How are you? How are things in Paris?'

They had talked for almost ten minutes, 'François' relating the story of his journey home via Marseille, the narrative of his lies still watertight, his facility for deceit as accomplished as any Amelia could recall. She wondered if the man Kell had identified as 'Luc' was seated alongside CUCKOO in Paris, listening to his conversation, just as Kell was listening to hers: two sets of spies, in London and Paris, both working under the assumption that they held the upper hand.

'What are you doing this weekend?' she asked.

'Nothing,' CUCKOO replied. 'Why?'

'It's just that I wondered if you would be free to come and stay at my house in Wiltshire?'

'Oh . . .'

'Perhaps it's too soon?'

'No, no.' CUCKOO sounded enthused, as well he might; the invitation would be welcomed by his masters in Paris. 'Will Giles be there?'

'No.' She glanced at Kell, who frowned, as though confused by CUCKOO's interest in Amelia's husband. 'I think he's away this weekend. Why, do you want to meet him?'

'At this moment I prefer if it's just the two of us, you know?' CUCKOO replied. 'Is that OK?'

'Of course, darling.' She generated a perfectly timed pause. 'Does that mean you'll come?'

'I would love to.'

'That's wonderful news. I can't wait.' Amelia recalled CUCKOO's insistence on taking the ferry to Marseille, rather than a flight direct to Paris and decided on a quick test of his cover. 'Can I send you a ticket for the plane?'

'I prefer not to fly, remember?' he replied instantly, and she could only marvel at the speed of his lies. What a fool she had been, what a dupe. And now she would have to live a lie of her own, to ensure that there was no difference between her behaviour in Tunis and her behaviour in Wiltshire. She would have to play the part of a caring mother, embracing him, smiling at his conversation, taking an interest in his affairs. Amelia dreaded that and yet she longed for the moment when she would have her revenge. From the great joy of the reunion in Tunis she had been cruelly returned to the tunnel of her working life, a place

263

of ambition, of dedication to a cause, but a place without personal fulfilment. Perhaps it was where she belonged.

'I'm starving,' she told Kell after she had hung up. She saw her hand lingering on the sleeve of his coat, one of her habitual ways of controlling men. 'Take me somewhere to eat?'

'Of course.'

They had walked a few hundred metres to a Lebanese restaurant on Westbourne Grove and set about formulating the plan to find François. Sitting over open menus, waiting for a bottle of wine in the bustle of the dining room, it was decided that, in order to keep the operation secret from Truscott, Haynes and Marquand, Kell would assemble a small team of trusted contacts off the books at Vauxhall Cross. He suggested bringing Barbara Knight over from Nice and told Amelia that he would call her in the morning to arrange the trip. Having ordered their food, he sent a text to Elsa Cassani, asking if it would be possible for her to take the next available flight to London. Elsa responded within fifteen minutes ('For you, Tom, anything!') and Kell smiled. He knew a former MI5 Tech-Ops officer named Harold Mowbray, now private sector, who would be able to work in tandem with Elsa on CUCKOO's email servers and mobile phone networks. They would also need a surveillance man to tail CUCKOO once he had left Amelia's house in the country. Kell had an old contact from his days working a desk in London, a former Royal Marine named Kevin Vigors, who would work in return for cash-in-hand.

'I'll need money,' he told Amelia. 'A lot of it. These are good people and they'll all need paying.'

'It can be arranged.' He wondered if she would lean on

Giles for the cash. 'I'll see what I can dig up on Luc Javeau, but I can't be away from the Office this week. You'll be on your own until I get down to Wiltshire on Friday. The next few days are wall-to-wall with meetings, then the PM on Wednesday. Is that all right?'

Kell nodded. 'It's fine.' It was better that she should remain out of the picture once CUCKOO had returned to Paris. If anything went wrong, Amelia needed to be deniable. 'What about our military options?' he asked.

'What about them?'

He tried to plant the idea as delicately as he could. 'If we find François, it may be necessary to go in with force. If it goes to ransom, they will almost certainly attempt to kill him, whether or not you pay.'

'I understand that.' By now, they were halfway through their meal. Amelia pushed what remained of her food to the side of her plate. Kell mistook the silence as she wiped her mouth for disquiet.

'All I'm saying is, we need to get to them before it gets to that stage. We will need to enjoy an element of surprise . . .'

'I know what you meant, Tom.' She looked across the room, a clatter of plates and glasses being cleared from a nearby table. 'We have people in France, in northern Spain, who could do a job like that. But I don't know how to get it past Simon. To use SAS would require . . . finesse.'

'Forget SAS. We'd have to go private sector.'

Amelia touched the simple gold chain around her neck, tugging at it for ideas. 'As long as they're not gung-ho. Those guys sit around for weeks on end, cleaning their bloody rifles, dreaming of the good old days at Hereford. I don't want them going in all guns blazing. I want people

265

with experience, people who know their way around France.'

'Of course.'

'I'd want you to go in with them, Tom. Can you promise me that? Keep an eye on them?'

It was an astonishing request, not least because, throughout his long career, Kell had never so much as fired a shot in anger. Nevertheless, he was in no mood to deny Amelia what she wanted.

'I promise,' he said. 'Of course, if it comes to that, I'll go with them.' He found a half-smile that seemed to reassure her. 'We will get to François,' he said. 'Whatever happens, we will bring him home.'

50

Vincent Cévennes arrived at St Pancras station at 19.28 on Friday evening, his appearance noted by an ex-Special Branch associate of Kevin Vigors named Daniel Aldrich, who sent an email via BlackBerry to Kell with photo confirmation of the target passing the statue of Sir John Betjeman on the station concourse. Amelia, reluctant to spend any more time in CUCKOO's company than was absolutely necessary, had arranged for a taxi to collect him from St Pancras and to drive him south-west to Wiltshire. Standing in a crowd of pedestrians at the edge of Euston Road, Aldrich watched as the driver held out a sheet of A4 card on which he had written 'Mr Francis Mallot' in black marker pen. CUCKOO, spotting the message, handed him his bags, which were placed in the boot of the car.

The taxi was soon pulling out into the pell-mell of Friday evening traffic. Aldrich did not attempt to follow the vehicle from London, nor had Kell's team wired it for sound; it was extremely unlikely that Vincent would risk making a telephone call to his controllers in the presence of a driver whom he would surely assume was employed by Amelia. Instead, Aldrich sent a second email to Kell.

> Confirm CUCKOO has two bags. Black leather computer shoulder holdall + black moulded plastic suitcase, wheeled. Carrying m/phone, also Hermes gift bag. Vehicle leaving StP now, 19.46, navy blue Renault Espace n/plate X164 AEO. Driver heading west along Euston Road.

Kell received the email on a laptop in the kitchen of Amelia's house and announced to the assembled team that CUCKOO would likely arrive in Chalke Bissett at around nine-thirty. Harold Mowbray, with Kell's assistance, had spent the previous twenty-four hours equipping the house, top to bottom, with surveillance cameras and voice-activated microphones. Amelia had come direct from Vauxhall Cross at lunchtime and suggested that Vincent should sleep in the larger of two spare bedrooms. On the assumption that he might ask to move to a different room, the bedroom to the left of the landing had also been fitted with cameras and microphones, the first in a gilt mirror fixed to the north wall, the second in the frame of an oil painting hanging to the left of the bed.

There were two bathrooms on the first floor of the house. The first was en suite in Amelia's bedroom, the second located between CUCKOO's room and a short, wallpapered corridor that connected it to the landing. This was the bathroom Vincent would use and it had also been rigged by Mowbray.

'My experience, people do all sorts of strange things in toilets,' he muttered, installing a miniature camera in the socket of a towel rail about six inches above the floor.

'CUCKOO comes in here, thinking he's got some privacy, he might drop his guard as well as his trousers. If he makes a call, we can catch it on the microphone. If he's got stuff in his bags, we might see him go through it. Unless your frog goes looking for this shit, he's not going to have a clue we're watching him.'

There was a risk of French surveillance on the house, so Kell remained in the property as much as possible, to avoid being recognized as Stephen Uniacke. Susie Shand, Amelia's literary-agent neighbour, had given permission for her house to be used as a base by Kell's team. Shand herself was on holiday in Croatia, a signed copy of The Official Secrets Act tucked into her suitcase. The owners of the third house in this isolated corner of Chalke Bissett, Paul and Susan Hamilton, were used to strangers from London staying at Shand's home and did not approach any member of Kell's team to enquire what they were doing in the village. In the event of a conversation in the neighbourhood, the team had been briefed to pretend that they were members of the family visiting for the long weekend.

Shand's house was a run-down cottage with low, worm-eaten beams about a minute's walk from Amelia's front door. Both houses looked out over a lush valley on the northern side and a steep hill to the south. Shand's garden backed on to the western perimeter of Amelia's property. The rooms in which the team had installed themselves were damp but comfortable and Kell found that he enjoyed the relative peace and tranquillity of the countryside after days of travel and cities. Their main operational centre was a large library lined with books given to Shand by the cream of London literary society. Barbara Knight, a lifelong bibliophile, found first editions of works by William Golding,

Iris Murdoch and Julian Barnes, as well as a signed copy of *The Satanic Verses*.

It was in this room that Elsa Cassani set up shop, placing three laptop computers on a large oak dining table and nine separate surveillance screens on bookshelves that she dusted and cleared of books. The screens showed live feeds from each of the rooms in Amelia's house; during a brief rain shower on Friday morning, the images blurred and flickered, but Kell was satisfied that they would have complete coverage of CUCKOO at all times. The only 'black hole' was a utility room in the northern corner of the house that he was unlikely to use.

Underneath the main window in the Shand library, Elsa had placed a mattress on which she slept at intermittent hours of the day beneath a duvet without a cover. She kept a bottle of Volvic beside this makeshift bed, some night creams and perfume, and an iPod that screamed and grunted whenever she plugged it into her ears. Harold was billeted upstairs in the smaller of two spare rooms. Kell was across the hall on a mattress that sagged like a hammock. Barbara, on account of her advanced years, was given the master bedroom.

'The Gillespie's not a patch on this,' she joked. She spent the majority of her time alone, sitting in the room, reading a new biography of Virginia Woolf and working through the plan for Saturday morning.

'It'll be Miss Marple all over again,' he had told her. 'Put on a show like the one in Nice and we'll put you up for a BAFTA.'

Spying is waiting.

On the Thursday evening, with Amelia still in London

and Vincent still in Paris, Harold and Barbara had driven into Salisbury to watch a film, leaving Kell and Elsa alone in the house with nothing to do but reminisce about Nice and to work through the final details of the operation.

'Amelia is going to try to persuade Vincent to go for a walk with her on Saturday morning. If the weather's bad, she'll suggest visiting a pub near Tisbury for lunch. Either way, we should have enough time to get into his room and soak his gear. There's no mobile reception in the valley, so if we're lucky, he might have switched off his phone and left it behind as well.'

'This would be *very* lucky, I think,' Elsa replied. She had three separate gold studs in her left ear and Kell kept staring at them, thinking of her other lives. 'All I need is fifteen minutes with the laptop. I can copy over everything from his hard drive, then bring it back here for analysis. If he's getting emails from his people, we can start to read them. If they are being careless, we might be able to trace where the messages are coming from.'

'What do you mean "if they're being careless"?'

'Anybody serious wouldn't email from the location where they are holding Amelia's son. They would drive a few kilometres away, do it from there. People often keep a device for that purpose away from the base. But it can be a pain working like this and sometimes people get lazy.'

Kell thought of Marseille, of his own computer stripped down by Luc and handed back, complete with key-logger software and the tracking device. He had told Elsa about the attack in Cité Radieuse and she had touched the scar on his face, a tenderness which had surprised him. In Nice, he had been concerned that Elsa was playing him, most

271

likely at Marquand's request, but there was surely now no reason to doubt her.

'You were a little dismissive with me the first time we met,' she said.

'I was working,' he replied.

'This is fine. I expected it. Jimmy told me that you could be . . . what is the word?'

'Wonderful?'

A swipe of laughter. 'No. Impatient. A little arrogant . . .'

'Brusque.'

Elsa had never heard the word before. She tried it out, rolling it around, and decided that it was adequate enough as a description of Thomas Kell. 'Brusque, yes. Then later on, much kinder to me. I liked our conversations.'

He was surprised by her flirting, but enjoyed it. She had a way of dismantling his professional veneer, of strolling into the more private rooms of his personality with what felt like the fearlessness of youth.

'You did a fantastic job,' he said, and meant it. The research Elsa had done into Malot's background had unlocked the DGSE operation and led him to Christophe Delestre.

'Let's eat,' she replied.

The day before, Harold had stocked up on ready-meals for the team at a supermarket in Salisbury. Opening the fridge at lunchtime, looking for something to eat, Elsa had dismissed the food as 'disgraceful' and duly set about making a batch of fresh pasta in the kitchen. Within half an hour, she had transformed the room into a bombsite of bowls and dough, flour hanging in the air like the dawn mists over the Chalke Valley. Now she cooked the pasta for Kell, who opened a bottle of wine from Shand's cellar and sat at the kitchen table, watching as she chopped courgettes, frying them in garlic and olive oil.

'You look like you know what you're doing.'

'I am Italian,' she replied, happy to bask in the stereo-type. 'But in return for your supper, I want to hear all of Thomas Kell's secrets.'

'All of them?'

'All of them.'

'That may take a long time.'

He did not want to talk about his marriage; that was his only boundary. Not out of loyalty to Claire, but because the story of their relationship was a story of failure.

'Start with why you left the Service.'

He had been drinking wine and stopped the glass against his lips, surprised that Elsa had broached the subject of his disgrace.

'How did you know about that?'

He was not angry; indeed, he felt an odd sense of relief, finding that he wanted to speak candidly of what had happened.

'People talk,' she replied.

'It's a complicated situation. I'm not supposed to discuss it.'

Elsa had put a pan on to boil. She looked at him with a quick, mock contempt and threw salt into the water.

'Nobody is going to hear us, Tom. We are alone in the house. Tell me.'

And so he told her. He told her about Kabul and he told her about Yassin.

'After 9/11, I did a lot of work alongside the Americans. They were angry about what had been done to them. Understandably so. They were ashamed and they wanted revenge. I think that's a fair assessment of their state of mind.'

'Go on.'

'Late 2001, I went into Afghanistan with a team from the Office. Joint operation with Langley. All of us had been caught off guard by what had happened in Washington and New York. We were playing catch-up, making things up as we went along.'

'Sure.' Elsa was watching the pan, her back to him, waiting for him to find his rhythm. She was wearing blue denim jeans and a white T-shirt. Kell stole a married man's glance at her body, all the time falling into the trap of trusting her.

'I made seven separate visits to Pakistan and Afghanistan over the next three years. In '04, the CIA arrested a man who you may have heard of. Yassin Gharani. He'd been in Pakistan where he'd attended an al-Qaeda training camp in the north-west. He told the Yanks he was a British citizen, had the passport to prove it. He'd subsequently been moved to their operations centre in Kabul, which is where they started to interrogate him.'

'Interrogate.'

'Interview. Question. Cross-examine.' Kell wasn't sure whether he was giving Elsa an English lesson or whether she was one step ahead of him on the semantics. 'He had not been mistreated, if that's what you're driving at. Langley was informed by MI5 that they had a file on Yassin. He'd been on a watch-list of terrorist suspects in the north-east of England. Not a flagged threat, not a target, no surveillance. But they knew about him, had been worried about him, they'd wondered where he'd gone.'

'So it makes sense to everybody that a young man like this goes to Pakistan and trains to fight?'

'It makes sense.' Kell poured himself more wine and stood to refill Elsa's glass. She had fried the courgettes and set them to one side in the pan and now slowly lowered the pasta into the water.

'Thank you,' she said, nodding at the glass. 'The tagliatelle, it takes only a couple of minutes.'

Kell took two bowls from a dresser beside the kitchen door, retrieved spoons and forks from a drawer. He put the cutlery on the table in front of him, the bowls next to the stove so that Elsa could reach them. Then he picked up the story.

'Now here's Gharani, a twenty-one-year-old student from Leeds, pretending to be visiting friends in Lahore, but the Americans have photographic evidence that Yassin is a jihad tourist who just got taught how to fire a rocket-propelled grenade in Malakand. I told him he had to be careful. I told him that his best prospect lay in talking to his own government. If he was honest about what he had done, about the people he knew back home, then I could help him. If he wasn't, if he decided to keep quiet and keep playing the innocent, then I couldn't be responsible for what the Americans would do with him.'

'I know this story,' Elsa said. She tested the pasta, pulling a single strand from the water and pressing it between her fingers. She wrapped a tea towel around the handle of the pan, took it to the sink and poured the contents into a metal colander, steam fogging into her face. She reared back and said: 'The CIA tortured him, yes?'

Kell felt a quick burst of irritation at her easy assumption of American guilt. He wondered if Elsa had worked on the case in some capacity or had merely read about it in the European press.

'Let's just say that the Yanks were tough on him,' he said. 'We all were.'

'What does that mean?'

Kell shifted in his seat, choosing his words carefully.

'It means that we were a long way from home. It means that we were trying to break up terrorist cells in the UK and US. We felt that Yassin knew things that would be useful to us and we ran out of patience with him when he wouldn't talk.' Kell found himself coughing. 'Eventually certain individuals became aggressive.' He composed himself, still protecting the identities of American colleagues who had stepped over the line. 'Did I physically touch him? No. Did I push him around? No, absolutely not. Did I threaten to get to his family in Leeds? At no point.'

Elsa did not visibly react. Her face was still as she said:

'So the interview was as they described it?' It was as though she had stopped herself using the word 'torture', like somebody stepping around a puddle. 'What happened, Tom?'

Kell looked up. She was no longer serving the food, as if the meal was being held in quarantine. She was not judging him. Not yet. But she wanted to hear his answer.

'You're asking a man you're about to sit down and eat supper with if he water-boarded a suspect? If I pulled out a man's fingernails?'

'Did you?'

Kell felt all of the despair of his final weeks at Vauxhall Cross rushing up to confront him.

'Do you think I would be capable of that?'

'I think we are all of us capable of doing anything.'

Yet the tone of Elsa's reply implied that she trusted Kell to have behaved within the law and within the boundaries

276

of his own decency. He felt a great affection for her at this moment, because such an accommodation was more than Claire had ever been able to provide for him. At times in the preceding months, turned out of SIS in quiet disgrace, he had felt like a criminal; at others, like the only man in England capable of understanding the true nature of the threat from men like Yassin Gharani.

'I did not torture him,' he said. 'SIS does not torture people. Officers from both services do not break the codes of conduct with which they are issued whenever they go into . . .'

'You sound like a lawyer.' Elsa opened a window, an airlock being cleared. 'So what's the problem?'

'The problem is the relationship with the Americans, the problem is the press and the problem is the law. Somewhere between those three points you have spies trying to do their job with one hand tied behind their backs. The media in London took the line that Yassin was a British national, innocent until proven guilty, who was tortured by Bush and Cheney, then flown to Guantanamo and stripped of his dignity. Habeas corpus. They charged that MI6 turned a blind eye to what went on.'

'What's your view on that? Did you ask where they were taking Yassin? Were you concerned about his condition?'

Kell felt the flutter of guilt, the shame of his own moral neglect, yet the certainty that he would not now act differently. 'No. And no.'

Elsa looked up and met his eyes. Kell remembered the cell in Kabul. He remembered the stink and the sweat of the room, the wretchedness on Yassin's face, his own lust for information and his contempt for everything that Yassin stood for. Kell's zeal had obscured even the slight possibility that the young man in front of him, starved of sleep and care, was anything other than a brainwashed jihadi.

'What I did, what several intelligence officers did, what was wrong in the eyes of the law and in the eyes of the press, was to allow others to behave in a way that was not in keeping with our own values. They found words for what we were accused of doing. "Passive rendition"; "Outsourced torture". This has always been the British way, they said, since imperial times. Get others to do your dirty work for you.' Elsa placed two pieces of kitchen roll on the table as napkins. 'Yassin was taken away.' Kell gathered his thoughts as he drank a mouthful of wine. 'The truth is – yes – I didn't really care what happened to him. I didn't think about what methods the Egyptians would use, what might go on in Cairo or Guantanamo. As far as I was concerned, here was a young British man whose sole purpose in life was to murder innocent civilians – in Washington, in Rome, in *Chalke Bissett*. I thought he was a coward and a fool, and the truth is I was glad to see him in custody. That was my sin. I forgot to care for a man who wanted to destroy everything that it was my job to protect.'

Elsa poured olive oil on to the pasta and stirred the courgettes and garlic into the long broad strands of tagliatelle. Kell could not interpret her mood nor sense where her opinion lay.

'So you're the fall guy?' she asked and he knew that he must be careful not to moan or complain. The last thing he wanted was for this lovely girl to feel pity for him.

'Somebody had to be,' he said, and remembered how Truscott had cut him loose: authorizing an SIS presence at the Yassin interrogation from a desk in London thousands of miles away; then brazenly accusing Kell of acting beyond the law when, years later, it looked as though the Foreign Secretary was going to get cooked by the *Guardian* over rendition. Kell had been thrown on the mercy of the courts, given a suitably anonymous, Orwellian codename – 'Witness X' – and pitched out of the Service.

'I'll tell you this,' he said, 'and then I'll stop talking. We are in a political and intelligence relationship with the Americans that goes deeper than anybody realizes and deeper than anyone is prepared to admit. If British spies see their American allies engaged in methods with which they disagree, what are they meant to do? Ring up Mummy and say they disapprove? Tell their line managers that they want to come home because they don't feel comfortable about things? This is a *war* we are fighting. The Americans are our friends, whatever you thought of Bush and his chums, whatever your feelings on Guantanamo or Abu Ghraib.'

'I understand that . . .'

'And too many people on the Left were interested solely in demonstrating their own good taste, their own unimpeachable moral conduct, at the expense of the very people who were striving to keep them safe in their beds.'

'Have some food,' Elsa said. She rested her hand on Kell's neck as she set the bowl in front of him, the softness of her touch a gesture of a friend's understanding as much as it was an indication of her desire for him.

'The kindest thing you can say about Yassin is that he was young.' Kell suddenly didn't feel like eating. He would have pushed the bowl to one side if it had not seemed rude or petulant to do so. 'The kindest thing you can say is that he didn't know any better. But try telling that to the fiancée of the doctor he would have blown up on the Tube, the grandson of the old man obliterated on the top deck of a bombed-out bus in Glasgow. Try telling that to the mother of the six-month-old baby boy who would have died of his injuries if Yassin had blown himself up in a Midlands shopping centre. Looking back at the evidence, they might have pointed out that a man like Yassin Gharani, with that back story, wasn't likely to be in Pakistan retracing the steps of Robert Byron. He was getting high on hate. And because of what happened to him, because we allowed ourselves to hate him in return, Yassin was given a cheque by Her Majesty's government for eight hundred and seventy-five thousand pounds.' Elsa sat down. 'Almost a million quid, in our age of austerity. Compensation for "ill treatment". Now that's a lot of taxpayer money for an individual who would, in all likelihood, happily have blown up the very High Court that found in his favour.'

'Eat,' Elsa said.

And for a long time neither of them said anything.

51

Seated at an outdoor table at the Coach and Horses, a well-regarded pub on the Salisbury road at the eastern edge of Chalke Bissett, Kevin Vigors looked up from his second pint of Old Speckled Hen to see a navy-blue Renault Espace, number plate X164 AEO, coming around the corner. He stood up from the table, crossed the road to a telephone box and rang Amelia's landline.

'285?'

'CUCKOO just turned into the village. Should be with you in three minutes.'

'Thank you,' Amelia said.

She replaced the receiver and looked at Kell, who was standing beside the Aga.

'That was Kevin,' she said. 'Time for you to be going. He'll be here in two minutes.'

Kell wished her good luck and walked to the back door, leaving the garden via the gate that connected Amelia's house to the Shand property. Within moments he was standing with Elsa, Harold and Barbara Knight in the library, staring at the banks of surveillance screens, like traders anticipating a crash.

'We should see him any second now,' Kell said, taking off his coat and throwing it on a chair. Elsa looked up and caught his eye, smiling a private smile.

'Here he comes,' she said, returning her gaze to the screen in the upper left-hand corner.

A camera, high on a pylon with clear sight of the dark lane ahead, had picked out the approaching taxi. The twin headlights bumped along the road until the vehicle came to a halt. Kell watched as CUCKOO opened the rear door and stepped out on to the road, stretching his back after the long journey. He was wearing the same black leather jacket that Kell had searched in the hotel room in Tunis.

'Wanker,' Harold muttered, and everybody tried not to laugh.

Right on cue, entering the frame in the lower left-hand corner, came Amelia, her head and body in silhouette against the glare of the headlights. Though the reunion was taking place less than a hundred metres away on the lane, the team could hear no sound as she stretched out her arms and enveloped CUCKOO in a mother's bone-crushing hug.

'God, I hope she is all right,' Elsa said, but Kell ignored the sentiment, because he knew that Amelia Levene would be just fine.

52

She buried her hate, tamped it down, hid it somewhere inside herself where it couldn't get out.

She'd always been good at that. Compartmentalizing. Adjusting. Surviving. Ever since Tunis.

When she saw CUCKOO climb out of the cab, for a split second Amelia experienced the same untrammelled joy she had felt in Paris at seeing her beautiful son for the first time. Then it passed and the man she had known as François was an affront to her, a malign presence in her home. Yet she showed none of this with her eyes. Instead she reached out to hug him and found that she could easily say her lines.

'Darling! You made it! I can't believe you're here.'

Even the smell of him was a betrayal, the aftershave he had worn at the hotels, his oils beside the pool. At times Amelia had felt an almost sexual desire to hold this man, to touch his skin, the sweet ache of a mother's love for her child. She had thought of him as so handsome and sophisticated; she had marvelled at the job Philippe and

Jeannine had done in raising such an interesting young man. And now this. An agent of French Intelligence in her own home, seeping into every crevice of her privacy and self-esteem. The days since Kell had broken the news to her in London had been, without question, the most wretched of her adult life; worse than the months following François' adoption; worse than the death of her brother. She had only two consolations: the knowledge that she was a better liar than Luc Javeau, the snake Paris had sent to deceive her; and the real possibility that François was alive and that Kell could get to him in his captivity.

'Come inside and unpack,' she said, the taxi driver heading further down the narrow lane in order to find space outside the Shand house in which to turn around and set off on the long journey back to London. 'We have the whole weekend ahead of us. Nothing in the world to worry about. What will you have to drink?'

At first, Kell did not recognize the voice; it was almost as though he had been speaking to a different man in the ferry disco. But then the cadences, the slick phrasing, the bizarre self-confidence of the CUCKOO personality came back to him, and he realized that he was listening to a master liar, a man who had all but absorbed another personality and embodied that which he had been instructed to impersonate. It was one of the quiet, shaming secrets of their secret trade; how quickly the spy *wanted* to set his own character aside and to inhabit a separate self. Why was that? Kell had no answer to it. He remembered how much his dissembling, the layers of his persona, had distressed Claire. He thought of her in America, far away among vineyards and Californians, and had to force off a surge of jealousy.

Elsa was beside him at the table, staring at the live feed from Amelia's sitting room, listening to CUCKOO's conversation through the speakers that Harold had set up in the library.

'Who's hungry?' Harold asked, standing in the doorway holding a stack of ready-made pizzas.

'This is not pizza,' Elsa replied, looking at the boxes and making a clicking noise with her tongue. 'This food is a disgrace. Wherever you get this, Harold, the supermarket should be closed down.'

'Hang on a minute . . .'

One of the screens had caught Kell's eye. Two white lights were flickering along the lane in what might have been a replay of the final stages of CUCKOO's journey.

'Who the fuck is that?' Kell said. The car was moving steadily towards them, about thirty seconds from the parking area above Amelia's garden. 'Get Kevin on the phone.'

'No reception,' Harold said.

'He's got a radio, hasn't he?' Kell felt his temper rising, the threat of the operation going wrong almost before it had begun. 'Elsa, check the radio.'

She scraped away from the table, found the radio in the kitchen, came back into the room.

'Switched off,' she said.

Kell couldn't believe what he was hearing. He swore at Harold, because the link to Vigors had been a Tech-Ops responsibility. Harold was still holding the pizzas, like a delivery man waiting for a tip. 'Put the fucking food down, Harold. Find out who this is.'

He pointed at the screen, the car now moving past Amelia's house, beyond the scope of CCTV. Kell could hear the low growl of the engine as it approached.

'It could just be people coming to supper next door,' Barbara suggested. 'Might even be the taxi. CUCKOO may have left something in the cab.'

'It could be anybody,' Kell replied, and ran outside.

53

He was just in time to find a burgundy Mercedes turning around in the lane. He closed the gate to the Shand house and stood in the road, holding a hand up to catch the driver's eye. Kell knew who it was. He recognized the hunched figure at the wheel, the Blair-era sticker in the rear windscreen: 'Keep Your Bullshit in Westminster'. The Mercedes came to a halt, mid-turn, and Kell heard the noise of an electric window sliding down.

'Yes?' came a voice. 'Can I help you?'

He walked around to the driver's window and leaned in.

'Giles. Fancy seeing you here.'

Giles Levene was not a man noted for his ebullient personality, nor for a particularly wide range of facial expression. He greeted Kell with the same bland inconsequence that he might have reserved for an electrician who had come to read the meter.

'It's Tom, isn't it?'

'It is. Any chance you could switch off the engine?'

Giles, polite and accommodating to a fault, switched it off.

'And the headlights please.'

The headlights snuffed out.

'What's going on?' he asked. If he was surprised to find Thomas Kell standing outside his house at ten o'clock on a Friday evening, he did not betray it.

'Well.' Where to begin? Kell looked up the lane towards the tree-shrouded light in CUCKOO's room. 'We're running an operation in your house. Amelia is in there . . .'

'I know Amelia is in there.' Giles was looking ahead, through the windscreen. His Mercedes was mid-way through a three-point turn, facing the Hamilton house. 'I wanted to surprise her. I was hoping we would spend the weekend together.'

Kell heard movement in a nearby tree, the clack of a bird. He could not work out what was more extraordinary: the idea that Giles still believed, after more than a decade of marriage, that Amelia would welcome a 'surprise' visit from her husband; or the fact that she had forgotten to tell Giles to stay away for the weekend.

'I'm afraid that's not going to happen,' he said.

Again, Giles did not seem unduly perturbed. 'Not going to happen,' he repeated, as though in a kind of daze. Kell felt like a policeman redirecting traffic away from the scene of an accident.

'Is there any chance you could go back to London tonight; turn around and head for home?' he suggested.

'Why? What's going on in there?'

Kell feared a long, drawn-out conversation. It was an unseasonably mild night and he was wearing only a short-sleeved shirt. He was reluctant to invite Giles into the comfort of the Shand house, not least because all those computers, all those TV screens, might prove too much for him.

'Is this about her son?' Giles asked. He made a minute adjustment to his rear-view mirror, as though something might be coming up behind the car. 'Has she got François in there?'

Kell was about to say: 'In a manner of speaking' but didn't want to overplay his hand. He knew that Amelia had told Giles about Tunis, about Jean-Marc Daumal, but her husband had no idea that CUCKOO was an impostor. Knowing that Amelia's husband was a stickler for protocol, Kell retreated behind the convenient screen of the Official Secrets Act.

'Look, I'm afraid I can't say anything at this time,' he said. 'Even with your clearance level, Giles, I'd be hauled over the coals if . . .'

He was interrupted by a sudden animation in Giles's face. He was frowning like a bad actor as he said: 'Weren't you booted out?'

Kell felt a muscle twist in the base of his spine and stepped back from the car, standing up to free it. 'Brought back in from the cold,' he replied. He placed his hands on the roof of the car, which was already damp with dew. 'Look. If it's too far to drive, the Office can put you up in a hotel in Salisbury. I'm profoundly sorry. I can see that this is very inconvenient. Amelia should have let you know . . .'

A characteristic stillness returned to Giles's features, the emotional reticence of a stalled and defeated man. 'Yes,' he replied quietly, still staring out of the windscreen. 'Perhaps she should have.'

There was a silence to which Kell contributed only the scuffing of his feet on the damp ground and a quick tap-tap of his hands on the roof. He knew why Amelia had married Giles Levene – for his money, for his loyalty, for his relative lack of ambition, which would never be allowed to impede her own – but in this moment he felt that Giles had made a wretched choice in accommodating Amelia's many faults. He would have been better off alone, as the dysfunctional bachelor he seemed so closely to resemble, or with a younger wife, who might at least have been able to provide him with children. Kell's heart went out to Giles, but he wanted nothing more than for him to switch on the engine and to head back up the lane to the village. As if in answer to his prayers, Amelia's husband conceded defeat and turned the key in the ignition.

'It seems I have no choice,' he said. 'If you see Amelia, will you tell her I was here?'

'Of course I will,' Kell replied, and felt a strange and disconcerting kinship with his fellow cuckold. 'Best if you avoid talking to her on the phone or by email this weekend.' It was like seeing off a friend whom he had betrayed. Giles nodded, as though absorbing yet another disappointment in a long ritual of humiliations. 'I'm sure Amelia will explain everything on Monday.'

'Yes,' he said. 'I'm sure she will.'

54

'Who was it?' Barbara asked when Kell came back into the house.

'Amelia's husband,' he replied, taking a bottle of Heineken from the fridge and popping the cap. 'He's gone back to London. Any change over there?'

Kell nodded in the direction of Amelia's house and a chastened Harold immediately set about making amends for his earlier mistake.

'CUCKOO's gone upstairs,' he said. 'Unpacking in his room. Amelia suggested he take a shower before dinner but so far all he's done is admire himself in the mirror and smelled the sheets to see if they're clean.'

'Have we still got decent visuals?' Kell asked, moving behind Elsa, in her habitual seat at the table. He looked up at the three screens feeding video surveillance of CUCKOO's bedroom and bathroom. In the lower right-hand corner, Amelia was taking a roast chicken out of the Aga.

'You want sound?' Harold asked.

291

'Only if he talks. Has he got a radio on in there? Any music?'

'Nothing.'

In a silent row, Kell, Elsa and Harold watched CUCKOO, near-hypnotized as he took pairs of folded underpants and balled-up socks from his suitcase, placing them in a wardrobe at the edge of the screen. He hung three shirts on hangers and draped a pair of linen trousers against the back of a chair. A book came out, a framed photograph. Kell took a sip of his drink.

'Where's Kevin?' he asked. 'Did you get him on the radio?'

Harold's voice was tight with apology. 'Yes. Sorry, guv. Amateur hour. He's parked now in the lay-by but didn't get there in time to see Giles's car. Anybody else appears, he'll flag them down and radio in straight away. I'm sorry it was switched off. I was busy with the live feeds, let it slip . . .'

Kell put him out of his misery. 'Forget it.'

Again they turned their attention to the footage from the house, three faces lit up by the flickering feed. Amelia was setting a table for two in the kitchen. CUCKOO had made his way into the bathroom.

'This is where he gets his kit off,' Harold said, but the joke fell flat. Kell wondered if he had been drinking to calm his nerves.

'What's he carrying?' he asked.

In his right hand, CUCKOO was holding an open laptop, which he rested on a stool beside the bath. He then locked the door, sat on the closed toilet seat and proceeded to tap in a sequence of letters.

'Can we see that, can we see what he's typing?' Kell asked.

'It's being taped,' Harold replied. He had put a camera in the ceiling light precisely for this purpose. 'I can go back and look at it later.'

'Do that,' Kell replied, though there was an edge of doubt in his voice. Had Harold picked the best angle? It looked as though the lid was obscuring the keyboard. 'Elsa, can you read the wi-fi?'

'Bringing it up now,' she said, and he looked down to see a screen of code on her primary laptop, an analysis of the Internet activity in Amelia's house. 'Must be something he wants to hide,' she said. 'Why else would he lock himself away?'

CUCKOO spent five further minutes checking email on Wanadoo; Elsa could not be certain what he was reading or writing.

'It's encrypted,' she said. 'I need the laptop. I need to get into the guts.'

'Tomorrow,' Barbara told her, her soft, mellow voice a welcome corrective to the tension in the room.

Kell turned and smiled. He was grateful that Barbara was on the team; she had a dignity and strength of character that obliged people around her to behave as they would in the presence of a grandmother or distinguished matriarch. In a lower screen, Amelia was removing the cork from a bottle of wine.

'Hang on.'

Harold had seen something. CUCKOO had placed the laptop on the floor and was standing up. From his back pocket he took out a mobile phone and opened the casing. He then reached into the ticket pocket at the front of his jeans and removed what appeared to be a SIM card.

'Good luck with that,' Harold muttered as CUCKOO put

the SIM into the phone, closed the casing and powered it up. 'More chance of getting a signal at the bottom of a swimming pool.'

The team looked on as Vincent stared at the phone, waiting for a signal from what Kell assumed was a French network. After two minutes, he switched it off and replaced the SIM in his jeans.

Everybody was thinking the same thing. Kell turned to Barbara.

'Tomorrow,' he said, 'you need to get your hands on that.'

'Of course,' she replied. 'All part of the service.'

55

Kell set an alarm for five o'clock and was downstairs before sunrise. He found Elsa awake in the library wearing a T-shirt and a pair of sleeping shorts, watching the live infra-red feed from the darkened rooms of Amelia's house. She turned as he walked in and seemed startled to see him.

'Oh, it's you. You gave me a fright.'

He stood behind her.

'Have you been awake all this time?'

The team had watched Amelia and CUCKOO eating dinner: they had listened to their conversation; to Amelia's flawless impersonation of a loving mother; to CUCKOO's word-perfect portrayal of François Malot. At midnight, CUCKOO had yawned and gone upstairs to bed, running a bath under Harold's unforgiving gaze – 'Bubbles? What kind of a man gets into a bath with *bubbles*?' – before getting into bed and reading a few pages of the novel that he had removed from his suitcase. Amelia had emailed Kell a report at half-past twelve, confirming that Barbara should appear at the house just after nine o'clock in the morning.

Kell had then gone upstairs to bed, where Barbara was already asleep.

'Harold woke me at three,' Elsa said, popping a stick of chewing gum in her mouth. 'He said nothing had happened. CUCKOO has been asleep since about one.'

Kell looked at the screens. He could hear the low, regular sighs of CUCKOO's breathing and felt like a doctor watching a patient in intensive care.

'No sign of Amelia?' There were no cameras in Amelia's bedroom or bathroom; Kell had afforded her that privacy.

Elsa shook her head.

'None.'

But Amelia was the first up. She appeared in the kitchen just after six in a pale silk dressing-gown tied tightly at the waist. She switched on Radio 4, made herself a cup of tea, then returned to her bedroom, away from the gaze of the cameras. Moments later, Harold came down into the library.

'Day Two in the Big Brother House,' he intoned in a thick Newcastle accent. 'Amelia is in the Diary Room.' He walked over to the table, stood behind Elsa and looked up at the master image from the bedroom. 'CUCKOO is fast asleep. He has no fooking idea that today he faces eviction.'

Kell laughed. Elsa did not understand the joke.

'What are you talking about?' she said.

It was another two hours before CUCKOO woke up, climbed out of bed, walked into the bathroom with a pyjama-tenting erection, stared at himself in the mirror, squeezed a spot beneath his chin and emptied his bladder in the toilet.

'Here we go,' said Harold. 'Elvis is in the bathroom.'

Kell went into the kitchen to find Barbara seated and dressed, a bowl of muesli and yoghurt on the table in front of her.

'CUCKOO's awake,' he told her.

'Yes. I heard.'

She looked alert and focused, her make-up slightly different, as though she had deliberately put on another face for the part.

'Amelia wants you there at nine,' he said. He glanced at his watch. 'That looks about right. CUCKOO had a bath before he went to bed, so chances are he'll be downstairs when you come in. How are you feeling?'

He remembered their first meeting in Nice, Barbara's shy, apologetic smile, the bustle and speed of her mind. A couple of days in the old country, away from Bill, appeared to have rejuvenated her. She was enjoying being back in the game.

'Oh, I'm looking forward to it,' she said, and grinned as she met Kell's eye. 'Let's hope we get the bastard. Let's hope we really *get* him.'

56

Vincent Cévennes – dressed as François Malot, channelling François Malot, *being* François Malot – was sitting alone in the kitchen of Amelia's house when a figure appeared at the door, tapping on the glass. For a split second he thought that it was François' mother coming in from the garden, but soon realized his mistake. The lady looking through the window had a slight arthritic stoop and was several years older than Amelia Levene. She appeared to be in her mid-sixties and from a different social class. She was holding up a set of keys. A cleaning lady, Vincent assumed. And so it proved.

'Good morning,' she said, a broad and friendly smile spreading across her face beneath a bloom of white hair. She was wearing a pair of Wellington boots and he presumed that she had walked from the village. 'You must be François?'

Vincent stood up to shake her hand. 'Yes,' he said, feigning an inability to understand English. 'Who are you, please?'

'You look a bit startled, love. Bless you. Did Mrs Levene not say I was coming?'

Amelia walked into the kitchen.

'Ah, I see you've met. Barbara, you're so kind to have come on a Saturday.'

'Wouldn't have missed it for the world,' Barbara replied, removing her overcoat and boots and taking them into the utility room. Vincent turned to Amelia.

'Your housekeeper?' he asked.

'My housekeeper.' Amelia nodded towards the sink. 'Hence the piles of washing-up. I was too tired to do it last night. She's marvellous, comes whenever I'm down. My brother employed her when he was living here, knows the place from top to bottom. She's getting on a bit, but still very fit and absolutely insists that she's not ready to retire.'

'And she knows who I am?'

Amelia smiled and shook her head. 'Of course not.' She reached out and touched Vincent's arm. 'I've told her that you're Giles's godson, staying for the weekend en route to Cornwall. Is that all right?'

'Perfect,' Vincent replied.

Barbara came back into the room. She had changed into a pair of old tennis shoes and was wearing a nylon smock. A ritual of small talk began. Vincent looked on as Amelia filled the kettle and prepared a cup of tea for the cleaning lady, knowing that she liked milk but no sugar. A short-bread biscuit was produced from a tin. Amelia tried her best to involve him in their tedious chit-chat, but Vincent – having insisted that François Malot had never learned to speak English – could not and did not wish to participate. If anything, he found that he was slightly offended by Barbara's presence, not because it affected the operation, but because Amelia had neglected to mention that a stranger would be joining them in the house. He hoped that she would not be staying long. As Barbara put on a pair of yellow rubber gloves and set about the washing-up, Vincent excused himself from the kitchen and went back upstairs to his room. After locking the bathroom door, he switched on his laptop and saw that there were no messages waiting for him on the server. He sent an email to Luc updating him on the housekeeper's arrival, then shaved with the electric razor that he had set to charge overnight. It was one of the little changes Vincent had made in his morning routine. François, he had decided, preferred the deeper stubble left by an electric razor; Vincent himself had always opted for the greater closeness of a wet shave. He had also changed his aftershave, taken up smoking – Lucky Strike Silver, the same brand as François – and removed a Cévennes family ring from the little finger of his right hand. All of these gestures were small, if vital details that had assisted Vincent in what he liked to call his 'chameleonic shift', a phrase that pleased him. Having closed the lid of the computer, he poured a glass of water from the tap and sipped at it as he contemplated the day ahead. Thus far, he could be reassured that the weekend was proceeding as planned. Dinner the night before had been a success; he felt that he had built on the relationship between François and Amelia that they had established in Tunisia. However, his primary objective for the next twenty-four hours, as agreed with Luc, was to lay the groundwork of a possible move to London. This he would do at a conven-ient opportunity, perhaps at dinner that evening or lunch on Sunday prior to leaving for Paris.

Vincent had only one reservation, which he would

necessarily conceal from Luc. The previous night he had set aside a strange and unsettling feeling of desire for Amelia, an anomaly that – in the clear light of a new day – he put down to alcohol and to the solitude of his position. He needed a woman at least once every week – he had come to realize this about himself as a young man at the Academy – and stressful situations often raised in him an inconvenient desire.

Ignore it, he told himself, and went back to the mirror to check his appearance. He brushed his teeth, combed his hair, then walked down to the kitchen.

57

'Choices,' Amelia was saying. Kell could hear her voice coming through the speakers in the Shand library. 'We could go into Salisbury and see the cathedral, if that would interest you. We could go for a walk. There are lots of lovely pubs in the area if the idea of lunch appeals. What do you feel like doing?'

Amelia was seated opposite CUCKOO in the sitting room, drinking a cup of coffee. In more than twelve hours of interaction, she was yet to put a foot wrong: the loving mother; the consummate hostess. CUCKOO, wearing a different pair of trousers to those in which he had concealed the SIM, was smoking a cigarette, a habit that had raised Barbara to new heights of mischief.

'Oh, he's a *smoker*, is he?' she had said to Amelia, spotting CUCKOO's packet of Lucky Strike Silver on the kitchen table. Her remarks were well within earshot of CUCKOO, who was pretending not to be able to understand. 'Well, if a Frenchman wants to kill himself, I'll not be stopping him. You tell Mr Levene he should have done a better job looking out for his godson's health.'

In due course, Amelia was able to persuade CUCKOO to join her on what she described as 'a short walk around the village'. Kell's preferred option, of a longer lunchtime trip into Salisbury, was rejected.

'That gives us an hour, at best,' he told the team. 'Depends how long Amelia can keep him out there. As soon as they reach the gate behind the house, we go in.' Kevin Vigors, the surveillance man, had been tasked with following them at a discreet distance; in the event that they turned for home, he was to alert Kell so that the team would have time to evacuate CUCKOO's room. Amelia was not carrying any kind of communication device with which to contact the team. That was standard SIS tradecraft; if CUCKOO spotted it, the game would be up.

It was another hour before they left the house, time in which Elsa and Harold, who had assembled their technical kit in three small bags, made last-minute checks while Vigors kept an eye on the live feeds. Finally, as the grandfather clock in Amelia's hall struck half-past eleven, Amelia and CUCKOO emerged from the house wearing matching green Wellington boots and Barbour jackets culled from the utility room.

'They should be coming past in less than a minute,' Kell announced. He looked at Elsa's face and she was suddenly a stranger to him, a hard edge in her expression, an absolute focus. Harold, so often the joker, was pacing in the kitchen, waiting for the word to go. Vigors, already outside in the garden, clicked his radio twice to confirm that he had seen CUCKOO and Amelia passing the Shand house on the lane.

'Everybody OK?' Kell asked, trying to convey a sense of calm and common purpose to the team even as he felt the under-skin crawl of disquiet. It was always like this; there was cruelty in waiting. Once they got into the house, once they were working, he would be fine.

Three clear clicks on the Vigors radio. That meant CUCKOO and Amelia were at the gate which connected the perimeter of the village to a meadow that ran west towards Ebbesbourne St John. Kell was in the hall. Harold came to the kitchen door and looked at him, waiting for the nod. He had one of the kitbags slung over his shoulder; Elsa was carrying the others. Kell counted to ten in his head, then opened the door.

It was ninety seconds from the Shand house to CUCKOO's bedroom via the short-cut in the garden; Kell had timed it. Harold reached the dividing gate first, opening it up and then moving quickly across Amelia's lawn to the house.

Barbara had already opened the back door. She said: 'Shoes off,' as they pulled up outside. She checked the bottoms of their trousers for mud, pronounced them clean, and within fifteen seconds, Elsa and Harold were in the CUCKOO bedroom.

58

'SIM,' said Kell.

Barbara had already been into CUCKOO's room, picked up his denim jeans, looked in the ticket pocket and found the SIM. She passed it to Kell as they stood beside the grandfather clock.

'All yours,' she said.

He went up to the bedroom and handed it to Harold. He had left one of the kitbags outside in the corridor. He removed an old Security Service encoder, switched it on and inserted the SIM, setting the machine to copy. Kell left him to it. Meanwhile, Elsa had taken out a computer and several cables of varying colours and sizes, one of which she connected to the mains. She took CUCKOO's laptop from the black leather holdall and flipped open the lid. Kell watched but did not disturb her. The plan was to crack the DGSE security encryption on the laptop and to transfer all hard-drive data on to her host machine. Harold had revisited the footage of CUCKOO tapping in the password in the bathroom, amplified the image and established three possible options.

Elsa tried the first of them – the French word 'DIGESTIF' followed by a three-number sequence – but the firewall remained in place. Her second attempt, substituting '2' for '3' at the start of the sequence, broke the security.

'You had it right, Harold,' Elsa said, but there was no sense of triumph or elation in her voice.

'You're in?' he asked.

'I am in, I think so, yes.' She was speaking quickly, tripping on her words. 'I tried the second code, it has put me through into a new interface.'

Kell looked around the room. The world of technology – of hard-drive encryptions, of phone triangulations – was as alien to him as some lost tribal dialect from the Amazon. Throughout his career, he had felt lamentably ill-informed in the presence of Tech-Ops teams and computer wizards. Leaving Elsa to begin transferring the data from CUCKOO's laptop, he looked around the room, making a mental note of the objects on display. He saw many of the personal items from CUCKOO's room at the Ramada: his 35mm camera; the gold cigarette lighter engraved with the initials 'P.M.'; the framed photograph of Philippe and Jeannine Malot; the Moleskine diary, every page of which he had photographed and sent to Jimmy Marquand. Beside the bed was the Michael Dibdin *roman policier* translated into French, a bottle of Highland Spring water and a pair of earplugs. Kell opened up the novel and – sure enough – found the fake letter to François, dated 4 February 1999, supposedly written by Malot's father. In a chest of drawers he found CUCKOO's counterfeit passport resting on the socks and underpants that he had unpacked the night before. His black leather jacket was hanging on a hook behind the door, beside a white cotton dressing-gown. It was the same story in the bathroom: the same shaving products, the same pills, the same bottle of Valium that Kell had seen in Tunis. How easily he had been deceived.

'How are you getting on?' he asked Harold, still crouched over the encoder in the corridor, frowning.

'At least another fifteen minutes,' he said.

'You?'

'Same applies to me,' Elsa replied. 'Relax, Tom, please.'

Kell felt as though he was intruding on events over which he had no power or influence. He went downstairs, removed the shoes from the hall, and found Barbara dutifully dragging a Hoover up and down on the sitting-room carpet.

'Any sign of CUCKOO's phone?' he asked.

'None,' she replied. 'Must have taken it with him.'

59

Barbara was correct.

Pausing in front of the first stile in the meadow, about four hundred metres from the Shand house, CUCKOO reached into his trouser pocket and powered up his mobile phone.

'I'm afraid you're unlikely to get a signal,' Amelia told him, asking for his hand so that he could steady her as she crossed over the stile. 'I normally have to drive across to Fovant if I want to check my messages. Occasionally one can get a feeble signal on the hill.'

She pointed ahead of her, in the direction of Ebbesbourne St John.

'Why don't you have a booster fitted to your house?' CUCKOO asked, an edge of surprise in his voice. 'Don't MI6 like to be in touch with you?'

'That's the whole point of this place.' Amelia watched as CUCKOO swung a leg over the stile, following her. 'Isolation. Retreat. I like to be somewhere that nobody can find me. My privacy is very important to me. You know what it's like to be at the mercy of text messages, constant calls on one's BlackBerry, endless emails from colleagues. My weekends are sacred. When I take over next month, they'll be posting security guards in the lane, wiring the house for CCTV. These are the last moments of solitude you and I will know for years.'

It was a deft coda, planting CUCKOO with the idea that Amelia envisaged their relationship stretching far into the future. She found it curious to reflect on how much she was enjoying turning the tables; she had expected to feel physically ill in his presence, but after only a few minutes in the house, CUCKOO had become little more than a cipher to her. Those aspects of his character that she had once found endearing – his sensitivity, his shyness, his careful and enquiring intellect – she now viewed as faults, weaknesses. She considered most of his conversation to be repetitive and lacking in insight; anecdotes and jokes were already beginning to be repeated. His physical attractiveness, which she had once, embarrassingly, prided herself on, was now evidence only of an extreme vanity, bordering on narcissism. The process by which Amelia had come to loathe CUCKOO was not all that different, she reflected, to the process by which she came to resent her former lovers. Those things she had most adored about him were now those things that she abhorred. She felt only an unequivocal determination to destroy him, borne of shame and the desperate desire to find François.

'*Merde*,' said CUCKOO.

He was patting his trousers, front and back, searching the inside pockets of his Barbour.

'What is it?'

'I forgot my cigarettes.'

309

Amelia felt an itch of alarm.

'Does it matter? I hate it when you smoke.'

He looked at her as though she had betrayed him, a sudden sullen expression of his contempt.

'What? Even outside, in the open air?' It was the first time that he had raised his voice against her. Why the shift in his mood? Did he suspect that something was going on at the house, the forgotten cigarettes a ruse to go back? But then CUCKOO seemed to remember the need for tact and good manners and his characteristic charm returned. 'I just like to smoke as I walk. It helps me to think, to relax.'

'Of course,' Amelia said. 'But we'll be home fairly soon.' She gestured ahead at a wooded glade about a quarter of a mile to the west. 'We can turn around at the end.'

CUCKOO was shifting from foot to foot. 'No, I'll run back,' he said, and before Amelia could stop him, he had vaulted over the stile and started jogging towards the house. At that speed he would be there in less than a minute. She looked back along the valley for a sign of Kevin Vigors. He was nowhere to be seen.

'François!'

CUCKOO stopped and turned around, frowning.

'What?'

Slowly, Amelia took herself back over the stile and walked towards him, buying time with every step. When she was a few metres away, she reached into her coat pocket and took out her keys.

'You'll need these.'

'Barbara can let me in,' he replied, turning and starting to jog. He called back: 'I'll only be five minutes.'

And all Amelia could do was watch and wait.

60

Less than two hundred metres away, secluded behind a screen of chestnut trees, Kevin Vigors saw CUCKOO running towards the house and immediately radioed through to Kell.

'Serious problem,' he said. 'CUCKOO is coming back.'

'What? Why?'

'No idea. But get out of there. You've probably got less than a minute before he reaches the house.'

'Can you stall him?'

'He'll smell a rat. Just get out of the bedroom.'

Kell was standing in the sitting room. He went into the kitchen, opened the bin, pulled out the contents and handed them to Barbara.

'Get outside,' he said, grabbing a pile of papers from the kitchen table, as well as Elsa and Harold's shoes and a recipe book from the shelf above the Aga. He stuffed them into the bin liner until it was full. 'Walk down the lane towards the Shand house. There are black dustbins between the two houses. CUCKOO is coming back. You'll have to stall him or we won't have time to clear out. Get him to help you with the bin.'

Barbara nodded but said nothing. She went to the door, walked up the stone steps towards the lane and headed slowly downhill in the direction of the Shand house. At the same time, Kell grabbed the vacuum cleaner from the sitting room and ran upstairs, holding it in his arms like an outsized child.

'Get the fuck out of there right now,' he called to Elsa and Harold, plugging the Hoover into a socket in the corridor. 'Grab everything. We are going into Amelia's room.' He was scooping up one of the kitbags in the corridor. He heard Harold say: 'Jesus fucking Christ' and watched as he picked up the encoder and took it past him, down the passage. Harold then came back into CUCKOO's bedroom and threw the rest of his hardware into a second bag that he slung over his shoulder and removed to the master bedroom.

Kell heard three clicks on the radio. CUCKOO was at the gate. In twenty seconds he would be opposite the Shand front door, in forty, at the back door of Amelia's house.

Elsa, repeatedly whispering 'Shit, shit' in Italian, had shut down the DGSE laptop and was putting it back in the leather carrying case.

'Hurry,' Kell hissed at her, coiling loose cables into the third bag. He unplugged her computer from the mains and ushered her out of the room, bundling the bag into her arms. He left the Hoover in the corridor to make it look as though Barbara had been cleaning upstairs. 'Go, go,' he said.

CUCKOO's bedroom was now empty. Kell checked the carpet. There was a small piece of yellow plastic beside the chest of drawers that he picked up and put in his pocket. There seemed to be a strong odour of work and sweat, but he could not decide whether the smell of Elsa's perfume was in the room or in his memory. He opened the window, on the basis that Barbara could have done so, and ensured that the team had left no trace of themselves in the bathroom.

Two clicks on the radio. CUCKOO was passing the Shand house.

Kell looked out of the bathroom window and saw him coming. He turned, walked into the corridor, reached the landing, went into Amelia's bedroom and closed the door.

It was only then that he realized they had not replaced the SIM in CUCKOO's jeans.

61

Barbara saw CUCKOO as she reached the dustbins. He had stopped jogging and was walking towards her, passing the Shand house and frowning in surprise at the sight of Amelia's cleaning lady struggling down the lane under the weight of a bin bag.

'You are OK?' he called out.

Barbara, tilting to one side for maximum visual impact, nodded her head in a demonstration of unbuckled stoicism and moved forward towards the dustbins.

'What are you doing back here, love?' she asked, resting the sack in the centre of the road so that CUCKOO's path was partially blocked.

'Smoke,' he said, miming a cigarette going in and out of his mouth. 'I help you?'

At least he's got some manners, Barbara thought, breaking into an effusive speech of gratitude as CUCKOO lifted the bag from the lane and carried it the short distance to the large black dustbins at the edge of the road.

'*C'est lourd*,' he said. *It's heavy*. As if to confirm this, the

Frenchman held his bicep as though he had suffered a sprain. For a split second, Barbara was about to reply in fluent French, the language of her life in Menton, but she checked herself and instead continued in her role.

'That's so kind of you, François,' she said, slowing her words down, as though talking to a child. 'Thank goodness I ran into you.' She was aware that, no more than ten metres away, behind the windows on the first floor of the house, Kell, Elsa and Harold were most probably in a perfect storm of panic, clearing out of the bedroom as fast as possible. She drew CUCKOO's eyes down towards the ground with a stern warning: 'Now, I don't want you going into the house with those muddy boots on.'

It was to the Service's advantage that CUCKOO was obliged to pretend that he did not understand what she had said.

'What, please?' he said. 'I not follow.'

Barbara repeated the warning, buying yet more precious time as she slowly explained, in nursery-level English, that she would not allow dirty footwear in Mrs Levene's home.

'Come with me,' she said eventually, channelling all of the charm and the mischief of her brief encounter with the receptionist at the Hotel Gillespie. She took CUCKOO's arm and walked him slowly up the lane towards the front of the house. When they had reached the kitchen door, which was still ajar, she again gestured to his feet.

'Your cigarettes are on the table, aren't they, love?'

CUCKOO pointed at the packet of Lucky Strike, which were indeed on the kitchen table, partially concealed from view by a peppermill and a bowl of sugar.

'I'll get them for you,' she said, squeezing through the door. 'That way you won't have to come in.'

'And the lighter,' he said. 'I must have my lighter.'

She passed the cigarettes through the door and asked for its whereabouts.

'In my room,' CUCKOO replied. 'But I can get this.'

'No, no, you stay there, love,' and Barbara climbed the stairs to the first floor, which was now a ghost town of inactivity. She walked into CUCKOO's bedroom, spotted the gold cigarette lighter on top of the chest of drawers, slipped it into the front pocket of her smock and returned to the kitchen.

'*Voila!*' she said with an air of triumph, handing the lighter across the threshold. It sounded as though it was the only word of French that she knew. 'Now you get back to Mrs Levene. She'll be wondering what's become of you. And if I don't see you again, it's been lovely meeting you. Enjoy the rest of your weekend. Safe trip back to Paris.'

62

Lying flat on the floor of Amelia's en-suite bathroom, so that their silhouettes would not show in the windows, Kell, Elsa and Harold could pick out only the mumble of Barbara and CUCKOO's conversation. Taking slow, near-silent breaths, side by side like campers sleeping in a three-man tent, they listened as Barbara closed the kitchen door, then heard what sounded like the footsteps of CUCKOO returning to the lane and walking back past the house, heading in the direction of the meadow. About a minute later, Kell received two low-volume clicks on his radio, then a pause before Vigors confirmed, with three further clicks, that CUCKOO was passing through the gate on his way back towards Amelia.

It was another minute before Kell dared to break the spell of their silence. Standing up, he swore quietly and looked down at Elsa and Harold. Slowly, like survivors from an earthquake, they clambered to their feet.

'*Cazzo*,' she whispered.

'Squeaky bum time,' said Harold and Elsa said: 'Shhhhh!' as though CUCKOO was still in the next room.

'It's all right,' Kell replied, opening the bathroom door. 'He's in the meadow. Gone.'

Barbara appeared at the top of the stairs.

'Do mind my language,' she said, 'but bloody hell, how did that happen?'

'What did he want?' Elsa asked.

'Cigarettes,' she replied. 'He wanted bloody *cigarettes*. Imagine if he'd come upstairs.'

'I'd have smoked one with him,' Harold muttered, and everybody went back to work.

63

Akim was woken the next morning by the sound of Luc and Valerie fucking in the next room. Always the same routine: Luc increasingly struggling for breath as he chugged against the headboard; Valerie smothering her moans with what was probably a sheet or the edge of one of the pillows. She was like a teenager or newlywed bride: wanting it every morning, wanting it every night. A cast-off from Internal Security, Valerie was the one random element in the operation, brought in by the boss because he could not function without her, but kept secret – as far as Akim knew – from Luc's masters in the DGSE. Even Vincent himself had only met her for the first time a few days earlier. Luc had sworn him to secrecy, knowing that Paris would pull the plug if they so much as suspected that Valerie was so intimately involved in the HOLST operation.

Akim looked at the clock beside his bed. It was just after six on a Sunday morning; he could have done with the extra hour's sleep. Now he was just thinking about pussy, about how much longer it was going to be before he could go back to Marseille.

'Arseholes,' he muttered and hoped that his voice would carry into the next room and stop the scrape of the bed against the floorboards, the soft muffled squeak of the springs. Eventually there was a groan from Luc, louder than most mornings, and the bed stopped moving, like a car coming to a halt in a lay-by. Moments later Valerie was padding barefoot next door and running the tap on the bidet. Akim heard Luc cough a couple of times, then the radio, the volume turned down low. Always the same routine.

Akim was due on duty at seven fifteen, relieving Slimane from the night shift. Three days earlier, he had gone down to find Slimane and the prisoner talking, HOLST's door wide open, his eyes filled with rage and tears. Later on, walking in the countryside near the house, Akim had asked for an explanation and Slimane had told him – laughing about it, like it was the funniest thing in the world – that he'd been taunting François about Egypt, about what they'd done to his 'fake mum and dad'. Akim, who had grown to like François, to respect him for the way he'd handled himself since the grab in Paris, had launched at his friend, a lot of the stress and the tension of their long confinement suddenly coming out in a frenzy of rage. The two men had fallen to the ground and scrapped like kids in the street, only to stop after a minute or two and look at one another, laughing at the dust on their clothes and trainers, flicking away the flies that buzzed around their heads.

'Who gives a fuck about him anyway?' Slimane had said, and then they'd ducked behind a tree and lain close to the ground because somebody had come past on a tractor.

Who gives a fuck about him anyway? Akim had given a lot of thought to that question. *Do I give a fuck about François? Should* I give a fuck about François? He'd hurt his dad, sure. He knew that. But it was Slimane who'd had the blade in Egypt, just like it was Slimane who'd wanted to finish off the spy at Cité Radieuse. Akim didn't want anyone, especially François, thinking he and Slimane were similar. Akim was a soldier, he did what he was told to do; he stayed true to whoever was paying him. With Slimane, you never knew where his loyalties lay, what he was thinking, what wildness was going to spring from him next.

Who gives a fuck about him anyway? Akim had gone to bed the previous night knowing that he might have to kill HOLST. Maybe that was what was bothering him. He didn't want to have to do it but he knew that Luc or Valerie were crazy enough to give him the order, just to test his loyalty. At about seven o'clock, after he had finished his nightly swim, Luc had received a document from Paris that effectively ended the first phase of the operation. It was a transcript of a conversation at Christophe Delestre's apartment in Montmartre, recorded by DGSE microphones five days earlier but only now, thanks to a typical Paris fuck-up, making its way to Luc. The conversation was between Delestre, his wife, and an MI6 officer calling himself 'Thomas Kell'. Kell, Luc had realized instantly, was Stephen Uniacke, the same man who had talked to Vincent on the ferry, the same man Akim and Slimane had been instructed to rough up at Cité Radieuse. Kell had run Delestre to ground, shown him a photograph of Vincent and worked out that HOLST had been switched. Luc, running downstairs, a dressing-gown tied slackly around his belly, wet legs still dripping water on the floor, had shouted for Valerie.

'Fucking MI6,' he said. 'Fucking Amelia Levene. I was right. She worked it out. She knows about the second funeral.'

There'd been an argument between the two of them, then Luc had dressed and driven north to Castelnaudary, where he'd bought himself half an hour at the Internet café and sent an email to Vincent's dedicated server.

They know about the second funeral. Stephen Uniacke is an MI6 officer named Thomas Kell. He found Delestre in Paris. Levene must know and is playing you. Abort immediately. Crash meeting, Sunday midnight.

When he got back, at around nine, it had looked as though they were going to abort and go home. Then Valerie had done what she always did. She had talked Luc round.

'Look, nothing has changed,' she said, smiling the whole time like she knew everybody was going to agree with her in the end. 'This operation was always top secret. Only six or seven of your colleagues in Paris knew the full extent of what you were trying to do. Even the Elysée was in the dark. Am I right?'

'You're right,' Luc had said quietly.

'Good. So you just close it down. You tell them François will be taken care of. Paris will be disappointed that they didn't get their leverage against Levene and they'll want to question you when you go back. But you don't go back. *Fuck* Paris. We keep François alive for a few more days and send a ransom to Levene. He's *priceless* to her.'

'MI6 doesn't pay kidnappers,' Luc had replied, which was when Valerie had snapped.

'Don't give me that shit.' Akim had looked across the room at Slimane who was grinning like it was all just a game. His face was still marked from the fight in Marseille, a blue-black stain under his injured eye. 'Her husband is a *millionaire*. She has access to tens of millions of dollars in offshore MI6 accounts. She'll pay up. She'll pay because we *make* her pay. She knows that if she doesn't, the boys will kill her son. That's a motivation, wouldn't you say?' There had been all that sarcasm in the room, like a test of their courage, Luc looking defeated and uncomfortable and Slimane almost laughing in his face. 'And when she finally pays' – Valerie was lighting up a cigarette – 'we give the guys their share, we take the money, we kill this prick' – a flick of her blonde hair in the direction of HOLST's cell – 'and then you finally get to quit the job I've been trying to get you to quit for the last three years. Or are you scared about that? Are you worried your bosses will catch you out?' It was a deliberate provocation in front of the team. Even Slimane looked at the ground.

'I'm not scared, Valerie,' Luc had replied, like he wanted to take the conversation next door. 'I just want to be sure we know what we're getting into.'

Akim could still picture what she did next. She stood up, walked across the room, and buried her tongue in Luc's mouth, at the same time grinding her hand into his cock so that Akim felt himself grow hard.

'I've always known what I'm doing,' she had said. 'All you guys have to do is follow me.'

Soon after that, Luc agreed to everything: the timing of the ransom; the date when they would kill HOLST; the sweetness of his revenge against Levene. Like Slimane always said, Luc was weak around Valerie, prepared to do whatever she wanted. There was a kind of flaw in his character that kept him permanently under her spell. Unlike with everybody else, he never argued back, never stood up for himself, never questioned her decisions. This tough guy of the DGSE seemed to be under a kind of hypnosis. It was embarrassing to watch a man behave like that. Slimane called him 'the carpet'.

The toilet flushed next door and Akim heard Valerie padding back to the bedroom. He wanted to fuck her – he'd felt that way since they'd met – and lit a cigarette, pulling on his tracksuit and shoes. Then he opened the curtains. That amazing view down to the Pyrenees. Akim always liked looking at it first thing in the morning. Like a new country, a heaven. Then he went to work.

Slimane was asleep in the armchair at the bottom of the stairs, his hand down the front of his trousers, spittle coming out of one side of his mouth. Akim looked through the spyglass and saw that HOLST was lying on his bunk, eyes fixed on the ceiling. He woke Slimane, was sworn at for his efforts, then went into the kitchen to fix a cup of coffee. Moments later, Luc appeared, naked except for a pair of white cotton boxer shorts. There were tattoos on his biceps, flakes of sunburn on his shoulder blades. Akim caught the funk of their sex, like Luc wanted him to know that he'd just nailed Valerie. He opened the door out on to the back porch.

'Big day.' The boss went to the fridge. He took a long swig of orange juice direct from the carton. When he had finished, he put the carton on the kitchen table and fixed Akim with one of his lazy stares.

'Vincent still isn't responding,' he said. 'We've only had two emails from him since he got to St Pancras, one on

Friday night, one yesterday morning when the housekeeper arrived. The message we sent to abort has gone from the server, so he must have seen it. Valerie has left a voicemail telling him to go to Paris, but there's no reception for mobiles at the house.'

Slimane strolled into the kitchen, spotted the carton of orange juice and went to pick it up. Luc grabbed his forearm, holding it above the table like there was a flame underneath.

'You two not listening to me?' he said. He was stronger than Slimane, who had a look on his face like spilled acid. 'We have a problem. Vincent was lured into a trap and we don't know if he's been arrested, if he's still at the house or if he got the message to abort.'

'Fine,' said Slimane. 'So you can tell him when he gets back to Paris.'

'No.' It was Valerie, coming in behind him in jeans and a T-shirt. 'I want *you* to tell him, Akim.'

'Me?'

Luc released Slimane. Valerie spread her arms to embrace the two Arabs, holding them around the neck. 'We want *you* to talk to him.' Akim enjoyed the feeling of her skin against his neck. 'Find Vincent when he gets back to Paris. He'll be holed up at the Lutetia. Find him and then do what you do best. Smartest thing we can do now is clear the trail.'

64

Luc's email to Vincent had been seen almost instantaneously by Elsa Cassani in the Shand library, where she had saturation coverage of CUCKOO's lines of communication. The message appeared on the dedicated DGSE server, where it would be encrypted the moment CUCKOO logged on.

> They know about the second funeral. Stephen Uniacke
> is an MI6 officer named Thomas Kell. He found Delestre
> in Paris. Levene must know and is playing you. Abort
> immediately. Crash meeting, Sunday midnight.

'Tom,' she said. 'Christ. You need to see this.'

Kell was in the kitchen. By now, Barbara had gone to Gatwick, en route home to Menton. Harold was upstairs in the Shand house watching *3:10 to Yuma*.

'What is it?'

Kell came into the library carrying a mug of tea. Elsa pointed at the third laptop, on the right-hand side of the oak table. The pressure of her index finger blurred the screen.

'This just came through?'

'Less than a minute ago. How do they know about you?'

Kell put the tea down on the table.

'They must have bugged Delestre's apartment,' he said. It was the only possible solution he could think of.

'But you were there on Monday. How can it have taken them so long?'

'Manpower,' Kell replied, knowing that, when it came to following up every lead, listening to every conversation, the French were just as stretched as the Security Service or SIS. 'They probably have microphones all over Paris, checking Malot's friends and colleagues. Could have taken them several days to work out I was there.'

'I'm finding the name Vincent Cévennes all over CUCKOO's files,' said Elsa, drinking from a bottle of Evian. 'Also Valerie de Serres, probable girlfriend of Luc Javeau. You think that's an alias for Madeleine Brive?'

'Almost certainly.' Kell scribbled down the names on a piece of paper. 'Where's CUCKOO now?'

They looked up at the bookshelves, nine screens in rows of three, like a game of noughts and crosses. It was just after eight o'clock on Saturday evening, Amelia preparing a fish stew in the kitchen, CUCKOO reading Michael Dibdin in the sitting room.

'Can you hold the message on the server?' Kell asked.

'I don't think so.' Elsa typed something into the lines of code on the second laptop. 'I could delete it. That way he won't find out until he leaves tomorrow. I guess they'll be trying to call him on the phone.'

'Harold!'

Kell shouted upstairs. There was a grunting noise through the floor, then the sound of Harold scraping away from his western and thumping downstairs.

'Yes, guv?'

'Can you take another look at CUCKOO's mobile phone activity? Chances are there's a text message or voicemail waiting for him, instructing him to abort.'

'To *what*?'

'They know about us. They know their operation is blown. They're trying to tell him to go back to Paris.'

Kell made the decision to buy time and to delete the email from the DGSE server. He then sent a message across to Amelia telling her that the operation was blown. At breakfast, she was to tell CUCKOO that there was an SIS emergency in London and that a car was coming to pick her up. For security reasons, she could not offer 'François' a lift to St Pancras, but a pre-paid taxi had been booked to take him back to London. Kell knew that as soon as CUCKOO was a mile outside Chalke Bissett, he would come within range of a mobile phone signal and hear any of three messages left for him by Valerie de Serres. The first was explicit enough:

François, it's Madeleine. I don't know why you haven't responded to your email but you must abort, OK? Call me immediately please. We will crash meet Sunday midnight. We can explain everything. I need to know that you have received this message and that you will be there.

Harold had hacked into CUCKOO's voicemail, allowing Kell to re-acquaint himself with the tense, petulant voice of his ferry seductress, Madeleine Brive. CUCKOO, having heard the message, would then make every effort to evaporate into the English countryside, shaking off SIS surveillance as he did so. The trail to Amelia's son would be lost.

65

Vincent realized there was a problem when he heard Amelia knocking rapidly on the door of his bedroom shortly before eight o'clock on Sunday morning. He had been awake for almost an hour, finishing the Dibdin and listening to the bleating of the lambs on the steep hill behind the house.

'Are you awake, darling?'

She came into his bedroom. She was already dressed, in the uniform she wore for Vauxhall Cross: a navy-blue skirt with matching jacket; a cream blouse; black shoes with kitten heels; the gold necklace given to her by her brother as a present on her thirtieth birthday.

'You look like you're going to church,' he said.

He was shirtless in bed, propped up against the headboard, deliberately provoking her with his physique. He knew that Amelia felt an overpowering love for him, but also a physical desire that conflicted with her duties as a mother. He could sense it in her; he could always tell with women.

'I'm afraid there's an emergency in London. I have to leave. There's a car coming for me at half-past nine.'

'I see.'

'I'm so sorry.' She sat on the end of the bed, imploring forgiveness with her eyes. Vincent remembered his first sight of her pale skin beside the pool, the swell of her breasts. He had often thought about the taste of her, the transgression of a sexual relationship. 'The worst of it is I can't offer you a lift back to London. The Office doesn't know about you and my driver would cotton on. But I've arranged for a taxi to pick you up at nine fifteen. Is that all right? Does that give you enough time to pack?'

It seemed as though he had no choice. Vincent pulled back the duvet, climbed out of bed and put on his dressing-gown.

'It's a real pity.' Was Amelia being honest or had she somehow discovered the truth about him? 'I was looking forward to spending the rest of the day together. I wanted to talk about the move to London.'

'Me too.' She stood up and put her arms around him, and it was all that Vincent could do not to press his body against hers and to kiss her. He was convinced that he could possess her, that she would offer no resistance. 'I can't even let you stay, I'm afraid. Too many people would start asking awkward questions if . . .'

'Don't worry.' He broke free. 'I understand.' He began pulling out clothes from the chest of drawers and placing them in his suitcase. 'Just give me five minutes to take a shower and pack. I'll come downstairs. We can have breakfast. Then I can go back to Paris.'

66

As Kell had predicted, Vincent Cévennes was exactly one mile east of Chalke Bissett when his mobile phone began to come alive with a symphony of beeps and tones that lasted the better part of a minute.

'Blimey, you're popular,' said Harold Mowbray, sporting the casual weekend attire of a Wiltshire taxi driver as he accelerated towards Salisbury.

Vincent, sitting in the back seat of the taxi, did not respond. He saw that there were messages on his voicemail and clicked 'Listen' on the read-out.

François, it's Madeleine. I don't know why you haven't responded to your email but you must abort, OK? Call me immediately please. We will crash meet Sunday midnight. We can explain everything. I need to know that you have received this message and that you will be there.

At first, he did not understand what Valerie was telling

him. Abort? Why was it necessary to hold a crash meeting in Paris within twelve hours? Vincent took out his BlackBerry and checked the inbox. There were no messages, just as there had been no emails on his laptop the night before. Perhaps, in the confusion of the weekend, unable to reach him as easily as they would have liked, Luc and Valerie had simply panicked.

He dialled the number in Paris, heard it reconnect to Luc's cell phone.

'Luc?'

'Vincent, Jesus. At long fucking last. Where the hell have you been?'

Back at the Shand house, Elsa was able to feed the conversation into Amelia's Audi as she and Kell tailed the taxi on the Salisbury road. Within seconds, Vincent had realized that he was completely compromised. Luc told him everything: that 'the guy on the ferry was an MI6 officer'; that 'Uniacke was an alias for Thomas Kell'; that 'Kell talked to Delestre in Paris and put two and two together about the funerals'. Luc and Valerie were certain that Amelia had known about Vincent's deception 'for at least five days'. That was why she had invited him to her house in the country; not to get to know him better, but to find out who was behind the Malot conspiracy. Vincent asked if MI6 knew that François was being held in captivity.

'Assume that they know everything,' Luc replied.

Sitting alongside Kell in the passenger seat, Amelia shook her head and said: 'We'll never get to François. They'll kill him or move him in the next forty-eight hours.'

'Not necessarily,' Kell replied, but it was baseless optimism. Unless Elsa could trace the origin of Luc and Valerie's communications more precisely, their hopes of success were slim. He suspected that François was being held within a five-mile radius of Salles-sur-l'Hers, the village in Languedoc-Roussillon where Arnaud had dropped Vincent in the cab, but without accurate coordinates it would be like droning caves in Tora-Bora. Vincent was their only hope, but with only two specialist surveillance officers at his disposal, Kell's chances of following him to the crash meeting were near non-existent. How could he expect Harold and Elsa, two tech-ops specialists given only a basic grounding in surveillance techniques, to tail CUCKOO without being spotted?

Up ahead, Vincent had hung up on Luc and was already making plans to disappear.

'Listen,' he said to Harold. 'That was my boss. I need to get to a train station as quickly as possible. There's been a change of plan.'

'I thought I was dropping you in London, sir?' Harold replied, enjoying the role. 'Cleared my whole day.'

'Just do as I say,' Vincent told him, his faultless English now punctuated with rage. 'You'll get paid just the same.'

Amelia, listening alongside Kell in the pursuing vehicle, turned up the volume as Harold responded: 'All right, all right. No need to lose your rag. You're the one changing his mind, mate, not me.' His voice was muffled by road noise and static, but the words were clear enough. 'Salisbury OK for monsieur? Trains run from Tisbury as well if you prefer.'

'Just take me to the closest train station.'

About a quarter of a mile further along the road, Kevin Vigors was travelling in advance of the cab with Danny Aldrich. They were coming into Wilton when Kell contacted them on the radiolink.

'You hear that?'

'We heard it,' Vigors replied.

'Harold's taking CUCKOO to Salisbury. If he tries to get clear of us, that's where he'll do it.'

'Sure.'

All night, Kell had tried to anticipate how CUCKOO would behave in the aftermath of his exposure. His instinct would be to return to French soil as soon as possible. But how? In addition to the major London airports, there were airlines running flights to France from Southampton, Bournemouth, Exeter and Bristol. It was unlikely that Vincent would go direct to St Pancras without first trying to shake his tail, but he might pick up a Eurostar to Paris at either of the two stations in Kent, Ashford or Ebbsfleet. There was an option to hire a car and to drive it on to the Eurotunnel service at Folkestone, but Vincent would assume that SIS had access to number-plate recognition technology and would quickly be able to identify his position. A train south from Salisbury would take him to the cross-Channel ports.

'You think he'll take the train?' Amelia asked.

'Let's wait and see.'

On the outskirts of Salisbury, the cathedral spire drifting right-to-left across the windscreen as Harold negotiated a roundabout, Vincent announced that he needed to find an ATM. Three minutes later, Harold had pulled into a lay-by opposite a branch of Santander in the centre of town.

'Can you wait here, please?' Vincent asked him, leaving his suitcase and laptop on the back seat as he opened the door.

'It's a double yellow line, mate,' Harold replied. 'How long are you gonna be?'

There was no answer. Harold could only watch as the Frenchman crossed the road, stepped around an elderly couple, and joined a short queue at the ATM.

'I'm parked outside a cinema,' he announced. 'Mock Tudor, branch of Black's beside it.' Harold was talking into the void of an empty car, and hoped that the commlink was working. He put in an earpiece and twisted in his seat, trying to get his bearings. 'I'm in a parking bay at the side of the one-way system, looks like the street is called New Canal. Got a branch of Fat Face behind me, Whittard's coffee next door.'

Amelia's voice came through with a burst of static. 'We have you, Harold. Tom's coming around the corner. I know exactly where you are. Confirm CUCKOO's position?'

'Across the road, taking some cash out at Santander. He's left everything on the back seat. Suitcase, laptop. Only thing he took was his wallet.'

'What about a passport?' Kell asked.

'I'll have to look.'

'Is he wearing the leather jacket?'

This from Aldrich, who was parked with Vigors in the market square only three hundred metres away.

'Affirmative,' Harold replied. The leather jacket contained a tracking device that he had sewn into the lining the previous morning.

'He'll take it off,' Amelia muttered.

And so it proved.

Think, Vincent told himself. *Think*.

He put three successive cards into the ATM, taking out four hundred pounds on each. His heart had pounded him into a sweat of fear. He felt the distilled anger of a shamed man and wanted to find Amelia, to destroy her as she had destroyed him. How long had she known? How long had they all been playing him?

Think.

Stuffing the last of the money into the hip pocket of his jeans, he looked to the right. Past the local cinema, just a few doors down, was a branch of Marks & Spencer. It would be open on a Sunday and he could perhaps find an exit through the back. The cab was behind him and he turned towards the driver, who wound down his window and peered out.

'What's that mate?'

Was he one of them? One of a team of ten or twelve surveillance officers now scattered around central Salisbury? Vincent had to assume that everybody was a threat.

'I want to buy a sandwich in Marks & Spencer,' he shouted across the road, gesturing towards the store. 'Can you wait two more minutes please?'

He heard the driver's response: 'Mate, I told you. I'm not allowed to stop here,' and, for a moment, Vincent wondered if Amelia was the only one in town, the only one following him. There were so many questions in his mind, so many variables to contend with. He recalled what Luc had told him on the phone. *'Assume that they know everything.'* It was all so degrading, so hopeless and sudden. Vincent tried to remember what he had been taught at the Academy, but that was long ago and he found it difficult to think clearly. They did not prepare me for this, he told himself and began to blame Luc, to blame Valerie, because the whole operation had been crazy right from the start. How did they ever think they were going to get away with it? Was he going to be the fall guy? Would they wash their hands of him now?

Think. The doors of Marks & Spencer were automated and Vincent found himself in a long, strip-lit room of nightdresses and skirts, of Salisbury housewives, bored kids and trudging husbands. He followed signs upstairs to the men's department, turning around on the escalator so that he could look back at the shop floor in the hope of spotting a tail. Was Thomas Kell here? Vincent had warned Luc on the ferry, warned him about the threat from Stephen Uniacke. That was what was now so infuriating. All of his hard work, all of his talent and emotional investment in the operation wasted because Luc had been slack. How had they allowed themselves to be duped like that? *He's just a boring little consultant,* Valerie had said. *You're getting paranoid. We've been through his phones. We've looked at his computer. The Englishman is clean.*

Vincent reached the top of the escalator, wondering how long it would take the taxi driver to come after him. They could just arrest him for not paying his fare. He found socks, a pair of underpants, some deck shoes, a pair of denim jeans, a red polo shirt, a black V-neck sweater and a checked sports jacket. Cheaply made, ugly clothes, he would look bad in them, not his style or even the style of François. He bought a small leather shoulder bag, paying for everything in cash. There was a food section downstairs and Vincent bought a sandwich, because he did not know when he would next be able to eat, and also a litre bottle of water, swallowing at least a fifth of it before he reached the counter. He was so thirsty. The constant sense of apprehension was like a sickness stretching his skin. The staff kept smiling at him, even a young mother tried to catch his eye. Nothing could have been further from Vincent's mind. He knew that he hated women again, despised them, because you could never trust the way a woman talked to you, what she said with her face. Their words meant nothing. Even mothers lied. He told himself: *I am no longer François Malot*, but it was like sloughing off a skin that was still caught up in his soul. *I am Vincent Cévennes and the game is up. They are coming for me.*

He walked through the lingerie section, tanned models on posters lying with their eyes, and found an exit that brought him out into a narrow passage with a bakery directly ahead. To the left, a car park, with shoppers milling around automated ticket machines; to the right, an uncovered, pedestrianized shopping zone with branches of Top Man, HMV, Ann Summers. *Think.* Vincent slung the leather bag over his shoulder and walked west, looking for a café or hotel, somewhere to conceal himself. He came out under a walkway into another section of street closed to traffic. Ahead of him, beside a boarded-up branch of Woolworth's, there was a busy café with tables out on the street, plenty of customers inside and out. The Boston Tea Party. He walked through the door, found the eyes of a bottle-blonde waitress with a bob and asked if he could use the toilet.

'No problem,' she said. She had an Eastern European accent, probably Polish. She waved him upstairs.

Vincent moved quickly now, because he was cornered and they could come for him at any time. He went into the toilet, locked the door and began to take off his clothes. He took the new outfit from the leather bag and put on the underpants, the jeans, the deck shoes, the polo shirt and the tweed jacket. He left his wallet and his phone in his black leather jacket and hooked the jacket on the back of the door. There was a half-empty box in the corner of the toilet filled with bottles of washing-up fluid and he stuffed the clothes on top of them. He must leave no trace of himself. At the start of the operation, three passports had been left for him at locations across London for just this sort of emergency. At least that was one bit of forward-planning that Luc had got right. One of the passports was at Heathrow Terminal Five. As long as nobody had moved it, he would be free to leave. All he had to do was get to the airport.

Amelia Levene had been buying tights and ready-meals at that particular branch of Marks & Spencer for over ten years. She knew the layout of the store, knew that CUCKOO would find the car park exit and vanish within minutes if they didn't get close to him. So she had sent Aldrich round the back while Kevin Vigors, leaving his car in the market square, kept an eye on the New Canal entrance.

Kell and Amelia had parked alongside Harold's taxi and were trying to raise Aldrich on the radio. Vigors, twenty metres across the street, had already sat down in a bus stop, looking, for all the world, as though he waited there in the same seat, at the same time, every day of the week. Meanwhile, Kell had telephoned Elsa and told her to make her way to Charles de Gaulle on the first available flight. He was gambling that the crash meeting would take place in Paris and knew that CUCKOO had to be there by midnight. There was no point in Elsa continuing to monitor email and telephone traffic when the French knew they were compromised. Better that she get over to the French side so that she was in a position to tail CUCKOO from the airport or from Gare du Nord.

Six minutes went by. Still no word from Aldrich, still

no sign of CUCKOO. Amelia told Vigors to go into the store. Seconds later, Kell's mobile vibrated on the seat beside him. Amelia looked down at the read-out.

'It's Danny,' she said, putting the phone on loudspeaker.

'I have a visual. CUCKOO just came out the back. Passing HMV. Everything's closed, not that many people about.' There was a momentary loss of contact, as though Aldrich had lowered his phone. Then: 'He's carrying a new bag. You saw that, right?'

'We haven't seen anything,' Amelia replied. 'He probably bought a new set of clothes in M&S. He'll assume we've wired whatever he's wearing.'

'He'll assume correctly.' Aldrich coughed like a smoker. 'Hang on. CUCKOO just went into a café. The Boston Tea Party. Can you get Kev outside? There's an old Woolworth's opposite, Waterstones on the corner to my right. I'll go round the back, make sure there's no exit.'

Within two minutes Vigors had left the bus stop and jogged three hundred metres along New Canal, turning beside the branch of Waterstones. Aldrich saw him and nodded, confirming to Kell by phone that there was no back exit. Vigors sat down on a bench next to a teenager wolfing an onion-oozing, mid-morning hamburger. They saw CUCKOO coming out wearing a red polo shirt, a tweed jacket, blue deck shoes and denim jeans.

'Well, well, well,' Aldrich muttered into the phone. 'If anyone wants four hundred quid's worth of vintage leather jacket, looks like CUCKOO left his in the gents.'

'He's changed clothes?' Amelia asked.

'Just like you said he would.' Making eye contact with Vigors, Aldrich set off in pursuit, one man on one side of

341

the street, one man on the other. 'Not sure the look really suits him. Confirm, Kev and I are tailing.'

'Watch yourselves,' Kell said. 'He'll use windows, he'll stop and let you come past him. Go one at a time and keep some distance.'

'We've done this before,' Aldrich replied, though without reprimand.

'He'll almost certainly try for a taxi,' Amelia added, catching Kell's eye. 'Whatever you do, boys, don't lose him. Without the jacket, we don't have a fix on his position. If Vincent disappears, everything disappears with him.'

67

Vigors and Aldrich tailed CUCKOO to a branch of Waitrose on the outskirts of town, Vigors guiding Kell towards them so that there were three sets of eyes on the Frenchman, staggered along the route. Having spent ten minutes in the store, CUCKOO found a taxi outside, just as Amelia had predicted. She had brought the Audi to a petrol station within two hundred metres of the Waitrose car park and picked up Kell as CUCKOO's cab passed them, heading out on to the Salisbury ring-road. A minute later, Harold scooped up Vigors and Aldrich and the two vehicles followed Vincent's taxi in parallels as far as Grateley, a small village fifteen miles east of Salisbury.

CUCKOO pulled into Grateley station shortly before eleven o'clock. He paid the driver and bought a train ticket from an automated machine. The station was deserted and Kell knew that he could not afford to risk putting one of the team on to the platform. Instead, he sent Aldrich, Vigors and Harold ahead to Andover, the next stop on the line and told Elsa, who was driving past

343

Stonehenge, to divert to Salisbury station, in case CUCKOO doubled-back.

In the end, he boarded a London train. For eight minutes, Kell lost CUCKOO in a surveillance black hole until Vigors, whom Harold had driven to Andover at a steady 85 mph, joined the train. As he passed through Whitchurch and Overton, Vigors was able to assure Kell and Amelia, by text, that he was in visual contact with CUCKOO. Harold and Aldrich then effectively chased the train on parallel roads while Kell and Amelia remained behind in Andover. Basingstoke was the first major intersection on the London route and Kell anticipated that CUCKOO might attempt to leave the train and to switch to another service. Aldrich, arriving on the Reading platform just thirty seconds before CUCKOO's train pulled in, was informed by Vigors that he had decided to remain on board. So Aldrich and Harold continued east towards Woking, where CUCKOO did indeed switch routes, stepping off the London service at the last moment and joining a Reading train, leaving Vigors stranded on board. His sleight of hand, however, was observed by Aldrich, who managed to catch the Reading service, albeit three carriages down, while Harold looked on from an opposite platform.

Kell had never known a more complex and operationally challenging period. The Audi was a mess of road maps, sat-navs and communications equipment. By the time CUCKOO was on his way to Reading, with Aldrich trying to find him by walking down the carriages, Vigors was out of the game and Kell effectively down to two pairs of eyes. He rang Vigors and told him to go to London and to wait at Waterloo station, on the off chance that CUCKOO would try to head into the city. If he did so, Vigors might have an opportunity to follow him out to Gatwick or Luton, or even on to a Eurostar service from St Pancras. Meanwhile, Elsa had been sent ahead to Heathrow.

In the end, the Frenchman kept things simple. At Reading, he again switched services. Aldrich had more than enough time to follow him off the train, even to wait alongside him on the platform, and to travel back towards Woking, where he called Kell to tell him that CUCKOO had boarded a RailAir bus to Heathrow. Harold was more than twenty miles away, snagged in traffic on the outskirts of Reading with one bar of power on his mobile, but Aldrich was still able to follow the bus in a cab while Kell and Amelia went ahead to the airport.

They were sitting in the car park of a Holiday Inn, at the edge of the M4, when Amelia's mobile phone rang. The number was unknown, an echo-delay on the line as she put the call on speaker.

'Is this Amelia Levene?'

Kell knew immediately who was calling. A Frenchwoman, fluent English with a strong American accent.

'Who am I speaking to, please?'

'You can call me Madeleine Brive. I met your friend, Stephen Uniacke, on a ferry to Marseille.'

Amelia locked on to Kell's eyes. 'I know who you are.'

The voice became both louder and clearer. 'I want you to listen very carefully to me, Mrs Levene. As you are aware, the primary operation against your service has failed. You will never know who was behind it. You will never find the people responsible.'

Kell frowned, wondering what Valerie's remarks revealed about her state of mind. Was she concerned that they knew her location?

'I doubt that,' Amelia replied.

'You may be interested to know the whereabouts of your son.'

Kell felt a coil of blind anger and could only imagine what Amelia was faced with.

'Mrs Levene?'

'Please go on,' she said.

A young couple, trailing suitcases and jet lag, walked past the Audi on their way towards the Holiday Inn.

'You speak French, am I correct?'

'You are correct.'

'Then I will speak in French to you, Mrs Levene, because I want you to understand every . . . every *nuance* of what I am about to tell you.' She switched to her native tongue. 'This is now a private operation. François Malot is being held at a location in France. In order to secure his release, five million euros should be paid into a Turks and Caicos trust within three days. The details of the account will be sent to you in a separate way. Do I have your cooperation?'

Kell could have no bearing on the decision. He looked quickly at Amelia, sensing that she would capitulate.

'You have my cooperation,' she said.

'Within the next twenty-four hours, we will send you proof that your son is alive. If I do not receive the sum of money requested by Wednesday at 1800 hours, he will be executed.'

The mobile phone began to beep. A second call was coming in. Kell looked down at the read-out and saw that Aldrich was trying to reach them.

'Hang up,' he mouthed, gesturing to Amelia, who had reached the same conclusion. They were at war with these people; everything was now about power and control.

'Fine,' she said, 'you'll have your money,' and shut off the call. Amelia allowed herself only a moment's reflection before connecting Aldrich to the car.

'Go ahead, Danny,' she said.

'Terminal Five. CUCKOO just got off the bus. Must be looking to fly BA to France.'

68

Within ten minutes, Elsa Cassani, sitting patiently in a Terminal Three branch of Starbucks with only a laptop and an iPhone for company, had scribbled down every flight leaving for France from Heathrow airport in the next five hours.

'CUCKOO has a lot of choice,' she told Kell, who was en route with Amelia to Terminal Five. 'There are flights to Nice, Paris Charles de Gaulle, Paris Orly, Toulouse Blagnac and Lyon. They go all the time.'

Kell dismissed Lyon and Nice, but Toulouse remained a possibility, because the city was within an hour of Salles-sur-l'Hers. Yet Paris still seemed the most likely destination. He called Aldrich inside the terminal building for an update. CUCKOO had sat down at a table in Café Nero, a stone's throw from passport control.

'He went straight there, guv.'

'Didn't buy a ticket? Didn't go to the BA desk?'

'No. Hasn't bought a coffee, either. Just sitting there.'

Kell explained the situation to Amelia, who hazarded what turned out to be an accurate guess.

'He's either meeting somebody or picking up a package. They may have cached a passport for him. Tell Danny to sit tight.'

Needing the jolt of a cup of coffee, Vincent stood up, queued at the counter and bought a double espresso. His table was still free by the time he returned to his seat. For hours he had felt an almost fatalistic sense of imminent capture; everything he'd done in Salisbury, every move he'd made on the trains, wouldn't have been enough to throw off a decent British team. There were cameras at the airport, police in plain clothes, customs officials, security personnel. What if his photograph had been circulated among them? How was he going to get on to a plane? If he could just get through passport control, he might throw off MI6 on the Paris Metro. They wouldn't be able to operate as effectively on French soil. But even that loophole seemed to close in front of Vincent's eyes; there was an MI6 station in Paris and Amelia had had more than enough time to arrange blanket surveillance across the capital.

Think.

Try to see it from her perspective. She doesn't want her secret to get out. If it does, her career is over. Only a handful of her most trusted colleagues will know about François Malot. Maybe she's just as confused, just as rattled, as I am. Buoyed by this thought, Vincent sank his double espresso and did what he had come to do.

The Multi-Faith Prayer Room was a few paces away. He walked through the door from the main terminal and came into a short narrow corridor with prayer rooms on either side. To his left, a bearded Muslim was kneeling on a mat, in the act of praying. To the right, three veiled African women were seated on plastic chairs. They watched Vincent as he passed. The bathroom door was open. He went inside and locked it.

The bathroom stank of urine and patchouli oil. Vincent waved his hand under the automatic drier to create a covering noise and stood on the toilet, pushing one of the ceiling tiles above his head. It came free and jammed at an angle as small particles of dried paint and dust fell into his hair. Vincent looked down to protect his eyes while feeling blindly with his right hand, pushing through what felt like tiny nests or cobwebs, little piles of dust. His arm began to ache and he switched hands, turning around on the toilet seat so that he could search in the opposite direction. The handdrier cut out and he flushed the toilet with his foot, hearing voices outside in the corridor. Was it the police? Had they followed him into the prayer rooms so that they could make a discreet arrest?

Then, something. The crisp edge of a large envelope. Vincent went up on tiptoes and pushed the loose ceiling tile further back, stretching to reach what he had come for. It felt like his first piece of luck in hours. It was the cached package, covered in a scattering of dust. He flushed the toilet with his foot a second time, replaced the tile, sat down and opened the seal. Five hundred euros in cash, a French driving licence, a clean phone, a passport, Visa and American Express cards. Everything in the name 'Gerard Taine'. Vincent flicked the dust from his hair and clothes, left the bathroom and carried the package out into the terminal.

Time to go home. Time to get a plane to France.

'So that was interesting.'

Danny Aldrich had watched the scene unfold from a queue at one of the automated check-in machines.

'What happened?' Kell asked.

'CUCKOO went into the multi-faith rooms, came out five minutes later carrying something. Now he's fifth in the queue at the BA ticket desk.'

Kell looked at Amelia. They were both thinking the same thing.

'He must have had a passport cached in there,' she said. 'We need to know where he's flying to. Can you get into the queue behind him?'

'No chance,' Aldrich replied. 'Not a good idea to get that close after Reading. He'll make me.'

'You carrying any ID?' Kell asked.

'Sure.'

'Then find a member of airport staff on the security side, preferably somebody high up the food chain. Tell them that they need to talk to whoever serves Vincent at the BA counter. Be discreet about it. Make sure he doesn't see what's going on. Get the flight number, get the name on the passport, credit-card details if he doesn't pay cash. Can you manage that?'

'No problem.'

Amelia nodded in mute agreement. 'Nice idea,' she said as Kell hung up. The Audi was parked on the second floor of a multi-storey short-term car park, less than a minute's walk from where Aldrich was standing. Against the grinding roar of an aeroplane passing low overhead, Amelia adjusted her position in the passenger seat so that she was facing Kell at an angle. 'Something has occurred to me,' she said. Kell was reminded of a gesture Amelia had made at the office in Redan Place, a quiet resignation in her features. It was uncharacteristic of her to be so shaken. 'I should go to Number 10. We should try to set up a line to the French, cut some sort of deal. Falling on my sword may be the only way to save François.'

Falling on my sword. Kell disliked the phrase for its pointless grandeur. Amelia was better than that.

'That won't save him,' he said. 'Whoever these people are, Paris will tip them off. Even if it's a rogue operation, which I suspect it now is, there will be factions within the DGSE loyal to the perpetrators. There'll be an internal leak, François will be killed, Luc and Valerie will catch the next boat to Guyana.' When he saw that he was making no progress with his argument, Kell took a risk. 'Besides, if you go, my career is finished. The minute Truscott gets his hands on the tiller, he'll throw me to the wolves over Yassin Gharani. If you don't survive, I'm looking at growing tomatoes for the next thirty years.'

To his surprise, Amelia smiled.

'Then we'd better make sure nobody finds out what we're up to,' she said, reaching for his hand. It was as though she had been testing him and was now assured of his loyalty. 'I'll talk to some military friends, put a unit together in France. And get Kevin on the phone. We ought to send him up to St Pancras.'

69

It took Vincent Cévennes seven minutes to reach the front of the queue at the British Airways ticket desk, where he was observed looking at a flight schedule on the teller's computer screen before handing over a French passport and a credit card, in return for a ticket. With CUCKOO's attention fully occupied, Aldrich had taken the opportunity to flag down two patrolling police officers and to inform them that he was a surveillance officer with the Secret Intelligence Service. One of the officers agreed to approach the BA desk and to interview the female member of staff who had just sold CUCKOO a ticket. Aldrich made it clear that any conversation must take place out of sight of other passengers in the terminal.

They waited until CUCKOO had taken a lift upstairs to the duty-free shopping level. The more senior of the two policemen then approached the BA desk, indicated to the teller that he would like a discreet word, and managed to hold a brief conversation with her in a small staffroom secluded behind the ticket desks. The entire exchange took less than five minutes.

Aldrich called Kell with the news.

'Right. Got a pen? CUCKOO is travelling under the name Gerard Taine. Just paid five hundred and eighty-four pounds on an American Express card for a business-class seat on the BA flight to Charles de Gaulle, leaving Terminal Five at eighteen fifteen.'

Kell, who was still in the car park, looked at his watch.

'That's in less than two hours. Get two tickets on the same plane. One for you, one for Elsa. Travel separately. When CUCKOO comes out the other side, I'll try to be there.'

'How are you going to manage that?'

Kell had looked at the list of flights leaving Heathrow for Paris before six.

'There's an Air France to Charles de Gaulle leaving Terminal Four fifteen minutes before you take off. We're going there now, I'll try to get on board.' Kell had already started the engine and was pulling out of the parking bay. 'Kevin is en route to St Pancras. Amelia will stay here and organize hire cars at Gare du Nord and Charles de Gaulle. If we're delayed or you don't hear from me, try to stay on CUCKOO's tail as long as you can. He'll probably take the Metro, try to shake you off in Paris. If we get lucky, he'll hail a cab.'

Fifteen minutes later, Kell was barging the queue at the Air France desk in Terminal Four and hustling himself on to a packed Sunday-night flight to Paris, shelling out more than seven hundred euros for the last seat on the plane. By eight fifteen local time he had touched down at Charles de Gaulle, only to be told that CUCKOO's BA flight was delayed by half an hour. That gave him time to pick up the hire car and to drive it in loops around the airport, waiting for a call from Aldrich with the number plate of whatever taxi CUCKOO hailed outside the terminal. In the end, CUCKOO caught an RER train to the city, standing for the duration of the journey just three rows from Elsa Cassani, looking, for all the world, like any other washed-out twenty-something Italian returning from a hedonistic weekend in London. Danny Aldrich boarded an Air France bus to Etoile. Kell took the A3 autoroute south-west into Paris, but his Renault became snarled in peripherique traffic and he lost contact with the RER. By the time Elsa had pulled into Chatelet ten minutes later, she was the only member of the team within two miles of the target.

CUCKOO lost her in less than fifteen minutes. Emerging from Chatelet, he crossed the Seine and boarded a metro at St Michel, heading south towards Porte d'Orleans. At Denfert-Rochereau station, having spotted Elsa three times since Charles de Gaulle – once on the RER, once while crossing the Pont Notre Dame and once in his carriage between Saint-Sulpice and St-Placide – CUCKOO forced open the doors as they were closing and jumped out on to the platform, watching Elsa glide past him in a state of mute obliviousness.

Five minutes later she had surfaced at Mouton Duvernet and called Kell with the news.

'Tom, I am so, so sorry,' she said. 'I lost him. I lost CUCKOO.'

70

My name is Gerard Taine. I am no longer François Malot. I work for the Ministry of Defence. I live in a small village outside Nantes. My wife is a schoolteacher. We have three children, twin girls of two and a son who is five years old. I am no longer François Malot.

Vincent remembered the mantra of his emergency cover but did not know Taine in the way that he had known François. He knew nothing of his interests, nothing of his proclivities; he could not imagine the grammar, the *archi-tecture* of his soul. He had given no thought to him in the way that he had thought about François, day and night, for months. Taine was just a fallback; Malot had been his life.

Vincent sat on the bed in the Hotel Lutetia, unsure if the British had followed him, unsure if Luc or Valerie would ever come. He felt as though he would never leave this place. He felt as though he was a shell, a failure, a man who was being made to pay the heaviest price for a sin he had never committed. It was like that time at high school

356

when he was fourteen and his whole class, every friend he had ever made, every girl he had ever liked, turned on him because he had reported a case of bullying to a teacher. Vincent had been trying to do the right thing. He had been trying to save his closest friend from the turmoil of the older children's attacks, but was betrayed by the very teacher in whom he had confided. As a result, they had all rounded on him – even the friend whose neck Vincent had tried to save – and for many months afterwards had humiliated him in the classroom, caking his clothes in food and shit as he walked home, screaming 'Bitch!' and 'Rat!' whenever he passed. Vincent's whole sense of justice, of right and wrong, had been inverted by that experience. He had learned that there was no truth, there was no kindness. Even his own father had disowned him. *You never betray your comrades,* he had said. *You never betray your friends,* as though Vincent was one of the soldiers he had fought alongside in Algeria. But he was just a fourteen-year-old schoolboy with no mother, no sister, no brother to love or understand him. *They were hurting my friend, Papa,* he said, but the old man hadn't listened and now he was long dead and Vincent wished that he was in the hotel room so that he could tell him what had happened in England, what had happened to François, and maybe try to explain all over again that all he had ever wanted to do was protect his friend and to make his father proud.

He stood up and went to the window, looking down on to Boulevard Raspail. The curtains were open, the window ajar. He poured himself a whisky from the mini-bar, opened the carton of cigarettes he had purchased at Heathrow and raised a silent toast to François Malot, blowing smoke out into the damp Paris night. It was the wrong thing to think

– he knew that – but he missed Amelia, he missed their talks and the meals they had enjoyed together, the time they had spent at the pool and the beach. He no longer wanted her; she had betrayed him and had ceased to exist as a woman. But he missed her as François might have missed her, because she was his mother, because she had cared for him and would have gone to the ends of the earth to protect her son. A woman that powerful, a woman that strong. Imagine possessing a mother like that. François was so lucky to have her.

Vincent drained the whisky, poured another from the mini-bar, even though Luc and Valerie might arrive at any moment and smell the alcohol on his breath. He began to dread what they were going to do. It was the sense of isolation he couldn't stand; everything he had known about himself, everything he had trusted and believed, had been stripped away from him in just a few hours. Like the bullying at school: one minute he had been one person, the next he was somebody else. A rat. A traitor. Their bitch. He had been right never to trust anybody after that. It was what he had thought going into the first interviews with the Directorate, what they must have seen in him, what they must have liked.

My solitude is my talent, he thought. My self-sufficiency is my strength.

There was a knock at the door.

71

By midnight, Kevin Vigors had arrived in Paris, picked up a Peugeot hire car at Gare du Nord and driven south to Boulevard Saint-Germain where he found Kell, Elsa and Aldrich at a table in Brasserie Lipp, nursing their sorrows with four plates of choucroute and a couple of bottles of Chinon.

'I don't know what to say,' Elsa whispered as Vigors slipped on to the banquette beside her. 'I did not have the experience that Danny has, that you have. I am so sorry that . . .'

Kell interrupted her. 'Elsa, if you apologize one more time, I'll get you a job fixing computers in Albania for the rest of your life. There was nothing you could have done. One of us should have got on the train with you. It's impossible to follow a trained target without back-up.' He looked up at the three faces gathered around him and raised his glass of wine. 'All of you were fantastic today in extremely difficult circumstances. It was a miracle we got as far as we did. There's still every chance that we can find

François once Luc and Valerie make contact with Amelia tomorrow night.'

He had already given the bad news to Amelia, who had been obliged to stay in the UK so that she could put in an honest day's work on Monday for the benefit of Truscott, Marquand and Haynes. To avoid spending the night with Giles in Chelsea, she had taken a room at the Holiday Inn, where she was gradually making her way through the various items that CUCKOO had left on the back seat of Aldrich's cab. She kept the gold lighter, engraved with the initials P.M., but put everything else back into Vincent's suitcase and the black leather holdall, wondering what she would do with them. Sitting alone on the sixth floor of the hotel, looking out over a gridlocked M4, her sense of frustration was akin to the powerlessness she had felt in the face of her late brother's cancer. Despite all the resources at her disposal, all of her experience and expertise, she could do nothing to influence the events unfolding in France. Her trust in Thomas Kell was absolute, but she could hardly believe that she had left François' safety in the hands of only three men and an Italian computer specialist with non-existent experience in the field. Amelia had managed to organize a three-man team of 'security experts' – an Office euphemism for ex-SAS soldiers moon-lighting in the private sector – who would leave for Carcassone in the morning. But she could only afford to have them on stand-by for forty-eight hours, not least because she had drained one of her bank accounts to pay for them. Unless Kell discovered François' whereabouts in that time, there would be no military option for seizing her son. And how were they going to find François without CUCKOO? The trail had gone cold.

Amelia was checking her emails at regular intervals, staying in touch with Kell and confirming arrangements with Anthony White, the commander of the security team. At twenty past eleven, she heard the ping of a message coming through on her laptop.

It was from GCHQ, with the subject heading 'Amex'.

You requested live trace on American Express card 3759 876543 21001 / 06/14 / GERARD TAINE
Card use (abbreviated):
British Airways (Sales) / LHR T5 / 16.23 GMT   £584.00
World Duty Free / LHR T5   / 17.04 GMT   £43.79
Hotel Lutetia / Paris / 00.05 GMT+1   €267.00

She picked up the phone and dialled Kell.

72

The Hotel Lutetia was a five-star Parisian landmark known to Kell from his brief tenure in the city a decade earlier; he had held meetings with SIS and DGSE colleagues in the lobby and knew something of the hotel's history as a base for the occupying German army during World War II. It was less than a mile from Brasserie Lipp and would logically make a safe, discreet location for CUCKOO's crash meeting with Luc and Valerie.

Within four minutes of receiving the call from Amelia, Kell had paid the bill at Lipp, walked south-west with Elsa down Rue de Sèvres and told Danny Aldrich and Kevin Vigors to park as close to the hotel as possible.

Aldrich found a space for the Peugeot on the eastern side of Boulevard Raspail and kept an eye on the entrance. Vigors went straight to the reception desk and booked a double room in his own name before settling into an armchair with clear sight of the main bank of lifts. Kell and Elsa walked into the hotel arm in arm, like lovers returning from a midnight stroll.

'We're staying here,' he told her as they ambled past reception. 'Dirty weekend. We're going to have a drink in the bar before we go up to bed.'

'Promises, promises,' she replied, and squeezed his arm tight against her chest.

The bar was in a large rectangular lobby the size of a real tennis court. About ten guests were seated in scattered groups on armchairs upholstered in scarlet and black, *digestifs* and cups of coffee on low wooden tables between them. A lone waiter moved briskly among the art deco sculptures, the tinkle and cough of polite conversation accompanied by a bald pianist covering show tunes at a grand piano in the corner. Kell sat in an armchair facing out towards the main entrance; Elsa was opposite him, watching the bar. For half an hour they conversed in English about Elsa's childhood in Italy, while Kell sent and received occasional text messages to Amelia, Vigors and Aldrich.

'If you were my lover and you spent this much time on your phone, I would leave you,' she said.

Kell looked up and smiled. 'Sounds like I've been warned.'

Seconds later, pushing through the revolving doors of the hotel, a young Arab man came in from the street wearing denim jeans and a leather motorcycling jacket emblazoned with the Marlboro logo. Kell could not at first make out his face, but as he passed the reception desk, he saw to his astonishment that it was one of the two men who had attacked him in Marseille.

'Jesus Christ.'

Elsa, reclining sleepily in her chair, leaned forward. 'What?'

'It's the guy from the . . .' He had to think quickly. There was no time to alert Vigors. 'Go to the lifts. Don't hesitate.' Elsa was out of her seat, her consternation plain for anyone to see. Kell lowered his voice. 'There's a young French Arab heading there now. He's part of their team. Follow him. Try to find out which floor he's going to.'

The waiter paused beside Kell's table as Elsa walked away.

'Is everything all right, monsieur?' he asked.

'Just my girlfriend,' he replied. 'She thinks she saw her cousin going past.'

'I see.' The waiter glanced after Elsa, noticing that a guest in the corner of the lobby was trying to seek his attention. 'Would you like anything else before I close the bar?'

Kell saw Elsa arriving at the lifts.

'No, no thanks,' he said, turning back to the waiter. 'Could I please just have our bill?'

73

As Akim stepped into the lift, sweating beneath the heat and weight of the leather jacket, he heard a woman's voice behind him and turned to find a dark-haired girl, speaking in Italian, running towards the lifts. If she had not been young he would have allowed the doors to close, but he pressed the button at the base of the panel and they parted just in time to allow her to squeeze into the cabin.

'*Grazie*,' she said, breathless and gratefully catching his eye, then corrected herself, remembering that she was in Paris: '*Merci*.'

He liked the naturalness of her, a raw girl from nothing who had made it to a place of money. She wasn't a whore; maybe somebody's mistress or a guest at a family reunion. Looked like she knew how to be around a man; looked like a woman of experience. He breathed in the smell of her, the way he sometimes walked into a woman's perfume a second after she had passed him in the street.

'*Prego*,' he said, a little late, but he wanted to make a

connection with her. Akim switched to French and said: 'My pleasure.'

She was not exactly beautiful, but pretty enough and with that glint in her eye that made everything come together. He wished he could have more time to be with her. He had pressed the button for the fifth storey and she now pushed six.

'We are almost going to the same floor,' he said.

The lift climbed through the building. The Italian girl did not respond. Maybe the adrenalin of the job was making him seem pushy. As the doors opened on the fifth floor, Akim muttered *'Bonsoir'* and this time she did respond, saying *'Oui'* as he walked outside. He waited until the lift had closed, then turned left towards 508.

The corridor was deserted. He came to Vincent's door and knocked quietly. He heard the soft padding of approaching footsteps, then the slight contact of Vincent's head as it touched the door, staring through the fish-eye lens. The latch came off and he was invited inside.

'Where's Luc?'

Not: *How are you, Akim?* Not: *What a nice surprise.* Just: *Where's Luc?* Like Akim was a third-class citizen. Vincent had always made him feel like that.

'They're coming later,' he said.

The room was large and smelled of cigarettes with a breeze blowing through it. There was a window open, a plastic pole on the curtain tapping against the glass. Vincent was wearing a white Lutetia dressing-gown over blue denim jeans with bare feet and looked, for the first time in Akim's memory, like he had lost control of himself.

'What do you mean "coming later"?'

Akim sat in a chair facing the double bed. Vincent's head

had made a neat dent in one of the pillows on the left-hand side, like a kid had done a karate chop. There was a remote control on the bedcover, two miniature bottles of whisky beside the TV.

'Are you going to answer me?' Vincent placed himself between the bed and the chair, like it was Akim's duty to tell him whatever he needed to know. 'How did the British find out about me? Who told them? What's happening with François?'

'I thought *you* were François, Vincent?' Akim replied, because he couldn't resist it. They'd all laughed about how seriously Vincent had taken the job. 'Brando', Slimane called him, even to his face, because at the house he'd never once dropped out of character.

'You making fun of me?' Vincent said. He possessed some physical strength and his temper was quick, but he had no guts. Akim knew that about him. Nothing to respect.

'Nobody would ever make fun of you, Vincent.'

Akim watched as Cévennes moved to the side of the bed and sat down. The Academy pin-up, the DGSE golden boy. Vincent had always had a high opinion of himself.

'Where's Luc?' Vincent asked again.

Akim was already bored by the questions and decided to have more fun. 'What about Valerie? Don't you care about her, too?'

'Luc's the boss,' Vincent replied quickly.

'You reckon?'

There was silence between them now, time in which Vincent seemed to come to terms with the anomaly of Akim's presence in his room.

'What's this about?' he said. 'You got a message for me?'

'I do,' Akim replied.

It was simple after that. Just a question of commitment. He unzipped the motorbike jacket, reached inside for the gun, moved it level with Vincent's chest and fired a single silenced shot that lifted him back towards the wall. Akim stood up and stepped forward. Vincent's eyes were drowning in the shock of what had been done to him; there were tears in his eyes. His face was white, blood gargling in his throat. Akim fired two further shots into his skull and heart; the first of them shutting Vincent down like a doll. He then picked up the spent cartridges, secured the gun inside the jacket and moved towards the door, checking that nothing had fallen out of his pockets when he had sat on the chair. He looked through the fish-eye lens, saw that the area outside was clear, and walked into the corridor.

74

Kell did not bother to call Amelia in London to get clearance for what he was about to do. He told Vigors to look for a security camera blind spot near the fifth-floor elevator and to wait for any sign of the Arab or other members of the DGSE team entering or leaving Vincent's room. He instructed Aldrich to wait in the car outside and told Elsa to go to the room that Vigors had booked at the Lutetia.

'There's nothing more you can do,' he told her. 'Get some sleep. I may need you in the morning.'

Then he waited outside the hotel. He smoked a cigarette and paced the pavement. It was past one o'clock on a Monday morning in Paris, still warm and humid. A man in his mid-fifties came past Kell and walked up the steps of the hotel. Everybody a stranger, everybody a threat. Kell turned and looked at Aldrich, still as alert and as reliable as he had been all day long. The best of the best. They nodded at one another. A police car with yellowed headlights moved disinterestedly north along Raspail.

The Arab had been inside for less than ten minutes when

Kell's phone began to pulse in his pocket. It was Vigors.

'He's already leaving. Just took the stairs. I'm in the lift.'

'You sure it was him?'

'Same guy. Red-and-white motorcycle jacket, heading down. He'll be there . . .'

The signal cut out. Kell motioned to Aldrich who started the engine on the Peugeot. He looked up the steps of the hotel and in the glass of the revolving door caught the movement of someone walking towards the entrance. He knew that Vigors would be ten seconds behind him. Eye contact with Aldrich. This was it.

The Arab came down the steps of the hotel, saw Kell to his right, did not appear to recognize him from Marseille but moved left, as if to avoid contact. This took him towards the Peugeot. Vigors had got out of the lift, run across the lobby and was already through the revolving doors. Kell waited until the Arab was two metres from the car, then ran at his back, driving his right hand into the upper section of his skull and steering him with his left as Vigors came past them, opened the rear door of the Peugeot and turned to help. Kell remembered the Arab's weight, his wiry cunning, but Vigors was far stronger and with the element of surprise had forced him into the back seat of the car within seconds. Aldrich lurched out on to Boulevard Raspail as the door slammed shut behind him. Vigors pushed the boy's head back as Kell encircled his body, trapping his arms against his chest. The Arab was shouting, struggling to get free, spit hitting Kell's neck and face.

'Shut the fuck up or I will break your arm,' he hissed in Arabic, and then was pushed against the door as Aldrich made a fast-right down Rue Saint-Sulpice. Kell had no idea where they could take him, no idea what they would do

370

with him afterwards. He was not even sure that the kidnapping had passed unnoticed on a quiet Paris thoroughfare in the small hours of the morning.

'Head south-west,' he said. 'Pantheon. Place d'Italie.'

Beneath the thick leather of the motorcycle jacket Kell could feel the hard outline of a weapon.

'Kev, take his arms.'

Kell loosened his grip on the Arab and Vigors wrenched the arms backwards so that they were pinned behind the Arab's back. He had stopped struggling, but there was thick white spittle, like wet chalk, in the grooves of his mouth. Kell reached for the zip on the jacket and the Arab tried to bite at his hand, lowering his chin. Kell said: 'Don't be a baby' and tugged his head back. He lowered the zip, reached inside the jacket and immediately felt the butt of the gun. He pulled it out.

'Why are you carrying a silenced automatic?' he asked in French. All of them could smell the cordite. 'More to the point, why have you just fired it?'

Vigors recognized the gun as a SIG Sauer 9mm. Kell removed the silencer. There were eight rounds still in the magazine. He leaned forward and placed the gun in the footwell of the passenger seat, then continued searching the jacket. He pulled out a wallet, a mobile phone, a packet of cigarettes. He told the Arab to pitch forward so that he could search his back pockets. Aldrich, a block east of the Pantheon, removed his own belt and passed it to Vigors, who fashioned a basic wrist restraint around the Arab's hands. Kell then took out his phone and sent a text to Amelia.

Going to need a safe house ASAP. CUCKOO probably down. Suspect in car. One of two from Marseille attack.

75

The message forced Amelia to involve SIS Station in Paris, a move that she had always been reluctant to make. Widening the circle of knowledge, even in a secret organization, increased the chances that word of the DGSE operation would spread through the Service. So she chose somebody young and ambitious, a fast-stream bachelor of twenty-seven who would be only too happy to help out the Chief-designate in the hope of seeing his skill and discretion rewarded further along the line.

Mike Drummond was woken from his bed just before three o'clock. By four, he had dressed and driven twenty-five minutes south of Invalides to Orsay, a commuter town where SIS rented a detached, two-bedroom house in a quiet suburban neighbourhood a few minutes from the railway station. Kell waited until Drummond confirmed that he was inside the property, then asked Aldrich to proceed to the address. By four fifteen, he was showing Akim into a modestly furnished living room with a small, flat-screen television in front of the window, vases of dried flowers above a gas fireplace, a half-finished bottle of Stolichnaya standing alone on a tray near the door.

'Drink?' he said.

'Water,' Akim replied.

In the car, things had calmed down between them. Akim had told them his name, denied killing CUCKOO, denied any involvement in the kidnapping of François Malot and issued a threat that his 'friends' in Paris would come looking for him if he didn't get home by noon. But the rage and physical aggression in his behaviour had subsided. It had been replaced by a more sanguine attitude that Kell believed he could exploit.

'What about food? Are you hungry?' He looked at Drummond, a ginger-haired Brummie with freckles and a snub nose who seemed to have taken a decision only to speak when spoken to. 'There's food in the fridge, right?'

''Course,' Drummond replied.

Vigors had been to the bathroom, fixed three cups of instant coffee and taken one of them out to Aldrich in the car. The street was black and still, not a twitch of curtain, not a stray cat or dog. Vigors offered to switch places with Aldrich, who had been driving for the better part of two hours. He sat in the vehicle on watch while Aldrich went inside.

'Here's the situation,' Kell said, welcoming him into the room as he directed his words at Akim. 'We are all of us officers with the Secret Intelligence Service, better known to you, I suppose, as MI6. We have a twelve-man team in Paris on standby and a larger operation in London monitoring this conversation from our headquarters on the Thames. You are perfectly safe. We used force against you at the Lutetia because we had no choice, but our discussion now is not going to be as uncomfortable as you think. As

I said in the car, I remember you from Marseille, I know that you were just doing your job. I am not in the business of revenge, Akim. I'm not interested in seeing that justice is done for the murder of Vincent Cévennes.'

The young Arab looked up, confused by his interrogator's strategy. Drummond had been into the kitchen and now wordlessly passed the prisoner a glass of water before retreating into a chair. Akim's hand shook as he drank it.

'I looked through your phone in the car,' Kell continued. It occurred to him that Drummond would be taking mental notes, both with a view to improving his own interview technique and to see how far the infamous Witness X would pursue the softer lines of enquiry before resorting to threat and malice.

'I need to make a call,' Akim replied. They were speaking in French. 'Like I told you, if I don't tell them I am coming back, they will take action.'

'What kind of action? Who are the people you want us to contact?'

Kell was gambling everything on a calculation he had made about Akim's personality. He was a thug, yes, a man who would kill on orders, but he was not without decency. His phone had been full of photographs: of smiling girlfriends, of family members, children, even landscapes and buildings that had caught the young Arab's eye. There were text messages full of humour; messages of concern for a sick grandparent in Toulon; expressions of devotion to a benevolent God. Kell was certain that Akim was just a street kid who had been plucked from prison by French Intelligence and turned into what a long-ago colleague in Ireland had described as 'a useful idiot of violence'. He possessed the self-improving drive of a survivor born into no money, no education, no hope. But there was something sentimental about him, as though he had promised himself better things.

'I can't tell you that,' Akim replied, but Kell had not expected an answer without sugaring the pill.

'Then maybe I should tell you,' he said. He went towards the door and opened the bottle of vodka, wanting a couple of fingers to jolt his senses and carry him into the morning. 'I think their names are Luc Javeau and Valerie de Serres. I think they hired you to kill Phillippe and Jeannine Malot in Egypt earlier this year.' To Kell's surprise, Akim did not rebut the accusation. 'We know that François Malot was kidnapped shortly after his parents' funeral and that a DGSE officer named Vincent Cévennes impersonated him in an influence operation against a senior figure within our organization.'

Drummond crossed and uncrossed his legs, realizing that Kell was referring to Amelia Levene. Aldrich flashed him a cold, appraising glance, an experienced old hand quietly telling the young pup to take that secret to his grave.

'I don't know,' Akim replied, shaking his head. 'Maybe this is true, maybe it isn't.' He had been wearing a tight black vest under the motorcycle jacket and raised his hands in defence, the nylon fabric accentuating the long muscles in his arms.

'We know it's true,' Kell said firmly. There was a sofa in the room and two armchairs. He rose from the sofa and crouched in front of Akim, glass of vodka in hand. 'When Vincent was exposed by MI6, I think Luc and Valerie panicked, yes? The operation was now a failure and they told you to kill him. But what should they do about François? Kill him, too, or ransom the boy to his mother?' Akim looked away, but Aldrich and Drummond offered no solace. 'Did you know that Valerie telephoned my boss this morning requesting five million euros for the safe return of her son?' The sum brought Akim's gaze directly back to Kell, as though something had stuck in his throat. 'How much of that money have you been promised? Five per cent? Ten? What about your other friend, the one who did this to my eye?' Kell pointed to the scar on his face and smiled. 'Does he get more than you or the same?'

Akim's answer lay in his silence. He did not reply to Kell's questions because he could not do so without losing face.

'What's that?' Kell stood up, went back to the sofa. 'They haven't promised you a share of the money?'

'No. Only a fee.'

Akim answered in Arabic, as though to hide his shame from Aldrich and Drummond. Kell did not know if either man could understand as he said:

'How much?'

'Seventy thousand.'

'Seventy thousand euros? That's it?'

'It was a lot of money.'

'It was a lot of money when you started, but it's not a lot of money now, is it? Luc and Valerie take off with five million euros sometime next week, making it impossible for you to work for the DGSE ever again. You're being used. Tell me about them. Tell me about their relationship. They've already put three deaths on your conscience, maybe four if they make you shoot François as well.'

Akim sneered. Suddenly he had been handed a chance to retaliate.

'I won't be shooting François,' he said. 'Slimane, he wants to do it.'

76

François heard the noise of the key at eight fifteen. Sometimes they woke him earlier, sometimes – like when Akim was on duty – they let him sleep.

The first day he was there Luc had told him to remain on the bed whenever somebody knocked on the door. If he wasn't sitting down when they came in, if François didn't have his hands raised in the air, palms open to show that they were empty, they would throw his food across the floor and then there would be nothing to eat for the rest of the day. So François did what he had always done and remained on the bed and raised his arms above his head, like a soldier in the act of surrender.

It was Valerie this morning. That was unusual. Behind her, Luc. No sign of Slimane, no sign of Akim. In the middle of the night he had heard a car pulling up outside the house and thought that he recognized the voice of the man who came inside and was greeted by Luc in the hall. One of the temporary guards the weekend when Slimane and Akim had gone to Marseille; ex-Foreign Legion, a macho, stubble-headed Aryan named Jacques who couldn't cook like the others, had a kind of lazy, ruthless stupidity. François assumed that he was coming back on duty. He prayed that Slimane had been given a few days off. He prayed that he had seen the last of him.

'We need to make a film,' Valerie said, indicating that François should remain on the bed. She was carrying a newspaper. Luc had an iPhone in his hand.

'What kind of film?'

'The kind that proves you're alive,' Luc replied bluntly. Their attitude towards him was brusque, even nervous. François had always tried to read his captors' behaviour, feeling that it would bring him to a better understanding of their motives and designs. Whenever they were curt like this, whenever he felt that he was being treated badly, he feared it was because they were planning to kill him.

'Hold this,' said Valerie, handing him a copy of *Le Figaro*. It was that morning's edition. There was a lead story about Sarkozy, an advertisement for holidays in Mexico, something on the right-hand side about Obama and funding in Washington. Luc dragged a wooden chair from the hall into the cell and sat on it, facing François and pointing the back of the iPhone at his bed.

'Say who you are,' he said. Valerie was standing over him and moved slightly to the left when Luc told her that she was blocking the light.

'My name is François Malot.' Inexplicably, François felt as though he had done something like this many times before. He looked up at Valerie. She was staring at the blank wall behind him.

'What is the date today?' Luc asked.

François turned the paper around and recited the date, then showed the front page to the lens.

'This is fine,' Valerie said and indicated to Luc that he should stop filming. 'What else does she need to know?'

François looked at them, trying to ascertain what they were thinking. He knew that he was being ransomed; he had been told that his 'mother' would pay. He knew nothing of her, only what Slimane had whispered to him night after night through the door. He had not wanted to believe any of that. In the first few hours of his captivity, François had thought that he was a victim of false identity, that they had taken the wrong man, killed the wrong family. Now, less than a month after his parents' murder, he had begun to feel free of them in a way that made him feel shameful and guilty. Surely he should still be grieving, even though they had grown so much apart? What sort of a son cared only for his own survival and felt relief that his mother and father had been killed? He wanted to speak to someone about it, to Christophe and Maria; he believed that he might be going slightly mad. They never tried to judge him. They always understood what he was trying to say.

'Tonight will be our last night in the house,' Valerie announced. 'This time tomorrow, we move.'

'Why?' François asked.

'*Why?*' Luc repeated, imitating François' voice and dragging the chair back out into the hall. François looked out beyond the open door and glimpsed Slimane in the living room. He had a lurching premonition that he would never see the morning.

'Because too many people have been to this house, too many people know you were here,' Valerie replied. Slimane turned and smiled at François, as if he had been listening to the conversation all along. 'We are in the process of making everything very simple.' Valerie crouched down and ran a hand through François' hair. 'Don't worry, little boy. Mummy will soon be coming to get you.'

77

Kell finished the vodka and wondered if he had read Akim wrong. Drummond had reacted as the Arab said: 'Slimane, he wants to do it', coughing in surprise and then pretending to clear his throat. Aldrich, suddenly tired and edgy, took a step forward, closing up the space as if to make sure that Akim never said anything like that again.

'You think it's funny?' Kell asked in English.

To his surprise, Akim replied in the same language: 'No.'

Kell paused. He looked up at Drummond, glanced across at Aldrich. There was a tiny gap in the curtains and it was becoming light outside. *I am the Americans with Yassin*, he told himself. *I can ask what I like, I can do what I like. None of it will ever leave this room.* He wanted suddenly to strike at Akim, to land one good, jaw-smashing punch to his face. But he stuck to his principles. He knew that everything he wanted to learn from the Arab would come if only he took his time.

'Do you have children, Mike?'

At first, Drummond didn't react, but then, in his surprise

at being addressed, said: 'No, no I don't' so quickly that he almost tripped on the words.

'Danny?'

'Two, guv,' said Aldrich.

'Boys? Girls? One of each?'

'A boy and a girl. Ashley's eight, Kelley's eleven.' He stretched out a hand and indicated the difference in their heights. Kell turned to Akim.

'How about you?'

'Children? Me?' It was as though Kell had asked if Akim believed in Father Christmas. 'No.'

'I'm a great evangelist for children,' Kell continued. 'I have two of my own. Changed my life.' Neither Drummond nor Aldrich would know that this was not true. 'Before I had them, I did not understand what it was to love self-lessly. I had loved women, I love my wife, but with girls you always expect something in return, don't you?'

Akim frowned, and Kell wondered if his French was being fully understood. But then the Arab nodded in tacit agreement.

'When I go home, after a long trip like this, if it's late at night, the first thing I'll do is go into their bedrooms and see that they are safe. Sometimes I'll sit there and just watch them for five or ten minutes. It calms me. I find it re-assuring that there is something in my life that is larger than my own greed, my own petty concerns. The gift of my son, the gift of my daughter *renews* me.' He used an Arabic word to emphasize this last phrase: *tajdid*. 'It's a very difficult thing to convey to people who don't have a young family. Children complete you. Not a wife, not a husband, not a lover. Children save you from yourself.'

Akim pulled a tissue from the pocket of his jeans and

wiped his mouth. He had been offered a chocolate biscuit from a packet in the kitchen and eaten three in the space of a few minutes. Kell wondered if his strategy was having any effect.

'Are your parents still alive, Akim?'

'My mother died,' he said. Before Kell had a chance to ask, he added: 'I never met my father.'

It was a gift that Kell seized upon.

'He abandoned your mother?'

Again, Akim's sustained silence provided an answer.

'And I guess you wouldn't have much interest in meeting him now?'

A quick surge of pride forced its way through Akim's body like a movement in dance and he said: 'No way,' even as his eyes, in a moment that passed in an instant, seemed to pray that Kell would somehow produce him.

'But you have other family here in France? Brothers, sisters, cousins?'

'Yes.'

He wanted him to be thinking about them. He wanted Akim to be picturing the laughing niece in the photograph on the phone, the sick grandfather in the hospital in Toulon.

'The mother of François Malot, my friend, my colleague, gave him up for adoption when she was just twenty years old. She never saw her baby again. That's difficult even for me, a father, to imagine. Things are altogether more complicated between a mother and her child. That's a bond that never leaves you, a cord going right back into the womb. What your organization did was to taunt her with the most basic feeling we possess, the most elemental and decent thing about us. A mother's love for her children. Did you understand that when you agreed to help them?'

Akim wiped a crumb from his mouth and looked down at the floor. The moment had come.

'I'm going to make you an offer,' Kell said. 'In two hours' time, a chambermaid is going to knock on Vincent Cévennes' door at the Hotel Lutetia. She'll think he's sleeping so she'll leave him in peace. She'll come back a couple of hours later and she'll find his body. You were seen by three of my colleagues entering the hotel shortly before Mr Cévennes was killed. It's almost certain that the French authorities will seize CCTV footage of your presence in the hotel. The last thing they'll want is a scandal. But if, by some chance, they need to blame somebody for the shooting, if – say – the heat builds up from the British side about the kidnapping and murder of François Malot, say Paris needs to throw somebody to the wolves, we might be able to persuade them to release that footage. We also might be in the mood to show them audio and visual recordings of the conversation you and I have been enjoying for the last couple of hours.' Akim looked up at the ceiling, then quickly to the door and window, as if he might see the very cameras and the microphones to which Kell was referring. 'So you see where you stand? This man' – he indicated Drummond – 'works at the British Embassy in Paris. Within twelve hours, he can have you in a hotel room at Gatwick airport. Within twenty-four, he can issue you with a new EU identity and offer you permanent residence in the United Kingdom. Give me what I need to know and we will look after you. I see you as a victim in this, Akim. I don't see you as the enemy.'

There was a long silence. Watching Akim's face, his eyes distant and still, Kell began to wonder if he would ever speak again. He craved the answers to his questions. He craved success not only for Amelia, but for himself, as a salve against all the wretchedness and disappointment of the last dozen months.

Akim's shaved head lolled to one side, then came up at Kell, like a boxer recovering in slow-motion.

'Salles-sur-l'Hers,' he said quietly. 'The woman's son is being held in a house near Salles-sur-l'Hers.'

78

Kell was on the TGV to Toulouse when Amelia called to tell him that she had received a video of François in his cell.

'Proof of life,' she said. 'Filmed this morning. I'm sending it through to you now.'

Kell realized that it would have been the first time that Amelia had ever seen her son's face. He could not imagine how she would have felt at such a moment. The immediate tug of a new devotion, or a reluctance to be drawn into the possibility of yet further pain, further betrayal? Perhaps François was just another face on just another screen. Could she have felt any connection with him after expending so much love on Vincent?

'Any word from White?' Amelia asked.

The three-man security unit had taken off from Stansted airport just before six o'clock. Their plane had landed at Carcassone two hours later. One of the team – referred to only as 'Jeff' – had driven to meet a contact in Perpignan and picked up some basic equipment and weapons. White and a second man – 'Mike' – had gone to Salles-sur-l'Hers to scout the location and to try to establish the number of people inside the house. After booking rooms at a hotel in Castelnaudary, they had driven west to Toulouse, meeting Kell's train at two fifteen.

'One thing,' said Amelia. 'As far as they're concerned, I'm just another client. Any relationship they might have had with the Service in years gone by is history. We'll have no operational control.'

Kell had assumed as much.

'Everything will be fine,' he reassured her, and thought that he could hear the voice of George Truscott in the background, barking orders to an underling at Vauxhall Cross. 'If Akim's product is accurate, we will have François out by tonight.'

Kell was certain that Akim had been honest, not least because White's initial diligence on the farmhouse fitted Akim's description of the building precisely. Furthermore, Mike had been into a *tabac* in Villeneuve-la-Comptal and flashed a photograph of Akim at the proprietor and his elderly mother, who had recognized Akim as one of the two young Arabs who had been buying Lucky Strike cigarettes, newspapers and magazines from the shop for the previous three weeks. Her son reckoned they were living in the farmhouse on the hill, south-west of Salles-sur-l'Hers, which had once been occupied by the Thébault brothers and was now owned by 'a businessman from Paris'. That was confirmation enough.

'We took a look at the house this morning from a barn on the opposite side of the road.' White was a fourteen-stone, six-foot old Etonian with a Baghdad tan whose security firm, Falcon, had made annual seven-figure profits out of the carnage in Iraq and Afghanistan. He talked about the operation as though it were no more complex than a routine dental appointment. 'The layout matches the map you showed us. Exits east and west down the connecting track from the D625. Access from the south is foot only, but Jeff reckons he can use the windmill as sniper cover.' To such a man, extracting a French national from a poorly guarded farmhouse in the middle of Languedoc-Roussillon was plainly money for old rope. 'There's the fenced-off area on the western side of the property where we assume François exercises. The swimming pool is exposed out front. It's got to be the same place.'

'Have you any idea how many people are in there?' Kell asked. White and Mike were driving him east towards Castelnaudary on the A61 autoroute. 'Akim said they sometimes use two ex-Foreign Legion as back-up guards. He knows Slimane is in the house. After that, it may just be Luc and the woman.'

White overtook a prehistoric 2CV and settled into the inside lane, sticking to the speed limit. 'Jeff is still keeping an eye out. The worry in these situations is that they move the package on a regular basis. We haven't seen any sign of life at the house since we got there. Judging by what you said on the phone, these people have been careful to make calls and to use computers away from the location, but they've been there a long time and might be looking for a change of scene. How many times have they tried to reach Akim since the Lutetia?'

Luc had called Akim's mobile shortly after eight o'clock. Akim had confirmed CUCKOO's assassination by text message but Valerie had then rung back just after Kell had left for Austerlitz station. Under Drummond's instruction,

Akim had ignored the call. Valerie had rung back an hour later, leaving a tetchy message.

'Akim needs to talk to her or they'll get suspicious,' White said. 'Did he mention anything about a second location?'

Kell shook his head. There was an unspoken warning in White's analysis. *We're doing this as a favour to Amelia. Mate's rates. Two days, max, then we can't afford to stick around. If your boy isn't in there, we're going back to Stansted.*

Just then, like an augur of success, Jeff phoned to say that he had seen a young Arab walking along the lane past the ruined windmill, about three hundred metres south-east of the house.

'Slimane,' said Kell.

There was also a car in the drive, a white Toyota Land Cruiser that had not been parked there earlier in the day. Perhaps Luc and Valerie had returned to the house after making their calls to Akim.

It was enough to green-light the operation. In two connecting rooms at the hotel in Castelnaudary, White set out the plan.

'You said the boss likes to go for a swim in the evenings.'

'Akim mentioned that, yes.'

'Then we'll go when he goes. Get close to the house, Luc comes out to the pool, that's our trigger. Jeff takes him out in his Speedos from the windmill. If he stays indoors, fine, we'll wait for the sun. Mrs Levene said live rounds, body count.'

'She wants to send a message to Paris,' Kell confirmed.

White nodded. A routine dental appointment. He then set out further details of the raid. Jeff – curly-haired, mid-forties, looking for all the world like a hearty landlord from a pub in Shropshire – would walk along the track from the south side and take cover in the ruined windmill, two hundred metres from the pool. Mike would go in through the front door and secure the cell. Simultaneously, White would enter through the exercise area, removing the metal bars at the rear entrypoint of the cell and extracting François through the back. Kell would be waiting to drive them out on to the D625. In spite of White's insistence that the operation was 'a piece of piss', Kell had insisted on a role.

'As soon as we go in, block the track at the eastern intersection,' White told him. 'Something goes wrong and they come out and try for the Land Cruiser, get in the way and take out the tyres. Don't shoot anywhere higher than the bumper. Your boy might be in there if they've seen us coming.'

'Are they going to see you coming?'

Jeff laughed. Mike, who still had the build and buzzcut of the Regiment, looked like a cowboy preparing to spit a wad of tobacco on the floor. White smiled and passed Kell a Glock pistol. 'Fired one of these before?'

'Didn't you get the memo?' Kell replied, touching the barrel. 'That's all MI6 does nowadays. Assassinations.'

79

François was sitting on his bed when he heard Luc coming downstairs and telling Valerie that he was going for a swim. It was just before seven o'clock in the evening, probably another ten minutes before Slimane or Jacques brought him supper. It would be his last meal in the cell. He had heard the sounds of the house being packed up, boxes placed in the Land Cruiser outside, the slamming of car boots, the zipping of cases. At any moment François was expecting to be taken from his room and driven to a new prison, a new terror, one from which he would never be returned.

Five minutes passed. He heard the door of the microwave clunking shut and knew that he could expect another frozen meal: rice in a bag; sinewed cuts of beef or pork in a supermarket sauce. Sure enough, a few minutes later he heard the ping of the timer, then either Jacques or Slimane loading the food on to a plate. One of them would carry a tray into the cell, the other would watch to make sure that François made no attempt to escape.

Footsteps outside, the knock on the door. François raised

his hands above his head and heard the padlock clunk against the door as the key was inserted. Jacques came in, glanced at the television, dumped the tray on the floor and walked across the room to pick up the bucket of urine.

'Stinks in here,' he said. François had heard it all before.

Slimane was behind him, looking oddly detached, perhaps a little stoned. Usually he would mutter a few words, something spiteful or contemptuous, just to get his blood going, to ease his boredom. But tonight he stared into the middle-distance, his left eye still bruised and swollen, as though he had something else on his mind, like a sixth sense of imminent defeat.

A car passed on the track outside, cutting through from the south-east. Local knowledge; somebody who knew the rat run. Just then, from the first floor, François heard a woman shouting, not in panic or fear, but from a sense of outrage, of stunned surprise. Valerie. Jacques put the bucket on the floor, directly in front of François, looked at Slimane and went out into the hall, as if a fire alarm had gone off and he wasn't sure if it was a test. Then François heard the sound of Valerie running downstairs. In that moment, the front door flew open and something was thrown into the hallway. The house inverted with noise. Slimane and François blocked their ears, the room screaming, as Jacques dropped to the ground. At first it looked as though he had tripped or slipped on the floor, but François saw blood on the wall behind him, the barrel of a rifle, then the outline of a man wearing body armour and a black balaclava. His ears were numb. He had kicked over the bucket and was staring at the urine as it pooled out in front of him. Even then, he thought that Slimane would make him clear it up.

Valerie had come to the bottom of the stairs. She looked

into the cell and screamed at Slimane: 'Shoot him!' An instant later, blood had sprayed against the door of the cell as her body crumpled beside Jacques. The soldier had shot her point-blank in the head.

Slimane reached for the rear pocket of his jeans. This was where he kept his gun, the gun with which he had taunted François, the gun with which he had threatened him, day and night.

It was out and levelled at François' chest in one quick, trained movement. François looked beyond Slimane, at the masked face of the soldier who had shot Jacques and Valerie. An instant later the soldier had swung his own weapon towards Slimane, but it was too late; the Arab had stepped towards François, grabbed and spun his body as easily as a man moving the branch of a tree, and pressed the cold steel of his gun against François' right temple. Slimane's arm flexed around François' neck, he began to drag him backwards across the floor of the cell and away from the soldier.

François tried to twist free, but Slimane only held him tighter and pressed the barrel of the gun harder against his head, shouting: 'You put your fucking gun down.' It was not clear whether the soldier could understand. 'Go back out of the door!' the Arab screamed in French. 'Get outside. I'm taking this prick with me and we're leaving in the car.'

The grip on François' neck momentarily slackened and he grabbed at a breath of air, gulping and coughing. There was a wet slick of sweat all over François' face; it was as if the two men were transferring fear from skin to skin. To his dismay, François saw the soldier lower his rifle and step over Valerie's dead body, moving backwards towards the door, seemingly in the act of surrender. As he did so, Slimane moved tentatively forward, his hips banging against

François, shunting him towards the hall, all the time driving the gun into the side of his head like a screwdriver.

'I'm going to kill you, you know that, don't you?' he whispered; it was as though he was enjoying himself, adrenalized by the scene playing out in front of him. Terrified that the trigger would give way, François watched as the soldier reached for the door, preparing to retreat on to the driveway. At the same time, Slimane forced François up into the hall, picking his way between the two dead bodies on the ground.

François became aware of the movement behind them before Slimane, perhaps because he was so attuned to every detail and characteristic of his prison. He sensed the near-silent removal of the metal bars securing the rear door of the cell; he heard the sudden twist and push on the door handle as a second soldier burst into the room behind them. François twisted his head to the right to try to see what was happening, opening up a tiny gap between his head and that of his captor which gave the second soldier a clear target area. It was then that François learned, finally, of his own courage, because he wrestled free of Slimane and tried to turn on him even as he registered that the Arab's head had simply disintegrated before his eyes. François found himself tasting the warm blood, the brain tissue of his detested guard and began to spit it on to Valerie's body.

'Are you François?' the soldier who had fired shouted in French. He was also in body armour but his tanned face was not concealed by a balaclava. François, still in a state of shock, answered: 'Yes' as the first soldier came back into the hall and fired a silenced shot into Slimane's chest.

'Get behind us,' he barked in French. 'Who else is here?'

*   *   *

Thomas Kell had been listening out for the first shot from the windmill and heard what he thought was the snap of Jeff's silenced rifle just after seven o'clock. A second later he heard the sound of Luc's body splashing into the swimming pool, then a scream as Valerie de Serres reacted to what had happened from her bedroom on the first floor. On that cue, Mike burst through the front door, tossing a stun grenade into the hall; Kell guessed that he had fired his weapon at least three times in quick succession. Thirty metres to the east, he saw White moving low and fast behind a screen of trees, then disappearing behind the house as he approached the rear entrance to the cell.

Kell had his instructions. He switched on the engine of the rental car, reversed it into the drive so that the vehicle was within twenty feet of the house, then opened the rear doors on both sides. As he stepped out of the car, he heard a commotion inside the house, a man shouting in French, screaming at Mike to drop his weapon. Kell took the Glock pistol from its holster, sweat suddenly enveloping his neck and chest like a rash; in more than twenty years as an intelligence officer, he had never fired a weapon on active duty. He looked back at the front door and saw Mike stepping out of the house, like a man being pushed backwards towards the edge of a cliff.

Just then, to his left, a movement. Coming from the direction of the pool, across the terrace at the northern end of the house. A man in swimming shorts, soaked from head to foot, and bleeding from a wound to his neck and shoulder. The wound was bright red but the blood had blackened where it reached the shorts. Luc. Kell spun towards him and raised the Glock, shouting at Javeau to stop, but it was clear that the Frenchman was utterly disorientated and functioning solely on survival instinct. He seemed to recognize Kell from the interview in Marseille, but then turned back in the direction of the terrace and began to walk across an expanse of unmown grass, twisting like a drunk towards the track. Kell again shouted at him to stop. He walked up the steps, but could not fire nor follow him, because at any moment he might be required to go back to the car and to drive François away from the house.

He heard a gunshot, then White's voice, unintelligible. Kell looked back at the front door to see what was happening, then again at Luc who was still stumbling towards the road, now more than seventy metres away. In the next field, a tractor was obliviously ploughing. From the direction of the abandoned windmill, Jeff appeared at the edge of the terrace. Beginning to run, he raised his weapon to shoulder height and fired three shots at Luc's back, dropping him like a stag. Kell, stunned by what he had seen, turned and went back to the vehicle as Jeff followed behind him in a fluid, continuous movement, heading towards the house.

Mike came out first, François tucked in behind him, White half a second later.

'Move with me,' Mike was saying, 'stay behind me', as White shouted 'Clear!' and sprinted ahead to the car. They had Amelia's son on the floor of the back seat before Kell had even closed his own door. Jeff was the last one in, shooting out a tyre on the Land Cruiser as Kell put the Renault in gear.

'Anybody hurt?' he asked.

'Status, Jeff,' White replied, as though speaking into a radio.

'All clear, boss. Targets down.'

Kell accelerated away from the house.

Beaune,
Three Weeks Later

80

They waited on a bench in the centre of the square, a woman of fifty-three wearing a pretty skirt and a cream blouse, a man of forty-three in a linen suit that had seen better days, and a young French I.T. consultant wearing jeans and smoking a cigarette. He might have been their nephew, their son.

'He'll be here in a minute,' Amelia said.

It was a Saturday morning, just before eleven o'clock, young children playing in a small park at the centre of the square under the dutiful, exhausted stares of fathers who had promised their wives and girlfriends a few hours' respite from childcare. One of the children, a girl of about three or four, had a miniature pushchair in which she had placed a naked doll. She rattled it forward and back on the narrow path in front of the bench, falling once but immediately rising to her feet without fuss or tears, and without noticing that François had stood up from his seat to try to help her.

'Brave girl,' he said in French, sitting back down, but she did not appear to hear him.

Clockwise cars were circling the park, waiters at a brasserie on the far side of the square ferrying Perriers and *cafés au lait* to customers basking in the late summer sun. Kell turned and looked down Rue Carnot, glancing at his watch.

'In a minute,' Amelia replied and placed a hand on her son's knee.

Kell watched them, still not tired of their delight in one another's company, and reflected on how skilfully Amelia had played her hand. Jimmy Marquand promoted and sent to Washington, with school fees paid, salary boosted, and a five-bedroom Georgetown mansion to help convince him that SIS really had been left in good hands, despite one or two misgivings he might have had about a woman running the Service. Simon Haynes too busy thanking the Prime Minister for his knighthood to wonder how long Amelia had been keeping her illegitimate son a secret. And George Truscott eased offshore to the top SIS job in Germany before he could start asking any awkward questions about the sudden appearance in London of Monsieur François Malot.

At Amelia's instigation, Kell, Elsa and Drummond had spent two weeks looking into the possibility of a connection between Truscott and the elements in the DGSE who had carried out Malot's abduction, but they had found nothing, not even evidence that Truscott had known about DENEUVE. On the other hand, their investigation suggested that Kell had been correct in his assumption that the operation was linked to waning French influence in North Africa. Elsa had obtained copies of two cables, originating in Paris, which confirmed that senior figures in the DGSE had been 'extremely concerned' about Amelia's appointment as 'C'. Their misgivings proved well founded: within days of taking over from Haynes, Amelia had shut down nineteen separate operations in the Caucasus and Eastern Europe and re-directed more than forty officers to burgeoning SIS Stations in Tripoli, Cairo, Tunis and Algiers. As Head of Station in Turkey, Paul Wallinger was given *carte blanche* to amplify SIS influence from Istanbul to Tehran, from Ankara to Jordan. In London, other Levene allies, on both sides of the river, were instructed to sell this regional re-shuffle to a Downing Street already keen to reap the economic and security benefits of the post-Arab Spring era. By the time elections were being called in Egypt, the French government was reported to be 'paranoid' about aggressive SIS recruitment of sources within the Muslim Brotherhood and 'gravely concerned' about Libyan oil resources slipping beyond the control of Total S.A.

Paris itself had also embarked on a shame-faced internal investigation into the behaviour of Luc Javeau, details of which were leaked to Vauxhall Cross by Amelia's source in the DCRI. It was confirmed that Javeau had indeed been the officer tasked with cleaning up the mess left by DENEUVE's treachery. The scandal had stalled his career, a setback he blamed squarely on Levene and which his superiors were only too happy to avenge by waving through Javeau's plans for the Malot operation. In the aftermath of François' release, more formal channels saw the DGSE distancing itself from the 'unpredictable rogue elements' that had threatened to break the 'formidable and lasting intelligence relationship between our two countries'. Amelia's opposite number in Paris also stressed the importance of keeping what had happened in Salles-sur-l'Hers a secret, both to protect Mrs Levene's privacy but also 'to avoid any complications with our respective governments'.

It was taken for granted that Paris was outraged by the assassination of serving DGSE personnel on French soil by an unaccountable unit of British ex-Special Forces.

Information on Valerie de Serres was harder to come by, but it was demonstrated that she was a former GIPN officer, born in Montreal, who had met Luc while their respective agencies had been working on a joint counter-terrorism operation. Amelia characterized her baleful influence over Luc as 'Lady Macbeth stuff', and it was generally accepted that Valerie had managed to convince Javeau to quit the DGSE and to ransom François for private gain.

As for Kell himself, his forty-third birthday brought no great change in his circumstances. With the Yassin trial scheduled for the new year, Amelia had made it clear that she could not be seen to bring him back into the Service without the good name of 'Witness X' being cleared in court and the incident wiped from Kell's record. There had been no word from Claire since her return from California, so he continued to rent his bachelor bedsit in Kensal Rise, eating take-aways and watching old black-and-white movies on TCM. Amelia had arranged for Kell's salary and pension to be reinstated, yet her gratitude towards him for facilitating the release of her son had not been as fulsome as perhaps Kell had anticipated. He felt like a man who had spent a fortune on a present for a close friend, only to see them tuck it away, unopened, in a cupboard, embarrassed by such an act of generosity. In this atmosphere, Kell occasionally began to resent the risks he had taken on Amelia's behalf, the secrets he had consented to keep, but his affection and respect for her was such that he was prepared to give her the benefit of the doubt. Amelia's behaviour was bound to have been affected by what had happened in France, as well as by the demands – and status – of her new position as Chief. In time, he told himself, she would bring him back into the fold and give him the pick of any overseas job that caught his eye. Kell looked forward to that day, not least because it might offer him some respite from London and from the collapse of his marriage to Claire.

It was Kell who saw the old man first, shuffling along the road in a grey flannel suit. He knew his face because he had watched him, from this same spot, three days earlier.

'Here he comes,' he whispered.

François leapt up from the bench but Amelia remained seated, as though Kell and François were acolytes, her guardian angels. She heard François say: 'Where?' and looked up to see him squinting in the direction in which Kell was facing.

'He's coming across the street,' Kell replied quietly. 'The man with white hair in the grey suit. Do you see him?'

'I see him.' François stepped away from them, as if to give himself more time to take in what he was witnessing. Only now did Amelia turn. Kell would later tell himself that he had heard her gasp, but it may simply have been a trick of his imagination.

Jean-Marc Daumal seemed instantly to sense the presence of Amelia Weldon and stopped at the edge of the square, as though tapped on the shoulder by a ghost. He looked directly at the three figures on the bench but appeared to be having difficulty bringing them into focus. He took two paces forward. Kell and François remained where they were, but Amelia moved towards him.

His head began to shake as he saw her, everything that

he had recalled of her beauty still present in her face. Soon he was only metres away from the bench.

'Amelia?'

'*C'est moi, Jean-Marc*.' They came together and kissed one another lightly on both cheeks.

'What are you doing here?'

He looked beyond her and scanned Kell's face, perhaps assuming that he was the man who had finally won Amelia's heart. Then he looked to Kell's left, at the young man, and frowned, gazing at him as though trying to remember if they had met before.

'I knew you would be here,' Amelia told him, resting her hand on Daumal's wrist. She was shocked by how much he had changed, and yet the years had not extinguished all of her love for him. A person is lucky to know even one person in their life who understands and cares for them so completely. 'You look well,' she said.

Amelia caught Kell's eye in a moment of deep affection for him, a sudden reward for all that he had done for her. Then she turned so that she was facing her son.

'Jean-Marc, there is somebody I would like you to meet.'

Acknowledgements

My thanks to: Julia Wisdom, Anne O'Brien, Emad Akhtar, Oliver Malcolm, Lucy Upton, Roger Cazalet, Kate Elton, Elinor Fewster, Hannah Gamon, Tanya Brennand-Roper, Jot Davies, Kate Stephenson, and all the team at HarperCollins in London. To Will Francis, Rebecca Folland, Claire Paterson, Tim Glister, Kirsty Gordon and Jessie Botterill at Janklow and Nesbit UK and to Luke Janklow, Claire Dippel and Stefanie Lieberman in New York. To Keith Kahla, Hannah Braaten, Dori Weintraub, Matthew Baldacci, Sally Richardson and everybody at St Martin's Press. To Jon, Jeremy, Caz, Kerin and Alanna at *The Week* – thank you for the office. To Marwa Che Hata, Theo Tait and Noomane Fehri for Tunisian expertise. To Liss, Stanley and Iris, Sarah Brown, Ian Cumming, Tony Omosun, William Fiennes, Jeremy Duns, Joe Finder, Natalie Cohen, Caroline Pilkington, Siobhan Loughran-Mareuse, Mark Pilkington, Christopher and Arabella Elwes, Jeff Abbott, Bard Wilkinson and the eagle-eyed Sarah Gabriel (www.sarahgabriel.eu).

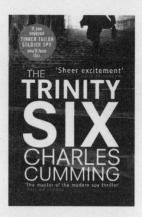

'This is today's spooks at their most ruthless... To give too much away would seriously damage the enjoyment you'll get from this exciting, ingenious, elegantly written thriller'
Guardian

'Shows why Charles Cumming has won so much praise for his contemporary spy stories... Impressive and convincing, with a stunning twist at the end'
Sunday Telegraph

'From the first page to the last it has the ring of absolute authenticity. Tautly written, cleverly plotted... It reminded me strongly of the early books of John le Carré'

Robert Harris, author of *Fatherland* and *The Ghost*